Ryan felt Hellstrom's mind reach out to touch him

The leader of Helskel leaned back in his chair, his eyes opened wide. "I underestimated you," he said quietly. "Consider yourself lucky."

"You're the lucky one, Lars. Most people who have underestimated me are sitting on the knee of Father Death."

Hellstrom eyed him for a long minute, then threw back his head and laughed. "You're a treasure, Cawdor. Helskel needs a man like you."

"Rather have you replace the tires of my wag, and we'll be on our way."

"Ah, well, that's the rub, isn't it? We need you, and you need tires. Can't we help each other?" Hellstrom grinned, his face taking on a cadaverous, skull-like aspect. "Because if you won't help me, you and your people will die in a manner far less spectacular and far more agonizing than the late Zadfrak."

**Also available in the
Deathlands saga:**

JAMES AXLER

DEATH LANDS®
Stoneface

A GOLD EAGLE BOOK FROM
WORLDWIDE®

TORONTO • NEW YORK • LONDON
AMSTERDAM • PARIS • SYDNEY • HAMBURG
STOCKHOLM • ATHENS • TOKYO • MILAN
MADRID • WARSAW • BUDAPEST • AUCKLAND

For Melissa Ellis and Will Murray,
and for all the mucksuckers they've helped
me to defeat.

First edition November 1996

ISBN 0-373-62534-0

STONEFACE

Prologue

Ryan opened his eye.

As usual he didn't know where he was after the mat-trans jump. But his mind was clear enough, and he was thankful he had been spared the horrible nightmares that were the frequent side effects of the gateway's quantum energy overflow.

With crystal clarity he remembered escaping Gert Wolfram's Tennessee fortress, leaving it aflame and overrun with stickies, the flight by hot-air balloon to the subterranean redoubt.

He remembered closing the door to the gateway chamber, and the disks in the floor and ceiling beginning to glow as the matter-to-energy converter assembly automatically powered up.

He remembered the spark-shot mist gathering overhead, seeping down, and the darkness closing in.

And then there was light again and he opened his eye, expecting to be somewhere else.

Most of the time, a change in the color of the armaglass walls of the chamber was the only thing that told Ryan and his friends that a mat-trans jump had been successfully completed.

In every redoubt, the octagonal design of the chamber remained the same, though each chamber was color-coded. The predark engineers had obviously decided color-coding was the simplest method of differentiating the chambers, evidently so the original gateway jumpers would know at a glance into which redoubt they had materialized. He'd often wondered why they hadn't simply put up signs identifying the locations. He chalked it up to yet another unfathomable mystery of predark scientific reasoning.

This gateway chamber had dingy white walls, and they weren't made of translucent armaglass. Instead, they were heavy, mortared concrete blocks. The door was a slab of steel set tightly in the wall, a wheel-lock jutting from the rivet-studded, cross-beamed mass.

A thin thread of light shone from a single overhead fixture, the glare stabbing painfully at his eye. There was a distant high-pitched whine he had never heard before, the sound of an engine or generator. He felt its regular pulsation through the floor beneath his hands and booted feet.

His five friends stirred. He heard a mutter from Jak, a grunt from J.B. and a groan from Doc. Krysty sat up, brushing a wisp of crimson hair from her face. "Everybody feel all right?"

As a matter a fact, everybody did, remarkably so. It had been one of the smoothest jumps in recent memory. Not only had there been no hideous hallucinatory nightmares, no one was complaining of nausea, dizziness, headaches or other symptoms of "jump sickness."

Jak and Mildred were the last to push themselves into sitting positions. The stocky black woman looked around and said, "This isn't a gateway chamber. Not exactly."

J.B. removed his spectacles from a capacious pocket of his coat, settled them on his bony nose and said, "Yeah. Never saw a unit like this before."

Doc climbed to his feet with the help of his swordstick. The ceiling was low, and he couldn't stand at his
full height. "Unusually cramped quarters. Inasmuch as
I have a touch of claustrophobia, I would prefer less
confined environs."

Ryan stood and went to the door. He had to stoop
slightly, too. He put his hands on the wheel-lock, giving
it a counterclockwise twist. It didn't budge. The wheel
obviously hadn't been turned in a very long time. Taking and holding a deep breath, he threw all of his weight
and upper-body strength against the lock.

With a tortured screech of rusted gears tearing free
from time-frozen stasis, the wheel turned. Slowly and
resistantly at first, then Ryan was able to initiate hand-
over-hand spin.

He threw his shoulder against the steel door and there
was a sucking sound of rotten rubber seals ripping. The
hinges squealed and the door opened. He stepped out,
blaster in hand. Everyone followed him, alert and
watchful. Then they stopped and stared.

"Dark night," J.B. breathed.

"Where this?" Jak demanded.

"This isn't a redoubt," Krysty said uneasily.

They were in a medium-size room with a dozen desks,
most of them covered with computer terminals. Sheets of
crumbling, flaking paper lay in pieces beneath discolored coffee cups and verdigris-eaten brass paperweights.

A control console ran the length of one wall, consist-
ing primarily of glass-encased readouts and gauges. A
fine layer of dust clung to everything, coating the floor
and instrument panels with a powdery gray film. They
could taste it on their tongues, and the floating particles
tickled nostril hairs.

On the other side of the wall, behind the console, the whining sound slowly faded.

Ryan silently agreed with Krysty. This place wasn't a redoubt. Almost all of the ones they had visited in the past had standardized layouts, adhering to the same design specs. Here there were no vanadium-steel sec doors, freestanding control consoles or flickering display monitors.

The door at the far end of the room was wood-paneled and had a simple knob rather than a lever or a sec-code keypad affixed to the frame. This place looked more like an office or a classroom.

"The Air Force," Mildred suddenly said.

Ryan turned toward her. She held a scrap of paper gingerly between thumb and forefinger. A small dark blue symbol was emblazoned near its top edge, a bird with outspread, upcurving wings.

"This is United States Air Force letterhead," she said, "a memo regarding the quantum interphase transducer experiments."

The vibrations of her voice and the soft touch of her breath were enough to cause the scrap of paper in her hand to crumble and float away in tiny fragments.

"I think we jumped into a military testing facility," she continued. "We jumped into a prototype gateway chamber."

Krysty looked around. "It's so old, there's probably very little of use to us here."

"Its power source is still operational," Doc pointed out.

Ryan walked to the door and put his hand on the knob. Following a procedure that was now ingrained habit, his five friends fanned out behind him, taking cover behind desks and drawing their weapons. Looking over his shoulder, he began counting in a soft voice. "One...two..."

On "three," he turned the knob, flung the door open and threw himself to one side. There was no sound from anywhere except the creak of rust-eaten hinges.

Ryan peered carefully around the doorframe, staring into semidarkness. He blinked. He was looking down a long, smooth corridor, a dim glow of light filtering from its far end. Cool air brushed his face, blown from a distant, unseen opening.

Gesturing behind him to the others, the one-eyed man stepped out cautiously, heel to toe. His footfalls sent up flat, faint echoes. His companions joined him, pushing quietly through the dimness. J.B. took the point, Uzi in hand.

The corridor turned to the left like an *L*. J.B. paused at the angle, gestured for the others to wait and crept carefully out of sight. They could hear the muffled slapping sounds made by J.B.'s boots on the dust-filmed concrete floor.

The footfalls ceased. A latch clicked and the glow of light widened, dissolving the darkness. The air current increased in volume. They heard J.B.'s footsteps again, fast and hard. He was running. Ryan's finger crooked tight on the trigger of his handblaster.

The Armorer sprinted around the corner. His normally sallow face was flushed with excitement, his eyes behind the lenses of his spectacles wide.

Panting, he called to them, "Come on! You won't *believe* what I found!"

Chapter One

Several days later

They heard the screamwings before they saw them.

Ryan Cawdor whirled, his hand making a reflexive move toward the butt of the SIG-Sauer holstered at his hip.

Jak Lauren inclined his white-haired head to the west. "Swarm screamwings. Stirred by vibrations wag's engine."

Ryan looked behind him at the flat curve of black roadway fifty yards away. The Hotspur Hussar Armored Land Rover sat there, the powerful turbocharged V-8 engine idling with a muted throb. On the far side of the road, Krysty Wroth's bright red hair shone through the underbrush like a torch. She was examining the shrubs, searching for edible berries. She hadn't heard the high-pitched whistling shrieks floating up from behind the western hills.

The one-eyed man turned back to the wooded foothills, which were at least a quarter of a mile away, dotted with large bushy growths. The shrieks were rising in volume.

At his and Jak's insistence, the wag had stopped so the companions could stretch their legs and relieve themselves after a six-hour drive. Ryan assumed J. B. Dix was inside the vehicle with Mildred Wyeth and Doc Tanner. At least he hoped so.

Jak jerked his thumb back toward the road. The scar-faced teenager's lips were set in a grim line, his ruby eyes narrowed. "Better move. Screamwings on top us soon."

Ryan and Jak returned to the wag at a trot, casting glances behind them. They still saw nothing, but the ca-cophony of eerie cries grew louder by the second.

"Everybody back aboard!" Ryan shouted. "Screamwings!" Krysty ran back up the slope to the roadbed. J.B. pushed open the side door panel. The wiry, bespectacled weaponsmith climbed out, holding his Smith & Wesson M-4000 shotgun tightly. His Uzi hung from a lanyard across his narrow chest.

"Where?" he demanded.

Jak gestured back toward the hills. "Hear?"

"Yeah. Getting close."

Poking his head into the wag, Ryan saw no sign of Mildred or Doc. He looked across the roof of the vehi-cle, then cupped his hands and bellowed, "Mildred! Doc!"

From the tangled underbrush on the other side of the roadway, he heard a faint response from Doc.

Krysty made a move in that direction. "I'll get them."

Ryan checked the move by grabbing her arm. "Stay put. Get inside and button up."

He turned to J.B. "Kill the engine."

The red-haired woman looked anxiously toward the foothills. Already the leathery rustling of hundreds of wings was mixing with the weird shrieks. "Can't we out-run them?"

Ryan shook his head. "Worst thing we can do. Screamwings can't see unless something's moving. If we can't be on the move before the flock gets here, we've got to stay put. Leastways, that's what I'm told.''

He unleathered his pistol and ran across the shoulder of the road, down the gentle slope, and blundered through the undergrowth. He glanced back once and glimpsed a dark, twisting mass uncoiling from the far side of the hills, silhouetted by the sunset.

Screamwings were rare, even in this region of Deathlands. Ryan had never seen them, but he had heard plenty of stories about isolated settlements being completely wiped out by ravenous hordes of the winged predators.

He ran through the undergrowth, waist-high weeds and tangled brush, heedless of the thorns snagging his clothes and tearing his skin. He kept shouting Mildred's and Doc's names. He reached a small clearing in the overgrown vegetation, just as the stocky woman and the tall, skinny man appeared on the opposite side.

Relief welled up inside him. ''You weren't supposed to wander far.''

Mildred ran a hand through her beaded plaits of hair. ''Sorry, Ryan.''

''My fault,'' Doc said. Small twigs and leaves were snarled in his shaggy silvery white hair. He gestured with his lion's-head ebony swordstick, which concealed a rapier of the finest Toledo steel. ''I'd hoped to find a blackberry patch in this morass. I fear my enthusiasm for pies and muffins infected the lady.''

''Let's hope our visitors don't have your sweet tooth,'' Ryan said.

Doc angled an eyebrow at him. ''Pardon?''

''Screamwings. A swarm is on its way.''

They heard the beat of wings, and their faces registered their fear.

"Don't move unless you have to," Ryan said. "Stand stock-still and hope the screamwings will pass us and the wag by."

The three formed a rough circle, standing back to back. Ryan faced the way he had come, the SIG-Sauer held in a two-handed grip, barrel pointed upward. He waited for the first glimpse of the screamwings and didn't have to wait long.

Several black shapes held aloft by furiously fluttering wings darted above the overgrowth, dipping and banking and diving. Ryan tried to keep them framed within his limited field of vision, but it was nearly impossible. The speed and maneuverability of the creatures was remarkable.

Ryan stopped trying to follow their blindingly fast movements and concentrated only on staying as motionless as he could.

Suddenly a screamwing landed on the upraised barrel of the SIG-Sauer.

The screamwing was barely six inches long, though its wingspread was over two feet. It was scaled and clawed, with a wide mouth full of rows of serrated, pointed teeth. Leathery, talon-tipped wings whipped the air. Longer, curving claws were on the hind legs. A long tail lashed around the built-in baffle silencer as it sought to secure its perch. Unblinking eyes, like chips of cold obsidian, glared around.

Ryan had seen any number of mutated animals in Deathlands, but he had never seen one that looked like predatory death stripped down to its bare essentials. He couldn't even guess at what predark life-form the screamwing had sprung from.

He remembered Mildred once commenting that most mutations were random, sometimes not a case of evolution, but *de*volution. Perhaps the screamwings were some species of hunting bird that had regressed to their reptilian roots. Like snakes, the screamwings had no conventional organs of hearing, but relied on supersensitive nervous systems to detect sound vibrations in the air and ground.

The creature crouched there, turning its head jerkily back and forth. Ryan saw its rear claws tear small scratches in the steel of the SIG-Sauer. It took all of his willpower to hold the blaster steady. He had no idea if a shriek from the thing would draw the flock to the clearing, or if it would decide to take an experimental bite out of his hand.

The screamwing opened and shut its jaws with a clashing of teeth, looking almost evil.

Then it launched itself from the barrel of the blaster, the point of its tail brushing the patch over Ryan's left eye, a puff of air fanning his right. It took all of the man's self-control not to flinch. Not too long ago an accident had taken the sight from his good eye, and he had been rendered completely blind. Though he had recovered his vision, he was still overly cautious about risking it again. Fortunately the screamwing showed no further interest in him. It flew in a rapid circle around the clearing, then flapped from sight.

Ryan lowered his arms, trying to steady his nerves and bring his breathing back to normal. He heard the shrieking and leathery slap of wings from the road, and an occasional muffled thud as if the little demons were trying to batter their way into the wag.

Since the wag carried three-inch-thick armor plate, he doubted the screamwings could inflict much damage, but the vehicle's six tires were another matter. If they found they liked the taste of rubber, he and his friends would be stranded in the hills.

Then, over the shrieks and flutterings, came the staccato hammering of J.B.'s Uzi.

Mildred tensed. "They may need our help."

Ryan nodded curtly. "Let's move. Doc, take the point. Your blaster has a wider spread."

The three went as quickly as they dared through the underbrush, eyes scanning the area all around and above. When they reached the perimeter of the brush, they sank to their knees.

The surface of the wag was acrawl with scaled black bodies, snapping teeth and beating wings. Though the engine had been silenced, the little predators had still zeroed in on the vehicle as the source of the vibrations. Another group swirled, swooped and screamed above it.

J.B. had one of the shuttered gun ports open just enough to accommodate the barrel of his Uzi. He was firing it in short bursts, not really aiming. Some of the creatures fell, dropping with thrashing thumps to the blacktop, where they were set upon by other members of the swarm.

A screamwing soared toward Doc, gliding on the air currents. Ryan unlimbered the eighteen-inch panga at his waist and sliced the creature in two with a single upward stroke. So razor keen was the edge of the blade that it met almost no resistance when it cut through the creature.

Unfortunately it had time to voice a thin scream before its hindquarters and torso parted company. Drawn by the sound of pain, a clot of screamwings detached themselves from the mass circling the wag and fluttered in the direction of Ryan, Doc and Mildred. Doc triggered the Le Mat. Deadly 18-gauge grapeshot ripped a huge hole through the swarm. Small bodies rained to the ground, blood and viscera spraying in all directions. The survivors swerved and rejoined the rest of the circling flock.

"By the Three Kennedys," Doc whispered. "Archaeopteryx. The earliest known ancestor of the modern bird."

"That's what the screamwings are?"

"Except the archaeopteryx was believed to have feathers. These things are more reptile than bird."

"Reptile or bird," Ryan replied, "they've got us in a bastard fix."

Ryan quickly considered and discarded several plans. Even if he, Mildred and Doc could brave their way through the gauntlet of deadly demons and get back inside the wag more or less intact, the single-minded predators might very well cling to it forever, or until they died of starvation. The only option seemed to be waiting them out, hoping the screamwings would tire of trying to chew armor plating and seek out more palatable prey.

Then another possibility arose. In the distance, clearly audible over the racket of the creatures, came the buzzing roar of a small engine.

Chapter Two

"Sounds like a motorcycle," Mildred said, craning her neck to see over the surface of the roadbed.

"Look," Doc said, gesturing with the long barrel of the Le Mat.

The screamwings crawling over the surface of the wag had fallen silent. With their heads darting to and fro, they looked like hounds sniffing the wind for a scent. The engine sound grew louder, rising and falling as gears were shifted.

With a piercing collective shriek, all of the screamwings flung themselves into the air. Like a cloud of black smoke, the flock rushed away, drawn toward the throbbing noise.

Ryan got to his feet and ran to the wag, Mildred and Doc at his heels. While they climbed inside, the one-eyed man gazed down the long flat ribbon of roadway. It stretched ahead, cutting through the foothills, then dropping across rolling plains.

Less than an eighth of a mile ahead a figure sat astride a motorcycle. Above it were dark fluttering shapes, like bundles of dirty cloth unfolding and folding in the air.

As Ryan got inside the wag, Jak said, "Lucky break us."

"Pretty damn unlucky for somebody else," J.B. commented. "We drew those monsters out. Now that poor bastard is paying for it."

Even as he spoke, the motorcycle toppled, throwing the rider to the road. The screamwings covered the bike and made darting passes at the rider, who tried to crawl toward the vegetation.

Ryan eyed the grade of the road and said to J.B., "Put us in neutral. Let's roll forward."

J.B. engaged the gears and the wag slowly moved forward. Peering between the front seats, Ryan kept his eye on the rider, who was swatting and batting at the winged demons. He picked out more details as the wag picked up speed. The rider was a man, and his long, dark blond hair was tied at his nape. He wore only cutoff jeans and a sleeveless denim jacket. He was bleeding from a score of fang and claw inflicted lacerations.

"J.B.," Ryan directed, "when we get abreast of that guy, just slow down. Don't stop."

"What're you planning?" Krysty asked, a line of worry appearing on her brow.

"I'm going to get him inside. Give me those gloves and a blanket."

After slipping on the heavy work gloves and draping a blanket over his head and shoulders, Ryan crouched by the door, holding the handle.

"I'll need both hands free," he said to Mildred. "Keep me covered."

Mildred moved directly behind him, her Czech-made target pistol held at the ready.

"Almost there," J.B. said. "Get ready."

"Keep the door open a crack and keep the wag moving. I don't plan to be out there more than thirty seconds."

"Touching the brakes," J.B. called.

In two smooth motions, Ryan slid open the door and leaped out of the vehicle. Since it wasn't traveling more than five miles per hour, he hit the turf running.

The man was on the ground, adding his shrieks to those voiced by the darting, slashing, biting creatures. He was trying to cover his face and protect his eyes. Three of the screamwings were on top of his head, sinking teeth and claws into his scalp. He wasn't fighting back, and he appeared to be completely unarmed.

The rest of the swarm was occupied with the idling motorcycle, or so Ryan hoped. Because of the blanket hooding his head, his peripheral vision was obstructed and he had no idea if any of the screamwings were turning their attention to him.

Even as the thought registered, he heard the sharp double crack of Mildred's revolver. Something limp landed on his right shoulder, then fell to the ground at his feet.

Not bothering to look down, Ryan kept his eye on the blood-streaked man howling and thrashing over the sandy soil. He reached him in two long-legged bounds and snatched one of the little demons from the man's head.

It came away clutching pieces of scalp and hanks of hair, yowling in protest and pain. It sank its teeth into the thick leather of Ryan's glove, and though the needle points didn't penetrate, Ryan felt the pinching pressure. He snapped its neck with his other hand.

Flinging the body away, Ryan slapped another screamwing from its perch on the man's head, at the same time swatting at the third. It took flight, hissing in anger and fear, its tail lashing from side to side like a miniature whip.

Ryan got his hands under the man's arms, lifted and heaved him up over his shoulder. Fortunately the man didn't weigh much. In fact, he was downright scrawny.

Securing a grip on a blood-slick wrist, Ryan ran back toward the wag, which had progressed only another fifty feet down the road. He loped across the shoulder of the road, ducking as several winged shapes swooped in front of him. The man draped over his shoulder suddenly stiffened and shrieked out a curse as one of the screamwings landed on him. He struggled and howled, "Bastard mutie's eatin' my balls!"

There was nothing Ryan could do but try to quicken his pace. Even Mildred, an Olympic-class shootist, would be hard-pressed to plug a target as small as the screamwing perched between the man's legs without the cure being worse than the disease.

Krysty and Mildred slid the door open just as Ryan reached it. He wasn't gentle about laying down his burden—he bent over and hurled the man into the wag. The back of his head struck the metal with a sharp bang, and the screamwing, pressed beneath the body, crushed against the floorplates, squealed and clawed its way out between denim-clad thighs.

Ryan leapt into the wag, and Krysty slammed the door shut behind him, the edge clipping his boot heel. At the same time, the screamwing took flight within the confined space of the wag, generating shrieking chaos.

No one dared to trigger a blaster, but there was plenty of flailing about with gun barrels. Jak had to duck to avoid being brained by Doc's Le Mat. Ryan managed to whip the blanket from his shoulders and fling it over the frantically fluttering creature. The weight dragged the screamwing down to the floorplates. Jak used the heels of his boots and the heavy butt of his .357 Colt Python to hammer out its life.

Finally the lump beneath the blanket no longer stirred. Doc wadded up the cloth, rolling the remains of the screamwing into a tight ball, and Krysty opened the door just wide enough for him to throw it out.

Mildred had scooted over to the examine the screamwings' victim. He was groaning, his eyes closed, face streaked with blood. She peeled back an eyelid and said, "Out of it. Pain, shock or that impact to the head. Maybe a combination of all three."

She reached over to tug out the first-aid kit stowed beneath the front passenger seat.

"Can we start the engine now?" J.B. asked. "This incline bottoms out in less than a mile."

Though there were no nearby sounds of the screamwings, Ryan said, "Let's just keep rolling until we stop. No sense in tempting them back to us."

Though the rear cargo compartment of the Hotspur could accommodate eight people, it wasn't the best place for a field hospital. Mildred had the wounded man stretched out on the deck, and she kept bumping everyone as she attended to him.

Ryan watched her methodically clean her patient's wounds, swab away the blood and check his vital signs. For the hundredth time, he thanked the twist of fate that had planted her within his little group.

Mildred Wyeth was a medical doctor, a former specialist in cryogenic sciences. Though she was in her mid-thirties, she was, chronologically, well over a century old. Mildred had entered a hospital in late 2000 for minor surgery, but a freak reaction to the anesthetic had necessitated her body being placed in cryonic stasis until a treatment could be found.

It never was. The world was blown apart before she was revived, and she slept, like a fly trapped in amber, for a hundred years. Ryan had found her in a shielded underground cell, her life-support system still functioning. He had brought her back to life, into a world she had never dreamed existed. The cryogenic process and suspension of life seemed to have reversed the ill effects of the anesthetic.

Besides her medical skills, Mildred had proved herself invaluable as a tenacious survivalist. She had also won a silver medal for free pistol shooting in the last-ever Olympic games.

Watching her ministrations with a clinical interest was another refugee from a past time period, Dr. T. A. Tanner. Unlike Mildred, who had bobbed unknowingly down the temporal stream, Doc was the subject of a cold-hearted scientific practice known in predark days as "trawling."

Since the 1940s, American military scientists and their counterparts in other countries had tried to reconcile Einsteinian physics with quantum mechanics. By the 1990s, the reconciliation attempts had spawned the ultra-top-secret experiment known as the Totality Concept. There were several subdivisions of the experiment, such as Overproject Whisper, Project Cerberus, and, finally, Operation Chronos.

With the use of a complex matter-transfer device called a gateway, the project scientists had tried time and time again to snatch subjects from a past temporal line and "trawl" them to the present.

Their only success was a man from 1896. Theophilus Algernon Tanner, Ph.D., scientist and scholar, was plucked from the bosom of his beloved family and deposited in a sterile subterranean chamber a century hence.

Though he learned all he could about the twentieth century, Doc never forsook the hope of returning to his wife and two children. His constant attempts to return to his own era so angered the overlords of Operation Chronos that they eventually used him as a trawling subject again. Rather than sending him back, they opted to transfer him decades into the future. Like Mildred, he missed the nukecaust by less than a month.

All that remained of the Totality Concept and its spin-off researches were the matter-transfer units tucked away in underground redoubts.

The other members of the group were the products of the hellgrounds known as Deathlands.

Sixteen-year-old Jak Lauren had all the hard, bitter experience of a man twice his age. An albino, with fear-some ruby eyes and a shock of bone-white hair, he favored bladed weapons over blasters. He bore scars from many near-fatal encounters, the least of which curved up from the corner of his mouth and across his high-planed face.

Jak had buried two sets of families during his young life—his folks back in Louisiana and his wife and infant daughter in New Mexico. He hid the tragedies behind a taciturn mask and an eerily calm, almost detached, manner.

Ryan Cawdor and John Barrymore Dix had been companions for well over a decade, since they traveled the Appalachians in a pair of huge war wags with the legendary Trader. The weapons dealer had been their undisputed leader and mentor, even something of a father figure to Ryan.

Trader had earned a considerable fortune by uncovering hidden stockpiles of weapons and fuel and using them to barter his way through the Deathlands. He had been a fearsome figure in his day, a reputation he fully lived up to and enjoyed.

Recently, after beating a case of rad cancer, Trader had been reunited with his former lieutenants. His long illness had changed him, leaving him sometimes confused, sometimes irrational, but still a dangerous man to cross. People had always treaded lightly around him, but his weathered skin had become so thin with age, it was anybody's guess as to what might provoke him.

He had resented that Ryan was his group's undisputed leader, and that the younger man no longer showed him the deference he believed was due. Their reunion had been punctuated by many disagreements, with Ryan and Trader frequently going eyeball to eyeball over tactics and even ethics. Everyone had feared that one day Trader wouldn't be the first to blink, and either he or Ryan would catch the last train west.

Though there was no denying that the grizzled veteran of Deathlands had gotten the group of friends out of a few tight spots, he'd gotten them into just as many, due to his temper and ego.

The last tight spot had been in California. Trader and Abe, the former main gunner of War Wag One, had apparently sacrificed themselves to save Ryan and the rest of the group from an enemy attack.

The love of Ryan's life was Krysty Wroth, who was, by definition, a mutie. She possessed the empathic ability to sense danger. The few others with these prescient powers were called "doomseers" or "doomies."

Krysty had been trained to hone this empathy by being in tune with the energies of Gaia, the great Earth Mother. By tapping into these energies, the power field of the planet itself, Krysty could gain superhuman strength for a limited time.

Ryan had an eleven-year-old son, Dean. The issue of a brief encounter between Ryan and Sharona, the wild wife of a frontier baron, Dean had been united with his father for only a short time. Ryan grew used to being called "Dad" and was totally devoted to the boy. Recently he had enrolled the lad for a year in the Brody School in Colorado. While his son received an education, the companions continued their journeys throughout Deathlands, with Ryan hoping to find that undefined something that would give his soul peace.

Frequently they used the gateway chambers to make mat-trans jumps, but those jumps had too many variables, since they never knew where—or even if—they would rematerialize.

As Doc had pointed out on more than one occasion, it was like deliberately jumping from a hot yet familiar frying pan into an unknown fire.

Though gateways were hidden in subterranean military complexes all over the continent, the vast majority were concentrated in the Southwest.

Mildred had said that even in her day, the public was aware that the government maintained secret underground bases in some Southwestern states. She claimed the official story was that the subterranean centers were part of the COG program, the Continuity of Government, in case of a national disaster, but most people suspected some kind of covert scientific research was going on. According to her, the gateway redoubts were probably only a small part of many hidden predark installations.

In fact, the wag the companions were traveling in had been found in an underground installation in Dulce, New Mexico, into which they had materialized from their last jump. It wasn't the same redoubt they had visited several times before, a few hours' journey from Jak's former ranch. They had realized in short order that the complex wasn't even a Redoubt. It was older and of a far different design. The mat-trans gateway was an addition to the original specs, almost an afterthought. There was little clue as to what function the installation had been built to serve. There were the usual No Unauthorized Personnel Beyond This Point warnings posted, but a curious symbol was imprinted at the bottom of every sign— a red triangle with three horizontal black lines running through it.

The Land Rover, one of several identical vehicles, was in almost perfect condition, with barely a hundred miles on the odometer. A former patrol wag, it was outfitted with a barricade remover, spotlight and public address system. There were a number of airtight containers of gasoline in the subterranean hideaway, and these had been used to power up a generator and recharge the battery. They had found a hand-operated air pump to reinflate the tires.

A cupboard in a side room yielded camping gear, which they loaded into the vehicle, plus an assortment of shirts and jeans, which they stuffed into a backpack and took along.

Though earnestly searched for, no spare tires could be found beyond the one they boosted from another Land Rover, but the supply of gasoline and spare cans was sufficient to carry them several thousand miles—up through Kansas and Nebraska, skirting a corner of Colorado and eventually to the ville once known as Calgary. After surveying that region, they intended to circle back around and pay a visit to Dean at his school.

For the past few days they had been following a remarkably well-preserved strip of road through South Dakota, toward the Black Hills. Ryan and J.B. had passed through the region before, and since in predark days it had been one of the most sparsely populated areas of America, they hoped violent encounters with muties or humans would be limited.

However, the injured man on the floor had obviously come from a settlement of some sort, either a ville or a barony. He had regained a sort of semiconsciousness, but he didn't speak, only murmured and groaned.

"Hitting the bottom of the grade, Ryan," J.B. stated. "What's the plan?"

"I'll take a quick look-see."

The wag rolled to a smooth, slow stop. Sliding open the door, Ryan cautiously poked his head out and checked their backtrack. He saw nothing, but the wind carried faint high-pitched cries.

"Looks fine," he said, shutting the door. "Start her up."

J.B. keyed the engine to rumbling life, threw the wag into gear and sent the vehicle rocketing up the road. Everyone lurched backward. Mildred, who was trying to affix a strip of gauze over one of the man's many lacerations, swore at him.

"Sorry," J.B. said with a grin. "Got carried away. This wag handles like a dream. Much better than that old LAV we used to have."

Mildred muttered something and returned to her task.

"One thing," J.B. added. "Got a pretty good look at that guy's bike when we passed it by. Looked like a Honda 150."

"So?" Jak asked.

"It was in great shape. Almost perfect."

"What's your point?" Krysty asked.

"Motorcycles aren't the safest form of transportation," J.B. answered. "Most of the ones I've ever seen were wired-together rattletraps."

Ryan considered J.B.'s words and agreed with him. Because they offered no protection from chem storms, mutie and human attacks or even bugs, motorcycles weren't the conveyance of choice in Deathlands. They were quaint, useless relics from predark days, holding a curiosity value only for kids Dean's age. Ryan could count on the fingers of one hand how many working models he had seen over the past thirty years.

An aspirated moan came from the man on the floor. "*Damn.* My balls hurt..."

"He's coming around," Mildred announced.

Chapter Three

The stranger propped himself up on one elbow, made a tentative move to touch his groin, blinked around, licked his lips and said faintly, "Hey."

"Hey yourself," Mildred replied. "Before you ask, you're not hurt too badly. Contusions, abrasions, a lot of lacerations, but most are superficial."

The man peered at her suspiciously. "You talk like a healer."

"I am. What's your name?"

The man scanned the faces in the back of the wag. "Those screamwings nearly chewed me to pieces. You got 'em off me?"

"Yeah," Ryan answered. "It was the only fair thing to do since we stirred them up."

"Accidentally," Krysty added. "The vibrations of the engine disturbed them."

Ryan made quick introductions all around, but the stranger didn't seem inclined to identify himself.

"Where are you from?" the man asked.

"Far and away, hither and yon," Doc replied with a smile.

"Never heard of them places," the man muttered.

"We're still waiting to hear your name," Mildred reminded him.

"Zadfrak."

"What?"

"Zadfrak," the man said impatiently. "I don't stutter, do I?"

Jak snickered, but fell silent when Ryan glanced his way.

"Where you from?" J.B. asked.

"Helskel."

Ryan's eyes narrowed. "That a ville, or what?"

Groaning, Zadfrak sat up. "A what."

Though the light was dimming, Ryan gave Zadfrak a close inspection. No longer covered in blood, he didn't look like a healthy man. His face bore a deep pallor that the sun could never touch, and his naked torso and limbs were fishbelly white. Between red-rimmed, watery blue eyes, an X was carved into the bridge of his nose. The scar looked like the result of a painful process involving a red-hot needle. Though the man appeared to be in his early- to mid-thirties, he was thin to the point of emaciation.

"Not carrying weapons," Jak said.

"So? That a crime?"

"No. Just triple stupe."

"How far to this Helskel?" J.B. demanded.

"What difference does it make to you, four-eyes?"

Ryan tensed, but J.B. only smiled gently. He took his foot off the gas pedal and allowed the wag to slow to a crawl. Turning his head to look at Zadfrak, he said in a quiet voice, "The difference is that I know just about every settlement, outpost and ville in Deathlands. I never heard of a Helskel."

In a quick flick of the wrist, J.B. picked up the M-4000 from the passenger seat, swung it around and pressed the bore against Zadfrak's back. "And since you were on a motorcycle, it means that wherever you came from isn't far from where we found you. And if you talk to me like that again, the screamwings will finish you off. Now—answer my question.''

Zadfrak seemed undisturbed by J.B.'s words and the pressure of the blaster. He coughed—a deep racking sound from the bottom of his lungs. He put a hand to his mouth, spit into it, examined the result and flung his hand down. The sputum made a bright pink blob on the dark metal of the floorplates.

''Rad cancer,'' Mildred commented, leaning back on her knees. ''I suspected as much.''

Zadfrak smiled sourly. ''Yeah. That's why I was out on my bike with no weapons. Didn't give a shit what came after me . . . screamwings, stickies, whatever.'' He half turned his head toward J.B. ''So go ahead and shoot. You'll beat the reaper by a couple of weeks, mebbe less.''

J.B. put his weapon back on the seat and returned his attention to driving.

''If that's the case,'' Ryan said, ''you want to be dropped off by the side of the road?''

Zadfrak shook his head. ''No. Figure I wasn't supposed to chill myself this way. Fate or destiny or some kind of shit brought us together. Might as well see where the ride takes me.''

''Getting dark pretty soon,'' J.B. said. ''Can we reach this Helskel of yours before nightfall?''

Zadfrak shook his head. ''It's a day's travel and a bit. Best make camp. You don't want to be on this road at night.''

''You know a safe place?'' Ryan asked.

''Yeah. A couple of miles up the road.''

Zadfrak moved around to face the shuttered windshield, leaning against the front seats. He directed J.B. to slow the vehicle, since the turnoff he was looking for wasn't easily detectable from the road, even in full daylight.

Ryan looked at Krysty and mouthed "Anything?"

She shook her head. "So far so good," she mouthed in response.

Though Ryan had the utmost faith in her abilities to sense danger, he wasn't comforted. Their new acquaintance appeared to be extraordinarily phlegmatic about his situation and his surroundings. He didn't make comments about the wag, or even the quality of the blasters everyone had in plain view. Many brave—or foolhardy—souls had tried to get their hands on the companions' weapons and had paid the ultimate price.

Following Zadfrak's instructions, J.B. turned the wag to the right, crossed the shoulder of the road and pushed through a few scraggly bushes. An old, almost completely overgrown gravel path pushed through the underbrush. The wag followed it slowly.

As the vehicle rolled farther down the path, the brush became sparser and they heard the sound of rushing water. Ryan looked past Zadfrak, his eye straining into the greenery ahead. He estimated they had penetrated two hundred yards into the underbrush when Zadfrak said, "Stop."

J.B. braked and sat with his hands on the wheel as he glanced over his shoulder at his guide. "Now what?"

"Now we get out. We got a supply of fresh water, nobody can see us from the road and we can kick back and bed down."

"The Black Hills are the hunting grounds of the Cheyenne and the Lakota."

Zadfrak made a derisive spitting noise. "The Family took care of the few that were around here. Tommorrow I'll show you what we do to redskins."

Mildred's lips compressed, but she said nothing.

Everyone disembarked, but no one wandered far. A small river was only a few hundred feet away. It wasn't very wide and didn't appear to be very deep, but judging by its lack of odor, the water was fresh enough.

Zadfrak leaned against the hood of the wag, not bothering to help pitch the tents or gather firewood. He accepted a sleeping bag from Jak without a word of thanks, as if it were his due.

They'd traded ammo for food in the last ville they'd passed through, and as Ryan helped Mildred break out the provisions, she said in a low, angry tone, "If that scrawny son of a bitch wasn't my patient, and wasn't terminal, I'd have J.B. teach him a lesson. I may do it myself if he doesn't watch his mouth."

Krysty and Jak prepared a meal, which was quickly consumed, and afterward they drank a pot of coffee sub.

Doc made a face after his first mouthful, and began his usual refrain that a coffee substitute should taste something like the original, not like boiled chicken droppings. He tried to enlist Mildred's aid in extolling the virtues of predark coffee, but she wasn't in the mood and told him so.

Ryan noticed that Zadfrak had eaten very little, but was sipping carefully at his cup of coffee sub. "Not much of an appetite?" he asked.

"My stomach always feels like it's full of broken glass. Can't eat much more than mush."

"Tell us about this Helskel," Krysty suggested.

He shrugged. "It's a place. In Manson's country."

"Man's Son's country?" J.B. echoed. "Sounds like some kind of religious retreat."

"It is, yeah. Kind of."

"That where got bike?" Jak asked.

Zadfrak nodded. "Yeah."

"Too bad lost it."

"Lots more where that one came from. Wags, too." He nodded toward the Land Rover. "Better than that one."

"What about fuel for them?" J.B. challenged. "That isn't easy to come by, unless you got a refinery setup."

"We do. And lots more. We got blasters of all kinds, all calibers. Plenty of ass, too."

"Sounds like heaven on earth," J.B. said sarcastically, trying to avoid meeting Mildred's icy glare.

Ryan doubted everything he'd heard. Colossal liars were legion in the Deathlands. But, to be polite, he asked, "Is all this stuff predark?"

Zadfrak took a sip from his tin cup. "Yeah. It all works, too. Lots of stuff stockpiled in the nose."

"The *nose?*" Doc asked. "Did I hear you right? The nose?"

Lifting his head, the man said, sounding suddenly fearful, "Forget it. I get delirious sometimes. My head gets mixed up."

"Whose nose?" Jak prompted.

"I said forget it! I may be half-chilled, but I'm still loyal to the Family."

"So your kin lives in Helskel," Mildred said. "How many?"

Zadfrak stood quickly, dashing the contents of his cup into the darkness. "I'm feeling like shit. Need to sleep."

With that, he turned and shuffled away, sleeping bag rolled under one arm.

"That," J.B. whispered, "is one of the strangest men I ever met."

"Story doesn't add up," Krysty murmured. "If Helskel isn't a figment of his imagination, then it's got to be a new ville."

"Especially with his talk about predark stuff in perfect working condition," J.B. agreed.

Ryan was too tired to weigh the truth of Zadfrak's tale. "Let's turn in. Doc, you got first watch."

"I'll spell you at midnight," J.B. said, checking his wrist chron. "After that, it's whoever I feel like rousing."

Mildred pushed herself stiffly to her feet. "Long as it isn't me."

Everyone retired to their tents. Ryan, as tired as he was, even with Krysty's head on his shoulder, found sleep elusive. His mind toyed with the images Zadfrak's words had conjured, settling on the man's sneering dismissal of the local Indian tribes in the region.

Hundreds of years ago, Pa Sappa, the Black Hills, were held in high religious regard by Plains tribes. They were holy places, power points watched over by Wankan Tankan, the Great Spirit. Since the nukecaust, many of the tribes had reasserted their ancient claims over lands stolen from them by the predark government. Though hostilities between the tribes and non-Amerindians weren't as bloody as two hundred years earlier, people still traveled through their lands holding on to their top-knots.

It was hard to believe that Zadfrak's family could have chased the Cheyenne and the Lakota and Ogallala Sioux out of the Black Hills, no matter how well armed he claimed Helskel to be.

Ryan finally fell into a fitful sleep, dreaming in fragments of a great bat-winged evil hovering overhead, of something as ancient as the land they traveled across. It was a dream of flight and pursuit and grinning, demonic faces.

The brief trilling of a songbird awakened him at daybreak. Peering out through the tent flap, he saw the sky was gray with "wolf's tail," the oyster hue of false dawn.

Careful not to disturb Krysty, Ryan took his gunbelt and crawled out of the tent, softfooting behind the wag to relieve himself. Buttoning up, he peered around the wag to see if Zadfrak was still asleep.

He was gone, his borrowed sleeping bag zipped open and spread out on the ground. Ryan made a quick circuit of the perimeter of the camp, but saw no sign of J.B. or anyone who had replaced him on watch. Checking the tents, he saw everyone was accounted for—except for Doc and J.B.

There was no sign of a struggle, and he knew, as uneasy as his sleep had been, the slightest odd sound would have snapped him awake. He saw by the lightening sky a few footprints in the hard-packed earth around Doc's tent, which led toward the riverbank.

Ryan started to walk in that direction and hadn't gone far when he heard laughing voices over the rush of the current. Though he couldn't make out the words, he identified the tones as belonging to J.B. and Doc.

Realizing he'd been holding his breath, Ryan released it in a sigh. He slowed his pace.

Then he heard the scream.

Chapter Four

An insistent bladder had prodded Doc awake in the pre-dawn darkness. Stumbling from his tent, he passed J.B. and Zadfrak sitting around the dying campfire, drinking cups of coffee sub. J.B. gave him a one-finger salute as he went into the shadows to urinate.

He was more awake by the time he returned to the fire. Knuckling his eyes, he asked, "Have you been up all night, John Barrymore?"

"Just since midnight, when I spelled you. Got at least an hour till sunrise. Why don't you go back to bed?"

Doc stifled a yawn and sat down next to Zadfrak, reaching for the coffeepot. "I believe I shall tarry here a moment."

"We're thinking about trying to catch a mess of trout for breakfast," J.B. said. "Zadfrak says there's some rainbow in the river."

The old man nodded eagerly. Fishing was one of his passions. "Sounds very much like a plan. I am certain everyone would rather have fresh fish than beef-jerky broth."

"Let's go then," Zadfrak said, getting to his feet. He covered his mouth, coughed, hawked, then spit into the embers.

Doc fetched a rod and reel and tackle box from the storage compartment of the wag. The black sky was turning gray, so they were able to negotiate the path Zadfrak led them down.

The river's current wasn't particularly fast, and the bank gave way to a fifty-odd foot curve of mudflats. Doc affixed a lure to his line and carefully picked his way out across the mud. Neither J.B. nor Zadfrak seemed inclined to join him.

The earth squished beneath Doc's feet, but he barely sank into it more than ankle deep. Reaching its edge, he cast the line as far as he could toward the center of the rushing water. He had only begun to reel it back in when the line quivered with a strike. Over his shoulder, he called, "I've made contact, gentlemen!"

Zadfrak stumbled and slogged out across the flats to join him. "Play him some, old man. Don't let the bastard run into the deepwater."

Doc didn't reply, though he found a backseat fisherman as irritating as J.B. probably found a backseat driver. Zadfrak kept up a steady stream of advice, encouragement and an occasional burst of profanity.

The pole bent at a forty-five-degree curve, the line was taut and Doc strained against the pull. His shoulder muscles began to ache, but he kept on playing out slack, reeling it back in and working his way to the left.

Finally, after about six or seven minutes of struggle, Doc landed the trout with Zadfrak's help. The fish was, as Doc proclaimed it, a genuine whopper.

The rainbow trout was at least three and a half feet long, weighing upwards of forty pounds. Doc and J.B. let out whooping laughs, with Zadfrak clapping his hands in spontaneous applause.

"To hell with breakfast," J.B. called from the bank. "Take us two full days to eat that whale!"

Doc shifted his position, finding some solid footing so Zadfrak could remove the feather-bedecked hook from the trout's mouth. Suddenly the mud heaved beneath the old man's feet with a convulsive shudder, and a spray of water and slime flew into the air.

Stumbling and slipping on the slick surface, Doc lost his balance and fell with a splat. In the watery sludge in front of him shone two cold, white-encircled black eyes, each the width and breadth of his outstretched hands. Less than a foot from his face, a huge rubbery-lipped maw with a shovel-shaped underjaw opened with a liquidy, slurping gasp.

Doc knew exactly what he was facing. For half a heartbeat, terror froze him motionless. Then he screamed, clawing and kicking himself away from the gaping mouth of the mucksucker.

The creature lifted itself out of the mud on finned, stiff-membraned lobes, its titantic toothless jaws closing on Doc's left ankle with a crushing force.

Propelled by its fins, the mucksucker made a wrenching backward heave, its fluked tail threshing the water into a white froth. It intended to drag Doc into the river with it. Digging his fingers into the mud, the old man kicked out with his right leg, which skidded across the slippery charcoal-gray skin of the mutie's blunt snout.

A small, rational part of Doc's mind told him the mucksucker wasn't really a monster, but only a mutated form of catfish, a lungfish that dredged its meals from shallow bottoms and mudflats. Straining its sustenance through a fibrous screen at the back of its throat, a mucksucker was mostly considered a nuisance, not a threat.

The larger part of Doc's mind, the irrational part in charge, told him he was in the grip of a twenty-foot-long, half-ton hellspawn that intended to eat him.

He cursed himself for leaving his swordstick behind. Bracing himself with one hand, Doc managed to draw his Le Mat from its holster, but another backward lurch of the mucksucker jerked the blaster out of his sludge-slick hand. The weapon fell into an algae-scummed puddle.

As he groped frantically for it, he heard J.B.'s shouting, splashing charge and he glimpsed Zadfrak lash the mucksucker across its broad skull with the fishing rod. It twitched in pain, but refused to release its grip.

Zadfrak planted one foot on its head, preparing to drive the rod into one of its eyes like a spear. Then, like a sail unfurling, a serrated dorsal fin unfolded vertically from the mucksucker's back. The sharp spines of the fin stabbed Zadfrak's right arm and slashed furrows along his side. He staggered backward, crying out, dropping the rod to hug himself. He fell onto his back full length with a splatter of mud and grunt of forcefully expelled air.

Blood sprang from half a dozen punctures on his arm, from shoulder to elbow. Doc saw crimson glistening along his rib cage as Zadfrak thrashed over, gaining a kneeling position. Shooting out his left arm, his surprisingly strong fingers closed around Doc's right wrist.

"Grab me with your other hand," Zadfrak gritted from between clenched teeth.

Doc followed his instructions, grasping the man's wrist with both hands. The next backward lunge of the mucksucker dragged them only a foot.

There was a sudden fusillade of shots. Doc recognized the sharp snapping stutter of J.B.'s Uzi and the suppressed crack of Ryan Cawdor's SIG-Sauer. One of the mucksucker's huge white-rimmed eyes broke apart in a spray of gelatinous fluid, and several holes were stitched across the blunt skull.

The creature's long tail flailed and slapped spasmodically. Mud flew in great sheets, covering Doc, stuffing his nose and blinding his eyes.

The crushing pressure on his foot relaxed, and Zadfrak yanked him forward and to his feet. He heard a muffled, mushy explosion, then a stinking wave of warm air washed over him.

Pawing the mud out of his eyes, Doc watched the death convulsions of the monster fish. Part of its long thick-barreled body looked oddly deflated, and he realized that a bullet had punctured one of its internal air sacs.

He was still snorting sludge from his nostrils when Ryan grabbed him by the shoulders and spun him.

"Are you all right, Doc?" he asked, bending over to probe his legs with searching fingers.

"Just bewildered, thanks to our newfound friend."

J.B. was attending to Zadfrak, who held his right arm at a stiff, unnatural angle. The skin around the puckered punctures was swollen and turning a livid purple.

"Damn thing finned me," he said with a grimace. "Got a dose of the poison."

"You're having the luck of a shithouse rat since you met up with us," J.B. said sympathetically. "Hope you did better on your own."

The rest of the group, roused by the gunfire, came running to the riverbank. Though in various states of dress, all brandished blasters, fingers on triggers, barrels swinging back and forth seeking targets.

"It's okay," Ryan called. "A run-in with a mucksucker. Taken care of."

Turning to Zadfrak, Ryan squeezed the man's left shoulder. "We thank you for that."

"Had to watch my son die," Zadfrak said faintly. "Rad cancer got him. Ain't fair to be chilled when you mean no harm."

Supported by Ryan, Zadfrak managed to walk rubber-legged to the bank. Mildred examined the wounds in his arm. "We'll have to try to draw out the poison."

"We have some fixings for a poultice in the wag," Krysty said.

Held up by Krysty, Zadfrak followed Mildred back to the campsite. J.B. studied the mucksucker's carcass.

"We spend a day salting it down, we'll have a month's supply of meat."

Doc pursed his lips, as if tasting something sour. "If the axiom 'you are what you eat' is indeed true, are you sure you want to consume the flesh of a creature that feeds on offal and excrement?"

"Eaten worse," Jak commented, unsheathing a long knife and striding out toward the mucksucker.

Doc retrieved his Le Mat and the rod and reel. J.B. glanced toward the river and said, "Your rainbow got away. Flopped back into the water. It was a genuine whopper."

Running his fingers through his mud-caked hair, Doc replied, "They all are, my dear fellow. They all are. And they always get away."

Under the watchful eye and blasters of Ryan and J.B., Doc waded waist deep into the river and washed the mud and slime from his body and clothes. Jak continued his single-minded task of cleaning the mucksucker. It wasn't particularly hard work, though it was bloody. Ryan reckoned the job almost too difficult for one man, but

Jak was from the Louisiana bayous and obviously had experience.

By the time the sun had topped the horizon, the white-haired youth had flayed the rubbery skin and excised the body from dorsal to ventral.

J.B. and Ryan returned to the camp, since Doc had volunteered to stay behind and watch the teenager's back. A fire had been built, and a noxious odor wafted from a bubbling pot hanging from a spit over it. Mildred was tending to the pot, stirring it with a long wooden spoon.

J.B. wrinkled his nose. "I hope that's not breakfast."

"It's Krysty's poultice," Mildred said. "I don't usually have a lot of faith in folk remedies, but it's the best we've got."

Ryan bent over Zadfrak, who was lying in his sleeping bag. Eyes closed, his face filmed with perspiration, he was shivering as if from a chill. His lips had a slight bluish tinge. Pressing a hand to the man's forehead, Ryan felt a terrible heat. "He's burning up."

"I know," Mildred replied. "He's having an extreme reaction to the toxin. A healthy man might be sick for a day, but our guest is anything but healthy."

Guided by Krysty's instructions, Mildred stirred the heated mixture of herbs and plants. She poured the pulpy paste onto a square of porous cloth, then tied the four corners together to make a leaky bag. Moving over to Zadfrak, she stretched out his swollen right arm and applied the cloth over several of the punctures.

"That's supposed to draw the poison out?" J.B. asked.

"Supposedly. Even so, the shock to his system may be too severe for him to rally." Standing, she wiped her hands clean against her pants. "All we can do is wait."

They waited. The prospect of remaining in the area another full day and night didn't disturb Ryan. He owed Zadfrak the chance to pull through. Besides, they had a supply of fresh water and, Doc's objections to mucksucker meat notwithstanding, plenty of food. Also, they were well hidden, or so he hoped.

Along toward late afternoon, while a mucksucker stew cooked over the fire, there came the stealthy sound of feet treading on leaves and dry twigs.

Everyone within earshot of the sound reacted immediately, rolling to their feet, blaster barrels snapping up, bodies assuming combat stances. A black-and-white pinto pony stepped lightly from the underbrush at the western perimeter of the campsite.

Astride the horse's back was a slightly built but lithe-looking Sioux warrior. He wore a fringed buckskin hunting shirt and leggings. His black hair flowed freely down his back, and red hawk feathers were pinned to the back of his head. His face, though unpainted, was a mask of restrained ferocity.

The warrior could have stepped from the nineteenth century or an old Western vid, except for the M-16 automatic assault rifle cradled in his arms. His sharp, dark eyes closely examined the faces of the people spread out in a semicircle around him, finally resting on Zadfrak.

Ryan and J.B. had picked up a smattering of the Lakota language in their travels, so Ryan said, *"Hou le mita cola."*

The warrior's grim slash of a mouth twitched ever so slightly at the flawed pronunciation of "Hello, my friend."

"Good afternoon," he said in perfect, unaccented English. "I am Touch-the-Sky. The *wasicun* call me Joe."

Noticing that the blaster bores pointing at him hadn't wavered, he added, "I mean no harm. I assure you I'm alone."

Ryan slowly lowered his blaster, and everyone followed suit, though J.B. did so reluctantly and slowly.

"I see you caught a mucksucker," Joe said.

"Would you like some?" Krysty asked. "There's plenty."

Joe made a face, but stopped short of sticking out his tongue. "No, thank you. I never acquired a taste for it. And, frankly, neither has anyone else I know."

Doc whispered into J.B.'s ear, "See, I told you."

Shifting position on his saddle blanket, Joe added, "Besides, this isn't a social call. Why are you giving aid to the marked man?"

"The what?" Ryan asked.

Joe traced an X on his forehead. "The man who bears the mark of the Family. It means he has crossed himself out of the flow of life."

"I don't follow you."

"You don't know he's from Helskel?"

"You mean there *is* such a place?" Mildred asked.

"There is, and if you value your lives, your spirits, you'll give it a very wide berth." He gestured toward Zadfrak. "Leave that carrion and go."

"We owe a life to that man," Ryan said. "Whatever he is, wherever he's from, he's sick and we owe him."

"I understand you must discharge such debts. Even in the darkest of hearts there is light somewhere, and that man's heart is very dark. But I don't intend to threaten you—only to warn."

"You're being very cryptic," Doc said. "Inscrutable, even."

Joe smiled. "In which case I'm living up to my stereotype. Very well. I'll speak with a blunt tongue."

Saluting the area around them, he said, "This land once belonged to the Cheyenne, the Lakota, the Crow, the Pawnee. When skydark came, we believed it was a time of deliverance for our people and divine retribution against the white man. Their religion, their outrages, their politics, all was swept away. The tribes of my people returned to the old ways. We hoped the predark evil was destroyed forever. Unfortunately, evil has a way of returning . . . or, in the case of Helskel's masters, never going away."

"You said you were going to speak with a blunt tongue," Ryan reminded him.

"A few survivors of predark politics and predark science banded together. They seek nothing less than to regain dominion of the world, to rebuild the ugly, soul-destroying societies and bureaucracies. They wish to revive the horrors of predark."

Pointing at Zadfrak, he continued, "That man and his so-called family are their servitors. If you return him to Helskel, then you'll learn the truth of my words. By then, it may be too late for all of you."

Reacting to the pressure of Joe's knees, the pony turned and trotted back into the brush.

A hoarse cough from Zadfrak drew their attention. He was conscious, but his eyes were glassy. They sought out Ryan.

"You going to do what that red man said? Leave me behind?"

Ryan kneeled beside him, feeling his forehead. His fever was down. "Is that what you would do in our place?"

Zadfrak tried to grin. "Probably."

"What do you want us to do?"

"Take me home. Let me die with the Family."

"We'll do it."

He nodded and closed his eyes. His breathing was shallow. Mildred lifted the poultice, noted the condition of the arm, listened to his heartbeat, timed his pulse and examined his pupils.

When she arose, her expression was grave. "His temperature's down, but not enough. His lungs are filling. He's got a day and a half, maybe three at the outside."

Eyeing Zadfrak sadly, Doc said, "Then we should to do what he wants. Get him back to his family."

"Have you noticed," Krysty interjected, "that he refers to 'the' family and not 'my' family?"

"An idiosyncrasy of speech," Doc said, "using the definite article. Maybe it's just local idiom."

"Don't forget those DNA suckers back in Louisiana who referred to themselves the same way," Mildred commented.

Krysty hugged herself. "I doubt we'll ever forget them, though I wish to Gaia I could."

Ryan studied the position of the sun. "Too late in the day to start now. Think he can last until tomorrow, Mildred?"

"I'll do what I can," she replied. "But at this point, it may be damn little."

Chapter Five

For seven hours the wag had been traveling across a stretch of highway that barely qualified as a footpath. The asphalt was cracked, split, furrowed, wrinkled and overgrown with scraggly weeds. On either side were wide featureless expanses of dark earth. Far ahead, the dome-shaped peaks of the Black Hills shouldered the sky. Rising above them was the snow-capped Harney Peak, the highest point in Deathlands east of what remained of the Rockies.

The relatively smooth surface of the highway had deteriorated with every mile they logged. Zadfrak, drifting in and out of lucidity, neglected to inform J.B. of that fact. More than once he had been forced to engage the wag's front-wheel drive to get them over sections of highway that had completely caved in. Everyone was jounced, bounced, tossed and thoroughly pummeled. It occurred to Ryan that if the rad cancer didn't kill Zadfrak, the trip home certainly would. However, they should have known that a halfway decent stretch of road was more of an anomaly than a standard. Over a hundred years earlier, "earthshaker" bombs had completely resculpted the Cific coast.

New mountains had appeared almost overnight, long-dormant volcanoes had erupted and month-long earthquakes had shaken thousands of square miles with cataclysmic shocks and tremors.

A time or two their rad counters registered readings wavering uncomfortably close to the orange sector, but the "warm zones" were quickly bypassed.

J.B. suddenly leaned forward, peering through the ob slit, and relaxed the pressure on the gas pedal. He pointed. "Something up ahead."

Ryan followed the pointing finger and for a moment couldn't identify the shapes he saw lining the right side of the roadway. Purely from habit, he drew his SIG-Sauer. Even when he finally identified the shapes as harmless, he didn't leather it.

Affixed to six-foot-tall wooden poles were grinning human skulls, bleached by the sun and scoured by the wind. Small holes had been drilled in the tops of the craniums, and projecting from them were colorful spinning pinwheels. The brightly hued vanes fluttered cheerfully in the breeze.

J.B. came to a stop near the first skull. Ryan counted ten more, planted at fifty-foot intervals on the edge of the road. Turning to the passenger compartment, he said, "Zadfrak. You awake?"

The man raised his head from the floor. His eyes were sunken, surrounded by dark rings. "Yeah?"

"What are these bastard skulls supposed to mean?"

Zadfrak's dry lips peeled back from his discolored teeth in a grin. "Signposts. And warnings to the Injuns. Those are the skulls of red men. Put a couple of 'em up myself. When you reach the last one, take a hard right."

He coughed and then, in a cracked, sandpapery voice, sang, "One little two little three little Indians—"

Mildred put a hand over his mouth and shoved his head back down to the floor. "Shut up," she said in a monotone. "Not another word or I'll gag you with the tip of my boot."

Ryan and J.B. exchanged a long look, then the wag began to move again. Just past the tenth signpost was a path that at first glance was no more than a shallow trench raked through the dirt. J.B. turned the vehicle onto it.

It was a rugged, rocky roadway surrounded by castellated hills. The suspension of the Land Rover creaked and groaned so loudly that Ryan wondered if the wag could take the roughing.

The narrow road swerved around rock formations and gullies, and Krysty swore as the vehicle yawed and she nearly fell from her seat. The area looked like hell with the fires out. An ancient sea bottom of clay strata worn by aeons of frost and flood had been shaped into forms resembling colossal pagodas and pyramids. Throat and eye-burning vapors arose from burning coal seams in the ground, cloaking their surroundings with a noxious fog.

The path swung down into a dry arroyo with a lazy serpentine motion. Pebbles rattled noisily beneath the Land Rover's wheels and chassis. J.B. suddenly slowed the vehicle to a crawl, hitting the brakes and downshifting.

It was late afternoon, with sunlight slanting through the dust. Children played in the warmth, mothers lay upon old mattresses on the ridge, dogs yapped and bounded all about.

The children, unnerved by the lion roar of the wag's engine, ran squalling up the sides of the bank. Their mothers beckoned to them and stared at the wag with a combination of fear, hostility and open curiosity.

"I think this is the place," Ryan stated.

J.B. urged the vehicle another two hundred feet into the arroyo and braked. The mothers and children stood above them on the edge of the ridge and stared down.

Turning to Krysty, Ryan asked, "Feel anything, lover?"

She narrowed her green eyes. "Not danger exactly, but certainly no friendliness. Curiosity mainly. Want me to get out and talk to them?"

"No, I'll make the contact," Ryan said, holstering his blaster. "Keep the engine running and your fingers on the triggers. Orange alert."

Opening the door, Ryan stepped out, hands held well away from the butt of his blaster. One of the women was closer than the others. She was a slim, curly haired female dressed in a ragged shift with the hemline at her upper thighs. A little boy was trying to crawl up one of her legs.

"Afternoon," said Ryan, pasting a friendly smile on his face.

The woman only nodded.

"Is this the way to Helskel?"

She nodded again.

"How far?"

She parted her pale lips. Her voice was creaky, as if she were unaccustomed to using it. "Half a mile. Less."

"Thanks. Do you know a man named Zadfrak? We're looking for his family."

The woman's small eyes suddenly narrowed. "Why?"

Before Ryan could answer, a whip crack split the air, and a fountain of dirt erupted from the arroyo floor a foot in front of him. Even as the dust spurted, Ryan lunged backward against the wag, the SIG-Sauer springing from its holster into his hand.

To jump back inside the Land Rover would require a couple of seconds, an eternity in which he would be exposed to bullets. Crouching behind one of the armored flanges protecting the wheel wells, Ryan peered up at the lip of the ridge. He saw the woman and children scuttling away.

The gun ports opened in the wag, and he heard the rear door handle turning. "No," he commanded sternly. "Everyone stay inside."

A second shot winged past, buzzing like a furious bee. Ryan looked over the wheel well, tracking for a target. He was angry at Zadfrak. He should have warned them to expect an attack, but then again, the one-eyed man should have expected one, as well. Ambushes were part and parcel of life in Deathlands.

A third steel-jacketed bullet spanged off the wag's heavy metal hide, leaving a shiny smear on the bodywork to commemorate its impact.

"Hey, you crazy bastards!" Ryan shouted. "I'm not impressed!"

There was a rustling from the brush at the crest of the arroyo's bank, and a hoarse voice inquired, "You armed?"

"Of course."

"What do you want?"

"We're returning a favor. Got a sick man here who says he's from Helskel. We're bringing him home."

"What's his name?"

"Zadfrak."

There was a long period of silence, then Ryan could hear faint whispers. The voice shouted, "Okay, it's cowboy time. Stand up, blaster by the barrel."

The six-inch barrel of Jak's Colt Python protruded from the gun port over his head, and Ryan heard the youth say, "Got in my sights. Three men rifles."

Ryan stood slowly, holding his blaster by the barrel. As if waiting for a cue, three men broke out of the shrubbery at the lip of the ridge. Their beards and long hair were matted with dust and twigs, and they wore the ragged remnants of shorts. Battered tennis shoes covered their feet, and though their rifles looked as if they had seen better days, they used them carefully to cover him and the wag.

A burly man with a mass of curly dark hair confined by a leather thong leapt down the bank, cradling a bolt-action Remington mountain rifle in his arms. Though he was grinning, his eyes held the alert, wary look of a half-wild animal.

He dropped lightly onto the arroyo's floor and approached Ryan, the wide grin never faltering. He looked over the Land Rover and said, "Nice wag. Where do you find the gas for it?"

Ryan shrugged. "Here and there. Can I put my hands down now?"

The man responded to the question with one of his own. "What's your name?"

"Cawdor."

He nodded. "Thought so. One-eyed man with a SIG-Sauer. Heard of you. Used to ride with the Trader. Yeah, you can put your hands down."

Ryan did so, but he didn't leather the blaster. "What's your name?"

"Phil. The other two gentlemen are known as Dog and Suds."

"Who's who?"

Phil indicated the taller of the pair. "This is Suds."

If Suds had ever introduced a drop of water to his face, he might have been fairly good-looking. As it was, his skin was almost black with encrusted dirt. Straight raven hair was gathered in a knot at the base of his neck. A cloud of gnats hovered around him.

"This here's Dog."

Dog was short and fair-complected, and he was one of the ugliest mortals Ryan had ever seen. The left side of his face was covered by red, puckered weal, a badly healed scar that lifted his lip on that side revealing brown, cavity-ridden teeth in a permanent grin. His hair was shaggy and dirty, and at one time might have been blond. The irises of his eyes were a yellow-brown.

"Dog ain't got no tongue," Phil went on. "Had it shot out of his head by a Lakota. Can't talk, but Jesus God, is he mean."

Dog looked at Ryan out his yellow eyes and grunted. Saliva dripped from his lip on the left side of his mouth.

Ryan noticed one similarity that all three men shared— a lack of an X carved into their foreheads.

"You're not Zadfrak's family," Ryan stated.

Phil shook his head. "Novitiates. We're Farers, trying out for Helskel's militia. Right now we're part-time sec men, not full-time X-men."

Farers were a loosely knit but far-flung group of nomads who traveled the midwestern Deathlands, trading goods, foodstuffs and even themselves to villes.

"Yeah, a real nice wag," Phil said, walking around the Land Rover and kicking the front tire. "What would you trade for it?"

"Nothing."

Phil grinned. "We could just appropriate it, if you don't want to bargain."

"Could try. I should point out that at least five blasters are pointed at you from the inside." Ryan lifted the SIG-Sauer but didn't aim it. "Not to mention the one out here. I doubt you small-timers could take all of us."

Dog made a slobbering sound. Ryan smiled coldly, knowing that the three men would either start a firefight they couldn't win or knuckle under.

Phil continued to grin, but there was a trace of uncertainty in his eyes. "Don't get fused, man. You said you had a passenger, a Family member?"

"Yeah. He's sick."

"Come on into Helskel, then. Strangers are always welcome."

He turned and began trudging down the arroyo. Dog and Suds lingered behind. When Ryan made a move to open the passenger-side door, Dog jammed the bore of the rifle into his spine.

Over his shoulder, Phil said, "You walk with us. Your pals are less apt to get nervy with their blasters if you're on the road with us."

The rifle barrel prodded Ryan's kidney, and whirling quickly, he backfisted the length of steel away. "Back off, friend."

Dog growled and lunged forward, swinging the rifle, trying to shatter Ryan's profile with the wood-grain stock. The one-eyed warrior dropped to the ground, knocking his adversary's legs out from under him with a swift leg sweep. Dog went down heavily on his back with a crunch of gravel.

Springing erect, Ryan put the bore of the SIG-Sauer on Suds and booted Dog expertly beneath the chin with his right foot. His victim's head snapped back and met the arroyo floor with a thud. Ryan kicked the Remington from his slack fingers, and it clattered over the rocks end over end.

Phil was staring at him. His grin had been replaced by an O of surprise. He looked at Dog, dazed and twitching in the dust, and said faintly, "I hope you didn't kill him."

"No. I'm riding into Helskel in my wag, with my people, with Zadfrak. You three'll lead us. You try to run, you try to lead us into an ambush, I'll put six bullets along the buttons of your spine. Acceptable?"

Phil nodded. He and Suds helped the groggy Dog to his feet.

Ryan climbed into the wag and said to J.B., "I guess we've been formally welcomed."

After less than a mile the arroyo opened into a wide flat plain with cultivated fields. The crops were wheat, corn and beans. Beyond the fields was Helskel.

The overall design of the place was a confusing mishmash of architecture: circus tents, geodesic domes, Quonset huts and lean-tos. The main part of the ville looked like a standing set from an old Hollywood western vid. The wag wheeled up the main thoroughfare, following Phil, Dog and Suds.

Helskel was one great open market, where nearly anything could be bought or sold. Shops and stalls were brightly painted. Vendors with wheelbarrows cried out the merits of their wares, jolt merchants were shouting "today only" special deals and wandering musicians played a discordant variety of tunes, few of them recognizable.

Men and women on motorcycles roared up and down, back and forth along the streets, throwing choking clouds of dust into the air. Ryan noted that all the cycles looked new, with fresh paint, highly polished chrome and the sounds of healthy engines.

A large number of people sporting Xs on their foreheads wandered everywhere, a curious conglomeration of all races and ages, dressed and undressed in every imaginable fashion. A few men sporting shaven pates and the X scars trooped about. They wore mirrored sunglasses, carried compact Tec-10 machine pistols and wore gray corduroy vests decorated with hanks of human hair. They might as well have carried signs labeling them sec men.

Most people on the street shuffled, stumbled or lay about, busily doing whatever occurred to them at the moment. One girl, completely naked except for looping whorls of blue paint, danced alone atop the rusting, wheelless husk of an old wag, moving in time to the soundless music of invisible instruments. The hot metal of the roof had to have been burning her bare feet, but she didn't seem to notice.

"The bastard spawn of the predark," Mildred muttered.

"Lilies of the field," Doc said. "They toil not, nor do they spin."

Zadfrak, on the floor of the Land Rover, was completely unconscious, not responding to Krysty telling him that he was home.

The dusty avenue went past hovel and tent and crude shack, until it opened in a large central square. Phil stopped in the middle of the street and pointed to a three-story wooden-frame structure, the only building in the square. "The Patriarch needs to look you over before any other business gets done."

Climbing out of the Land Rover, Ryan said, "Your man needs medical attention."

"That can wait. Got to make sure you fit in."

Everyone disembarked, J.B. making a very exaggerated show of pocketing the ignition key. Even if a thief cracked the steering column in an attempt to hot-wire the wag, an electric circuit was connected to a small but frightfully destructive package of plastic explosive inside the firewall.

Phil gestured toward the bat-winged doors, and Ryan led his party inside.

If it hadn't been for the electric light fixtures and silent, glowing jukebox in the far corner, the saloon might have been mistaken for a watering hole of two hundred years earlier. The bar top, the tables and the floor were exceptionally clean, and brass footrails and spittoons gleamed with a high polish. From the distance came the faint throb of an electric generator.

Mildred, standing beside Ryan, suddenly froze and said, "Oh my God. The Family. Helskel. I should've been able to put the pieces together. Zadfrak wasn't talking about Man's Son's country. He meant *Manson's* country."

"What mean?" Jak asked.

"Charles M. Manson," Mildred replied. "Look."

Following her pointing finger, they gazed at the huge mural mounted on the wall behind the bar. It depicted in gold and brown Charlie Manson's final ascent into heaven, amid joyous welcome from angels above and remorse from the deluded souls below. The deluded souls had human bodies, but their heads were those of swine.

Near the top of the mural stood God, smiling beatifically as he beckoned his second only begotten son with widespread arms.

"Blasphemy," Doc muttered. "Sick. Depraved."

"Who the hell is Charles Manson supposed to be?" J.B. demanded impatiently.

"Our spiritual savior," a soft, hollow voice replied. "He who shaped Deathlands into the image of paradise he foresaw over a century ago."

The vision of the mural had taken everyone aback for a moment, so they hadn't immediately noticed the man sitting against the north wall. He was a vision almost as startling as the mural.

The man's body was lanky, and very thin. Beneath a thick shock of upstanding jet black hair, rose a remarkably high forehead. It was impossible to gauge his age. He had one of those smooth, unlined faces that would always look the same between the ages of twenty-five and sixty-five. His eyes were in shadow, but there was something, some force swimming in them that raised the fine hairs on Ryan's nape. It was a spark of self-centered dedication to a single goal, a single-minded drive to attain an inexplicable objective.

The man's hands were very long, and he had them steepled before his pursed mouth. He was dressed completely in white—white blazer, white shirt, white tie, white trousers and shoes. There wasn't a single speck of color anywhere on him. He was sitting in a large fan-backed wicker chair.

"Shades of Somerset Maugham," Doc whispered to Mildred.

Phil stepped up to the white-suited man and ducked his head. He spoke to him rapidly in a low whisper for quite a while, then gestured to Ryan.

The leader of the companions approached the chair and the man suddenly waved a hand. "Far enough, kindly," he said. "You are covered with road dust and exude a frightful odor."

Ryan didn't bother to swallow his irritation. "If I'd known we'd be meeting, I'd have bathed in rose water and disinfectant."

The thin man eyed him broodily. "You've an intrusive tongue. Did I ask you a question? No matter. Phil tells me your name is Cawdor."

"That is true."

"*Ryan* Cawdor, I presume."

"Yeah."

"He tells me you've brought Zadfrak back to us."

"True again."

"Why?"

"Because he asked us. He's sick."

The thin man stirred. "I know that, Ryan Cawdor. I also know that I cast Zadfrak out of the Family. Disowned him, stripped him of his rights and set him loose in Deathlands to die. Returning him here is a great affront."

"Zadfrak didn't mention that. We owed him a debt, and he wanted to be returned to Helskel. That's all there is to it."

The man smiled in an odd, cold way. "I don't think I believe you. I think you came here to make mischief."

Ryan returned the cold smile. "Oh?"

"There could be no other reason."

There was a shuffling behind Ryan, then a barely audible click. He spun, hand darting to his blaster. In a jagged fragment of a second he saw that the entire wall backing the jukebox had swiveled open, disgorging seven of the shaven-headed X-scarred men, all aiming large-caliber handblasters. Some were automatics, some were revolvers, but all looked brand-new.

The cold tip of a gun touched the back of Ryan's neck. He heard the sound of a round being jacked into a chamber and froze, hand on the butt of the SIG-Sauer.

The thin man held up one narrow hand. "That bloodies the floor, much as you'd enjoy it. There are other ways."

The white-clad man stared at him with shadow-pooled eyes. Ryan's mind sensed a whispering touch, like an invisible, wispy cobweb brushing him with ectoplasmic tentacles. His heart began to pound. The man was a psionic, a line-of-sight telepath. He wasn't necessarily a mutie, but norms with true telepathic abilities were extremely rare. Extrasensory and precognitive perceptions were the most typical abilities possessed by muties who appeared to be normal.

The vague touch disappeared, and he heard Krysty draw in her breath sharply. The man in the white suit suddenly stiffened, and Ryan guessed that the mind probe had been directed at Krysty and met unexpected resistance.

"Your woman is a telepath?" the man demanded. He paused, then added in a meditative tone, "No, an empath. A doomseer. But with formidable abilities."

"You're not so unique after all," Krysty said.

A smile drifted onto the man's angular face. "Very true. My name is Lars Hellstrom." His tone was much more relaxed. "Sorry about the coldness of the reception, but we can't be too careful with all the anarchist crazies and night-creeping Indians running loose these days."

"I agree," Ryan replied. He could hear the person behind him breathing. The pressure of the gun bore was still against the back of his neck, and he considered disarming the bastard, but Hellstrom raised a languid hand.

"Hold on that, Fleur. I've scanned him. He's not an enemy. At least, not yet."

The pressure of the gun barrel was removed, and hearing the rhythmic clacking of boot heels on wood, Ryan turned slightly.

The tallest woman he had ever seen walked slowly around him, giving him the briefest of appraising glances. A black .380 Beretta 85-F dangled from her right hand. She looked to be only half an inch shy of Ryan's six feet, two inches. Her face might have been beautiful if not for the grave, joyless expression she wore, the X scar on her forehead and the gold-embroidered black patch covering her left eye.

There was an air of dangerous assurance about her, of knowing precisely what her abilities were and how superior they were to others. However, that quality, coupled with her manner of dress—brown leather jacket, skintight jeans and knee-high black boots—didn't detract from the femininity exuding from the smoothly chiseled features, one cobalt blue eye and the luxuriant waist-length fall of dark mahogany hair. A fourteen-inch bowie knife was scabbarded crosswise across her belly.

The woman squirmed into a comfortable position on Hellstrom's lap, and he absently fondled her upper thigh. "This is Fleur, my warlord. Looks like you and she have something in common, Cawdor, at least in the old glassie department. You both fall a little short of a twenty-twenty vid."

Fleur impaled Ryan with a blue glare. "I've never found it a problem," he said.

"You're a very adaptable fellow," Hellstrom replied.

Addressing the armed X-men, he declared, "Blasters down. It's secure for the moment."

Ryan made introductions all around and removed his hand from the SIG-Sauer, but went back to it when a commotion broke out behind him. Several sec men were dragging Zadfrak's limp form into the saloon. The backswing of the bat-winged doors dealt him a nasty crack on the head. He cried out, and Mildred made a move to intervene.

Krysty put a hand on her arm. "No," she breathed. "Great danger here."

Mildred subsided, but she favored the sec men with a ferocious glare.

Zadfrak was dropped roughly to the wooden floor, six feet in front of Hellstrom. Fleur arose from Hellstrom's lap and leaned against the back of his chair.

Crooking a long finger, Hellstrom gazed down at Zadfrak and said, "Come here."

The man tried to rise, but the meager reserves of strength contained in his diseased body were exhausted.

"On your belly, then," Hellstrom said. "By returning here after you were cast out, your status is less than an animal's."

Sickened, more than a little angered, Ryan watched as Zadfrak slowly and laboriously crawled toward Hellstrom's feet. His breath came in harsh, aspirated gasps.

"Why are you treating him like that?" Mildred asked, voice full of fury. "He's sick."

Without looking at her, Hellstrom snapped, "Mind your tongue. You have no idea of our Family's traditions."

"Agreed," Ryan said. "But the question still stands. Why are you humiliating this man?"

"You're a very cocky cat," Fleur said. She had a pleasant, melodic voice, despite the overtone of menace in it. "But guess what can chill you?"

"Another cliché?"

Fleur rushed from the back of the chair, cheeks reddening, hand raising the Beretta. Ryan drew the SIG-Sauer in one smooth motion. He had the bore on a direct line with her eye patch just as she centered the Beretta on his.

Hellstrom cried out, in a surprisingly pettish voice, "Freeze on that, Fleur, Cawdor!"

The woman froze, but she didn't lower her blaster. She reminded Ryan of a ravening beast of prey, preparing to spring. With a self-indulgent chuckle, Hellstrom reached up and drew Fleur back by the wrist.

He patted her buttocks, and she slowly tucked the blaster into a back holster beneath her jacket. She returned to her position behind the chair. She didn't take her eye off Ryan.

"You must forgive my warlord," Hellstrom said with a smile. "Fleur prefers a more active, physical type of debate rather than verbal one-upmanship. She can be rather difficult when she's feeling testy."

Ryan started to say something, thought better of it and leathered his pistol.

Zadfrak reached the base of Hellstrom's chair. His body went slack, but he managed to raise one violently trembling hand beseechingly. He spoke in a croaking whisper.

Ryan didn't understand what he said, but interest suddenly flickered in Hellstrom's dark eyes. Taking a white linen glove from the pocket of his blazer, he slipped it on his right hand and leaned forward. Grasping a handful of Zadfrak's sweat-drenched hair, he pulled the man's head up level with his knees and leaned forward.

When Zadfrak stopped whispering, Hellstrom gently lowered the man's head, allowing him to pillow it on his white-shod feet.

Stripping off the glove, Hellstrom tossed it on the floor and announced, "Zadfrak has been welcomed back into the Family, his past sins expunged, his status restored. He deserves a Family funeral and memorial service with all the attendant honors."

Gesturing to a pair of X-men, he said, "Take him to his old quarters. Make his last hours as comfortable and pain free as possible."

"Oversee the preparations of the pyre," he directed Fleur.

To Ryan, he said, "Of course, you and your people are invited to remain here. It was Zadfrak's last request that you be treated as honored guests of his Family."

Fluttering a hand through the air, he added, "Please avail yourself of Helskel's hospitality. There are spare rooms on the floor above, and you're welcome to them gratis. Your jack is no good here."

The skin between Ryan's shoulder blades crawled. He still sensed the half-dozen blaster bores behind him. None of the tension was evident in his voice when he said, "Thanks. We'll be pleased to visit for a while."

Chapter Six

Ryan and the companions took their gear from the Land Rover and stowed it in the three upstairs rooms reserved for their use. The rooms were small, but furnished with brass-railed beds and chairs. A bathroom was down the hall, done in gleaming porcelain with chrome-plated fixtures.

After getting settled, the six friends met on the street outside the saloon, then took a tour of the ville, letting the settlement flow around them. The mingled odors, the colors, the people and the strange music made by old predark instruments were interesting but also unsettling. All of them had been in odd places during their treks across Deathlands, but never had they visited a ville that throbbed with such a pulse of incredibly strong but joyful evil.

By engaging a few of the street merchants in conversation, they learned that the permanent residents of Helskel lived in an insular world, a universe completely separated from the rest of the ravaged continent. Their world was Helskel. Changes, rebuilding processes, old and new baronies were of absolutely no interest, and, in effect, didn't exist for them. This was their microcosmic kingdom, and anyone desiring to live among them had to think like them, believe like them and be like them.

After bumping into this thick-headed attitude a number of times during the afternoon, J.B. was irritated enough to ask Mildred, "What's all this crap they spout about Charlie?"

As they walked, Mildred explained in terse, low-voiced sentences. "Charles Manson was one of the most famous criminals of predark history. I was just a little kid when he was arrested, but I remember the publicity storm. He and his family were so famous, they became part of popular culture."

Noting the blank expression on Jak's face, Doc said, "The media, like television, radio, movies, magazines."

"Anyway," Mildred continued, "Manson was terrifying in a lot of ways. He relished publicity and even while he was in prison, his cult of followers who had murdered people at his command were still his subjects. Most of his followers, his 'family,' were women, and they shaved their heads as part of some ritual on his behalf. When he carved an X into his forehead, they did too."

"How many people did his family chill?" Ryan asked.

"God knows. There were a lot of unsolved murders they were suspected of, but Manson mainly targeted people he considered pigs."

"Pigs?" J.B. echoed.

"Pigs. That was his word for the upper class. The wealthy, the famous, the people who had the power in predark days." Mildred's eyes narrowed. "I believe the term 'creepy-crawl,' which is used so much in Deathlands, was derived from a family practice.

"Manson came along at the right time, or the wrong time, depending on your point of view. The period of history he walked through was a time of cultural experimentation—free love, spiritual liberation, drug use and a half-baked religiosity were all tenets of the so-called hippie movement.''

Doc cleared his throat. "I remember reading about it. The movement seemed exceptionally natural and idyllic, and along came Charles Manson and his family, living what appeared to be the typical hippie life out on a ranch near Los Angeles. It was a communal life-style, and Manson espoused his own cockamamy religion. His followers called him either God, Jesus or Man's Son. They believed he was the new messiah, the modern reincarnation of Christ. He reached the point where he believed it himself.''

Mildred nodded. "There was more to it than that, of course. Manson specialized in creating zombie-minded followers. His family had degrees of initiation, indoctrination techniques using isolation, hypnosis, drugs and discipleship to create a web to ensnare innocents.''

"As I recall,'' Doc said, "Manson believed that all people were part of one vast mystical whole, so there was really no such thing as death, and murder wasn't really a sin.''

Ryan shrugged. "I've run across crazier beliefs than that.''

"Maybe,'' Mildred said. "But one of Manson's articles of faith was that a popular British musical group were prophets, and if you listened very carefully to their songs, particularly one called 'Helter Skelter,' you could hear exactly what was going to happen in the not too distant future.''

"Which was?'' Krysty inquired.

"An apocalypse that would start when all black people rose up and killed all white people, except for Manson and his followers, who would emerge at the end of the battle to rule the world. As the story goes, after a few years, once the victorious blacks found they were unable to govern, they'd turn the reins of power over to him. The world he used to describe as coming to pass is very much like this one."

"Sounds like Helter Skelter had something for everybody," Krysty said with a wry smile. "Racist fantasies, violence-prone crazies, plunderers, rapists."

"Yes," Doc agreed dolefully. "Truly a dream world for ambulatory sociopaths. Every type of insanity could be indulged and encouraged in the land of Helter Skelter."

"Helter Skelter," Ryan repeated. "That was the name of Baron Zapp's tower stronghold in Greenglades, down in Florida."

"And don't forget that coldheart killer, Traven," J.B. reminded him. "Thinking about it, seems like he borrowed a lot from this Manson." Turning to Mildred, he demanded, "Why didn't you mention this stuff then?"

"Partly because the connection wasn't as obvious as this one. Besides, a Helter Skelter is a kind of slide in English amusement parks, and since we were *in* an amusement park, I didn't put the pieces together."

"The apocalypse didn't happen exactly the way Manson hoped it would," Doc said, returning to the subject at hand.

"No," Mildred replied. "So he tried to help it along by killing as many people as he could, or having his zombie family members do it. Manson would say, 'Helter Skelter is coming down' or 'now is the time for Helter Skelter.' When he made that proclamation, his family went out and butchered people. Some were strangled, hanged, disemboweled or shot. Or all three. They painted the words Helter Skelter on the walls in the victims' own blood.''

Ryan shook his head in disgust. "Even if those chillings brought about the war he wanted, how did Manson figure that he wouldn't be wiped out, too?''

Before Mildred could answer, a man wearing a sleeveless leather jacket sitting astride a chopped-down motorcycle roared in a dust-spurting circle around them, his toothless mouth grinning lasciviously at Krysty. Her hair stirred and snapped tight to her nape, and her right hand eased down to caress the butt of the .38-caliber Smith & Wesson 640 holstered at her hip.

The biker saw the movement, and he blew her a kiss before turning the motorcycle up the avenue and away from them. All of them saw the winged skull emblem sewn on the back of the jacket, and the legend Hell's Angels printed above it.

Mildred pointed to the biker. "Manson encouraged bike gangs to join the family and supply the military wing. Looks like Hellstrom is playing the same riff.''

"Bullshit,'' J.B. spit. "Those so-called Angels we ran up against in Snakefish a few years ago were triple stupes. Military wing, my ass.''

"Stupes they might be,'' Ryan said, "but it wouldn't surprise me a bit if some of these bikers weren't veterans of that fight. If they recognize us, we might have to fight our way out of Helskel.''

"What happened Manson?'' Jak asked. "Chilled?'' There was a hopeful note in his voice.

"Unfortunately, no,'' Mildred replied. "The murders weren't the catalyst for the great war he hoped for. Instead, Manson and a number of his people were arrested and sentenced to death. A change in the law commuted that sentence to life imprisonment. While he was in jail, his family of followers grew—sick people who were attracted to his vision of a ruined wasteland of a world."

Mildred paused and waved at the buildings of Helskel. "Looks like some people never forgot it and used his insanity as a blueprint. All because a depraved mass murderer had a talent for philosophy and hogwash a hundred years ago. This is the world according to Chairman Charlie."

Doc ran his fingers through his hair and sighed. "If the notion weren't so absurdly ugly, so ludicrously repellant, I would spend my visit here laughing. Or weeping."

"Whatever Helskel is or isn't, it has a lot going for it," Ryan commented. "Electricity, guns, gasoline. They're a damn sight better off than most villes and baronies we've seen."

"I must concur. But I find the amount of working predark technology in their possession rather unsettling," Doc commented. "If not outright disturbing."

"The question is," J.B. put in, "where did this group of triple stupes find it all?"

They continued their tour of Helskel through the gathering dusk. Ryan spied Fleur leaning up against the support post of a building, talking to the biker they'd seen earlier. Though she kept up her end of the conversation, she watched Ryan all the while, fingering the long knife at her waist, staring at him with her single eye of cold azure.

Something knotted in the pit of Ryan's stomach like a length of slimy rope.

They returned to the principal market square and listened to the performance of a band of minstrels. They weren't very good, and the lyrics nonsensical, but they were drawing nods of approval and applause neverthe- less. At the end of the performance, one of the musi- cians attributed the authorship of the song to Charles Manson.

Ryan felt a tap on his shoulder. Turning, he looked into Phil's smiling face.

"Enjoying yourself?" he asked.

"To a point." Behind him, Ryan glimpsed Dog and Suds in the crowd. Evidently Dog hadn't forgotten about the kicking incident, glaring at him over Phil's shoulder. Ryan knew the man was scheming a payback.

"Good," Phil said. "The patriarch wanted me to tell you about a Family function tonight, at midnight. You need to be in your rooms by then."

"Why?"

"Family and novitiates only. Everybody else off the street by nine."

As if no more could be said on the subject, Phil turned and drifted away into the crowd, Dog and Suds joining him.

Ryan repeated the message to the others.

"I say we pack up and get ourselves gone," J.B. stated.

Ryan eyed the dimming sky. "Be full dark soon. Too dangerous to navigate the route at night. Let's grab a bite, turn in and leave at first light."

There was an eatery only a few steps down the avenue. It was a small establishment, but seemed fairly clean. The proprietor, an overweight woman with leathery warts adorning her face, handed them handwritten menus. There was an X scar inscribed in her forehead.

Before they could look the menus over, she said, "Serving only one dish tonight, folks. It's all we got, so it's the best we got."

"In that case," Ryan said, "give us what you've got."

The meal was on their table in a jiffy, but after looking at it, Doc mumbled that he wouldn't have minded waiting a little longer.

The steaks were rump, and tougher than the old bull they came from. The vegetables—string beans, tomatoes and baked potatoes—were at least easy on the palate and the digestion.

The woman brought over a pot of coffee and cups. "Take your time, let yourself out when you're done," she announced. "I've got to get ready."

"For what?" Krysty inquired.

"Zadfrak's send-off."

"When did he die?" Mildred asked.

The woman heaved her downsloping shoulders. "Don't know if he has or hasn't. I just got told to get ready for the function. Attendance is mandatory."

With that, she hustled into a back room and disappeared from sight.

Doc poured himself a cup of coffee. "In my experience, a funeral is not scheduled until the subject is deceased."

He raised the cup to his lips, took a cautious sip and a sudden delight shone from his blue eyes. "By the Three Kennedys! Coffee! Real honest-to-Juan-Valdez *coffee!*"

No one bothered to ask who Juan Valdez was, but everyone else had a cup, too.

"Not much difference between this and sub," Jak said, after swallowing a mouthful.

"That's because your taste buds have been eroded by years of neglect," Doc replied, gleefully filling his cup again. "I can feel the caffeine caressing my nerve endings already."

Frowning, Krysty said, "Guns, fuel, electricity and real coffee. Can't think of a more undeserving lot to have all these blessings."

That remark subdued Doc's happy exclamations, but not his thirst for the brew. Everyone sat and waited, content with one cup apiece, while Doc finished the pot.

When they left the little eatery, night had fallen and the streets of Helskel were nearly deserted except for a few merchants closing down their stalls. Dust blew in the streets, a cold night wind eddying it along in eye-stinging clouds. Carried by the wind was the sound of activity, northward of Helskel's perimeter. The faint noises were of metal on metal, tools clinking, hammers pounding.

"Building something there," Jak stated, gesturing. "Half mile."

Ryan peered into the darkness. Fleur's thinly veiled threat about curiosity chilling cocky cats came to mind.

"Let's get to our rooms," he suggested. "Wouldn't hurt to lock the doors."

"If Hellstrom meant us harm," Doc said, "he's going the long away around the barn. He certainly would have disarmed us."

J.B. took off his spectacles and wiped the grit-spotted lenses on a sleeve. "Good idea to stay on orange alert, no matter what."

They entered the empty saloon and mounted the stairs to their quarters. Once in the room he shared with Krysty, Ryan chair-locked the door. Though they unbuckled their gun belts, they kept their blasters close to hand.

The feather mattress was comfortable, but Krysty's body was tense. She held Ryan's hand as he stroked her hair.

"This place is a black pit," she said quietly.

"A pesthole ville, all right," Ryan replied in the same low tone.

"No. There's a something really terrible lurking here."

"We'll be on the road at daybreak, lover. We'll never see Hellstrom or this place again."

"It's not Hellstrom or even Helskel I fear. It's the resurrection of a predark evil, an evil that may have helped pave the way for the nukecaust."

"So they managed to get their hands on a few working predark artifacts. Some people have managed to find stockpiles. It's not commonplace, but it's not all that rare, either."

"You don't understand," Krysty said in a faraway voice. "The people here, they're not really people. They're shadow duplicates."

"Shadow *whats?*"

"We've been taught that before the nukecaust, war, rape and murder were aberrations in an otherwise smoothly functioning world."

"So?"

"Mebbe maniacs like Charlie Manson were the advance guard of the new order that survives, even thrives in the Deathlands. This is their world now, and mebbe we're the abnormal ones."

"You mean we're the mutants now?"

Krysty hitched over on her side, her breath warm on Ryan's cheek. "We're worse than the mutants," she answered. "Because mutants at least fill some niche. Deathlands created them. But people like us, people who believe in a certain decency, and wish to live in peace with one another, may be in the minority. Mebbe skydark was autumn for the human race, and you and me and Dean and Doc and the rest who share similar values and dreams have been displaced by the shadow people. They love the atmosphere of random violence and constant fear. The shadow people have adapted to it, they feed off it, they revel in it. They're the hollow duplicates of humans, and they wouldn't want the predark world to return even if it were within their power to rebuild it.''

Ryan didn't speak for a long moment. When he did, his tone was barely above a whisper. "I hope you're wrong. I hope Helskel isn't representative of what the world will come to be.''

The brassy bleat of a trumpet came in through the open window, startling them both so much that they reached for their blasters.

They lay quiet in bed, listening for the sound again. When it came, Ryan rolled to his feet and went to the window. By poking his head and shoulders out and craning his neck, he saw of spots of distant torchlight beyond the limits of Helskel.

"Something's happening,'' he said over his shoulder.

He heard the horn again, and as he stared at the flickering pinpoints of light, an urge to see what was going on grew within him. It wasn't simple curiosity, or a tactical decision to recce a possible danger that tugged at him. It was a compulsion.

A quick rap on the door made him jump and smack his head painfully on the window sash. Krysty didn't laugh. She was sitting up in bed, holding her blaster in a two-handed grip, thumbing back the hammer.

"It's me,'' J.B. said in a hoarse whisper.

Removing the chair from beneath the knob, Ryan opened the door and allowed J.B. to enter. In the hallway stood Jak, his ruby eyes shining in the gloom. Behind him were Doc and Mildred, looking keyed up and anxious.

"You hear that horn?" J.B. asked.

"Yeah."

"What do you think it means?"

"Probably the function we were told about."

J.B. wasn't satisfied with the response. "I think we should check it out."

"I think someone wants us to check it out," Krysty said. She had put down her blaster and was massaging her temples with her fingers.

"Why?" Ryan asked.

Her green eyes narrowed, Krysty said, "Does anyone else feel an almost overwhelming need to go out there?"

"Yeah," J.B. replied.

"Me too," Ryan stated.

"Sure," Jak said.

Krysty worried her lower lip with her teeth for a moment. "I suspect we're on the receiving end of a psychic beacon. Very subtle, but very insistent. If I wasn't so sensitive to such influences, I'd just discount the call as impulsive curiosity."

"Hellstrom," Ryan stated flatly. "Bastard."

Standing up, Krysty strapped on her gun belt and tossed Ryan's to him.

"What are you doing?" he demanded.

"We've got a lot of questions about Helskel," she replied. "Time to get some answers."

"I thought you were afraid."

Momentary anger flashed in her eyes, then she smiled sardonically. "I am. But I'm more afraid of what might happen if we don't respond to the invitation."

Ryan sighed. "All right, let's move out. Everyone on red alert."

They left the saloon by the back door, moving stealthily, blasters in hand, every sense alert. As it turned out, their precautions were unnecessary. No guards were posted; no one hailed them or barred their way. Helskel was as empty of life as a rad zone.

The sky overhead was a deep blue-black, stars gleaming frostily around a weak quarter moon. The stars and moonlight provided enough light for them to creep through the sagebrush and scraggly vegetation without stumbling into holes or tripping over rocks.

They moved toward the glowing spots of torchlight until they reached the foot of a gentle slope. Ryan took the point, clambering up the deeply furrowed face to the crest. The others watched him peer over it, then drop flat. After a few seconds he gestured for them to join him.

Krysty lay down beside him and Ryan whispered into her ear. "I guess this is where it's at."

"Christ Almighty," Mildred murmured.

Chapter Seven

A glance at his wrist chron showed Ryan the hour of midnight was close at hand. "Looks like we're right on time," he whispered.

In the center of a natural bowl formed by several low hills reared a pyramidal structure. Made of long lengths of gleaming aluminum, it was at least fifty feet high and a hundred wide at the base. The interior of the skeletal structure was packed with cordwood, coal and paper. It was kept inside the pyramid shape by a high chain-link fence that stretched around it. At least a half ton of tinder was spread out beneath the fuel.

At the apex of the pyramid, where the four poles joined, was a block-and-tackle contrivance with a heavy rope pulled taut and out at a forty-five-degree angle. The end of the rope was affixed to a railed dais that was positioned about forty feet from the pyramid's base.

On top of the dais, lounging in the fan-backed wicker chair and still dressed in spotless white, was Lars Hellstrom. A black drum rested on his lap. His lean body was in a casual posture, but his eyes were penetrating and as keen as a hawk's. Ryan had the urge to duck his head, even though he knew it was impossible for Hellstrom to spot him and his friends.

The area around the pyramid and the dais was thronged by a murmuring crowd, all wearing strange, barbaric costumes. Many wore the hides of beasts, others nothing at all except body paint in multicolored patterns. Most of them wielded flaming torches.

Hellstrom lifted a hand, and the murmuring of the crowd died away. Every eye was upon him, staring with an intensity that came close to adoration.

"I greet you, my brothers and sisters and children." Hellstrom's voice was like deep, compelling music and carried a great distance. It was a voice that could sway crowds to madness.

Ryan looked at the rapt faces of the people gazing up at him, and decided that Hellstrom was one of the most dangerous men he had ever seen. To the men, women and probably even the children of Helskel, this rail-thin patriarch was already on the road to divinity, just like his savior, Charlie Manson.

"We have survived. That's our key word. Survival. The Family has survived for over a century. Everything Lord Charlie prophesied has come to pass. Helter Skelter did indeed come down. And we, his Family, have inherited the earth and we have prospered."

Absolute, uncompromising uniformity of purpose lay like a duplicated mask on all the faces turned toward him.

"We have seen the dawn of our success," Hellstrom continued. "We have risen like the phoenix from the ashes, and we occupy the place that was kept from us years ago by the duplicities of false gods."

The listeners stirred, venting their enthusiasm in an ovation of "Helter Skelter has come down."

"Even if the world had not choked to death and spit up its own guts and burned itself out, the Family would still have survived. Charlie's vision was real, his knives were

real and the blood he spilled was real. His teachings outlived his enemies. The age of pig magic is over!''

"Helter Skelter has come down!'' The throng went
wild. Hoarse shouts and cries of hysterical delight resounded.

"I can't believe this,'' Mildred said in horror. "I really can't believe it.''

Ryan knew what she meant. Hellstrom's presentation
seemed so staged, so contrived, so childish, it was difficult to understand how anyone could buy into it.

"The age of pig magic is over!'' Hellstrom thundered
again. He leaned forward in his chair. "We're the sor-
cerers now, baby!''

The night trembled with wild acclaim and wilder
screams. Everyone stamped their feet and shook their
torches madly. Hellstrom's eyes roved over the faces of
his audience. Slowly the shouts and hysterical shrieks
subsided into murmurs of heartfelt sentiment.

"Now, we must give one of our brothers a proper
farewell,'' he said. "And though he leaves us, and we will
miss him, we must not shirk our duties to our world, to
the rest of the Family.''

Hellstrom sat back in his chair and began to beat the
drum in his lap with slow, light blows. The brassy blare
of the trumpet split the night, and four people, all wearing hooded animal skins, marched toward the dais. They
were carrying Zadfrak, bound hand and foot to the
wooden frame of a litter.

The quartet placed the man on the platform near the
base of Hellstrom's chair and the crowd shuffled forward, forming a half circle around it, chanting mindlessly, "Helter Skelter has come down, has come down,
Helter Skelter has come down.''

As the crowd chanted, they flung their arms up in unison, weaving their bodies rhythmically from the waist up.

"Helter Skelter has come down, has come down..."

Suddenly a naked woman sprang into the space between the people and the platform, her long hair flying loose. Red and blue paint adorned her bare arms and legs. She brandished a fourteen-inch-long bowie knife over her head, and she exuded an erotic energy, a dangerous sensuality. With a start, Ryan recognized the woman as Fleur.

Bounding to the dais, Fleur straddled Zadfrak's body and shouted, "When you get to the bottom, you go back to the top of the slide!"

All the people shouted those words back. "When you get to the bottom, you go back to the top of the slide!"

Fleur began to slash Zadfrak's bound body with her blade. Hellstrom beat the drum faster and faster, louder and louder, and Fleur matched that frenzied rhythm with wild slices. Blood sprayed up, splashing her nude body, spattering in an artless pattern across her breasts.

Mildred made a gagging sound, but she didn't avert her gaze.

Fleur suddenly sagged against the rail of the platform, quivering and panting in exhaustion.

The crowd surged forward with a mad howl. "You may be a lover, but you ain't no dancer!"

Knives appeared in every hand, and they converged around the dais. Blades slashed and sliced, but Ryan noted that he saw no stabbing motions.

Hellstrom maintained the steady, fast drumbeat, then in stages he began to slow it. As he did, the throng began to wander away. By the time the drumming was a maddeningly slow *bom . . . bom . . . bom,* the red ruin of a human being lay on the litter.

Fleur, still breathing hard, untied the rope from the rail and knotted it around the top cross section of the litter. A man who was completely naked except for a hooded mask made from a huge wolf's head leaped to the dais and began hauling on the rope, hand over hand.

The litter and Zadfrak's mutilated body swung up and free of the platform, inching toward the top of the pyramid. At one point, the lupine mask slipped, and Ryan recognized the scarred face of Dog beneath it.

At the same time, men with torches scurried about the base of the pyramid, igniting the tinder. Several more men, carrying metal tanks with hoses and nozzles attached, squirted sprays of liquid onto the packed flammables.

Jak's nostrils twitched. "Gasoline. High-grade. Smell like predark stuff."

In almost all regions of Deathlands, predark gasoline was worth as much, if not more, than gold. To use it as an accelerant when alternatives were available meant one of two things—either the citizens of Helskel were unpardonably wasteful, or they had an almost unlimited supply.

By the time Zadfrak's body had been winched to the apex of the pyramid, the tinder had caught and flames were roaring upward through the fuel. They could feel the heat on their faces.

Zadfrak's body dangled there, held by the strength of Dog's brawny arms. When flames were licking at his blood-dripping feet, Dog released his grip.

The rope hummed through the pulley, and Zadfrak plunged into the pyramid of sheeting flame. An agonized scream floated over the roar of the pyre, the cheers of the crowd.

Mildred put her hands to her face, eyes blank with shock. "He's still alive."

Zadfrak's bound body went crashing through the burning wood, coal and sagebrush. A whirling column of fiery sparks and embers corkscrewed up into the black sky. A breeze blew the sweetish stench of roasting human flesh in their direction.

Ryan followed the spinning, glowing motes. Despite his best efforts not to, he visualized what was happening to Zadfrak: his skin would blister and peel, his organs would burst and his bodily fluids would boil and evaporate. The bones would be reduced to a gritty ash within a few seconds. He hoped the man had lost consciousness quickly.

Dropping his gaze to the dais, he saw that Hellstrom was still seated, tapping his long fingers on the drum skin. He was smiling, and he seemed to be staring past the throng to the ridge top hiding Ryan and his people.

Cold fear stole over the one-eyed man. Taking Krysty by the arm, he backed down the slope. "Let's get the fuck out of here."

As J.B., Jak, Doc and Mildred followed him and Krysty through the sagebrush, Ryan tried to shake the fingers of horror clutching at his mind and heart. The slashing with knives and the cremation of Zadfrak was the concoction of a deranged mind. It served no purpose other than ceremonial theater. It was a sham.

"Still want to wait until daybreak?" J.B. asked, jogging beside him.

Ryan shook his head. "Let's move out. If anyone tries to stop us, blast 'em down."

When they reached Helskel, Jak, Mildred and Doc volunteered to retrieve their gear from the rooms, while J.B., Ryan and Krysty went to prepare the Land Rover.

"According to the fuel gauge," J.B. said, "we have about a quarter of a tank. Let's get as far as we can on that, then stop and gas up."

"Good idea," Ryan replied.

They rounded the corner of the saloon, sprinting toward the parked vehicle. They ran only a few yards before J.B. rocked to such a sudden halt that Ryan nearly trod on his heels.

"Shit!" J.B. hissed.

Ryan stepped around him and inspected the Land Rover. "Fireblast!"

The armored wag's six tires were flat. They had all been expertly slashed.

Chapter Eight

There really wasn't a choice. To pack up and hike out of the area on foot was completely out of the question. Behind them were the badlands, and they had no idea of what lay ahead. Nor were they inclined to abandon the wag. It would be too much of a loss to simply shrug off.

"Perhaps it was the work of one of the men we met today," Doc offered. "That Dog fellow, for instance. A prank, a vindictive act of vandalism, and perhaps Hellstrom knows nothing about it."

Doc's theory sounded unconvincing, even to his own ears. After a brief discussion, it was decided that everyone would return to their rooms.

They entered the saloon through the back door and climbed the stairs to the second floor. Ryan took a position in a chair, facing the door, blaster in hand. Krysty sat on the bed, leaning against the headboard, her Smith & Wesson in her lap.

They spoke very little. They just sat and waited for something to happen.

Ryan checked his wrist chron every so often. At a little after three, he saw that Krysty had nodded off, still sitting upright against the headboard, eyes closed, breathing shallowly through her nose.

He thought about waking her, then decided to let her sleep an hour. He looked out the window and watched the distant fire-glow of the pyre for a few minutes. When he turned to look at Krysty, she was no longer there.

Instead, a vast, rocky plain stretched out all around him, the edges blurring into the horizon. He found himself standing completely still in a small depression made of dry, cracked earth, like the remnants of an ancient water hole. A bloodred sun shone down with a light that was sharp and painful to the eye.

He stared up at it with a horrid fascination. From its crimson center, tongues of flame roiled and churned in a scarlet maelstrom. From the molten core sprang a white shape, whiter than snow, whiter than bleached bone.

A man shape fell from the sun and landed gracefully in the small depression. Lars Hellstrom's bloodred eyes glowed, and a white-hot halo of energy crackled around him like a static discharge.

Hellstrom drifted toward him, ghosting over the ground, feet not moving, smiling a dreamy smile. Ryan reached for his blaster, but he knew it wouldn't be snugged in his holster.

He gestured for Hellstrom to come closer. "Come on, hell's spawn," he crooned. "I'll send you back to Charlie on a shutter."

Hellstrom floated closer. Ryan bounded forward, hands reaching for and closing around the man's throat.

Ryan's hands crunched through flesh and bone as though they were dry ashes. Snarling, he shifted his grip to the dreamily smiling face, and it crumbled to fragments beneath his clutching fingers.

Hellstrom's neck and head fell away, and from the empty space between his shoulders spewed a torrent of blackness. Like a stream of semiliquid tar, it coiled and curled, a piece of shadow somehow given life and movement.

Ryan struck at it, but the black fluid wrapped itself around his hand, then flowed up his arm. Sepia tendrils squirted into his mouth, his nostrils, his eyes.

Struggling wildly, Ryan clawed the black shadow-stuff from his face. He opened his eye, and found himself twitching on the floor of the room.

Krysty was kneeling over him, shaking him by the shoulder. "It's a dream, lover. Only a dream."

Ryan quivered and sat up, touching his face. He felt only sweat.

"It's all right now," Krysty said soothingly.

He tried to slow his breathing, ashamed to have made such a spectacle of himself. Early-morning sunshine shafted in through the window. Dust motes danced in abundance, given a glittery glow by the sunlight.

"I was asleep," Krysty said. "You transmitted your fear to me. It woke me up."

Smiling thinly, Ryan got to his feet and checked his chron. It was a little before seven. Out on the street he heard the hustle and bustle of Helskel preparing for another day.

"What did you dream about?" she asked.

Going to the wash basin, Ryan splashed cold water on his face. When his eye no longer felt like it was full of sand, he told her about it.

"Must have been a residue of our steak dinner. Or maybe your shadow-people story. Or even a psionic broadcast from Hellstrom."

Krysty shook her head. "I would've sensed that. You just had a garden-variety nightmare."

He pulled on his clothes, Krysty mirroring his actions. "I hope it wasn't precognitive."

A knock sounded on the door. Their blasters leapt into their hands, and they took positions on either side of the door.

"Who is it?" Krysty asked.

"Just me, Phil. I've got breakfast."

Ryan and Krysty exchanged quick, meaningful glances. Her hair stirred as if from a breeze, then she mouthed to Ryan, "Safe."

He moved aside while Krysty tucked her blaster into the waistband of her jeans and opened the door.

Holding a tray filled with covered dishes and a small pot of coffee, Phil said, "Compliments of the chamber of commerce."

Since both of the shaggy-haired man's hands were in sight and occupied, Ryan lowered his blaster, but he kept his finger resting lightly on the trigger.

Krysty took the tray with a word of thanks.

"The patriarch wants to see you after you've eaten," Phil said, pointing at Ryan.

"Just you. The rest of you are confined to your rooms until you hear otherwise."

"Not very hospitable," Ryan said, letting a steel edge slip into his voice.

Phil shrugged. "You got nice places to flop, three squares a day... I know a lot of people who'd cut their mama's throats to trade places with you."

He stepped out of the room and pulled a wheeled cart laden with breakfast trays down the hallway. "The patriarch will see you downstairs. Now, I've got to feed the rest of your crew."

Krysty shut the door with her foot and put the tray on the bed. The breakfast consisted of double portions of scrambled eggs, several strips of bacon, slices of freshly baked bread and a pot of the real coffee.

Neither Ryan nor Krysty felt much like eating, but they knew survival rules dictated they should force the food down. Both retained vivid and unpleasant memories of days passing between meals. Regular meals were the exception, not the rule, in Deathlands.

Once he'd eaten, Ryan felt more relaxed, the nervous tension ebbing away. After they finished the coffee, he stood, jacked a round into the SIG-Sauer and buckled on his gun belt. "Time to go. Do you sense anything?"

Krysty shook her head, frowning in frustration. "Just a void. I don't know if Hellstrom is broadcasting a shield I can't penetrate or if there are truly no hostile intentions."

"Only one way to find out."

Ryan stepped toward the door, and Krysty grabbed him from behind, encircling his waist with her arms.

"Let me go with you, lover."

Ryan turned, encircling her in an embrace. "Best we play out the hand the bastard's dealt to us, at least for now."

They kissed passionately, then Ryan disengaged himself from her arms and left the room.

Downstairs in the saloon, Hellstrom was seated in his wicker throne. Fleur, in her leather jacket and boots, lounged against the bar, nursing a glass of red liquid that Ryan hoped was tomato juice.

Hellstrom beckoned to him with a gesture, and Ryan approached, trying to keep his face inscrutable. Hellstrom's face was a bland mask. He linked his long fingers in his lap and leaned forward slightly.

"Few things ever change." His voice was no longer the strident roar of the night before, but it contained a note that lifted the hairs on Ryan's nape.

Ryan cocked an eyebrow at him, saying nothing.

"Even when building a world ordained by holy prophecies, there are always low-order swine who cannot understand and wish to tear it down. Regardless of your abilities, Cawdor, there is the stench of the sty about you."

Two men materialized out of the shadows and hit Ryan simultaneously, pressing him between them. They clawed at him, raking their hands over his body. Leather tore and his SIG-Sauer was gone. He was twirled about and thrown face first against the far wall. A quick frisk followed, with a knee positioned dangerously near his testicles. Then he was released and allowed to turn around. The entire process had happened so quickly that he hadn't even found time to blink.

Rearranging his clothing, Ryan looked around the saloon. Dog and Suds smirked at him, though with Dog it was hard to tell. He glimpsed the opening behind the jukebox and understood the sudden appearance of the two men.

Outwardly Ryan remained calm, but inwardly he was raging furiously at himself for being such a gullible stupe. He realized now why he had been provided with a hearty breakfast—to relax him, to throw him off guard. It was an old trick, and it had worked perfectly.

"What was the manhandling all about, Hellstrom?" he asked coldly.

One of the men behind him grunted, but Ryan didn't bother to turn. He knew who had made the sound.

"During your stay here," Hellstrom intoned, "several of my people recognized you and remembered you, especially from a little killzone called Snakefish."

"So?"

"I've also heard quite a bit about you, Cawdor. You're almost a legend, because you're not a child of Deathlands. You are a privileged pig, the son of a man who was one of the most powerful barons on the East Coast. You traveled the country with the swine-scum thief called Trader, stealing, plundering and terrorizing. Many of the people who suffered at your hands have ended up here."

Ryan snorted. "I ask you again—so?"

"So I think you're here to steal Helskel's bounty and sell it to East Coast barons so the Beforetime system can be rebuilt, so the power pigs can again rule the country."

"You psi-scanned me, didn't you?" Ryan demanded. "Did you find anything in my mind that led you to this conclusion?"

"You've got a mind mutie running interference," Hellstrom replied. "I can't be sure of the impressions I received."

"You're an insurgent," Fleur spit. "Admit it."

"You're a maniac," Ryan threw back, his temper getting the better of his judgment. "Admit it."

Ryan caught a blur of movement from behind him and he wheeled, sucking in his gut just in time to only partially suffer the punch that was intended to pulverize his right kidney. Still, the fist bouncing from his rib cage hurt, but so did the elbow he whipped up into Dog's windpipe.

The scar-faced man staggered back and dropped to the floor, gagging and clutching convulsively at his throat.

Suds swung at Ryan with the barrel of the SIG-Sauer. The one-eyed man bobbed to one side and lashed out with a right foot that struck squarely on Suds' kneecap. The cracking of bone was loud and ugly.

The man pitched forward, howling and plucking at his maimed leg. Ryan wrested the SIG-Sauer from his victim's nerveless fingers and leveled it at Hellstrom just as Fleur lunged forward, her hand drawing the Beretta from her holster.

"Tell this chill-crazy bitch to freeze," Ryan snapped.

"Freeze, Fleur," Hellstrom stated, a fraction of a second before Ryan squeezed the trigger.

The woman froze, her blaster only half-drawn, but Ryan kept his automatic on Hellstrom all the same.

"You're taking a big gamble," the white-clad man said. "Touch me and you're dead. Every hand in Helskel will turn against you, and every one of those hands will have a knife in it."

"I don't doubt that," Ryan replied. "But you'll board the last train West with me."

Suddenly he felt the delicate, wispy brush of Hellstrom's mind reaching out to touch, or to ensnare his. Ryan focused his thoughts on a single vivid image: he visualized Hellstrom's head exploding in a spray of blood, bone shards and brain matter. He concentrated on a vision of the white blazer turning red and wet, of that long, lean body flopping lifelessly to the floor.

He powered the image with a vicious conviction, packing it with a ruthless, unshakable certainty that the image would come true, and that he, Ryan, would be happy to arrange it.

Hellstrom leaned back in his chair with a jerk of his shoulders. His eyes opened wide, then they narrowed. "Get back, Fleur."

"He's just one man," his warlord snapped.

"Tell her, Lars," Ryan suggested. "Tell her what one man can do."

"Goddamn you, Fleur," Hellstrom said shrilly, fingers digging into the arms of his chair. "Back away from him!"

Fleur removed her hand from beneath her jacket and retreated reluctantly, glaring venomously at Ryan. Hellstrom glanced unhappily at the pair of pain-racked men sprawled on the floor, then back to Ryan.

"I underestimated you," he said quietly. "Consider yourself lucky."

"You're the lucky one, Lars. Most people who have underestimated me are sitting on the knee of Father Death."

Hellstrom eyed him for a long moment, then with a hand clap he threw back his head and laughed. "You're a treasure, Cawdor. Yes, you truly are. Helskel needs a man like you."

Ryan's one eye squinted at him. "I think I'd rather have you replace the tires of my wag, and we'll be on our way."

Hellstrom laughed again. "Ah, well, that's the rub, isn't it? We need you, and you need tires. Can't we help each other?"

Hellstrom grinned, and his face took on a cadaverous, skull-like aspect. "Because if you won't let me help you, you and your people will die in a manner far less spectacular and far more agonizing than the late Zadfrak."

Chapter Nine

Ryan kept the SIG-Sauer trained on Hellstrom, even when several sec men entered the saloon. They hesitated, hands straying to blaster butts, eyes darting from Ryan to Hellstrom to Fleur.

The white-clad man waved to Dog and Suds. "Never mind our visitor. Please attend to our injured novitiates. Mr. Cawdor and I are merely discussing business."

The sec squad collected the groaning, cursing, coughing men from the floor and carried them outside. When Ryan was sure they were gone, he said, "All right, Lars. Let's discuss business. I'll put my blaster away, providing you keep that warlord of yours on a short leash."

Hellstrom nodded. "Very well, Cawdor. Pray, take a seat."

Ryan tried tucking the SIG-Sauer back into its holster, but a leather seam had been split when Dog and Suds disarmed him. He stuck it in his cartridge belt and pulled a chair away from a table. Spinning the chair around, he thrust it between his legs and sat in a position where he could see the passage behind the jukebox, the saloon doors and Fleur all at the same time.

"Did you order our wag's tires to be slashed?" he demanded.

Hellstrom nodded. "I picked up your anxiety over not having spares when I scanned you yesterday. It was a small fear, tucked away in a corner of your consciousness."

"What about last night? You telepathically drew us to Zadfrak's barbecue, didn't you?"

"Excellent. I'd believed my influence was so subtle you would never detect it as intentional."

"Why did you want us there?"

Hellstrom fluttered a pale hand through the air. "Varied reasons, actually. I wanted to test the strength of your spines, and I wanted to provide you with a glimpse of the unity of the Family."

"And," Ryan interjected, "to see if you could scare the shit out of us."

Hellstrom smiled. "That, too. Did we succeed?"

Ryan grinned derisively. "Lars, in some places in Deathlands, we've participated in sing-alongs that made your little cookout look like a church service."

The smile on Hellstrom's lips faltered for a moment, but it returned. "Good. If you were easily distressed, we couldn't use you."

Ryan let that remark pass for the moment. "What about Zadfrak? Why had he been banished from Helskel?"

The smile fled Hellstrom's lips completely, and the messianic expression he had worn last night settled on his face. "He violated our racial purity laws. He laid with an Indian woman and tried to hide it from the Family."

"I wouldn't think you'd be so particular about rape."

"Rape, during a raid, is encouraged. It's a sound psychological warfare tactic. But Zadfrak fell in love with the red whore, and they even had a child."

"He told me his son had died of rad cancer," Ryan said.

"Yes, and afterward his squaw returned to her people. But Zadfrak tracked her down and tried to bring her out. She refused, and he killed her. He brought back her head, as though that would expunge his sin in the eyes of the Family. So he was banished, exiled to wander and die."

Ryan pursed his lips. "Yet you accepted him back into the fold when we returned him."

The smile crept back to Hellstrom's face. "That all depends on your point of view, doesn't it? From my perspective, Zadfrak returned with *you*. He returned with something of great value to the Family, and that canceled his crime of miscegenation."

His belly turning a cold flip-flop, Ryan asked, "How are we of great value? Zadfrak said you had better wags than ours, I've seen the quality of your blasters and I know you have access to gasoline. Your food is far better than that of most baronies, certainly better than what's available in an average ville."

"All true." Hellstrom linked his fingers and leaned forward. "What do you know about stockpiles, Cawdor?"

"No more than anyone else in Deathlands knows. Hidden caches of food, tools and merchandise laid down by the predark government before nukecaust and the big freeze."

"And you've found a few yourself." It wasn't a question, it was a statement.

"Yes." Ryan didn't elaborate on the many stockpiles found by Trader, or the redoubts.

"Then you've heard about the place of marvels somewhere in the northern extremity of Deathlands, haven't you? A place of wonders, a place free of muties, of rad zones, a place where there is enough of everything? A place where there is a vast treasure? A so-called land of lost happiness?"

"Of course," Ryan answered. "It's only a legend, or rumors based on old traders' tales."

Hellstrom tapped his two index fingers together. "You dismissed it, but regardless of 'legends' or 'rumors,' in the back of your mind it was always there. Don't lie, Cawdor. I saw that hope in your mind—deeper than your mind."

Ryan shrugged. "Who knows what dreams live on, unknown. That makes sense . . . just to survive."

Hellstrom smiled, grinned, then laughed. "Well, you've found that fabled place of plenty."

Ryan stared at him, wondering if Hellstrom was not only a psychic, but a psychotic, as well. "Here? Helskel?"

Hellstrom scowled. "No, not Helskel. The treasure place is nearby. Unfortunately Helskel is dependent upon it."

From her position at the bar, Fleur said, "He shouldn't be hearing this."

Without looking her way, Hellstrom hissed her into silence. "Our blasters, our wags, our gasoline, much of our food, even our electrical generators come from this place. But we don't have direct access to it. Everything is doled out piecemeal."

"By whom?"

"It's rather a long story," Hellstrom replied. "Much of it is surmise rather than fact."

"Until I get new tires, I appear to have plenty of time."

Hellstrom chuckled. "I begin to like you more and more, Cawdor. You intrigue me. However, I'll show you the place rather than tell you."

"Show me?" Despite himself, excitement pulsed within Ryan's chest. He had always assumed that the treasure place was no more than a hidden enclave full of secret predark technology. But there were those who deep down did believe in it. Krysty, for one, whose Uncle Tyas McCann had claimed some such knowledge.

"Sure. It's only a few hours' ride. If we leave soon, we can reach it well before sunset."

"I'd like my people to accompany us."

"No," Fleur bit out.

Hellstrom directed a dark glare toward her and she averted her gaze. "I see no problem with that. Besides, your woman may prove valuable in case we run across some dangers."

"Like what?"

"Like Indians," Hellstrom replied. "For some reason, they hate us."

Thinking about the skull signposts, Ryan said wryly, "I can't imagine why."

Hellstrom grinned, his face lighting up with an almost boyish glee. "This could be fun, a real outing! I'll have a picnic lunch prepared for us. Tell your people, Cawdor. Meet me back here in an hour."

Ryan stood and stitched a friendly smile onto his face. "Understood."

He moved toward the stairs, glancing back once. Fleur was staring at him reflectively, as if he were a bit of steak and she was wondering whether to devour him raw or rare.

Chapter Ten

For over three hours the AMAC had rumbled across the rocky plain, pushing deep into the Black Hills. Though the ride was much smoother than it had any right to be, Ryan was growing impatient.

When he'd first boarded the long, box-shaped Armored Mobile Anti-Riot Control unit, he had been so impressed that the rather slow speed and cumbersome maneuverability of the vehicle hadn't bothered him.

J.B. had been in just as much awe, especially when the prideful Hellstrom pointed out the blaster racks, the sixteen frag and CS gas grenade launchers and eighteen weapons ports.

Hellstrom explained that the AMACs were virtual wheeled fortresses and had been used in the late twentieth century to deter rioters. The vehicle was in perfect operating order, as though it had been built a year before, not a hundred. The big engine throbbed smoothly, the suspension didn't creak or squeak and the air-conditioning system kept the interior cool and comfortable.

"Where did you find this wag?" J.B. had wondered aloud, his voice full of envy. "It makes Trader's war wags look like baby buggies."

Hellstrom had only smiled a mysterious smile and touched a forefinger to his lips.

Ryan, Krysty, J.B., Doc, Jak and Mildred shared the passenger compartment with Hellstrom, Fleur and eight shaven-headed X-scarred sec men, who were identically armed with spidery-looking, lightweight SA-80 automatic rifles.

A pair of bipod-mounted, gas-operated M-249 machine guns were positioned at gun ports on either side of the vehicle.

Two men were in the control cockpit, one driving and the other constantly checking their backtrack with a periscope-type device that rose from the roof of the AMAC.

During the ride Hellstrom was acting as the perfect host. He had been carried into the AMAC, fan-backed chair and all, and he passed sandwiches and beverages around to everyone but the sec men.

He maintained a steady stream of inane chatter about crops, the weather and some of the odd people who had passed through Helskel. His manners were impeccable, and his vocabulary was large and almost as flowery as Doc's, without the use of anachronisms. He was a Deathlands anomaly—an educated man.

Still, his brittle conversation scratched at Ryan's nerves. He kept busy repairing the torn seam of his holster, but midway through the third hour of eating, drinking and listening, Ryan was irritated enough to ask bluntly, "How long has Helskel been in existence?"

Hellstrom broke off the anecdote about the four-breasted stickie he had once seen to say, "Feels like forever."

"Mebbe that's what it feels like," J.B. said, as anxious as Ryan to talk about something more substantial, "but me and Ryan have been in this general region several times, especially with Trader. Montana, Colorado, the edges of Wyoming. Never heard so much as a whisper about your ville."

"Not surprising," Hellstrom replied. "I wanted to keep Helskel an unknown quantity until we were strong enough to fend off incursions from rapacious insurgents like your friend Trader."

"If Trader had wanted us to take your ville," J.B. stated, "we would have."

Hellstrom shrugged. "It'd be interesting to see him try it now."

Ryan started to say something in defense of his missing mentor, but he shut his mouth. There was no point in engaging in a saber-rattling contest, extolling the warrior virtues of a man who might be dead. Besides, Hellstrom was right. Trader certainly had his rapacious impulses, and Ryan couldn't deny that Helskel looked to be too big a mouthful even for him to comfortably chew.

"We can't help but be curious, you know," Mildred said.

"I'll answer what questions seem fitting when we reach our destination." Hellstrom's tone was cold, barely civil. He didn't look in Mildred's direction.

Ryan reflected that since Hellstrom based his life on the racist beliefs of Manson, Mildred and her obvious relationship with J.B. was a source of great offense to him.

It never failed to surprise and sadden Ryan how the worst aspects of predark had survived; rarely had the kinder, more enlightened perceptions made it through the nukecaust, the skydark and the big freeze.

Ryan glanced past Hellstrom, focusing on the panorama of broken hills displayed beyond the windshield. He knew if he looked at Hellstrom, he wouldn't be able to disguise the loathing in his face.

In the distance, a mountain seemed to grow. Towering and dark, the play of sunlight on the broken, eroded edges of butte rock seemed to form faces. Then the mountain receded as the AMAC dropped down the side of a slope. There was grass in the shallow valley, and a creek ran between a grove of cottonwood trees. As the vehicle rumbled on, the walls on either side lifted higher, almost joining together at places, making a narrow passageway.

Krysty suddenly stiffened, her eyes widening.

"Danger," she said in a clear voice.

Ryan and his group drew their side arms. Hellstrom didn't question her announcement, but called to the man in the front peering through the periscope.

"What do you see?" he demanded.

"Nothing," the man responded, eyes pressed against the viewer. "Getting a three-sixty recce, but all I see are some birds— Oh, shit!"

The driver immediately lessened the pressure of his foot on the accelerator. Ryan moved forward, shouldering Fleur aside. He looked out the windshield, then lifted his gaze to the valley walls.

They sat on spotted ponies on facing rims of the arroyo, perhaps two dozen, twelve on each side. Scalps dangled from rope reins here and there. White, blue, red and yellow paint hideously distorted their faces into masks of naked, cruel hatred. They wore breechclouts and moccasins, with feathers in their long black hair.

The Sioux braced the butts of automatic rifles against their thighs, the barrels pointing upward. Their gazes were locked onto the vehicle as it rolled slowly beneath them.

At a word from Hellstrom, two of the sec men left their seats and crouched behind the M-249 machine guns.

"They're just watching us," Ryan said.

Hellstrom hitched over in his chair and looked up. "Like I figured," he said bitterly. "It's that fucking Touch-the-Sky and his band of zealots."

Ryan thought it best not to mention that he had met Touch-the-Sky, but he did say, "What can they do to us in here?"

Fleur looked at him contemptuously. "It's not what they can do, Cawdor, it's what *we* can do."

Hellstrom spoke to the sec men at the machine guns. "Explain it to them."

With rattling roars, the pair of M-249s opened up. Gouts of dirt exploded from the facing rims of the arroyo, flinging up rock and grit in high fountains. Spent shell casings clattered to the floor of the AMAC. Cordite stung the eyes and the nose. Behind it all was the steady double hammer of the machine guns. Even inside the AMAC, the whine of ricochets was audible, and they heard the patter of bullet-pulverized stone raining atop the vehicle.

The AMAC continued to roll forward slowly, passing beneath the position of the Sioux. The double streams of autofire kept on chewing up the edges of the arroyo, and Ryan saw that the Indians had disappeared from the rims. "They're gone!" he shouted angrily. "You're just wasting ammunition!"

Hellstrom swung his head, spearing him with an icy glare. The two men locked gazes. Without removing his eyes from Ryan's face, the white-clad man declared loudly, "Cease-fire."

The sec men complied immediately, the weapons falling silent at precisely the same time.

"Keep a lookout," Hellstrom ordered the man at the periscope.

Then he said sharply to Ryan, "It's my ammunition to waste, isn't it, Cawdor?"

"And it's our hair to lose," Ryan snapped. "It's an old trick of the Sioux, to keep an enemy hosing their ammo around, shooting at shadows until all the blasters are drained. That's when they mount an attack."

"Ah, I see." Some of the sharpness left Hellstrom's tone. "Have no fear, Cawdor. We have enough ammunition here to wipe out the entire tribe, not just Touch-the-Sky's group."

Swiveling his head, he bestowed a gallant smile upon Krysty. "And thank you, my dear, for your perceptions. I understand now how Cawdor has kept his life, when so many have wanted to take it."

Doc cleared his throat and asked, "So you are acquainted with that particular band of Sioux?"

Hellstrom nodded. "Touch-the-Sky is a traditionalist. He thinks that the nukecaust ceded the old Indian lands back to him and his people through divine intervention. He regularly patrols this area, killing any non-redskins who might cross into it. He's a vicious psychopath, completely unreasonable."

Doc raised his eyebrows in a "look who's talking" expression. He asked, "Why does he hold this area in such high esteem?"

The AMAC jounced as it climbed up a slope and out of the arroyo. As it topped the crest, Hellstrom gestured toward the windshield. "That's why."

The mountain filled the rectangular window, framed like a work of art. Though it was still miles in the distance, Ryan saw that what he had first interpreted as an optical illusion combined with erosion was indeed a grouping of carved faces on the mountainside—or what was left of them.

"Dark night," J.B. murmured, eyes wide behind the lenses of his spectacles.

"The nose," Jak said. He barked out a short laugh. "Get it now."

"By the Three Kennedys," Doc intoned in a husky whisper.

"No," Mildred contradicted him. "Roosevelt, Washington, Jefferson and Lincoln. Or they used to be."

Ryan surveyed the granite cliff looming above heaps of broken shale and scrubby trees. He dredged up a memory from his childhood education and said softly, "Fireballs! Mount Rushmore."

Chapter Eleven

All four of the sixty-foot-high heads of the predark presidents had been nearly obliterated, except for the colossal Abraham Lincoln effigy, and it was hardly intact. The top of Lincoln's head had been blown away, and one of his huge eyes was jigsawed by a network of cracks. The sight disturbed Ryan, as though he were looking at some symbolic image from years gone by, the leader of a nation with no mind, half-blind like himself.

Mildred didn't help matters when she said quietly, "It took fifteen years of preparation and over six years of actual work for an artist named Gutzon Borglum to design and begin construction of that memorial. He died before he could see it completed. Fifteen years—and it was destroyed in probably five seconds."

Ryan glanced over his shoulder and was surprised to see tears glimmering in Mildred's dark eyes. She said, "My Uncle Josh brought me here once, as part of a church tour group. I was about eight ... Over a hundred years ago." A hand flew to Mildred's mouth as she realized what had slipped out.

J.B. put an arm around her shoulders, and Hellstrom turned toward them. His lips quirked in distaste at the display of open affection and sympathy, but he didn't comment on it.

He asked, "What do you mean, woman? And tell the truth. I'll sense a lie."

Mildred hesitated a moment before stating boldly, "I was in cryogenic stasis during the nukecaust. Ryan and the others found me."

Hellstrom grinned. "You're a freezie!"

Mildred frowned. "So?"

"So, it appears that my first assessment of your little band was far more correct than I initially surmised. You *can* be a great help in my undertaking."

"You've mentioned that before," Ryan said suspiciously. "Mebbe it's time for you to explain."

Hellstrom waved a hand in a dismissive gesture. "Perhaps I will. After a demonstration."

The man at the wheel steered the AMAC toward a series of gentle grass-covered bluffs. He navigated the big wag expertly over the top of one, then followed a winding course between two of them. Hellstrom didn't provide him with directions. Evidently the driver had come this way before.

He braked the vehicle at the foot of a slope that was only ten feet high, more of a dirt dune than a hill. He keyed off the engine.

From a box attached to the wall, Fleur removed a hollow-bored Very pistol and a flare cartridge. The cartridge was color-coded yellow.

Hellstrom gestured to the sec man in the passenger seat and he arose, coming to stand beside Hellstrom.

"Take his place, Cawdor," the thin man instructed. "Man the periscope and watch everything that transpires with a close eye. Of course, in your case, you don't have much choice but to watch with an eye." Hellstrom laughed at his own wit.

Then, to the surprise of Ryan and his companions, Lars Hellstrom stood in a smooth, lithe motion, not even bracing his hands against the arms of his chair.

A pair of X-scarred men joined Fleur and the other sec man as Hellstrom unlatched the side door and pushed it open and out.

"What about the Indians?" J.B. asked.

"They never come this close," Hellstrom answered. "Some sort of tribal taboo. Or maybe they've got better things to do than get chilled."

Ryan waited until Hellstrom and his group had stepped out of the wag, then he pushed his way forward to the empty seat. The man behind the wheel ignored him, and Ryan returned the favor.

He examined the periscope, noting that each of the hand grips bore two buttons. On the right hand grip was a button marked with a plus sign, and another button with a minus sign. The left hand grip buttons were inscribed with arrows, indicating directions.

Ryan placed the upper portion of his face against the viewfinder and focused on the graven image of Lincoln. It was at least half a mile distant. He thumbed the plus button, and the great stone face swelled and enlarged until only the nose filled the viewer.

The right-side nasal passage looked different than its mate. It was a shadowed depression, like a hollowed-out tunnel.

Hearing Hellstrom's voice, Ryan removed his eye from the viewfinder and saw that he, accompanied by Fleur and the three sec men, had climbed to the top of the bluff.

At a word from Hellstrom, Fleur pointed the Very pistol skyward and pulled the trigger. The magnesium and thermite flare smoked through the air, ascending higher and higher until it exploded in a flash of bright yellow.

The flare hung there in the blue sky, shining with a brilliant glow. As it slowly descended on a miniature parachute, Hellstrom turned toward the wag and shouted, "Watch the nose, Cawdor!"

Ryan pressed his face against the viewer again. Nothing happened for what seemed to be a long time. "I don't see anything," he muttered, more or less to himself.

"Just keeping watching," the driver said.

Suddenly there was a flicker of movement in the hollowed-out nostril. Sunlight briefly gleamed off metal, then a shape appeared, seeming to crawl out of the nasal passage. It paused in the open air, just above the sculpted upper lip, and Ryan stared at it so intently and unblinkingly that his eye began to sting.

A mechanical device, barely two feet long, hovered in the concave depression of Lincoln's filtrum. Its body was made of interlocking metal segments, like the carapace of an insect. Extruder hooks and extensors studded its dully shining, silver gray skin. A photoreceptor shone red, like a cyclopean eye.

"Mildred," Ryan called, not taking his face away from the viewer, "come here."

When she reached him, Ryan pulled her onto his lap. "Take a look. Tell me what you think."

Mildred peered into the viewfinder and caught her breath. "Jesus."

"Ever seen anything like it?"

"No."

"Ever heard of anything like it?"

"Maybe." Her tone was doubtful. "Some sort of servo-mechanism. By the end of the twentieth century, robotic units were being used for a lot of different functions, including surveillance. You can see what looks like the lens of a closed circuit TV camera on it. But I've never heard of anything as sophisticated or advanced as that thing."

"We call 'em beetles," the driver offered.

"What's the motive power of the...beetles?" Ryan asked.

When the driver didn't respond, Mildred said, "Taking an educated guess, I'd say it probably utilizes local gravitational fields for propulsion. Extremely efficient."

"That's for certain," Ryan said. "Who would've built it?"

Mildred shrugged. "Hard to say. As you know, there was a lot of 'black technology' being developed by the government and military before the bombs fell—Whoops! It's moving."

She got up, allowing Ryan to take over the periscope again. He adjusted the magnification and direction so he could focus on the beetle. The little device flew in a straight line for Hellstrom's position. Ryan estimated its speed at around five miles per hour. In a little over a minute the beetle came to an abrupt halt, hovering twenty feet away from the bluff and twelve above.

Ryan looked away from the periscope and out the windshield. A light glowed on the gadget's metal shell and an amplified voice crackled from it.

"What do you want?"

Hellstrom's answer was smooth, relaxed and apologetic. "The harvest is requiring more time than I estimated. It'll be a few more days before we can make the delivery. I regret the deviance from the timetable."

"Is that all?"

"We spotted a war party of Indians on our way here. Have they molested you?"

"Isn't it your responsibility to ensure that they don't? We've supplied you with the means to place yourself in a superior posture to them. And much more besides."

Hellstrom bowed his head formally. "For which we are eternally grateful."

"Then live up to your end of our trade agreement. Is there anything else?"

"No," Hellstrom replied unctuously. "I trust I've not disturbed you."

"This communication is ended."

Soundlessly the beetle slid backward through the air, as though it were unwilling to turn its photoreceptor away from Hellstrom. After a hundred yards, it rotated quickly, ascended, and sped back toward Mount Rushmore.

Hellstrom, Fleur and the sec men returned to the wag. Ryan went back to the passenger compartment. Hellstrom was smiling, but it didn't reach his eyes. "Pretty impressive, huh, kids?"

"Very," Doc said.

Hellstrom shifted in his chair so he could look at Ryan. "What did you think, Cawdor?"

Ryan smiled wryly. "I think I've never seen a finer demonstration of the art of ass-kissing in my life."

Fleur spun toward him, lips pulling away from her clenched teeth. "Watch it, Cawdor."

Hellstrom scowled, then forced the smile to return to his face. "You're right, Cawdor. But if you knew the power behind that beetle, you'd want to weld your mouth to its ass, too.''

"Then why don't you tell us about it instead of making vague references?'' Krysty asked impatiently.

"In a little while.'' Hellstrom barked an order at the driver, who started up the AMAC and steered it back in the direction from which it had come.

Ryan consulted his wrist chron. "We'll never make it back to Helskel before nightfall.''

"I know,'' Hellstrom replied. "There is salubrious ground for a campsite a few miles away. Once there, we can relax and talk.''

"What wrong with here?'' Jak demanded.

"I want to put some distance between us and the nose. I'm not sure of the range of the beetles, and I don't want them getting a premature peek at the six of you.''

"Why not?'' J.B. wanted to know.

"Patience, Dix. All things come to those who wait.''

The wag rumbled back through the arroyo, and when they reached the small grove of cottonwood trees near the creek, Hellstrom ordered the driver to halt. Everyone disembarked and pitched camp.

Small tents, made of a lightweight fabric, were set up easily and quickly. There wasn't much deadwood for a fire, but there was no need for it. One of the men carried a metal cylinder from the wag, which was three feet long by three wide. At the touch of a lever on the side of the cylinder, chrome legs slid out from beneath it, and metal rings at the end of foot-high stalks projected from the top. Hellstrom explained that the cylinder burned a gas that furnished a smokeless fire for cooking and heating.

The sec men established a defense perimeter, assembling four tripod-mounted spotlights and alarm wires

around the campsite. One of the M-249 machine guns
was mounted at the rear end of the AMAC. Guards were
stationed every twenty feet outside of the perimeter. By
the time the sun began its slow descent, the area was
bathed in a bright white light.

Neither Ryan nor his friends felt particularly safe. As
Jak pointed out, Hellstrom seemed to be extending an
invitation for the Sioux to come in and lift their hair.

Doc agreed. "All he needs now is a ballyhoo balloon
to advertise our presence. This is not salubrious ground.
A deaf, dumb and blind multiple amputee could find us."

"Everything seems secure so far," Krysty said. "If the
Sioux are around, they're not planning anything violent."

"Yet," J.B. added. "The night is young."

"I thought Plains Indians didn't attack at night,"
Mildred said.

Doc chuckled. "And I thought you minored in American Indian history."

"Sociological groupings," Mildred responded with
some irritation. "Genotypes, cultural linkages in lin-
guistics and the like, not whether they preferred waging
war when the sun was up or down."

"It's true that Indians didn't attack at night a few
hundred years ago," Ryan replied, "because dew would
take the tension out of their hide-and-sinew bowstrings,
or dampen the powder in the pans of muzzle-loaders. The
warriors we saw carried automatic rifles, and they don't
have to worry about keeping their strings or powder dry."

"Thanks," Jak said. "Feel better now that cleared
up."

At least dinner was sumptous, which helped to offset
some of their anxiety. First, potatoes fried in fat, then

remarkably tender and juicy beefsteaks followed by baked ears of corn. Dessert consisted of thick slices of apple pie, swimming in cream. Afterward, sated, they drank the delicious genuine coffee. The repast relaxed them, the strong coffee notwithstanding.

Hellstrom sat in his chair and ate with a gluttonous gusto that surprised Ryan. If the volume of food he consumed that night was a normal meal, it was astonishing how he remained so thin. Fleur made several trips to the cookstove simply for him.

As they nursed their coffee, Hellstrom waved them over to him. "Gather 'round, boys and girls. Time to come clean and to speak of many things."

"'Of ships and shoes and sealing wax, and of cabbages and kings'?" Doc inquired with a rueful smile.

Hellstrom's lips twisted in a strange, mirthless rictus. "Sir, you are more correct than you could know."

Chapter Twelve

Contrary to the accepted dogma—Hellstrom said—the end didn't come as a nightmarish surprise to everyone. A select few had realized it was quite inevitable that the world would end in nuclear fire, and long before entire nations were bombed out of existence, this elite group, who were the most powerful men of their day, figured out a way to survive the apocalypse they were responsible for. They had the forethought, foresight and wherewithal to prepare for the worst.

Though this group may not have anticipated every repercussion from the nukecaust, such as skydark followed by the big freeze, they were well aware that a Deathlands would take the place of the North American continent.

As many as fifty years before the nukecaust, underground complexes were constructed under a program known as Continuity of Government, the ultimate insurance policy should Armageddon ever arrive. Many subterranean command posts were built, located in ten different regions of the country.

The most ambitious COG facility was code-named the Anthill because of its resemblance in layout to an ant colony. It was a vast complex, with underground sewage plants, railways, stores, theaters and even sports arenas.

Supplies of foodstuffs, weapons and anything of value were stockpiled, often times in triplicate.

Because of its size, the Anthill was built inside of Mount Rushmore, using tunneling and digging machines. The entire mountain was honeycombed with interconnected levels, passageways and chambers. The interior walls were reinforced with a special silicon foam, mixed with molten lead to provide shielding against radiation.

When the first bombs arrived on the twentieth of January, 2001, the Mount Rushmore facility had been in operation for some two months. At that time it was protected only by a skeleton force of soldiers. A group of scientists had taken up more or less permanent residence, sharing the complex with a few paranoid politicians and their families.

The world blew out on noon of that day, the safety measures kicked in, and everyone inside was safe and sound—or so they thought.

Despite all their precautions, radiation and fallout storms still reached them. The Earthshaker bombs caused extensive damage to the Anthill.

Since they had no choice but to remain in the facility in order to survive, and, hopefully, one day govern again, it took them awhile to realize that they were just as much victims of the nukecaust as those whom they refered to as the "useless eaters" of the world.

When this select few, this powerful elite, did realize it, they were upset. It wasn't part of their program. They had assumed that after ten years or so of waiting safely inside the Anthill, all the world would be theirs to rule.

However, the nuclear winter changed their plans, as did slow death from rad poisoning. Even if they managed to outlast the big freeze, they couldn't cure radiation sickness. Their bodies, not their intellects, would eventually betray them to Father Death.

So they embarked on a radical and daring plan. Cybernetic technology had taken great leaps since the era of prosthetic limbs and artificial hearts, and that self-same technology existed inside Mount Rushmore.

Operations were performed on everyone living in the Anthill, making use of the advances in techniques in organ transplants and medical technology. The select few within the bosom of the mountain, over a period of several years, were turned into cyborgs, a hybridization of human and machine.

Of course, such transformations didn't solve all of their survival problems, nor were they intended to do so. Compensation for the natural aging process of some organs was very difficult to arrange. The Anthill inhabitants needed a supply of fresh organs, preferably the organs of people who had died young with their bodies in generally good condition. Because of the nukecaust, this supply was severely limited, so they came up with the next best solution—cryogenics, or a variation thereof.

The temperature inside the facility was lowered just enough to preserve the tissues—not to such a low degree that the organs were damaged, but low enough to suspend the aging process. Combined with their cybernetic implants, the people in the Anthill achieved a kind of immortality. But they had only halted Father Death, not defeated him.

They had spent over a century in their little frigid world, looking out over the wasteland, prisoners of their own fantasies of power.

"THAT'S THE STORY," Hellstrom stated. "And who should know it better than I? All right, question-and-answer time."

"Who told you all of this?" J.B. asked suspiciously.

"The Beforetime pigs themselves oinked their tale to me, over a period of a few years. I filled in some of the gaps myself."

"So you're speculating," Mildred challenged.

"Surmising. As a freezie yourself, you should know what is possible."

"I do, and I'm more than just a freezie. I was a doctor of cryonics, and I know that for it to be effective the subjects have to be deep-frozen in liquid nitrogen at minus 196 degrees Celsius."

"They found a way around that," Hellstrom said.

"They, they," Jak said acidly. "Keep saying 'they.' Don't freezies have names?"

"Not as far as I've been able to learn. The only individual who has ever identified himself is a man calling himself the Commander."

"How many times have you been inside the Anthill?" Doc asked.

"None. All of my communications have been conducted through the beetles, which they use as surveillance and early-warning devices."

"How'd you arrange a trade agreement with them, then?" Ryan demanded.

Hellstrom tapped his temple with a forefinger. "A simple question of supply and demand. They demand certain products, and I supply them. I learned that from my father."

"Your father?" Krysty echoed.

"Baron Hustav Hellstrom. You and I are very much alike in background, Cawdor. Like you, I was the privileged son, the heir to a barony in the Northeast. When I was fifteen, it was wiped out by a combined army of muties and Forest People. I was one of the few survivors. I had received what used to be called a 'classical education,' and though I was exceptionally book-smart and knew the predark history of the Americas, I had little firsthand knowledge of how to survive Deathlands."

"It appears you managed," J.B. observed. "And very well, too."

"If you had met me only four years ago, you wouldn't have said that. For a long time I wandered and walked, learning the different cultures of the land, the local dialects, the topography, the varieties of flora and fauna. I walked and walked. I must've walked the entire length and breadth of Deathlands. The entire focus of my life was walking. That's why I hate to expend much energy on it now."

Fleur refilled his coffee cup and stood beside the chair, leaning a hip against it. She looked bored, industriously inspecting her nails.

Hellstrom took a sip of his coffee. "Where was I?"

"Making short story long," Jak said.

The white-clad man didn't appear to be offended, or, for that matter, to have even heard the young man's words. "I heard a lot about War Wag One and Two, about Trader and specifically about you, Cawdor. You appear to have a talent for insurrection. How many barons have you overthrown?"

"Only those who've needed it, Lars."

"I envied those barons, the lives they led, the people they controlled. I knew I could never reclaim my own birthright, but I knew I could establish my own barony, one so powerful that it could never be defeated. I was born to lead, to command, but there was one problem— I had no followers.''

Hellstrom leaned back in his chair, crossing one leg over the other and clasping the knee with both hands. He seemed to be enjoying himself immensely. ''In my late teens, I discovered my latent psionic abilities. I found that I could sometimes sense what other people were thinking, and I assumed everyone had this ability. Eventually, of course, I learned otherwise. My power was undeveloped, truly a 'wild' talent. I found I could read some people all of the time, some part of the time, and some none of the time. I needed a method, a doctrine to employ, so I could zero in on those individuals my raw powers would influence. Then I remembered reading about Charles Manson.''

''I remember reading about him, too,'' Mildred said bitterly. ''He was a sociopathic loser, a manipulator of the spiritually weak.''

Fleur made a growling sound deep in her throat. ''That's heresy, you Beforetime bitch.''

Hellstrom shushed her into glowering silence. ''He was a very successful manipulator, nonetheless. He spun out an entire apocalyptic mythology, which now, in hindsight, seems to be a prophecy. I figured that if people bought his mixture of mysticism, ritual and paranoia a century ago, they'd buy it again, especially with a new spin put on it.''

''And,'' Krysty interjected, ''especially if your mind influenced them.''

''Quite true. The more I used my psychic gift, the stronger it became, like strengthening a muscle. I began encountering people whose minds were vulnerable to my own. I not only could sense what they were thinking, I could project my own thoughts into their minds, and, in short, I controlled that mind on a modest scale. It's probable that Manson himself possessed and exercised this power to a very developed degree."

"But," J.B. pointed out, "you aren't a doomie."

"No," Hellstrom admitted. "My talent is of a different order. I interact with brain-wave patterns. Precognition and empathy operate on emotional states. For example, Ms. Wroth somehow intercepts the intent to cause harm, but she's not actually peeping into the future. Whereas I receive thought impressions, I'd guess that Ms. Wroth mentally picks up flashes of color, denoting emotions. Am I correct?"

Krysty nodded. "To some extent. The colors are very brief, almost subliminal. Orange for anger and red for murderous intent. If I hadn't been trained to interpret the bursts of color, I never would have realized what they meant."

"At first," Hellstrom continued, returning to the primary topic, "my followers were the walking wounded, the flotsam and jetsam, strictly the dregs of Deathlands. But as I continued my wanderings, I found followers, especially among the Farers and the bikers. Through them, the new Family managed to acquire a few decent blasters, but the life of nomads was wearing thin. It was too risky, especially after we drifted into this region. We lost several people to screamwings, and even more to the Indians. In fact, I rescued Fleur from the Indians during one skirmish, didn't I, Fleur?"

"Yes." She bit out the word, with no inflection or emotion attached to it.

"A little over three years ago, we arrived in this area, at the foot of Mount Rushmore. I'd heard about it in my youth and I wanted to see it. We had barely pitched camp when a band of Sioux came upon us. We managed to chill quite a few, but racked up some casualties ourselves. That night, while we were tending to our wounded, the Anthill—the Commander, in fact—made contact with me, via a beetle. The people up there had observed our fight and they wanted a trade."

"What kind of trade?" Doc asked.

"They wanted the bodies of the newly dead. They wanted the undamaged organs. I began a dialogue with them that built into a relationship. I persuaded them to supply us with what we would need to build a community nearby, and we would serve both as their protectors and their providers. They gave us seeds so we could plant crops, for them and us, and in return for fresh bodies, they traded us the means by which to provide them with even more fresh bodies."

"Let me guess this one," Ryan said, disgust thick in his voice. "You didn't want to chill members of the Family since you were so few in number, so you viewed the local Indian tribes as mobile organ banks."

Hellstrom laughed. "That's essentially correct. However, it's not as stone-cold as it sounds. It was also a matter of self-preservation. The Sioux wanted us and the people of the Anthill out of this country by any means necessary. We would have been forced to chill them anyway, and at least their organs weren't just food for the worms."

"Why didn't you trade our livers to the Anthill?" Ryan asked. "As outlanders, we were fair game."

"That you were, and indeed that was my original intention. I changed my mind when Zadfrak pointed out how you could be of service to Helskel."

"Helskel's been around now for three years?" J.B. asked.

"A little less," Hellstrom answered. "As the word about us spreads and more people join us, I estimate we'll be the most powerful barony in the entire country in a few years. If, that is, we end our dependence upon the Anthill."

"You want to take it over," Ryan stated. "To have all the predark tech to yourself."

"Wouldn't you, in my circumstances? Wouldn't your beloved Trader plan the same thing?"

"He might plan it," J.B. said, "if he believed the payoff worth the risk. How can you get inside the place?"

Hellstrom shrugged. "Up through the nose is the most obvious and most risky way. But there's another entrance."

"How you know?" Jak asked.

Hellstrom reached behind him and rapped his knuckles on the armor plating of the AMAC. "This wouldn't fit through the nose. No, they have a sort of matter transfer device up there, and a receptor unit nearby. When I receive large merchandise from them, like this wag, I pick it up in a cave about two miles from here."

Interested despite himself, Ryan inquired, "Why can't you use the mat-trans unit to jump inside the mountain?"

"It's strictly one-way, evidently single point to single point. There are no controls on the unit, and it's guarded by beetles."

"How do they receive your goods?" Mildred asked.

"Simple. They lower a platform from the nose, and when it's loaded, they reel it back up again."

"If you covet their possessions so much," Krysty said, "is there some reason you haven't staged a raid yet?"

"The best reason in the world. It would fail, our trade agreement would end and I would be placing Helskel in terrible jeopardy."

"So why bring up in first place?" Jak demanded. "Are you just armchair general?"

"Not quite," Hellstrom said softly. "A general needs soldiers, and I have them. But for this operation to have even a fractional succcss margin, I need very special soldiers. For instance, soldiers that can't be traced back to Helskel or to me. Soldiers that aren't Family."

Realization rushed through Ryan like a fountain of cold water. He fixed his gaze on Hellstrom, who met it with a thin, mocking smile.

"Shit," Krysty declared, her spine stiffening. "I'm getting a flash of triple red."

Then one of the tripod-mounted security lights exploded in a blaze of blue sparks. A microsecond later, the sharp, snapping report of an automatic rifle split the night.

"Oh, my," Hellstrom said mildly. "I do believe the Indians are upon us."

Chapter Thirteen

The bulbs of the other three security lamps were destroyed in rapid succession. Glass shattered, sparks flared, and within a heartbeat and a half, the lights were extinguished and the area was plunged into darkness.

Though Ryan and his people were on their feet, blasters in hand almost immediately, Hellstrom remained seated. Fleur shouted orders to the sec men as they ran to and fro across the campsite. Ryan peered into the encircling shadows, trying to force his vision to quickly adjust to the sudden darkness.

With a sigh of ennui, Hellstrom arose from his chair and nonchalantly ambled into the AMAC. He had just shut the door behind him when a bullet spanged off the wag's armored exterior, whining up into the night sky.

As Fleur shouted to the sec men to set up a fire zone inside the perimeter, Ryan and his friends took cover beneath and to the rear of the AMAC. They looked for something to shoot at and saw nothing.

The M-249 opened up with a staccato roar, smearing the darkness with bursts of orange flame. Fleur dashed to the sec man behind it and dealt him a fierce kick in the ribs.

"Head shots!" she shouted angrily. "Head shots, you piece of Farer shit!"

Ryan's eye grew accustomed to the gloom. The moon and the stars provided just enough light to make out the dim shapes of trees, brush and the sloping valley walls looming on either side.

There was another fusillade of shots from the shadows. Ryan counted at least ten rifles, firing more or less simultaneously. None of the bullets came near him or his people, but one of the sec men howled and fell in a sprawl of kicking legs and flailing arms. The sec men returned the fire with their SA-80 automatic rifles, triggering short, random bursts.

J.B. elbow-crawled up beside Ryan, his teeth bared in a humorless grin. "Mebbe we should have taken out Joe when we had the chance."

"You don't know if it's the Sioux out there," Mildred said.

A moment later, several undulating, high-pitched cries floated through the night sky.

"I guess you stand corrected—for once," J.B. told her calmly.

Another sec man made a run toward the closed door of the AMAC, but a storm of bullets struck sparks from its steel sheathing, and he was forced to dive beneath the chassis.

"If that's the war party we saw today," Ryan said curtly, "then we've got about two dozen to contend with. We're bastard outnumbered."

"But not outgunned. For some reason, they've got their blasters on semi," Krysty observed. "Not full-auto."

"Less chance waste ammo," Jak said, gesturing to the sec men raking the darkness with the SA-80s. "Not like these stupes."

Several full-metal-jacketed slugs ricocheted from the bodywork of the AMAC, screaming off in different directions. A sec man clutched at his leg and went down, screaming a curse. From a prone position, he squeezed the trigger of his blaster, sending streams of flame and lead into the shadows. There was no return fire until the firing pin of his SA-80 hit the empty magazine with dry, audible clicks.

Then a single shot cracked, a bullet zipped out of the darkness and caught him in the forehead, puncturing the X between his eyes. The impact bounced his head hard against the ground, the back of his skull breaking apart. His legs kicked, then he was still.

"Now that was a head shot," J.B. remarked sourly.

Ryan reflected that if the Sioux were looking for scalps, the shaven-headed sec men would be grave disappointments to them. On the other hand, he and his people had full heads of hair of varying colors, lengths and textures, and they might present a terrible temptation. Krysty's coppery mane in particular would be a valuable prize. He hoped that if Touch-the-Sky was with the war party, he would recognize them. An instant later he hoped the opposite. The Lakota had warned him and his people about Helskel, and he probably assumed they had thumbed their collective nose at his words of caution and, therefore, deserved everything that might come their way. Including scalping knives.

Hefting his SIG-Sauer in a two-handed grip, Ryan said, "Lay down a firing pattern. We may not know where our targets are, but we've got a pretty good idea of where they're not."

Krysty squeezed off several rounds from her Smith & Wesson 640, and the others followed suit, shooting into the gloom at different angles, trying to draw beads on shifting shadows, never knowing if they struck a target or just a piece of one. Doc's Le Mat was fairly useless as a long-range weapon, but its ear-knocking blasts provided them with a psychological edge.

A bullet whipped past Ryan's head, and he felt rather than heard the little slap of displaced air. It had missed him by no more than an inch, and it had come from behind.

Another bullet whistled past Ryan's face, splashing it with cool air, then flattened against the thick hide of the AMAC over his head. He twisted his body and blaster around, bringing the man-shape lunging from the darkness into target acquisition. Ryan and Doc fired at the same time. The Le Mat roared, spurting flame, and the rifle-toting figure back-somersaulted into the shadows.

Then the campsite was filled with running, shooting, half-naked men, shrieking out of the darkness from two directions. Not only did they carry automatic rifles, they carried tomahawks, knives and even a few feathered lances. Their faces were painted with ferocious designs. They bounded and leapt too quickly for Ryan to get an accurate count of their number.

The defense put up by Helskel's sec men was disorganized and sporadic. They retreated toward the wag, halfheartedly fighting a rearguard action without watching one another's backs or even taking the time to aim their blasters properly. They were in great danger of catching each other in a cross fire.

Ryan and his friends were veterans of dozens of battles, and they rushed out into the campsite in a wedge formation. J.B. took the point of the V, the rapid drumming of his Uzi clearing a path. Mildred, Krysty and Jak waited until their targets were clearly framed in their weapons' sights. When they fired, it was without haste and without mistake. At every shot, a painted warrior either tumbled limply to the ground or spun, grabbing at a wound.

Ryan had hung back to cover Doc while he adjusted the position of the Le Mat's firing hammer. The double-barreled weapon could be fired like a shotgun, or once the hammer was repositioned to fall on the revolver chamber, to fire nine .44-caliber rounds.

While Ryan waited, he watched several scenes at once: Fleur drilled one of the Sioux through the back of the head with her Beretta. She whirled on Krysty as the titian-haired woman put a .38-caliber slug in the center of a warrior's chest.

"Goddammit," she yelled. "I said head shots!"

Krysty didn't even glance her way as she said, "You don't tell me to do anything."

At about the same time, a sec man screamed as the flat razor point of a lance pierced his throat. The grinning Sioux withdrew it, and the sec man dropped to his knees, trying to stem the geyser of blood fountaining from a severed jugular.

Doc snapped shut the Le Mat and announced, "Ready and able, though not particularly willing."

He followed Ryan out into the battlefield. At such close quarters, the Indians were using their rifles as bludgeons and fighting hand-to-hand, uttering strident cries as they closed with their opponents. Ryan, trying to join his people's wedge, saw one of the warriors rush toward Krysty. He fired the SIG-Sauer point-blank, and the attacker dropped with a deep bloody cavity punched in his side.

Before he could shout for her to watch her back, a rush
of bodies knocked him sprawling, and a heavy weight
dropped directly onto his back, driving him face first to
the ground. Knees pressed into his buttocks and a pair of
large hands closed about his neck and squeezed.

Spitting out grit, Ryan heaved, bucked and twisted. He
managed to roll over onto his back and look up at the
hate-twisted, paint-distorted face bobbing over him. The
Indian was by far the stronger, and he resisted each of the
white man's efforts to throw him off. Then he thrust a
knife blade for his adversary's throat.

Ryan wrenched himself aside, and the edge of the blade
skimmed the side of his neck, drawing a thread of blood.
He fired his blaster at the Sioux, and a crimson spray
erupted from the bridge of the warrior's nose. His grip
loosened and he slowly fell forward. Elbowing the dead-
weight from his body, Ryan rolled to one side and got to
his knees.

A bullet plucked at his hair. He lurched forward,
facedown, and felt the cool passage of another slug
against his cheek. He sighted a feather-bedecked man
leveling a rifle at him. The one-eyed man rested his pistol on his wrist and sent a 9 mm wad of lead into the
Sioux's chest.

The campsite was screaming, bloody chaos. Blasters
blasted, lances lanced, knives sank into flesh and skulls
were split with gun butts. The sec men were finally fighting back now that they were overrun, and they shot,
slashed and clubbed.

He saw Jak use a snapping right-arm toss to bury one
of his leaf-bladed throwing knives into the breastbone of
a Sioux, before smoothly pivoting on one heel. With a

blade held in his left hand, he expertly slashed the throat of another attacker.

Doc shot a warrior who was drawing a bead on Mildred, and the big .44-caliber round knocked the man backward into the side of the AMAC, splashing the armor plating with a wet scarlet pattern.

J.B. let loose with the Uzi, the rapid-fire slugs smashing the faces and upper bodies of two Indians, twisting them off their feet, their arms waving in crazy floppings.

Mildred picked and chose her targets methodically, aiming for an extremity whenever possible. At one juncture, her ZKR target revolver shot the rifle out of a warrior's hands, causing no more damage than temporarily numbing his fingers. Of course, an instant later her humanitarian impulse was ruined by a sec man who blew the Sioux's chest out with a controlled burst from an SA-80.

A series of fat *pops!* reverberated through the air. Four cylinders spewing plumes of white smoke sprang from the launch tubes atop the AMAC and bounced across the battleground. The cylinders rolled and hissed, and almost immediately the campsite was engulfed by blinding clouds of vapor. Shrieks of surprise came in the wake of the grenades.

War cries, yells of pain and shouted obscenities became incomprehensible as the gas was inhaled by the combatants. The smoke seared eyes, lungs, nostrils and bare flesh, and the warring parties staggered around the killing ground, groping for whiffs of fresh air, not for each other.

Ryan crouched, trying to get beneath the clouds of gas. He inhaled some of it, and for a moment he gagged himself blind. Through the jiggling, burning water in his eye, he caught glimpses of shapes moving through the billowing chemical vapors.

The Indians seemed to be engaged in a slow, stubborn retreat back toward the shadows, hoping to melt into the night. They were obviously unwilling to give up the struggle despite the heavy losses they had incurred and the fact that they were all but incapacitated by the gas. Almost everyone was coughing, weeping and gagging. Here and there came the choking gasps of people vomiting.

Ryan heard a female cry of pain from behind him and the thud of a body hitting the ground. He feared opening his mouth to call out for Krysty, so he moved as quickly as he dared in the direction of the cry. Blinking hard, trying to focus through the fiery blur of his vision, through a part in the swirling vapors, he saw two figures at the far edge of the campsite.

For a heart-stopping instant, he thought it was Krysty facedown on the ground, but after he knuckled his eye, he saw a thin Sioux warrior kneeling on Fleur's back. One hand was tangled in the long mahogany fall of her hair. He was pulling her head up and back, exposing the white column of her throat to the knife he gripped in one fist.

Ryan sprinted toward them, firing the SIG-Sauer's remaining four rounds so rapidly the shots were a single solid sound. The warrior sprang from the woman's body and into the shadows. Because his eye was blurry and leaking tears, Ryan wasn't sure if the Indian had been knocked away by the 9 mm slugs or if he'd simply jumped.

Standing over Fleur, he reached down to help her up by one arm. She raked the hair out of her dirt-streaked face and looked up at him in astonishment.

"You helped me?" Her voice held an incredulous note.

"Actually I saved you," Ryan said. He sucked in a lungful of untainted air. "Are you all right?"

Before she could answer, a bare arm darted from the darkness, hooked around Ryan's neck and jerked him backward. Instead of resisting the force, Ryan kicked himself off the ground, throwing his full weight against the body behind him.

He and the warrior fell and rolled clear of the brush, down a slight incline and onto soft grass at the bank of the creek. The Sioux had lost his knife, and his right arm locked in a death grip around Ryan's neck, while the fingers of his free hand were pressing viciously against his larynx.

Ryan broke the hold by driving a powerful blow into the Indian's midriff with his elbow. The warrior grunted, and Ryan squirmed free and struggled to his feet. He clubbed down with the barrel of his blaster, striking the man between the shoulder blades.

From a kneeling position, the Sioux lunged forward and wrapped his arms around Ryan's legs. The one-eyed man fell forward, dropping the SIG-Sauer and toppling over the warrior. He managed to grasp the Indian by the hair and haul him into the stream with him. Both of them pitched into the water with a great splash.

The creek was shallow, barely waist deep, and the water was shockingly cold, but it flushed the burning effects of the gas from Ryan's eye and nostrils. The two men surfaced at the same time, gasping and blowing like whales. Ryan's closed left hand slammed into his adversary's jaw and knocked him off balance. He fell, disappearing beneath the surface.

The Indian clawed his way along the pebble-strewn bottom of the creek, using the gentle current as impetus to push him out of harm's way, but Ryan grabbed the Sioux by the back of the neck. He tried to rise, but Ryan held him down, using all of his upper body strength. The warrior heaved and kicked, thrashing the water into white froth.

Finally his struggles ceased. Ryan raised the man's head clear of the water and saw that his war paint had been washed from his face. He recognized the sharp, angular features of Touch-the-Sky, aka Joe. The lean-muscled Indian wasn't dead, though he was three-quarters drowned, his hair plastered flat to his head and shoulders, eagle feathers drooping and bedraggled.

Ryan allowed him to cough the water from his lungs and sneeze it from his sinus passages. The Sioux was in no shape to continue fighting. Ryan slogged up the creek bank, hauling Joe with him. He dumped the coughing man onto the grass, noticing as he did so that Joe bore two superficial bullet wounds, a blood-oozing hole in the upper thigh and a red-edged furrow across the small of his back.

After a few moments of groping, Ryan retrieved his blaster, ejected the spent clip and reloaded with bullets taken from his cartridge belt. By the time he had accomplished that, Joe was sitting up, inhaling shuddery breaths, his jet black eyes narrowed and seething with hatred.

"Kill me, *wasicun*," he hissed, sounding half-strangled. "I deserve it for failing to kill you when I first saw you."

"Someone has already expressed the same opinion about you," Ryan said. "I'm not going to chill you unless you force me."

There was a sudden, surprised intake of breath, and Joe demanded, "Aren't you with Hellstrom and his psychotics?"

"We're with them, but we're not of them. Get me?"

Joe opened his mouth to answer, but Krysty's voice, shouting Ryan's name, cut him off. She sounded very worried and hoarse, and her next call terminated in a coughing spasm.

Gesturing with the pistol, Ryan said, "Take off."

"What will you tell the others?"

"That you got away from me. That's the truth, isn't it?"

Joe didn't respond. He rose to a crouch and soundlessly merged with the darkness. Ryan climbed back up the slope and called to Krysty. She ran to him, green eyes clouded by worry and gas-induced tears. She squeezed his arms and touched his face. Fleur marched close behind her.

"You're wet," Krysty said. "You're not hurt, not wounded?"

"No. The Indian got away when we hit the creek. He swam underwater, I think."

"You think?" Fleur repeated suspiciously. "That was Touch-the-Sky himself! You didn't make sure?"

Ryan stared at her stonily. "Normally I would have, except that I emptied my blaster saving your life."

Fleur scowled, then wheeled away, taking long strides back to the campsite. Krysty and Ryan followed her. The area looked like an open-air charnel house, given an added unearthly atmosphere by the planes of drifting chemical fog. The gas had dissipated to some extent, but the survivors of the battle all looked and sounded miserable.

They stepped over the bodies of the slain and called to their friends. None of them bore injuries, beyond a few cuts and contusions, except for J.B., whose fedora sported a fresh bullet hole. He was angry about it, since he held one of the incompetent sec men responsible. Doc was suffering the worst from the effects of the gas, and Mildred tended to him as he gagged, wept and dry-heaved.

Ryan did an automatic body count. There were fourteen dead Sioux warriors sprawled on the ground, leaking fluids from a variety of wounds in a variety of places.

Out of the ten sec men he spotted only three were ambulatory, and one was cradling an obviously broken arm.

"Looks like we got big-time skunked," Ryan said.

"If not for the six of us," J.B. said, "this skirmish would've been a massacre."

The door of the wag banged open and Hellstrom stepped out with a grand, long-legged flourish. He held a handkerchief over his nose and mouth. Fleur quickly approached him, saying, "We have six dead, four wounded. Zezo won't last through the night, so he doesn't count."

"The opposition?" Hellstrom's voice was muffled and nasal, as if he were holding his nose behind the handkerchief.

"Fourteen, but only nine are worth salvaging."

"And the value of our people?"

Fleur made an exasperated gesture. "Four, if you include Zezo."

"A baker's dozen. Get to it. We'll attend to our own back home."

Fleur snapped her fingers toward the standing sec men, and they bent over and began arranging the bodies of the slain.

Hellstrom nodded in the direction of Ryan and his friends. "You and your group turned the tide, Cawdor. My thanks."

The white-suited man eased himself down in his chair and fluttered the handkerchief before his face. "Whew! Pungent, isn't it?"

Ryan strode over to him, put a boot against the support pedestal of the chair and shoved with all of his strength. The chair overturned, and Hellstrom was dumped unceremoniously to the ground, uttering a wordless cry of outrage and surprise.

The move had been performed on impulse, so Hellstrom had no opportunity to sense Ryan's intentions. As he gathered a handful of white jacket and yanked the skinny man to his feet, Ryan heard the clickings of rounds jacking into cylinders and hammers thumbed back. His people were covering Fleur and the surviving sec men.

Holding Hellstrom almost clear of the ground, Ryan shook him savagely. He weighed no more than a suit of clothes. "You son of a bitch, you knew this would happen. You wanted it to happen!"

There was a shadow of fear darkening Hellstrom's eyes, but there was also a monstrous anger. "You one-eyed prick, do you know how close to death you are?"

Snarling out a laugh, Ryan jammed the bore of the sound suppressor of the SIG-Sauer against Hellstrom's underjaw and cruelly forced his head back. "Nowhere near as close as you, you scrawny bastard."

He heard the snapping crack of Mildred's ZKR and then a sec man yelping in pain. "Just pierced his ear for him," Mildred called. "He makes another move, and I'll pierce his testicles."

Forcing a laugh, Hellstrom spread solicitous hands. "Okay, Cawdor. You're annoyed. I don't blame you. I understand it. But there was a reason."

Ryan stared at the man for another handful of seconds, then released him. He stepped back, lowering the blaster but not leathering it. Hellstrom rearranged his clothing, uprighted his chair and sank into its seat.

To Fleur, he said, "Get on with it. We don't have all night."

"All right, Cawdor. I apologize."

"It'll take more than that, Lars."

"And I'll offer more than that. Normally you would be put to a slow death for laying hands on me, or at the very least, scourged until you were crippled. However, I must make allowances for this circumstance. Yes, I expected the attack, and to some extent I needed it."

"Why?"

"Two reasons. Firstly I was curious to see how you people handled yourselves in a crisis. Very impressive, very professional. All of you kept your heads, which is more than I can say for my own people."

"Is that why you waited so long to use the gas, because you were testing us?"

"Yes."

"You sacrificed an entire sec squad for a test?"

"That's **what** they're here for," Hellstrom replied.

"What's the second reason?"

Hellstrom hooked a thumb in the general direction of Mount Rushmore. "You heard me tell the beetle that the harvest was delayed?"

"Yeah. So?"

With a hand wave, Hellstrom indicated the corpses spread out around the campsite. "Behold the harvest."

Ryan's face twisted. "The organs. That's why Fleur had such a hair up her ass about head shots."

"Exactly. We need hearts, livers, lungs and the occasional pancreas. Since I spared you people from the harvester's knives, I had to arrange a new crop from someplace."

"You lured the Indians to you. How could you be so sure they wouldn't have harvested all of our scalps?"

"I wasn't. Hence the gas attack."

Ryan sighed, shook his head and said, "You know what's really sick about this, Lars? It makes sense."

"I hoped you'd see it my way."

Doc, who had managed to regain most of his breath, husked out, "In the land of the ghoul, whoever has the most viscera wins."

A smile creased Hellstrom's lips. "Something like that, yes."

"You're overlooking one thing," Ryan said. "We now outnumber you. There's nothing to stop us from boosting your wag, dumping you here for the Sioux to find among the mutilated bodies of their friends and relatives and continuing on our journey."

Hellstrom shook an admonishing finger. "I'm surprised at you, Cawdor. You're overlooking one thing. A very obvious thing. Only someone who knows the correct sequence can start up the AMAC. If you fumble around, you'll blow it and yourselves to atoms. Besides, there's just enough fuel to return to Helskel."

"Lame bluff," Jak commented.

"Hardly. It's a standard security procedure to wire an antipersonnel device to the engine of a sec wag to keep thieves at bay. I'm sure your precious Land Rover is equipped with something similar. Am I right?"

He was, and it grated on Ryan's nerves to acknowledge it. The Helskel chieftain had them exactly where he wanted them. Different strategies cartwheeled through Ryan's mind. Even hijacking the wag once it was underway would be a pointless exercise, since they would be forced to go in the opposite direction of Helskel. And with a limited quantity of fuel and no idea where to obtain more, they would be stranded and vulnerable to the Sioux. He couldn't count on the sparing of Joe's life to save them from warriors seeking to avenge this night's chillfest.

Nor could they rely on J.B.'s expertise to deactivate whatever explosive device might be wired to the AMAC's innards. As the weaponsmith had mentioned more than once, it was quite possible to construct a bomb that would detonate no matter what you did to disarm it.

"You're right," Ryan admitted. "So what's the plan?"

"We'll harvest our crop and return to Helskel at daybreak." Hellstrom frowned as he looked over the bodies of his sec squad. "It appears that a few of our novitiates will have to be promoted sooner than expected."

"I'm surprised you don't want us to fill the vacancies," Ryan said sarcastically.

"Oh, by no means," Hellstrom replied cheerfully. "I have far greater ambitions in mind for you, Cawdor. Believe me."

Ryan believed him.

Chapter Fourteen

Fleur and the battered survivors of the sec squad worked the rest of the night and well into the early-morning hours, separating the victims of head and neck shots from those who bore wounds in their torsos.

Ryan was curious to see if they would remove the organs on the spot, but Fleur and her men employed another practice, no less grisly and bloody. Plastic body bags were removed from a rear compartment of the AMAC, and three corpses were snugged inside a single bag.

Of course, the bodies were first decapitated and the arms and legs amputated in order to facilitate easy packing. The limbs and heads were tossed down the incline toward the creek. Once the torsos were crammed belly-to-butt-to-belly inside the bags, containers of dry ice were emptied into them. The bags were then tightly closed with zippers and hermetic seal locks.

It was apparently an operation Fleur and the rest had engaged in many times before. Their skill with knives, bone saws and other surgical implements was very efficient.

Mildred watched the sawing and chopping with a clinical eye. "The dry ice will burn the epidermal tissues, but it'll preserve the organs, and I suppose that's the whole point."

"Disgusting," was Doc's observation.

Ryan and his party claimed tents as far away from the scene of dismemberment as possible without leaving the safety of the wag. But they were all too keyed up to sleep, and because their clothes still reeked strongly of gas, no one cared to share the close quarters of the tents just yet. Ryan was uncomfortable in his wet clothes, but fortunately the temperature didn't drop to an intolerable degree. Everyone sat and watched the organ harvesting and talked in low tones.

"We don't know if there's a bomb wired to the wag's ignition," J.B. commented. "He could be bullshitting us."

"True," Krysty said, "but Hellstrom doesn't strike me as the bluffing type."

"All bluff," Jak told them. "Seen kind before. Take away ass-kissers and nothing but coward."

"He's no coward," Mildred objected. "He's a pragmatist, just like we are. If we weren't, we wouldn't be sitting here."

Ryan grunted. "Yeah, well, I'm not sure we should be. It might be better if we take them prisoner, try to deal with the Sioux for safe passage, or take them back to Helskel and ransom them off for our wag."

"Both of those options have a certain merit," Doc said. But I fear they appear to have similar outcomes, as well."

"With us being chilled?" Krysty inquired.

Doc nodded sagely.

Around two o'clock, the torso packing was completed. True to Fleur's estimate, the wounded sec man called Zezo was pronounced dead shortly thereafter. Hellstrom gave the order to wrap his and the other sec men's bodies in canvas in preparation for the return to Helskel, then he retired to the AMAC.

Ryan drifted into a dreamless sleep, his head pillowed on his arms. He had gotten very little rest the night before, and the exertions and accumulated fatigue of the past two days caught up with him.

He was awakened almost immediately, it seemed, by Krysty whispering into his ear, "Wake up, lover. Time to go."

Ryan opened his eye. The blue-black backdrop of the sky was broken up by the pink and orange scraps of approaching dawn. He sat up, yawning, and Krysty sniffed the collar of his shirt and said, "Phew." She ran a hand along his jawline.

"I look bad, huh?" he asked.

Krysty smiled wanly. "Well, you aren't up to stickie standards yet, but I can see the start."

The sec men were breaking camp, laboring tiredly to disassemble the tents and carry the security lamps into the AMAC. The one with the injured arm was hampered by a makeshift sling. Of the body bags there was no sign, but the Sioux corpses that didn't fit Hellstrom's needs were left to lie where they had fallen.

The bodies of the slain sec men had been shrouded in canvas and were lashed to the roof of the vehicle.

All of the companions were baggy-eyed and disheveled. None of them had caught so much as a catnap, and Ryan experienced a momentary pang of guilt. As it was, he didn't feel the slightest bit refreshed. He felt rusty and mean.

One of the sec men strode over to them. "Knock down your tents and pack 'em out."

Ryan rose stiffly to his feet. "You knock 'em down."

The sec man's eyes were rimmed and netted with red. He probably hadn't gotten any sleep either. His growled retort was full of menace. "You heard me, one-eye."

"I've got a better idea," Ryan said. "How about I knock *you* down and pack you out," and he hit the sec man as hard as he could in the middle of the belly.

He doubled over, mewling. His hands clutched at his stomach convulsively, his breath fought to get back into his lungs. Sweat sprang out on his forehead.

"Let's get some breakfast," Ryan said, walking around the bent-over sec man and toward the AMAC. His friends followed him.

Hellstrom was inside the passenger area, looking fresh and clear-eyed. He greeted them with a rousing, "Good morning, good morning!"

He gestured to a hot plate on a shelf where a pot of delicious-smelling coffee warmed and sweet rolls were stacked on a tray. "Help yourselves."

After washing down a roll with a cup of the coffee, Ryan felt a little more human, albeit a very smelly, short-tempered and unshaven one. Hellstrom didn't bother chatting with them, for which everyone was grateful.

After Fleur and what was left of her sec squad boarded the AMAC, Hellstrom assigned two of the men to the control cockpit. The man whom Ryan had belly-punched passed him, steadfastly avoiding eye contact.

The broken-armed man sat near one of the M-249 machine guns, and Fleur sat beside the other.

Since there was much more room in the back on the return trip, Mildred stretched out across several of the chairs, her head in J.B.'s lap. Doc, who appeared so exhausted as to be ill, lay prone on the facing row of seats.

"Let's roll," Hellstrom commanded.

The engine of the AMAC caught on the second try, and though he tried, Ryan didn't see the driver's preliminary start-up sequence, which, presumably, prevented the wag from self-destructing.

The sun was clear of the horizon by the time the AMAC rumbled from the mouth of the valley and onto the flatlands.

Without preamble, Hellstrom announced, "Cawdor, I'm naming you a scion of the Family. Your official function will be to serve as warlord and adviser."

From the corner of his eye, Ryan caught Fleur whipping her head around in astonished outrage.

"You will share the title on equal footing with Fleur," Hellstrom went on smoothly. "And she should not have any objections, inasmuch as you saved her life last night."

Hellstrom stared past Ryan's shoulder at Fleur. "I am correct, am I not? My eyes didn't deceive me?"

Fleur murmured in a subdued tone, "You're correct. It's all in order."

Ryan uttered a short, weary laugh. "I appreciate the honor, Lars. However, I respectfully decline it."

"And I appreciate your candor, if not your ignorance. Unfortunately you can't decline it without declining your life and that of your friends."

Ryan sighed. "I'm fed up with your threats, Lars."

He made a move to pull his weapon, but Hellstrom threw up his hands in exasperation. "Blasters! Always with the blasters! Put that goddamn thing away, Cawdor, I'm not threatening you. By bestowing this rank upon you, I'm making you an untouchable, sacrosanct, blessed. You're protected, understand? If you turn me down and try to go on your way, you'll be fair game for every bladester, duelist, biker and chopmonger in the Black Hills.''

Ryan opened his mouth to respond, but Hellstrom held up a hand. "I know what you're going say. 'Just replace our tires and we'll be on our way.' I'm sorry, but the traditions, the protocols of the Family, must be observed, or I place my position as patriarch in jeopardy. I don't want to hurt you, I want to help you."

"What do you expect us to do?" Krysty demanded. "Stay in Helskel forever, so your population of scumbags won't come after us?"

Hellstrom shook his head. "Hardly. I have a business proposition for you."

Ryan guessed the answer to the question he put to Hellstrom, but he asked it anyway. It seemed to be expected. "Which is?"

Hellstrom shifted in his seat. "It's difficult for me to maintain the level of respect I deserve because I trade with the Beforetime pigs in Lincoln's nose for everything we have in Helskel. Some Family members are a bit disheartened by the fact that our very survival depends on those holdovers from the time of pig magic."

Hellstrom's expression became vaguely disconcerted. "Believe me, the Commander and the other freezie swine up there are a much greater menace to restoring the health of this country than Helskel could ever be."

J.B. snorted. "You're breeding a generation of chill-crazy maniacs. You're not a menace?"

Hellstrom ignored him. "I want—I need—those Beforetimers out of the way, and I need you to help me do it."

"How so?" Ryan asked. "You've got a pocket-sized army at your disposal. They're fairly well trained and very well armed, aren't they?"

"Yes, but there has to be an arsenal up there in the nose. As far as I know, they may have guided missiles to nukeblast Helskel from afar."

"What about a siege?"

"Same answer. From their vantage point, an assault force would be cut to pieces, and there would be no more trading."

"That's really what's worrying you, isn't it?"

Hellstrom tugged nervously at his long nose. "Of course it is. If we could stage a successful assault, we'd never have to trade again. Helskel would have everything it ever needs. There's a vast treasure of tech sitting up there, just out of reach."

"Do you have anything approximating a plan?" Ryan inquired.

Pinching the air between the thumb and forefinger of one hand, Hellstrom replied, "A germ of one. For it to succeed, it requires courage, cunning and a warrior's intrepidity. Which all of you possess in enviable amounts."

"Assuming, just for the moment, that we're inclined to go along with you," Ryan said, "what's in it for us?"

"You don't seem like a fool, Cawdor, but you certainly can sound like one. 'What's in it for us,' he asks." Hellstrom thrust his head toward Ryan. "What do you think? You'll be rewarded beyond your wildest dreams of avarice. Blasters, wags and an unlimited supply of fuel. If you're successful and you care to remain with us, you'll enjoy a position in Helskel second only to my own. If you wish to continue on your journey, I'll grant you a special dispensation. Everyone will be so happy with the new toys, they won't question any decisions I make. We'll be the most powerful barony in Deathlands, mebbe even on the whole planet."

"And if we're not successful," Krysty said, "you can always claim we were wild-assed mercies, not connected to Helskel at all, operating without your sanction or knowledge."

Hellstrom smiled. "The Beforetimers called it plausible deniability. Isn't that a lovely phrase?"

"The freezies in the nose may not believe you, lovely phrases or not," Ryan pointed out.

"That's an acceptable part of the risk."

Glancing over his shoulder, Ryan exchanged quick looks with Mildred, J.B., Jak and Krysty. He turned back to Hellstrom.

"I'm too tired to give your proposition the consideration it deserves. Let us get back to Helskel, rest up and have a chance to discuss it among ourselves."

"A fair proposal," Hellstrom replied. "From the moment we reach Helskel, you have thirty-six hours to reach a decision."

"And if you don't like our decision?"

Hellstrom replied with a smiling face, but there was no humor in his tone. "Then I'll be forced to make one of my own."

Chapter Fifteen

They arrived back in Helskel shortly before noon. The driver of the AMAC maneuvered it into a fenced-in compound behind the saloon, parking the vehicle between several motorcycles that were locked into stanchions and a pair of open-canopied dune buggies. There was a fueling station with two gasoline pumps situated on a concrete apron in the center of the lot. Two sec men armed with the compact Tec-10 machine pistols guarded it.

Everyone disembarked and trooped to the saloon. Fleur beckoned to a couple of the compound guards to carry Hellstrom and his chair out of the AMAC.

Upstairs, Krysty and Mildred made it plain that a bath was their first order of business. Doc, Jak and J.B. opted for naps. Ryan, who felt soiled and grungy, collected a fresh shirt and pants from the backpack and went to the first-floor bathroom.

The tub was old and deep, but it was equipped with running water. A cake of homemade lye soap the size of a ham was on a stool. Ryan filled the tub with hot water, removed his clothes and eased his body into it. He sighed with relief. For a few minutes he occupied himself with the ordeal of shaving by feel. He nicked himself twice before he'd rid his face of the stubble.

He scrubbed himself with the soap until his skin prickled, then lay back, closing his eye, hoping some of the tension and worry would ease from his muscles and mind. He was on the verge of dozing off when he heard the bathroom door click open. He reached for his blaster on the stool.

"No need for that, Cawdor."

It was Fleur, wearing a pink silk wrapper, the cuffs of the voluminous sleeves edged with brightly colored feathers. With her long hair tumbling about her shoulders, she looked astonishingly feminine, despite the eye patch and the X scar.

"What are you doing here?" Ryan demanded. Unconsciously his knees drew together.

With an easy smile, the woman replied, "I want a bath. No one told me this one was occupied."

"As you can see," Ryan said, "it is. Close the door on the way out."

"All right," Fleur said, but she didn't seem inclined to hurry.

Ryan angled an eyebrow at her. "Yeah?"

"That tub looks very accommodating. I think it might hold two."

"Don't even bother to test that theory."

Instead, Fleur strode forward. She casually raised the hem of her wrapper, sat on the lip of the tub, swung her legs over the top and plunged her feet into the water.

"What do you want?" he demanded.

"If we're to share the title of Helskel's warlord, we need to talk."

"I haven't made up my mind about accepting the appointment, yet."

"That's what we have to talk about, Cawdor."

"Why?" he asked.

Fleur's face acquired a solemn, quiet expression. "I don't care to share my position with anyone, unless it's someone I can trust."

"Makes sense."

"And I can't trust someone who doesn't know where I came from, or how I came to be."

"Tell me, then."

"When I was twelve, I was crossing the Rockies with my parents, as part of an overland wagon train. We were out of Seattle and were heading for Colorado. Turned out our guides led us into a trap. A bunch of mercies swept down out of the hills and chilled everybody."

"Except you," Ryan said.

"Except me. Since slavery was one of their sidelines, they figured they could trade me to Baron Alfred Nelson, leader of the Vista ville."

Ryan managed to keep the surprise he felt from showing on his face. Nelson was one of the many barons he and his group had run afoul of, and like many others, the man had lost his life when he sought to enslave or chill them.

"I tried to escape several times," Fleur continued. "The last time, I got this." She touched the patch covering her eye. "One of the mercies buttstroked me with his rifle. He was a little too enthusiastic, and I was instantly damaged goods."

"They didn't trade you to Baron Nelson, after all?"

The corners of Fleur's lips twitched in a small, bitter smile. "They didn't have the opportunity. The very next day a war party of Lakota swooped down. They butchered the mercies, just like the mercies had butchered the people on the wag train."

"Let the punishment fit the crime," Ryan intoned. "What did the Lakota do to you?"

"They took me with them. They knew I was a prisoner, so they more or less rescued me. They took care of me."

"How long did you stay with them?"

Fleur frowned. "Can't say for certain. Four years at least, mebbe five. It wasn't a bad life, though we were on the move a lot. I learned their language, they taught me to hunt, to track, to use weapons. To kill."

"How did you hook up with Hellstrom and his Family?"

"We came across the patriarch and his people struggling through a mountain pass in the winter. There weren't very many of them, and they were slowly starving to death. The patriarch wasn't taking any food, but gave what little they had to the strongest members. They were even eating their own shoes. My band of Lakota took pity on them and allowed them to share the winter camp."

Fleur closed her eye, as if viewing the past. "The patriarch and I made an instant connection. I knew, somehow, that he was a born leader, a messiah who would carve an empire out of Deathlands, one who would rule forever. I was shown that my white blood was far superior to that of the savages I'd been living with."

Disgust welled up within Ryan. He guessed that Hellstrom had psi-scanned everyone in the Sioux village and found Fleur's mind the most malleable, the easiest to influence.

"The patriarch and one of the tribal leaders, Touch-the-Sky, agreed to a pact," Fleur went on. "The Lakota would allow the whites to remain in this country as long as they didn't go anywhere near Mount Rushmore.''

"The Lakota knew about the freezies up there?'' Ryan asked.

Fleur opened her eye. "Oh, yes. It was a source of great anger to them. They viewed them as monstrosities, a monument to the predark evils that they had hoped were forever destroyed.''

"Of course,'' Ryan said with a mocking smile, "Lars broke the pact at the first opportunity.''

"And why not?'' Fleur demanded, her eye suddenly shining with near-religious fervor. "Who are the red savages to order their superiors around?''

"This is their land, for one thing.'' A thought suddenly occurred to him. "Was Zadfrak part of Hellstrom's group?''

"Yes,'' Fleur admitted reluctantly. "He fell in love with Touch-the-Sky's sister, Many Stars. When the patriarch and his Family left, Zadfrak took Many Stars with him.''

"And you went, too?''

"Of course. It was my destiny, wasn't it?''

"I think I understand now,'' Ryan said. "When Touch-the-Sky saw Lars had made a beeline for Mount Rushmore, he feared that he would ally himself with the freezies up there. A war party followed you, a fight broke out, Many Stars escaped and the seeds of the hatred between the Family and the Sioux were planted. Then, of course, after Many Stars gave birth, Helskel was established, Zadfrak returned to the Sioux just long enough to find that his son had died of rad cancer and he killed the woman.''

Fleur nodded. "And was cast out. Until you returned him."

"If I knew then what I know now, I would have left him for the Sioux or the screamwings."

"That's all past, Cawdor. We need to discuss your future with the Family."

"I don't see much of one, Fleur."

"You had better, or you won't have any future at all. That goes for all of your people, including your pet mutie bed mate."

Forcing down his anger, Ryan took a deep breath and said, "I'm listening. What's your take on my future as co-warlord of Helskel?"

Fleur leaned forward, her hand moving beneath the surface of the water to stroke Ryan's thigh. "After the ceremony, when your appointment is made official, you and I will enter into a contract. A bonding."

"Like a marriage?"

"Somewhat. My life belongs to you now, Cawdor. Together we will expand Helskel's influence, especially after you win the tech inside Mount Rushmore. You, me and the patriarch will be the most powerful people in Deathlands."

"You're forgetting a few things," Ryan said, trying to get control of his body. "I have a responsibility to my people, and I have a son."

"They'll enjoy a privileged status in Helskel."

"And my 'pet mutie bed mate'?"

Fleur lifted the corner of her mouth in a half-smirk, half-smile. "She'll just have to get used to the new arrangement, won't she?"

"No. Because whatever I decide, the arrangement you're talking about will never happen."

Fleur moved her hand farther up his thigh. Her fingers brushed his testicles, and her smile widened. "Don't let your pride lead you into making a foolish choice, Cawdor. After you're with me, you won't want any other kind of arrangement."

As her hand made a move to caress his penis, Ryan grabbed her by the wrist and yanked her arm, jerking her into the water. He used more force than was necessary, and she cried out in surprised anger.

"Get away from me," he said, his tone containing a deep, rumbling tone of menace. The scar that seamed his face glowed red. "Get away or I'll break your neck. You have my promise on it."

She didn't try to wrest away from his grip. "Our lives are intertwined now," she said, a note of urgency in her voice. "Mutual destinies. Between us, we have two eyes and can see further than anyone. We'll share one vision. Don't you understand?"

"I understand perfectly. Your life is your own. And I don't need your eye to see the truth."

He released her. Fleur stood in a rush and stepped from the tub.

"You've made an enemy today, Cawdor. Mebbe the last one in your life."

Ryan expected her to slam the door behind her, but instead she closed it with a quiet click. He swore and concentrated on regaining his sense of comfort. It wasn't easy. His mouth was dry, his heart was beating fast and a part of his body was still reacting to the woman—and not to his disgust and anger with her.

The water was turning cold, and he was grateful for it. His body was soon answering to his mind again. He climbed out of the tub, dried off and dressed quickly.

Back upstairs in his room, he found Krysty stretched out on the bed, wearing only a towel around her torso. Ryan sat down beside her and leaned over to kiss her lips, rubbing his smoothly shaven cheek against her face.

Krysty said playfully, "Now that I don't have to worry about beard burn..." She undid the towel and tugged at Ryan's belt.

Sighing, he reluctantly pushed her hand away. His eye drank in the womanly beauty of her form, from the full breasts tipped with hardening nipples, to the flat-muscled belly and down to the crimson tangle at the juncture of her rounded thighs.

"You have no idea how much I want you, lover," he said with a smile, "but I have to call a tactical meeting. With everybody present and fully clothed."

Krysty frowned for a moment, then sat up, reaching for her clothes. "It'll keep, I guess."

"God, I hope so."

While Krysty dressed, Ryan fetched the others. It took longer than it should have to rouse Doc. Ryan was a little concerned by how exhausted he was. The old man had often displayed a stamina astounding for what his body had been through at the hands of the whitecoats, but today he looked as if he were feeling every second of his two-hundred-odd years.

Back in his room, Ryan told everyone about his encounter with Fleur. No one made any jokes, for which he was grateful, but Krysty's eyes flashed with emerald fire.

"Do you figure Hellstrom sent her?" J.B. asked.

"Mebbe, though I doubt it. She trotted out the old 'my life is yours' horseshit, even though crawfishing on debts seems to be part of Helskel's basic philosophy."

"What you do?" Jak asked. "Be warlord?"

"It very much appears that is your sole option," Doc said. "Otherwise…" He drew a thumb across his throat.

"If I accept the offer," Ryan replied, "then we'll be bound to take on Hellstrom's mission to breach the Anthill. Mildred, you know anything about the Continuity of Government program? How much of Hellstrom's story about the installation can be matched up with actual history?"

Mildred shook her head, the beads in her plaited hair clicking. "Some of it, all of it, none of it. Keep in mind that paranoia was rampant during the last decade of the twentieth century. There was a historically high level of distrust in the government. There were rumors of secret deals and an exchange of technology with the Russians, and even, believe it or not, with extraterrestrials."

"Extraterrestrials?" Krysty echoed.

"Yeah. One school of thought was that the Star Wars defense program was designed to protect earth from an invasion from space, not to intercept nuclear missiles. Anyway, Ryan, to answer your question, all I can say is, I don't know. Since the technology existed to time trawl and teleport living matter across the world a century ago, I don't find the concept of bionically altered predarkers living in a cryonically controlled stronghold all that incredible."

J.B. took off his spectacles and breathed on the lenses. "If it is true, we'll have access to the mother of all stockpiles. We could write our own tickets, anywhere in Deathlands."

"And Lars Hellstrom can and will punch those tickets," Krysty said grimly. "We can't trust him to keep his word."

"It is a rigged game he wants us to play," Doc said. "And there is only one way to win at a rigged game. That is to quit."

"Or rig the game in our favor," Ryan replied. "Any suggestions?"

"Chill Hellstrom," Jak said.

"That'll be our final hand to play. No, I think our best tactic is to keep a low profile for the next three days. Mebbe during that time we can find an ace on the line."

"And if we can't?" J.B. challenged. "Then what?"

"Then I'll accept the appointment to warlord and we'll go from there."

Krysty shook her head in frustrated anger. "I hope this teaches us to be more careful about what we promise dying men in the future. A good deed never goes unpunished."

Ryan nodded thoughtfully. "That's one way of looking at it."

Chapter Sixteen

Ryan and his people saw and heard nothing from Hell-strom throughout the remainder of the afternoon or the following day. They walked around, sampling the sights, sounds and tastes of Helskel, and tried to ward off the fingers of dread and apprehension that clutched at them.

Jak was the most impatient. He was feeling claustro-phobic and more than a little trapped. He sorely wanted to boost the AMAC and tear out of there, with no re-gard to the consequences, shooting, slashing and slug-ging anyone who stood in their way. However, he was intelligent enough to realize that all six of them were en-meshed too tightly in Hellstrom's web to escape safely.

On the evening of the second day, a ceremony to in-duct novitiates into the sec squad was staged in the bar-room of the saloon. Unlike the funeral of Zadfrak, this ritual was very quick, almost casual. Ryan, Mildred and Krysty watched it through the front door.

Dog, Phil and three other men kneeled before Hells-trom, while their heads were shorn of hair by the use of clippers and razors. The men performing the tonsorial chores weren't very careful, and the scalps of all the in-ductees bore little bleeding cuts and slashes by the time the barbers were done.

Once their heads were shaven, Fleur took an ice pick that had been heating in a brazier filled with red-hot coals and inscribed X's on all five men's foreheads. The operation took only a few seconds per man since she was heedless of their blood and pain.

Afterward, as blood streaked down their faces, they bowed to Hellstrom, who proclaimed them warriors and servants of Helskel. He dismissed them with a bored wave of the hand. The bleeding men clutched fistfuls of their own hair and left.

"A new generation of cannon fodder," Mildred murmured.

Catching sight of the companions, Hellstrom gestured for them to enter. Ryan walked in as the new X-scarred sec men walked out. Dog gave him a sidewise glare as he passed. Fleur studiously avoided looking in his direction.

"At seven-thirty tomorrow evening," Hellstrom said, "I will have your decision. A war council has been called in the restaurant and your attendance is mandatory."

"What if I make up my mind before then?" Ryan asked.

"Then you'll wait until the council convenes, Cawdor. I don't grant private audiences on war council days. You may go now."

Though he earnestly tried to conceive of a plan through that night and most of the next day, Ryan couldn't come up with a suitable strategy to delay making the decision.

The jaws of the Helskel trap had snapped shut neatly and painlessly, but very securely. There was no choice but to go through with the pretense of accepting the position of warlord. Gloomily, none of his friends could offer an alternative, either, except to engage in a firefight they couldn't hope to win.

At seven o' clock, a little after twilight, Ryan was alone, walking toward the eatery, when Fleur sauntered around the corner of the building. She had her thumbs hooked into the belt loops of her jeans, and when she caught sight of him, a hesitant, almost shy smile played over the finely chiseled planes of her face.

"Evening, Cawdor," she said.

Tension lizards crawled along the buttons of his spine, but Ryan returned the smile. "Evening."

Casually he placed his right hand on his hip, just above the butt of the SIG-Sauer. If Fleur caught the movement, she gave no sign.

Taking a deep breath, she said, "I regret the incident the other day. I was out of line, expecting you to abide by customs that are new to you. I apologize."

Ryan said nothing, but one of Trader's favorite—and most tiresome—phrases popped unbidden into his mind. "Never apologize. It's a sign of weakness." And if there was one thing Fleur wasn't, it was weak.

"The patriarch has finally decided upon a plan to get inside the Anthill," she said after a moment.

"Good."

"Will you be a part of it?"

"I'll tell that to Lars."

Fleur nodded, and as Ryan made a move to step around her, she said hurriedly, "Not all of our sec force has assembled. One of the newest members, for one."

"Who might that be?" Instantly Ryan regretted asking the question.

"You know him. Dog." Seeing his eye narrow, she added, "He made the grade, but he's addicted to a certain vice. He'll be up to his ears in it by now, and somebody has to get him in shape for the council. He respects you. Mebbe you can see to it.''

It was such an obvious attempt at entrapment that Ryan almost spit on the toes of her boots. ''Why should I? I'm not Family.''

''You may not realize it, but your position in Helskel is very precarious. The patriarch doesn't trust you. If you bring Dog in, he may alter his thinking and believe you're cooperating from your own free will. Besides, it's the duty of a warlord to look after the warriors.''

Ryan stared unblinkingly into Fleur's single eye for a long silent moment. She stared back. He asked, ''Where can I find him?''

Fleur hooked a thumb over her left shoulder. ''Last house on the last lane.'' She smiled cryptically. ''Be prepared to use your fists, Cawdor. Dog may not want to come.''

Ryan smiled just as cryptically. ''I'll do my best.''

He walked around her, down the dusky, dusty streets of Helskel. Cooperating with Fleur's flimsy story was a big risk, but he couldn't back down in front of her, nor could he resist the urge to find out what she had planned.

He followed a twisting side lane, passing a number of shoddy shanties at the far end of the path. He heard the faint whine of reedy music emanating from the last of the slapdash structures. It was little more than a lean-to, with crudely hewn clapboard walls and a door that hung crookedly from leather hinges.

As he approached it, keeping to the lengthening shadows, the door banged open and a man stumbled out into the lane. Ryan stepped back in the murk, not moving, hand resting lightly on his blaster. The man passed within a few feet of him, and by the light of the rising moon and the setting sun, Ryan saw his face.

It was the face of a mindless brute. Ryan had seen more intelligence in the eyes of animals. The man mumbled to himself as he staggered, then barked out a snarl of a laugh.

With a thrill of loathing, Ryan realized that the vice Fleur had spoken of was the werewolf weed.

It was a rare drug, hard to find even in the hinterland of Deathlands. Composed of a mutated form of marijuana and various hallucinogens like peyote, the werewolf weed stimulated the hindbrain, causing an atavistic regression. It was at the same time an unpopular and popular drug. Its sole attraction for the user was to wallow in artificial bestiality for a time. Ryan had heard that some bands of marauders appreciated its influence before a raid, since it made them fearless and predatory. Unfortunately they would just as soon turn on their own comrades as an enemy while in its brutal grip.

Ryan catfooted up to the shanty and peered into the open door. The yellow glow of a kerosene lamp was dimmed by a wall of hot, acrid smoke. A skinny man playing a wooden flute crouched in a corner. On the floor lay a number of naked men and women, engaged in various sex acts. Their faces were slack, they growled like animals, they clawed and bit and slapped at each other. A man was bleeding profusely from a bite at the base of his neck, and a woman, her naked body glistening with sweat, was tolerating anal penetration from a grunting biker. There was no sign of Dog.

Stomach churning with sour bile, Ryan turned away and headed back up the path. A scuffling of feet from the shadows to his right drew his attention. He fisted his blaster and whirled.

A stooping, naked figure crept out of the pool of darkness. For a moment Ryan didn't recognize the slack-jawed, blank-eyed, gape-mouthed face staring into his own. Then, with a sense of revulsion, he recognized the naked man as Dog. The X slash on his forehead had scabbed over, and his ears protruded from his shaven skull.

Ryan stepped back. Dog shambled forward, a grin splitting his foam-flecked lips.

"Stay back," the one-eyed man warned. "I'll chill you where you stand."

Dog didn't seem to hear or care. In his regression, he probably didn't even recognize the purpose of the SIG-Sauer aimed at him. He laughed, a deep, wet, slobbery sound.

Ryan backpedaled carefully, his finger on the trigger, even though he knew full well the repercussions of killing Dog. It was a very neat trap Fleur had set. If he, an outsider, killed Dog, she would demand bloody retribution from the Family. It would be a legal execution, since Hellstrom hadn't yet officially named him a scion of the Family. And if he didn't chill Dog, the man was sure to murder him. Either way he would be removed from the equation, and Fleur would be restored to her former status as the sole warlord.

Ryan considered shooting to wound, but he knew that powered by the drug, even a 9 mm slug in an arm or leg would be only an insect sting to Dog. There was really only one option.

The one-eyed man pivoted suddenly and took to his heels, running full-out toward Helskel. If he could reach the saloon so that Hellstrom could see Dog pursuing him, there would be no question that he chilled the man in self-defense.

But he didn't get anywhere near the saloon. He barely made it to the mouth of the lane. Dog was more than half animal now, and with his slobbering snarls sounding in his ears, Ryan heard him loping swiftly behind him.

Trying to force more speed into his pumping legs, Ryan increased the length of his stride. In less than a hundred feet Dog caught up to him.

One hand locked in Ryan's hair and the other gripped the back of his neck with an agonizing pressure. He tried to fight free, but he staggered, losing his balance on the uneven ground.

He went down heavily. His head struck the ground, and the SIG-Sauer clattered and bounced noisily from his grasp. Still, Ryan continued to roll, throwing his body in a frantic somersault toward the lights of Helskel.

Dog landed on him with his full weight, his teeth sinking into the collar of his shirt. Ryan hammered at the frothing face pressed against his, not giving in to the impulse to cry out in pain.

Talonlike nails raked at his face, and knees jacked into his midsection, seeking his groin. Dog swarmed all over him, pounding, clawing and savaging. Snarls and thick-throated laughter filled his ears as Ryan struggled to shake him off.

Dog grabbed handfuls of Ryan's hair and banged his head against the ground, once, twice, three times. Maybe more. Ryan was unable to count beyond the third time. He could barely think.

He tried to draw up his legs, hoping to get in at least one solid kick, but Dog was all slavering madness, his steely fingers shifting from Ryan's hair to his throat. He struck in a blind frenzy of desperation, but Dog didn't feel the blows.

Ryan stretched out one arm, groping for his blaster, and his fingers brushed a rough, pitted surface. His right hand closed around it and he heaved up a rock the size of a small pumpkin. Not even trying to gauge the accuracy of the blows, he smashed the rock again and again against the side of Dog's head.

The man uttered a peculiar growling yelp, and the death grip on Ryan's throat relaxed a bit. With his free hand, Ryan slammed the steely fingers away. Dog bounded up and away from him, using Ryan's torso as a springboard, and very nearly drove all the wind from his lungs.

Ryan scrambled to his feet, bleeding, sick and dizzy, while Dog crouched on the ground only a few feet away. Blood streaked the side of his face and dripped down over his cheeks and mouth. The X scab had opened up and was leaking twin scarlet streams down either side of his nose. He touched the blood with his fingers, sniffed it, then put his fingers in his mouth, sucking them clean.

Snarling, Dog glared at Ryan, eyes gleaming balefully. His muscles tensed and coiled, then he sprang out of his crouch directly at Ryan's throat.

Instead of trying to avoid the leap, Ryan bounded forward, rock-weighted right hand swinging forward in a short, adrenaline-charged arc. The arc ended as the rock caught Dog in the center of his scarred, sallow face.

He howled as the force of the blow drove him flailing ten feet across the ground. The force also crushed his nose, driving the bone splinters through his sinus cavities, then into what was left of his brain.

Dog jerked, twitched and rolled in the dust. He came up to his knees, blood flowing from his nose. He opened his mouth as if to voice another howl, and a crimson torrent spilled past his lips, splashing on the ground. His eyes lifted to stare skyward, then he fell face first to the ground.

Ryan stood and watched as Dog's death spasms slowly ceased. He was gasping in lungfuls of air and probing gingerly at the raw abrasions on his face. Every tendon, every muscle in his body was alive with pain. His head throbbed, in cadence with his pulse. The world tilted around him and he sank to his knees.

Then voices were roaring, shouting and cursing all around him, and rough hands hauled him to his feet. He blinked his eye against the glare of torches and flashlights. Around him he could see members of the Family, all white with fury and outrage.

"The son of a bitch murdered Dog. Hold him, gimme my knife!" shrilled a male voice that Ryan recognized as Phil's.

Ryan struggled against the hands and arms pinioning him, but he was held fast. Fleur, silhouetted by the flickering torchlight, came striding toward him.

"It's as I said," she shouted. "He's a pig, an insurgent, an East Coast spy!"

"You're full of shit!" Ryan croaked. "Dog was a drugged animal, and you set me up to kill him, you lying—"

The back of Fleur's hand smacked across Ryan's mouth, his teeth cutting into his lower lip. He reeled backward and spit crimson at her feet.

"Blood for Family blood!" Fleur shouted. "It's the justice of Charlie!"

Then Hellstrom was there, borne in his chair by four sec men. His face was hidden by the shadows, but light was reflected from his eyes like a pair of tiny stars.

"What is going on here, Cawdor?" he demanded.

Fleur began shrieking before Ryan could collect his wits. She began a furious tirade about how Ryan was deceiving Hellstrom and everyone in the Family, how he had been plotting to betray them to the freezies in Mount Rushmore, about how he was on a secret mission from East Coast baronies, how he had tried to convince Dog to turn traitor, cold-bloodedly murdering the hapless sec man when he was in a sedated condition, simply because he refused to be party to the treachery.

Raging, Ryan roared, "She lies, Hellstrom! She's jealous of me, she hates me because I saved her life and then spurned her—"

A fist struck Ryan painfully and with terrific force in the belly, and he was robbed of all breath. He sagged in the grips of the men holding him. Hellstrom motioned for Ryan's captors to release him. He found that his legs wouldn't support him and he fell to his hands and knees, hanging his head and sucking in lungful after lungful of air.

Hellstrom patiently waited for Ryan to stand up again before he spoke. His angular face was expressionless, but he was in a bind, and Ryan saw the knowledge of it in his eyes. He didn't believe Fleur's accusations, and he still had a use for Ryan and his people. However, he had to assert his patriarchal status in the eyes of the Family.

"I want no more violence between you two. If you're making me choose between the pair of you, it'll have to be settled in combat."

Fleur said angrily, "He's an outsider, not Family. We kill outsiders who violate our laws. He hasn't earned the right."

"Shut up!" Hellstrom roared. The unexpected fracture in his icy, controlled reserve startled everyone into shamed silence. "I'm ceding him the right! I'll put off the war council until this matter is settled."

Fleur ducked her head and murmured, "I beg forgiveness."

Then a smile crossed her face. She eyed Ryan with a murderous glee and declared, "A track stand."

Ryan didn't say anything for a moment. He remembered what he had overheard of track stands—two combatants, both astride motorcycles, each armed with only a whip, a knife and the individual warrior's skill. He wasn't at all certain he was qualified. His experience with motorcycles was limited. Nor was he confident he could handle Fleur, a cold heart whose crazed ego demanded Ryan's life.

"Well?" Hellstrom challenged. "Are you up to it?"

Ryan wiped a thread of blood from his lower lip, surveyed the expectant faces all around him and said, "Name the time and place."

Chapter Seventeen

Ryan awoke at dawn, feeling as if all the bones in his body were stitched together at the joints by wire. Everyone was awake, and they crowded into the room he shared with Krysty.

Mildred brought him coffee, and J.B. handed over the eighteen-inch panga. "I've spent the last hour sharpening it," he said. "It ought to cut through plate steel."

"Or that bitch's throat," Krysty said coldly.

Heavy footfalls sounded out in the hall, and a knock came at the door. Ryan opened it. Six sec men, all holding Tec-10 machine pistols, stood there. Phil was in the lead, though because of his freshly shorn appearance, Ryan didn't recognize him at first. His scalp was crisscrossed with tiny scabbed-over lacerations. He wore one of the corduroy vests decorated with locks and hanks of his own hair.

"I like the new look," Ryan said. "Suits you."

"We're here to escort you to the track," he said in a clipped, businesslike tone, not responding to the gibe. "Everybody leaves their blasters here."

Ryan exchanged a long, warning look with Krysty. Her finger tensed on the trigger of her Smith & Wesson, but with a curse she tossed the weapon onto the bed.

Phil jerked his head toward the hallway. "Let's go."

"Is the escort a courtesy?" Doc asked. "Or a guard detail?"

"None of your fucking business, you old sack of shit."

Doc smiled gently and rapped the ferrule of his swordstick against the floor. "I shall remember you said that, my good man."

There was a carnival air around the gathering in the large open field a half mile outside of Helskel. Children squealed and chased one another, climbing over the mothers who were dressed in holiday finery. There were scarfs, headbands, shawls and quilted cloaks of every conceivable color and style. The men wore deerskin tunics, ruffled silk shirts and talismans of animal claws and mummified human fingers.

Ryan shivered in the chill air of early morning and inspected the field of battle. It was the same area where Zadfrak had been cremated a few nights before, but all signs of the huge funeral pyre had been removed, except for the raised dais. A dozen poles, ornamented with colored glass prisms and feathers, formed the boundaries of a giant circle, at least five hundred yards in diameter.

Two motorcycles were parked at opposite ends of the field. J.B. identified them as a Husqvarna 450 and a Honda Motosport 250 trail bike. Both were clean and seemingly in good running condition.

Phil indicated the Motosport with the barrel of his blaster. "That one is yours, Cawdor."

Ryan and his people walked over to it. J.B. gave it a quick inspection, checking the tire treads, the gas tank and the transmission gearing. "Looks in good shape, Ryan, probably easier to maneuver than that Husky. So far, I think they're playing fair."

"Just don't try to pop a wheelie," Mildred stated.

"I won't," Ryan replied. "Sounds like it could hurt."

Hellstrom arrived, borne in his chair by a three-man detail. They placed him atop the dais, which Ryan noticed was positioned directly in the center of the field. It presented an obstacle as well as a viewing station. Hellstrom caught his eye and beckoned to him with a finger.

After giving Ryan a quick hug and kiss, Krysty led the rest of the companions toward the throng at the sidelines.

Ryan joined Fleur as she stood before Hellstrom. There were no words of encouragement, no briefing concerning rules. He merely studied them silently with his hooded eyes, then raised a hand. A great shout was voiced from the eager throng ringing the field, and the two combatants trotted toward their mounts.

Fleur jogged toward the far end of the field and straddled the seat of her motorcycle. She quickly kicked it into roaring life, and a man handed her a whip and her bowie knife. She grasped the whip in her right hand and placed the long knife between her teeth.

Taking a deep breath, Ryan received the whip from a sec man, coiled it in his right hand and slid the sheathed panga halfway between his crotch and the motorcycle's seat. He experimented with it until he had the weapon in a position where he could easily and quickly grasp the handle.

"Begin!" Hellstrom shouted.

Ryan kick-started his Motosport and shifted it into gear. At the opposite end of the field, Fleur rode toward him, engine roaring. He moved out, revving the engine, testing the gears, heading toward his adversary at an oblique angle.

Fleur turned straight toward him, on a collision course, the whip lashing out. Ryan evaded the steel tip by ducking low over the fuel tank, shifting gears and jumping the cycle out of her path. Fleur hurtled past, almost to the edge of the field.

Swerving expertly, lifting her bike up on its rear wheel, she brought it around without the front tire touching the ground. A volley of cheers and a medley of whistles broke from the spectators.

Ryan was impressed, but he wasted no time gaping at her. Throttling up, he crouched behind the handlebars and swooped at Fleur before she could set her wheels firmly and upshift to a higher gear.

She evidently expected such a tactic, because her whip flailed out and opened a rent in the left sleeve of Ryan's shirt. It stung like liquid fire, but the skin remained intact. As he turned the handlebars, abruptly changing direction, his cycle's front wheel struck Fleur's machine a glancing blow. She swayed in the saddle but managed to keep her balance.

Whirling the whip over his head, Ryan snapped its weighted end toward her, aiming for her face. She avoided it by leaning gracefully to one side.

The two motorcycles whirled apart, churning up a great cloud of dust. Fleur roared up the field. Ryan massaged his left arm and directed his Motosport to follow in her wake. The observers shouted their approval.

The battle of skill went on as the sun rose higher over the arid field. The Motosport and the Husky circled, feinted, raced at each other, hurtled at appallingly unsafe speeds around the field. Twice Ryan was nearly forced out of the ring by Fleur's bikemanship. Once, she nearly caused him to pile up on the support posts of the dais.

Dust hung heavily in the air, like curtains of dirty chiffon. Ryan rolled through one of the curtains, which induced a short coughing spell. With his right hand, he tried to wave the grit and dirt particles away from his face.

Fleur chose that instant to ride up on his right side, his blind side, lashing at him all the while, her hair flying in tangled witch locks around her head. The whip ripped Ryan's pants and the thigh beneath it. Another stroke shredded his shirtfront and raised a welt across his rib cage. He managed to catch the snaking metal end of the whip. He gave it a yank, at the same time feeding the Motosport more throttle. Fleur had to release the whip's handle or be pulled from her mount.

She relinquished it with a screamed obscenity, then pursued him with her bowie knife held aloft. Sweat pouring down his face, the wind whistling in his throat, Ryan kept up the acceleration, roaring up, then down, then diagonally across the field, never giving Fleur a clear opportunity with her knife. He was beginning to feel his vitality ooze from the wounds he had received from Fleur's whip and those from Dog's manhandling less than twelve hours before.

Fleur came abreast of him, on his left, and struck with her knife. Ryan managed to block the disemboweling thrust with the handle of his whip, but in doing so he was nearly unseated. He was forced to drop the lash to keep from laying down his bike. He unsheathed the panga but was unable to use it. He had to keep both hands on the handlebar grips to maintain his balance on the wobbling machine.

Fleur crowded him, backing the Motosport to the edge of the field. She hacked at him with her bowie, and he parried her thrusts with his knife. Though the panga was longer, it was all Ryan could do to block her swipes and stabbing thrusts. A couple got through his guard and opened superficial cuts on his right forearm.

Trying to maneuver away from her, he felt himself slipping out of the saddle, losing control of the bike. All Fleur had to do was ride hard and bump the Husky into the Motosport, and he would be sprawled out on the ground, helpless. Ryan fought to hang on, to keep the bowie from spilling his guts all over the field.

She slashed at him again, the knife inscribing a figure-eight pattern through the air, and he felt the cold fire of a graze across his left shoulder blade. Ignoring the ticklish sensation of flowing blood, he raised the panga to parry another thrust from the bowie, and steel hilt locked against steel hilt with a clear musical note. She maintained the pressure, pushing against his knife with all her strength, their sweaty, dirt-streaked faces only inches away from each other.

The strain against the force exerted by Fleur overbalanced him, and Ryan had no choice but to drop his blade or fall. Letting go of the panga, he twisted his torso to one side, and the bowie blade skimmed past his upper arm, the point snagging and tearing the cloth.

Fleur was unable to react in time, and she nearly toppled face first from the saddle. Putting both hands on the grips and twisting the front wheel to the right, Ryan cut back on the throttle at the same time.

The woman sped past him and Ryan slipped out of the trap, riding off in the opposite direction. He regained control of his mount, wincing at the pain in his shoulder blade, concentrating on a new problem.

Fleur knew he had dropped his weapon, and when she charged him again, she would be completely on the offensive, doing her best to slice, stab, eviscerate and decapitate him.

Ryan's quick assessment was correct. Fleur staged sortie after sortie, swinging her bowie, her single eye ablaze with triumph and fury.

To evade her savage slashes, Ryan leaned forward, then backward, at one juncture almost lying prone while he rode his Motosport in an ever-tightening circle. Fleur dogged him all along, her blade slicing and snicking through the air.

This went on long enough for Ryan to note that at the end of every stroke, the momentum of her arm would pull up her far knee and loosen the grip of her thighs on the saddle.

As Fleur veered toward him again, swinging the Bowie in a downward chopping arc, Ryan planted the sole of his boot against her rib cage. All things considered, it was more of a prod than a kick, and not very powerful since he had only the motorcycle to brace against. Nevertheless, his foot jolted her sideways. She shrieked, struggling to maintain her balance and keep her grip on the knife.

Ryan broke away from the circle and rocketed in a straight line across the field. He leaned down, at full speed, and retrieved his fallen panga. Even as he did so he heard her Husky roaring in pursuit. Spinning the Motosport about, he turned to face the infuriated Fleur.

She rode toward him full tilt, throttle wide open, engine moaning, knife held out like an accusing finger. Before Ryan could maneuver, the Motosport and the Husky collided with a screech of metal tearing into metal. Fleur struck at him, Ryan parried with the panga, then both of them were hurled to the ground.

Though he tried to shoulder roll, he hit the ground with his head. The shock of impact jarred Ryan, causing the sky to grow dim for an instant and set his head to throbbing. He rolled over just as Fleur, knuckling grit from her eye, arose and rushed at him, knife plunging downward.

Ryan moved to one side, and the bowie bit into bare earth. At the same time, he threw up one leg, and the toe of his boot sank into her lower belly. She jackknifed over his foot and fell, snapping desperately at air.

Ryan was on his feet in an instant, and as the woman started to rise, he side-kicked the hand that held the bowie. Wrist bones popped, Fleur screamed and the long knife skittered across the ground, finally plopping into the dust.

She gaped at him in horrified surprise, then lunged sideways, scrabbling with her good hand across the ground, reaching for the knife. Ryan brought the heel of his boot down on the back of her hand. She screamed again as he pressed down with all of his weight. When he heard the delicate bones crunching, he removed his foot.

Fleur, hissing curses in an aspirated voice, tried to get to her feet again, using only her legs. This time the heel of Ryan's boot connected squarely against her forehead. Her one eye rolled back in her head, and she flopped flatly on her back.

Ryan stared down at her, the panga hanging from his hand. The onlookers went berserk, screaming and shouting, "Knife her! Chill her! Kill the bitch!"

The screams whirled and spun in the air around him. His body ached, his shirttail was a sodden, soaking mass from the blood leaking from his shoulder wound, and he was expected to kill an unconscious woman.

Ryan surprised the spectators and, to an extent, himself. He slid the knife through his belt, turned and started walking toward the dais where Hellstrom sat.

People swarmed out onto the field, yelling, laughing and shouting congratulations. Ryan looked around and saw Krysty and Jak in the crowd. He hoped J.B., Doc and Mildred were nearby.

As Ryan reached the foot of the platform, Hellstrom waved a hand. "This is it, Cawdor. Fleur is yours. Chop her to fish bait or take her as a slave. Your prerogative."

He glanced over his shoulder. Two men had propped up Fleur and were dragging her forward. Glancing back to Hellstrom, Ryan muttered, "The law of the jungle with a relish."

Hellstrom smiled in genuine amusement. "The law of Charlie, the law of Helskel. The law of Deathlands."

Someone handed him Fleur's knife. Ryan turned as the woman was dumped unceremoniously at his feet. She was conscious now, though dazed and disoriented. She stared up at him as he stood over her. Her one eye expressed fear, but her lips curled in a sneer.

Ryan looked at her for a very long moment, from the toes of her dusty boots to the top of her tangled mass of hair. Finally he rested his gaze on her hands. They were discolored, swollen, twisted at unnatural angles.

He stooped over, not averting his eye from her face. He laid the bowie knife beneath the heel of his boot, stamped down and yanked up sharply on the handle at the same time. The blade snapped at the hilt with a chiming sound.

Turning away, Ryan dropped the useless hilt on her lap and turned back to face Hellstrom, who was smiling a faint smile of bemusement.

"Let's hear your decision, Cawdor."

Chapter Eighteen

Ryan and his friends were accompanied back to Helskel by a jubilant crowd. There was no sound reason for their good humor, though the sight of blood and violence had obviously started their day on a high note.

Back in his room at the saloon, Mildred bathed, disinfected and examined Ryan's wounds, pronouncing them superficial. Only the shallow knife slash on his shoulder blade warranted stitches.

Ryan stoically sat through the operation.

Watching Mildred's deft movements with the needle and surgical thread she had taken from the first-aid kit, Jak asked, "What you tell him?"

The one-eyed man started to shrug, but a sharp spasm of pain made him turn it into a short nod. "I told him yes. He wants us downstairs by noon for the swearing-in ceremony."

Krysty winced. "I hope he doesn't intend to carve X's in our foreheads."

Mildred snorted. "Ryan's got so many scars already, one more won't make much difference."

"Hellstrom won't want to mark us as Family," Ryan said. "If we're captured in the Anthill, we're not supposed to have visible connections to Helskel."

When Mildred was done, Ryan put on a new shirt, his last one. "We better request that our other clothes are laundered, or I'll be wandering around buck-ass naked soon."

"Who'd notice in this place?" J.B. asked dourly.

"Maybe a clothing allowance is one of the warlord's perks," Mildred suggested.

At noon a sec man fetched them. He ordered them to leave their blasters behind, since the theme of the ceremony was one of trust. Reluctantly they did as he said, trooping downstairs to the barroom. There were twenty-seven sec men standing in sloppy "parade rest" postures aligned across the far wall. They were all gazing stone-faced toward Hellstrom. None of them appeared to be armed.

Hellstrom greeted Ryan warmly and bade him to stand on the left side of his chair. In a whisper, Hellstrom said, "Since our time is short, we'll dispense with the public ceremony and the ritual marking."

Ryan didn't ask why the time was limited; he figured Hellstrom would tell him sooner than later.

In a ringing voice—the same powerful, persuasive tone he had used at Zadfrak's cremation—Hellstrom announced, "This is Ryan Cawdor, a warrior of superior abilities. He has performed splendidly in the service of Helskel, in the service of our lord Charlie. As patriarch, as keeper of the sacred prophecies of Helter Skelter, I name him a scion of the Family. I further name him warlord, the master of all of you. His every command is to be obeyed without question, without hesitation."

A murmuring broke out among the ranks of the sec men. For a moment Ryan thought they were voicing their discontent, but he realized they were muttering, "Helter Skelter has come down."

Still, a few pairs of gimlet-hard eyes bored defiantly into his. One pair belonged to Phil.

"It is done," Hellstrom declared. "You are dismissed. Be happy, be loving, and remember the watchwords—vigilance is survival. Go forth and work for our world. Charlie's world."

As the sec men filed out, Hellstrom called, "Phil, Clem, wait."

"Painless enough," Ryan commented. "Now what?"

"Now I'll brief you on the plan. We lost precious time because of that idiocy last night and the track stand today."

At a gesture from Hellstrom, the pair of sec men lifted the wicker chair and carried it toward the saloon doors. "Follow me, warlord and company."

They followed Hellstrom and the sec men down the street to the eatery. A hand-scrawled Closed sign hung in the dust-streaked window, but the door was unlocked.

Hellstrom was carried to the largest table. After they placed him at its head, the sec men took up sentry positions before the door. Ryan and his friends took seats around the table. Krysty was gazing at Hellstrom distrustfully, her sentient hair lying tight to her nape.

From inside his white blazer, Hellstrom produced a large folded square of paper and spread it open on the tabletop. It was hand-drawn map, and Ryan could tell that an experienced hand had made the drawings. When he saw a dotted line leading west from a hilly area labeled MT. PIG, he realized the map depicted the region around Mount Rushmore.

Hellstrom began talking quickly, without wasting a word. "I have no idea what lies inside of Mount Rushmore, the layout of the Anthill complex or even how big it is. However—" his finger traced the dotted line that terminated in a series of wavy lines "—the cave where we pick up our trade goods is here. The distance between the nose and the cave is 2.3 miles, so there has to be a tunnel system."

"I thought you said there was just a single-destination receptor unit in the cave," J.B. said.

"I've always assumed it's one way because there are no control consoles there," Hellstrom replied. "However, the station has to get its power from somewhere, and it's reasonable to assume the gateway is connected to an energy conduit. Unfortunately we can't search the cave for it because of the beetles. The only way into the complex is through the nose. Once someone gains entrance, the gateway controls can be located and used to transport an assault force inside."

"Won't the Commander become suspicious if he sees an armed squad hanging around the cave?" Ryan asked. "You can't just sit around waiting and hoping that the gateway controls will eventually be under the control of your people."

"Of course not," Hellstrom responded. "I'll be in contact with the scouts who enter through the nose. I have an excellent electronic communications system at my disposal."

"Have comms?" Jak asked.

"Small but exceptionally powerful radios. They can transmit voice or electronic signals over a five-mile radius. Still, there will be a time lag to put the assault force in position, so they'll need to remain out of the scanning range of the beetles."

"You stated you were unsure of the range of the bee-tles," Doc pointed out. "It could be less than five miles, or as much as ten."

"Part of the risk, Doctor."

J.B. shook his head in disapproval. "Since you don't have a damn germ of information about what's up there, how do you figure your scouts will survive long enough to signal the assault force? Hell, for all you know, there's a legion of sec droids just waiting for a stupe to crawl up the nose."

Hellstrom squinted at him. "Sec droids?"

"Hunter androids," Ryan answered, "programmed to chill intruders."

"Take care of any you might meet in the Anthill, and you'll have nothing to worry about."

"How do you expect to get up the nose in the first place?" Krysty asked.

Hellstrom stood. "Come with me."

They followed the man through the dining area, into the kitchen and to a heavy door sheathed in aluminum. Grasping the lever handle, he popped the latch and swung open the door. Mist and an icy draft wafted over them. Breathing the very cold air was difficult and dried out their mucous membranes. Hellstrom marched into the meat locker, pushing a path through the sides of beef swinging from hooks. He paused by a pair of large metal containers. They were about four feet deep and five feet long, three wide. They resembled utilitarian coffins.

He waited until everyone was clustered around, and he raised the lid of one of the airtight oblong boxes. He waved away the cloud of vapors rising from it. Protected by transparent plastic wrappings, lying on beds of dry ice, were various human organs: hearts, livers, a set of lungs, even a pair of eyeballs.

Krysty made a gagging sound and turned away. Even Ryan felt a quiver of nausea.

Smiling, Hellstrom shut the lid. "The other box contains what's left of the redskins we became acquainted with the other night. Since the freezies are expecting this shipment, you'll be able to gain entrance into the Anthill with a minimum of fuss."

"How is anybody supposed to breathe in there?" Jak demanded.

"You'll be equipped with small oxygen tanks and the proper cold-resistant clothing."

"How many of these containers do you intend to ship?" Mildred asked.

"Just these two. Normally each container carries four organ trays stacked on top of one another. If two are removed from each box, then we've made sufficient room for a pair of you, one to a box."

Reaching behind the container, Hellstrom made an adjustment and the entire back panel lifted upward, connected by small hinges on the inside of the container.

"There's a latch on the inside. A quick and easy way to get in and out." He shivered in the freezing temperature and turned to leave. "Let's go."

As they followed him out of the locker, J.B. said, "Only two, you said. Are you planning for the ones who don't go up the nose to be your assault force?"

Hellstrom waited until everyone had filed out and he had shut the door before answering. "No."

Ryan exchanged quick, disconcerted glances with his friends, then they fell into step behind Hellstrom as he returned to the dining room.

As the man took his seat, he said, "Obviously, Cawdor, you will be in one of the containers. You'll be supplied with weapons and whatever ordnance you might need. I'll leave it up to you to pick your partner."

"What about rest?" Jak demanded.

"Oh, that's been covered," Hellstrom replied airily. "You'll remain here, in Helskel. As my hostages."

Ryan and his friends reacted immediately, reaching for blasters that weren't there. At the same time, Clem and Phil snapped up compact Tec-10 machine pistols that had been hidden beneath their clothing.

Ryan stood there in baffled rage, fists balled, teeth clenched. "What kind of lousy deal is this, Lars?"

Hellstrom steepled his fingers at his chin. "The only deal is that there is no deal. We reached no agreements, came to no terms."

The corner of his mouth lifted in a disdainful smile. "Did you truly expect me to trust you? You had to be coerced to accept the honor I bestowed upon you. Even without a psi-scan, I knew you were only playing along, waiting for your chance to escape. In any event, I wouldn't allow all of you to get inside the Anthill. You know too much about us and could make your own deal with the Commander."

"I still could," Ryan bit out.

Hellstrom shook his head. "No, I think you'd rather do anything than put the lives of the friends you leave behind in jeopardy."

"And what if we're captured or killed? What happens to them?"

"Then we'll turn them over to the freezies upon demand. I'll state I heard of the plan to breach their stronghold and imprisoned them."

"They won't buy that," J.B. snapped. "Not if they learn that two us were smuggled inside their complex by hiding in merchandise boxes."

"I'll have a Family patsy ready," Hellstrom replied smoothly. "Fleur is a good choice—disenfranchised, stripped of her rank, embittered. She'll be the perfect scapegoat to pin it all on."

"Plausible deniability," Mildred muttered.

"What if they still won't believe you?" Krysty asked.

"I'm not under the delusion that they won't be suspicious, but as long as some culprits are caught and punished, they'll be too worried about losing their organ shipments to cut off their trade entirely."

"Got all figured out," Jak said bitterly. "Big plans for big man. No matter how big, you can still die."

"Of course," said Hellstrom with a patronizing smile. "I trust you are aware of the reverse."

Turning toward Ryan, he said, "We leave tomorrow morning at first light. You have until then to choose with whom of your gallant crew you wish to share the dangers."

Hellstrom pointed toward the door. "Be ready tomorrow at dawn. Don't make me come looking for you."

The six people marched back to the saloon in such a fury that no one dared speak to them. None of them reacted with much surprise when they reached their rooms and found their blasters missing. They assumed the heavy weapons they had stowed inside the Land Rover had also been confiscated, such as Ryan's Steyr SSG-70 rifle and J.B.'s M-4000 shotgun.

Ryan sat on the windowsill and surveyed his five friends. "Guess I waited too long to find that ace on the line."

"That's because Hellstrom is holding them all," Krysty said gloomily. "We should have expected a double cross."

"Not that it matters," Doc said, "but I certainly did. However, let us not dwell on past 'should haves.' Ryan, my dear fellow, I volunteer to accompany you into the lion's den, even though Daniel had only his faith to sustain him. I am, after all, your greatest liability and therefore the most expendable."

"You?" J.B.'s tone was incredulous. "Sure you're up to a challenge like that?"

Before Doc could retort, Ryan said, "J.B.'s right, Doc. This smells like a fireblasted hellground, and I'm afraid the pace will be too intense for you. I appreciate the offer, though."

Squaring his shoulders beneath his frock coat, Doc said stiffly, "You forget that I have knowledge of the technology in use."

"Superficial layman's knowledge, not hands-on experience," Mildred reminded him. "Whoever goes with Ryan will need a grounding in cryonic science."

She pasted a false shy smile on her face and batted her long eyelashes. "I wonder who, out of the five of us, has those qualifications?"

"No way, Millie!" J.B. exclaimed hotly.

"I agree," Krysty said. "I can sense danger, and that's more of a necessity than knowing about predark freezie tech."

As an aside to Mildred, she added, "No offense."

That was the cue for a general bickering session to commence, with everyone talking and arguing at once. Ryan inserted two fingers into his mouth and produced an ear-splitting whistle. When everyone fell silent, he said calmly, "This is too critical, too important for me to make a snap decision. Give me some time to think, all right?"

Krysty shooed everyone out of the room, but not before they grumbled and cursed a bit. Ryan eased down on the bed, gingerly shifting so he wasn't applying pressure to his shoulder wound. Krysty sat beside him and ran her fingers through his hair.

"I'm bastard tired," he said.

"I'm not surprised. You've had a strenuous last few days."

"No, not that kind of tired. Weary, I guess is the word. Weary of chill or be chilled. Weary of never knowing which one of us will be the next one to board the last train West."

"That's life, lover," she said softly.

"Is it? Is life supposed to be this way?"

Krysty sensed his mood and bent over to kiss him. Feeling the warmth of her face against his lips, he could also feel the heat of her firm body through his clothes. He was desperate to feel more of that heat, so he peeled first his, then her clothes away.

They pressed together in a full, naked embrace. Lying down on the bed as afternoon shadows gathered outside the window, they clung to each other. They didn't talk. There wasn't time or the desire for conversation. As Krysty gasped beneath him, he thrust deep inside of her, relishing the passion she invoked in him and the sweet release of their union.

Afterward, they lay together, holding each other tightly. For a long time, neither one spoke. Then Ryan said, in a whisper, "I've made my choice."

Chapter Nineteen

The day dawned white and ghostly. The AMAC rumbled across the barren plains, towing a four-wheeled trailer. Beneath a canvas covering were baskets and crates brimming with loaves of bread, ears of corn, wheat and even hand-loomed bolts of fabric. In the distance, across acres of thorny shrubs, towered Mount Rushmore.

Ryan glanced over at Mildred. She tried a jittery, reassuring smile on him, but he was too tense to even try to return it. He knew she was more worried about the people left behind in Helskel than what awaited them.

Hellstrom sat in the back with them and ten sec men. He had dropped all pretense of the relaxed, friendly host. He snapped orders to the man driving and the one operating the periscope. Everyone's speech was faster and clipped, their movements tense, their eyes never still for an instant. They were like soldiers preparing for battle.

Ryan wore his long fur-collared leather coat. Beneath it was a combat harness, and from it hung four grens; two were V-40 minis, and the other two were DM-19 incendiaries. Though the SIG-Sauer was snugly holstered at his hip, a midsized Walther MPL submachine gun was clipped to the harness. The metal stock was folded sideways to allow for carrying comfort, and the perforated barrel could spit out 550 rounds per minute. Four extra clips of the 9 mm ammunition were attached to the harness. He had decided against carrying his Steyr bolt-action rifle—if any fighting was to be done, he figured it would be up close and dirty. The SSG-70 was strictly a long-range weapon.

His silk scarf with the lead weights sewn into the lining was wrapped around his neck.

Mildred was similarly attired and outfitted, with the same kind of grenades. Though she still packed her ZKR 551 target pistol, she had chosen, at J.B.'s recommendation, a Heckler & Koch MP-5 from Helskel's impressive armory as her second blaster. It was a fairly lightweight and compact submachine gun, constructed largely of stamped metal parts and heat-resistant plastic. It used a 20-round magazine, and its eight-inch barrel was equipped with a noise and flash arrester.

Ryan had considered the MP-5, since he had fond memories of his Heckler & Koch G-12 caseless rifle, but he felt its fixed wooden stock would interfere with his movements. Still and all, he was glad Mildred had chosen it.

As the journey continued, Ryan found himself drifting off, lulled by the rocking motion of the AMAC. Despite the almost superhuman stamina he possessed, he had his breaking point. Too much tension, too much bloodshed, and even his endurance could drain away.

He kept replaying the scene with Krysty the afternoon before, when he had told her Mildred was his choice to breach the Anthill. He had been prepared for a long argument, and when it didn't arrive, he felt a little let down.

His decision was logical, based primarily on Mildred's knowledge of twentieth-century history, psychology and technology. If the Anthill was indeed a cryonic deep freeze, as Hellstrom had said, then her background would prove invaluable. Also, she was a good person to have at your back if the going got tricky.

Krysty had seemed to accept his reasoning, though J.B. wasn't quite as calm when Ryan told him of his choice.

That evening, after apprising Hellstrom, Mildred and Ryan were allowed into Helskel's arsenal to pick out weapons. There were hundreds to choose from, all in mint condition. Hellstrom had commented on the irony of using the Anthill's own traded-in blasters against its inhabitants.

"You bored, Cawdor?"

Ryan opened his eye and gazed at Hellstrom. The man's face was strained, although he was trying to smile. "Just thinking."

"About what awaits you after you get up the nose?"

Ryan shook his head. "No. About what I'll do to you when I come back and find out you've mistreated my people."

Hellstrom's forced, stitched-on smile faltered. "A little premature, aren't you? Besides, there's no need to worry. Unless circumstances warrant otherwise, their status as guests won't change."

"That's good, that's real good," Ryan said. "But listen to me, Lars, and believe what I say. Harm any of them, and all hell won't hide you from me."

Hellstrom's shoulders stiffened. He glared at Ryan and opened his mouth to say something. Then he shut it and glanced away, shouting at the man at the periscope for a recce report.

Ryan settled back, repressing a smile. Though Hellstrom held the high cards, he was still unnerved enough by Ryan's self-confidence to take the threat seriously.

The AMAC retraced the route of five days before, rolling through the valley, past the Sioux battlefield and across the bluffs. There was no sign of the Lakota whatsoever, and Ryan wasn't sure if he was happy about that.

Once the wag was parked, Hellstrom took the Very pistol and inserted a red flare cartridge into it. Accompanied by a trio of sec men, he left the vehicle and climbed to the top of the ridge. He fired off the flare and waited.

Looking out past the windshield, Ryan watched the mechanical beetle zip from the direction of Lincoln's nose and hover above and before Hellstrom.

"You have the merchandise." The amplified, metallic voice wasn't asking a question, it was making a statement.

"Yes," Hellstrom replied. "All of the highest quality, too. What do you offer for it?"

The beetle pivoted slowly, its glowing photoreceptor eye turning toward the AMAC. Ryan ducked back out of sight.

"We will make that decision once we examine your goods and ascertain if they meet our present needs."

"Then we shall remain in the area until you contact me with your offer," Hellstrom replied. "Is that acceptable?"

"If you withdraw back to the valley, then it is acceptable. Return to this spot forty-eight hours hence. Understood?"

"Understood. Will you now make preparations to receive the merchandise?"

"Yes. You are familiar with the procedure."

As it had done before, the beetle retreated across empty air, ascended, twirled and skated back toward Mount Rushmore.

Hellstrom entered the AMAC, face glistening with a sheen of perspiration. He mopped his brow with a hand-kerchief and said to Ryan and Mildred, "Almost time."

Ryan threw him a mocking half-smile. "Hot out there, is it?"

Hellstrom's lips compressed in a tight line. "Where you and that Beforetime woman are going, you'll be praying for some hot."

The driver started up the AMAC and rolled it over the bluff, heading for the boulder-strewn base of Mount Rushmore. Above it, vast and exuding an ancient sad-ness, towered the ruin of Lincoln's head.

As the vehicle rumbled closer, something lowered it-self from the huge pit of Lincoln's right nostril. Like streams of metallic mucus, four steel cables connected to a long, flat platform descended from the nasal passage.

"Rapunzel, Rapunzel, let down your golden hair," Mildred murmured in a singsong tone.

Ryan didn't bother asking her what she meant.

When the platform scraped rocky earth, two sec men left the wag and pulled it away from the cliff side, while others busied themselves unloading the crates of crops and homemade goods.

Hellstrom announced, "Your transportation has ar-rived. Time to get ready."

Ryan and Mildred ran a quick inventory of their equipment and ordnance. The pair of small radio trans-ceivers were tucked into the pockets of their coats, and they donned the headsets, inserting the receiver plugs into their right ears. They made sure the comm devices were tuned to the same frequency and the circuits were open. Then they walked to the pair of metal containers at the rear of the AMAC.

"Hurry up and climb in," Hellstrom said anxiously. "I don't want to make them suspicious."

They slid into the metal-walled containers feetfirst. Each held a small oxygen tank, with a length of flexible hose extending from the nozzle. The hoses terminated in breathing masks, which fit securely over the nose and mouth.

It was an extremely tight fit for Ryan. He had to lie in a fetal position beneath the bottom tray that held human organs and dry ice. A sec man pushed in the back panel of the box, and when Ryan tightened it with the inner latch, it squeezed against a flexible seal. It was dark and cold, but the air was breathable. Still, he felt a stirring of claustrophobia.

After what seemed like a long, cramped, cold wait, Ryan felt the container being heaved up and carried out of the AMAC by at least four men, judging by the voices. He was dropped none too gently onto the platform, and he winced. The knife wounds on his shoulder and arm hadn't yet begun to heal, and the jolt set them to stinging. A few minutes later he heard a thud he assumed was Mildred's container being loaded onto the platform beside his.

A jerk shook the container around him, and he experienced a giddy, rising sensation in the pit of his stomach. Faintly Ryan could hear the steady creaking of a winch. He could feel the platform swinging gently back and forth, and he tried not to think of what might happen if the container slid off into empty space, spilling him, dry ice and human viscera all over the rocky ground.

The cranking, creaking sounds grew louder, and a moment later they were echoing hollowly. Ryan figured the platform had reached the nasal passage. Dimly he heard the steady throb of an engine.

The rising motion suddenly ceased. The platform swung forward, dropped a few inches, and he heard the crunching of rock as a heavy weight was dragged over it. The scraping of stone set his teeth on edge. The engine sounds abruptly ceased. When that sound stopped, Ryan held his breath, listening for more noise.

Suddenly a flat male voice intoned, "Barter and exchange report, record of the month of July."

The sound of the voice was human enough, but its colorless monotone motivated Ryan to grasp the butt of the SIG-Sauer.

The voice continued speaking, reciting a monologue concerning, barley, wheat, corn, surpluses, overages and shortages. Numbers were mentioned, over and over and for a very long time. Ryan was considering showing himself and shooting the boring bastard just to shut him up.

The droning voice ceased, then he heard the sound of footsteps slowly receding. They seemed to have a peculiar echo. The footfalls disappeared, swallowed up by a hissing noise. Ryan waited for a count of sixty, then touched the transmit stud on the comm in his pocket. In a very low whisper, he asked, "Mildred? You with me?"

In an equally faint voice, filtered through the plug in his ear, she replied, "So far. I think we're alone."

"Me too. On the count of three, let's open up."

"Do you mean one-two, open, or one-two-three, open?"

Ryan couldn't help but smile. He placed his fingers on the panel latch. "One...two...three...open!"

Pushing the latch to its down position, he shouldered the panel up and squirmed out as quickly as he could. Fortunately his legs weren't as stiff as he feared they would be. As he got to his feet, he saw Mildred rising from behind her container. They grinned at each other, then surveyed their surroundings.

A naked light bulb provided a dim overhead glow from a low ceiling. Feeble light filtered in from the tunnel in Lincoln's nose. A few feet away yawned a doorway chiseled out of solid rock. A series of worn stone steps led up to a dull gray metal door.

The circular chamber wasn't very spacious. A large winch occupied most of the space. Ryan noticed that it was powered by a gasoline engine. He also noticed that it was very cold in the room.

Shivering, Mildred pulled a pair of black leather gloves out of a coat pocket and slipped them on. "Must be around forty degrees Fahrenheit in here."

Ryan grunted. "Tolerable."

"If you enjoy winter sports."

Both of them were speaking in whispers.

Turning toward the doorway, Mildred said, "Time to see what there is to see. Keep a watch for those beetles."

Ryan unleathered the SIG-Sauer and jacked a round into the cylinder. "Stay on triple red."

As they eyed the metal panel, searching for a doorknob or latch, it suddenly rolled upward with the whooshing squeak of hydraulics. Both of them leapt for cover on opposite sides of the stone chamber. Ryan crouched down behind the cable-wrapped drum of the winch, and Mildred melded into the shadows at the far corner.

A man strode into the chamber, walking down the steps with long, deliberate strides. He carried a clipboard in one hand. He was a pale, burly man of medium height, his gray hair so close-cropped that the scalp could be seen beneath it. His face was as craggy and as furrowed as the stone walls around him.

His attire was a dark blue coat and slacks, with a white shirt and red tie. Ryan had seen pictures of costumes like that. They were referred to as "business suits." However, the coat was threadbare, and the trousers so worn through at the knees that flashes of pale flesh beneath could be glimpsed through the fabric. But despite the poor condition of his clothes, his black shoes were impeccably polished. Ryan noticed he wore a rectangular plastic-coated badge on his lapel that bore his likeness. There was only one word on the badge. It read simply: BOB.

The man marched purposefully to the container that had concealed Ryan and opened the lid. Without hesitation, he plunged his free hand into the bed of dry ice and picked up a plastic-shrouded heart. He examined it closely, grunting a time or two. He hefted the organ in his hand like a butcher trying to gauge its worth by weight alone.

Replacing the heart, he shut the lid and moved toward the other container, the one that had conveyed Mildred. As he did, he noticed the rigged back panel on Ryan's box hanging open a few inches.

The man didn't look alarmed, but he glanced quickly around the chamber, dark eyes wide and bright. He reminded Ryan of a very alert bird, trying to focus on the source of a mysterious sound. Those darting eyes swept over Ryan's hiding place, then just as quickly returned.

Rising up, Ryan leveled the SIG-Sauer at him, saying in a cold, clear voice, "Don't move. Just stand there."

The man stared at him in silence, an awesome disdain in his eyes. "I wondered when one of you perverted little shits would try something like this."

He moved, unafraid, to a small metal panel inset on the wall beside the doorway. A half-dozen colored buttons studded its surface. Ryan hadn't noticed it before.

"Don't try it, Bob," Ryan said, his blaster floating along with him.

Bob granted him one glance of disgust and continued reaching. Ryan held the SIG-Sauer in both hands, straight out in front of him, brought the sights into line and squeezed the trigger. The blaster bucked in his hand, and a 9 mm slug screamed across the yards that separated Bob from the gun bore.

The slug hit the man with the force of a sledgehammer, smashing him off his feet and ripping his right arm off at the shoulder socket and sending it pinwheeling across the chamber.

Ryan stared, astonished. He had shot to wound, not to kill or maim. He hadn't expected the man's arm to be ripped off. Then he saw why it had happened. There was no blood, either from the ragged shoulder socket or from the stump of the arm. Instead, he glimpsed a gleaming tangle of twisted metal, cables and wires.

Bob glanced down at his disembodied arm, then back to Ryan. "*Damn* you! That construct alone cost the government sixty thousand dollars. You've ruined it, you fucking renegade!"

Lurching to his feet, Bob stumbled toward Ryan. The echoes of his footfalls resounded hollowly within the stone vault.

"I don't want to kill you," Ryan snapped. "Don't move."

He didn't seem to hear or care. Clumsily he rushed at Ryan. Sidestepping quickly, the one-eyed warrior delivered a roundhouse kick to his belly. The man didn't cry out or even gasp as he folded over Ryan's leg. With the back of Bob's head exposed, Ryan brought down the barrel of his blaster against his skull.

Bob slid limply down Ryan's leg and fell face first to the stone floor. He made no movement afterward. As Ryan kneeled beside the man, he was joined by Mildred. She peeled off a glove and pressed two fingers against the man's carotid artery.

"He's alive, but his pulse is weird," she said. "Very fast and irregular. His body temperature seems unusually low, too. Turn him over, will you?"

Ryan obliged so Mildred could examine the stump of the shoulder. Within a raw orifice, color-coded wires intertwined and a complex network of circuitry glistened wetly.

Touching a fractured cylinder protruding several inches from the stump, Mildred said, "Looks like a Teflon socket."

A small transparent plastic tube corkscrewed within the hollow socket. A pale greenish liquid dripped from it to the floor, crawling across the stone. Ryan touched it, rubbing the fluid between thumb and forefinger. It was oily and viscous.

"This isn't blood," he said. "A lubricant, mebbe."

Frowning, Mildred dipped a finger into the spreading puddle, brought it to her nose and sniffed. Then, tentatively, she touched the tip of her tongue to her finger. Quickly she turned her head and spit.

"A sort of sweetish taste," she said, still spitting. "I think it might be some kind of coolant."

Ryan's eyebrows rose. "A coolant?"

"Yeah. Like Freon or something."

Mildred undid the man's shirt, tossing his tie aside. His flesh was very pale, an unhealthy mushroom shade. A five-inch pink scar ran down his clavicle, marked on either side by a saddle-stitched pattern.

She grunted. "He's one of the zipper club."

"What's that?"

"Old medical slang. Means he either had open-heart surgery, like a bypass operation, or he's had a heart transplant. See if you can get his mouth open."

Mystified, Ryan did as she said, squeezing the hinges of the man's jaw until his mouth gaped open. To his surprise, Mildred stuck a finger inside Bob's mouth, under his saliva-slick tongue. After a moment she withdrew it, wiping her finger on her jacket.

"Why did you do that?" he demanded.

"Testing his body temperature. If it was normal, his mouth would be hot even if his epidermis isn't."

"Well's it hot or not?"

"Not," she replied. "Very cool. In fact, probably not over seventy-five degrees Fahrenheit. It's almost as if the poor bastard is walking around in a constant state of hypothermia."

The doctor straightened and went to retrieve Bob's arm. Ryan studied the badge pinned to the man's lapel. It bore very little information beyond his picture, his name and a red dot about a quarter of an inch in diameter. The dot looked as if it had been affixed to the card somehow, and it bore an odd reflective sheen.

Mildred returned with the arm. Holding the limb by the wrist and the bicep, she bent the elbow back and forth. "This is extraordinary, Ryan."

"How so?"

"It's a bionic prosthesis, but it's about ten years beyond anything in use before the holocaust. Touch the hand."

Ryan poked the hand, pinched it and shrugged. "Feels like skin."

Nodding, Mildred said, "Exactly. Not latex or rubber, but a synthetic, organic equivalent of flesh. Perfect in every detail, right down to the texture and implanted hair follicles, which is pretty amazing, considering a human hair is only sixty microns wide."

"You doctors didn't have this in predark days?"

"We had something like it, used mainly to speed the healing process of burn victims, and it was hardly the best solution. This stuff is almost indistinguishable from normal epidermal tissue."

"How's it made?" Ryan asked.

"In my day, we used a form of silicon gel and plasma. A synthetic skin this close to the original has to be developed by genetic engineering, maybe through a form of cloning."

"So," Ryan said musingly, "it looks like Lars was telling the truth about this place."

"As much truth as he understood. Make no mistake—from what we've seen so far, and that's very damned little, I'd judge the people who live here are a hell of a lot more dangerous than the Helskel crowd."

Ryan stood, prodding the senseless Bob with the toe of a boot. "Yeah, Lars said that, too. What do you want to do with this guy?"

Mildred shrugged and tugged on her glove. "Your call. You shot him."

Dragging Bob to a far corner and laying him on his stomach, he used the man's tie, belt and shoelaces to gag and bind him. It was difficult since he had only one arm, so Ryan bound his wrist to his ankles, bending his legs up behind him. He briefly contemplated dumping the man down the nasal passage. Trader would have done it, and a few years before, he might have done it, too. But it didn't seem right to take the life of a helpless man.

Aside from that, there was a tactical wisdom in sparing the man's life; he and Mildred were the invaders here. Unwilling interlopers, maybe, but interlopers nonetheless. If there was even a marginal chance of reasoning with the Anthill residents, it made sense not to arouse their anger.

He returned to Mildred and they approached the doorway. The panel was still up. The woman suddenly put a hand on his chest and said, "Wait!"

Eyeing the panel, she said, "I think there's a photoelectric eye there. Just strolling through the beam might trigger an alarm."

Ryan produced Bob's ID badge and clipped it to the breast pocket of his coat. "Already thought of that. This dot looks like a light-sensitive cell. Seen them before, in other installations."

Mildred smiled and nodded in understanding. "I get it. If the cell is of the same electrochemical spectrum as the beam, it will interact with it, not react to it. Like a pass key."

"You said it better than I could have, Mildred. Let's give it a try."

Hands on their blasters, they walked up the steps and through the doorway, past the wall panel. Nothing happened.

"You were right," Ryan said, relief in his voice.

"You thought of it first," Mildred replied, sounding just as relieved.

They found themselves in a squarish tunnel. The light from two wire-encased electric bulbs glistened from the cold rock walls. The crude marks of tools showed on the stone. Ryan pointed them out.

"So far, this place doesn't seem to be the high-tech heaven Hellstrom made it out to be," he said. "Even the worst redoubt we ever visited wasn't chipped out of rock."

A faint musky but cloying odor took them by the throats and tried to force out coughs. Ryan stifled it, walking steadily along the passageway, his SIG-Sauer leading. A powdery coating of dust covered the tunnel floor, and each footstep caused a small cloud to puff up beneath their boots.

"They wouldn't win any awards for good housekeeping, either," Mildred commented, holding a finger beneath her nose to prevent a sneeze.

A wedge of light glimmered before them. They slowed their pace and sidled along the wall. The tunnel opened out into an enormous vaulted chamber, its ceiling almost lost high in the darkness. Both of them jolted to unsteady halts, forgetting the killzone they were braving. They had to blink and shake their heads, fighting to absorb what they were seeing. Ryan in particular wondered if it was indeed real and tangible and not a hallucination.

Mildred opened her mouth, gaping, her staring eyes sweeping the chamber. "Mother of God and sweet baby Jesus in her arms."

Ryan didn't say anything. He seemed to have lost the capacity for speech. He caught his breath in awed wonder.

The vast room was filled, almost as far as the eye could see, with crates, boxes, stacks of books, electronic gadgets, furniture, sleek and shining wheeled vehicles, paintings and musical instruments. The huge room was a museum of mechanics, art, literature, seemingly of the entire predark culture. There was simply far too much to absorb, much less identify.

Many of the objects and items were unfamiliar to Ryan, but he knew the thousands of items in the gargantuan vault represented the destroyed aspirations of a destroyed and dead society.

Ryan finally regained his voice. "What was that J.B. said? The mother of all stockpiles?"

Mildred husked out a small, faint laugh. "John had no idea, did he?"

Chapter Twenty

The sun rose in the east and streaked red ripples on the roof of the departing AMAC. Dust rose in gray spirals from beneath the tires as it rumbled through Helskel.

Krysty, Doc, J.B. and Jak stood outside the wag compound and watched as the big armored vehicle shrank in the distance. Krysty's eyes were wet as she murmured, "Please, Gaia, watch over them and keep them safe."

J.B. took off his spectacles and made a show of cleaning the lenses. "Goddamn dust...gets on everything." His voice was unsteady.

Behind them, a sec man swung the wire gate shut and clicked a heavy padlock into place. "Best move on, folks," he said.

Doc cleared his throat and recited softly, "'The lamentable change is from the best. The worst returns to laughter.'"

Jak glanced at him. "What supposed to mean, Doc?"

"It is from Shakespeare. I disremember which play or sonnet. I surmise the meaning is simple—as long as we can still laugh, we have not met the worst."

Krysty shook her head. "I don't feel much like laughing."

"Me either," Jak said. "Feel more like breakfast."

As they turned and trudged up the street, Krysty whispered, "You get an eyeful, J.B.?"

"Yeah," he answered in a low voice, ducking his head. "One of the dune buggies looks to be our best bet. Small, fast, maneuverable. Simple to hot-wire. Even if there's a plas-ex theft deterrent connected to the ignition, it'll be a cinch to disarm."

As the four people walked toward the eatery, no one else ventured forth on the streets. As early as it was, there should have been a few people, if only those staggering home from an all-night drunk.

Doc shouldered his cane jauntily and murmured, "From the oppressive atmosphere, it appears friend Ryan's assessment was correct."

· No one responded. All of them had stayed awake most of the night, huddled in Krysty and Ryan's room, talking in whispers, planning courses of action.

The question that never arose among them was, should they trust Lars Hellstrom to allow them the run of Helskel during his absence?

They were, all of them, battle-hardened and scarred veterans of Deathlands. One reason they were veterans and not victims was their almost instinctive distrust of anyone who wielded power over others.

This distrust was similar to a code, as necessary to survival in the wastelands of post-nukecaust America as food and water. So they had devised an escape plan, with Ryan briefing them on the location of the armory where their blasters were stored and how much opposition they could expect.

They had also settled on an escape route, using Hellstrom's map of Mount Rushmore and the surrounding environs as a blueprint. For the plan to work, it was crucial that they all behave as if they suspected nothing, to maintain the facades of trusting souls, worrying only about their loved ones, off on a mission in the service of Helskel.

They entered the eatery. The heavyset, wart-faced woman behind the counter glanced at them with sullen eyes. She didn't greet them.

"Breakfast, my good woman!" Doc shouted good-humoredly, rapping the countertop with his swordstick. "First and foremost, deliver to us a pot of your delectable coffee."

The four companions took seats around a table, and cups and a steaming pot were set before them. The woman didn't look them in the eye.

They ordered their food. The woman didn't write down their requests, but her eyes suddenly flickered, casting an anxious glance toward the doorway. Quickly she turned and slipped into the kitchen.

The four sec men entered quietly, lining the counter, leaning against it lazily. A couple of them stifled yawns. Phil seemed to be the leader of the quartet. He met Krysty's gaze and grinned. "Got tired of breakfast in bed, little princess?"

She returned the grin. "No, I got tired of seeing your ugly face first thing every morning. But as long as you're here, fetch us some bread and butter."

Phil stiffened, brows drawing low over his eyes. His hand strayed to the butt of his blaster. "You mutie whore. I'll show you some fetchin'."

Jak was in the process of pouring coffee into his cup. As Phil's fingers brushed the Tec-10, the pot and cup fell from his hands. Long before they struck the floor, a black leaf-bladed throwing knife was in his right hand. He threw it, with a blurring snap of wrist and forearm.

The blade pierced the back of Phil's hand, the razor point slicing through the palm and pinioning it to his upper thigh. His splayed fingers contorted, like the fluttering wings of a butterfly transfixed by a pin.

Before the three other sec men could react, Krysty, Jak, J.B. and Doc were on their feet, overturning the table. They flipped it toward the counter, smashing it against the four men, making a wooden sandwich with a human fill.

One of the sec men managed to draw his blaster. His first few shots crashed through the window and killed a drowsy, unsuspecting merchant who was opening his stall across the street.

The sec man's breath had been driven out of him by the table edge, and he tried to adjust his aim to find the proper range. Another knife appeared magically in Jak's fist. The blade inscribed a short arc, and the sec man dropped his blaster, his jugular jetting blood.

J.B. scooped the Tec-10 from the floor, but the sagging weight of the throat-slashed man, coupled with the force exerted by his three companions, flipped the table outward, bottom edge first. The wooden disk slammed squarely against J.B.'s face. Still bent over, the Armorer staggered sideways, glasses hanging askew, crimson gushing from his nostrils.

Roaring in wordless fury, a sec man flung the table away from him and closed on Krysty. He was either too drunk with rage or humiliation to draw his weapon.

Krysty braced herself, ducking a roundhouse right that ruffled her hair, and she slashed savagely upward with the stiffened edge of her right hand. Her hand chopped into her attacker's throat like the stroke of an ax. The sec man spit a hideous gurgle of pain and surprise, and he stumbled backward against the counter.

Clutching at his throat for a moment, his eyes went wide and wild. Dark vermilion erupted from between his slack lips, and he fell, first to his knees, then to his face.

At the same instant Krysty was avoiding the sec man's blow, Phil yanked the throwing knife from his hand and clawed for his blaster. Fingers slick with blood, they couldn't gain an immediate purchase on the grip.

As Phil fumbled, Doc snapped away the ebony sheath of his swordstick and assumed the classic posture of the fencer. "I told you I would remember what you called me, sir," he said, blue eyes alight.

"Fuck you, you old prick!" Phil grated. His injured hand finally closed over the butt of his weapon.

Doc lunged forward, the point of the rapier sinking into, then quickly withdrawing from, the left side of Phil's chest. A stream of blood followed it. Grunting his disbelief, Phil covered the wound with his left hand. Scarlet squirted from between his fingers. He raised the Tec-10 with his right hand.

"You old son of a bitch," he croaked, his unsteady hand trying to put Doc's body before the barrel of his blaster. "You've chilled me."

"'Priscian a little scratched,'" Doc quoted. "'Twill serve.' *King Lear,* act 4, scene 2, I believe."

Phil leaned against the counter for support. Jak reached out, wrested the pistol from his nerveless fingers and aimed it toward the final sec man, who was breaking for the door in a panicked run. The man screamed shrilly for help.

Before Jak squeezed the trigger, J.B. fired from a half-crouched position, following the sound of pounding feet.

The sec man pitched through the doorway and into the street, his back blown out by a dozen 9 mm rounds.

It was over in thirty seconds. J.B. straightened, adjusting his spectacles. Blood ran unnoticed from his nose. Jak, dangling the blaster in his hand, looked over the carnage of bodies and grunted, "Stupes. Triple stupes."

"And so are we if we stay here," Krysty said, swiftly taking the Tec-10 from her assailant. "All we can do now is make a run for the compound."

Doc resheathed his sword, armed himself with one of the machine pistols and moved toward the door. "I could still do with another cup of coffee."

The streets of Helskel were no longer empty. People were converging on the eatery from all points of the compass, some shouting questions, others looking only mildly interested. Krysty, Jak, Doc and J.B. held them at bay with gun barrels and threatening scowls.

They trotted up the street, trying to cover all directions with their eyes, ears and blasters. Their pace wasn't slow, but it should have been faster.

From ahead, they heard the sec men running to cut them off, the creak of leather boots, the thud of footfalls and the metallic clink of weapons. There were over a dozen of them, racing from the direction of the wag compound. They fanned out in a circle, gun barrels bristling, eyes glinting with the desire to kill.

Krysty took it all in, surveying the blasters and the men behind them. "Time for a judgment call," she announced.

Her Tec-10 dropped into the dust, and she placed her hands on top of her head. One by one, her companions did the same.

Chapter Twenty-One

Mildred and Ryan looked about them. The floor was surfaced with a highly polished light blue material, as were the smooth, curving walls. Bending, Ryan rubbed his hand over the floor, then looked at his fingers. "Clean. You could eat off it. Looks like it's made of some kind of vanadium alloy. How do they keep it this way?"

Mildred squinted at the floor. "A low-level electrostatic field, probably. Right before skydark, hospitals were experimenting with similar devices to keep operating rooms completely sterile. The field in here prevents dust and foreign particles from entering, pushing them toward the tunnel, like a giant whisk broom. That's the detritus we walked through when we came in."

Though they looked for them, there was no indication of spy eyes or security cameras. They moved carefully among the boxes, crates, vehicles, sculptures and tables holding electronic parts and even more crates. There seemed to be an order in which the artifacts were stored, though none was cataloged by name or even number. It required all of Ryan's willpower to resist the temptation to stop and examine everything.

"Kind of reminds me of crazy old Quint's redoubt in Alaska," Ryan said. "Except this place seems even bigger, and the relics aren't touched by time. Mebbe that electrostatic field you mentioned protects them.''

Mildred only nodded. She remembered J.B.'s tales of the strange complex operated by an incestuous madman.

As they wended a path through the artifacts, both noticed it was growing colder. The temperature seemed to have dropped by ten degrees. Ryan finally put on his gloves, the ones with the index fingers snipped off to allow easy access to triggers.

''Any ideas on how they keep it so cold in here?'' Ryan asked.

''Must be a huge air-conditioning system,'' Mildred answered, ''with giant circulating fans somewhere, like the blast freezers they used to have in food-processing plants. Must be a terrific energy drain to pump air this frigid through the entire complex.''

''Probably have nuclear power, like most of the redoubts we've seen.''

They passed several yellow four-wheeled contraptions outfitted with long, front-projecting prongs that Mildred identified as forklifts.

''What happens to the people when we knock out the cold circulation system?'' Ryan wanted to know.

Mildred shrugged. ''That depends.''

''On what?''

''If their metabolic rates have been artificially reduced, through cybernetic alteration and organ transplants, just so they can survive in such low temperatures, the result of raising the temperature could be catastrophic. Depending on the age of their original soft tissues and organs they could begin to decay almost immediately. That's what happens in cryonics when a subject is accidently thawed out.''

They continued walking through the vast space, the floor and walls echoing oddly to their footsteps.

Mildred craned her neck, looking up at the ceiling. ''The shielding in here must be fantastically absorbent, not just for radiation, but for sound.''

Gesturing behind him to a long, massively built wag bearing a chrome-plated Winnebago logo, Ryan said, ''There's got to be a big cargo mat-trans gateway in here. There's no way a fleet of that many wags could have gotten up here any other way.''

Mildred smiled. ''Unless they packed them up part by part and assembled them later.''

''What we really need is a map of the layout of this place. We could wander around in here for more than the twenty-four hours Hellstrom gave us.''

Because he was speaking in a whisper, he failed to hear the first footfall settle in front of him, but he grabbed Mildred by the arm before the second one had fallen. They crouched behind a table and watched a man, dressed similarly to Bob, sauntering between the aisle of artifacts. He was walking directly toward them.

The man passed them without a glance. Ryan realized he was heading toward the chamber inside Lincoln's head. After a warning glance to Mildred, he crawled among the tables, the wags and the furniture. He couldn't allow Bob to be discovered.

Dodging between the antiquities, Ryan managed to reach a point to the left and well ahead of the tunnel entrance. The man walked purposefully past. Ryan glided behind him, his left arm crooking around his throat. The man uttered a small gagging sound of shock as he was dragged behind a large bright red vehicle.

The man struggled for breath and clawed at his attacker's arm. Ryan kicked his legs out from under him, and he fell heavily, banging the side of his head on the vehicle's gleaming bumper. A small cut was opened in the pale flesh. He put a hand to it and stared as Ryan showed him the SIG-Sauer. He was middle-aged and slight of frame, with tiny eyes surrounded by puffy pouches of wrinkled skin.

The man made a choking sound of rage. "Are you insane? Are you a fool? Get out of here!"

Like Bob, this man showed no fear, only surprise and contempt. Curious, Ryan pushed his hand away from the cut in his temple. It was superficial and bleeding only slightly, but the blood oozed sluggishly. The color wasn't a deep red, it was more of a dark pink, with a crimson tinge. He wore a badge like Bob's, which identified him as DOUG.

Grabbing the man's tie, Ryan hauled him to his feet, put him in front of the gun and marched him back to Mildred. He gave her a look as though he were regarding a pile of excrement on a breakfast table.

"You're from Helskel," Doug said in a voice sibilant with spite. "Undisciplined maniacs, aren't you?"

The remark irritated Mildred. She drew her ZKR and pressed the muzzle against his forehead. "Not exactly. In Helskel, murder is indiscriminate and meaningless. I have a method. You don't talk, you die."

"From my view strata," Doug replied, "your methodology of data synthesizing is reactive, rather than proactive. You've assumed a posture which is simplistic and adversarial, rather than cooperative, inasmuch as your rationale for trespassing on restricted property is based on an insufficient grasp of the legalities involved and the disposition thereof.''

"What the hell did he say?" Ryan demanded.

Mildred smiled sardonically. "Used to be called new-speak. Authentic corporate jargon. One of the few things I don't miss about the predark days."

Pressing harder with the bore of her pistol, Mildred said, "What you just spouted was bullshit a hundred years ago and it's bullshit now. In simple, unadorned language, I want you to tell us the layout of this place."

By threatening and poking and prodding with their guns in more delicate portions of the man's anatomy, he finally agreed to take them to a map. They marched him ahead of their blasters toward the nearest wall. With a grin, Mildred whispered, "I guess not every one of Doug's organs is prosthetic."

Doug walked over to one of the walls. He stood and looked at it, saying, "Complex display."

Suddenly a three-by-three-foot square came alive with countless lines and dots of many colors. One of the dots was throbbing. Pointing to it, Doug said, "That represents my current position, indicated by the locator lozenge on my badge. Since I was the one who activated the display, the computer shows my position first."

Fixing their position in the confusing webwork of colors and intersection points and angles, Ryan and Mildred saw that the central core of the Anthill was indicated by a large pattern of blue lines and several big green dots.

Tapping Bob's badge on his lapel, Ryan asked, "Does the computer respond to your voice or to the locator lozenge?"

Doug was reluctant to answer. It required Mildred poking his kidneys with her blaster for him to say, "The lozenge."

"Locate the Commander," Ryan said.

One of the dots in the central core suddenly flared brighter and began to throb.

"Locate the circulating and pumping station," Mildred stated.

Nothing happened. Responding to Ryan's glare, Doug said, "It's only programmed to locate the installation's personnel. It was assumed that everyone in here was supposed to be in here and would therefore know their way around."

Studying the map again, Ryan traced a network of glowing grid lines with a forefinger. "We're here, almost on the top level. The Commander is below us...looks to be—" he counted quickly "—four levels. Where's the nearest elevator?"

Doug inclined his head to the left. "That way, about a hundred yards. Follow the curve of the wall."

Ryan pulled him away from the map. "Show us."

As they walked beside the wall, Ryan asked, "How many people are in this place?"

"Would you believe me if I told you?" Doug replied.

"Probably not. But answer me anyway."

"Sixty-eight active, one hundred and twelve inactive."

"Inactive? Do you mean dead?"

Doug shook his head disdainfully. "I say what I mean. If I'd meant to say 'dead,' I would have said 'dead.' I said 'inactive.' Are you unable to comprehend English, as well as simple survival-oriented common-sense measures?"

Angrily Ryan rapped the back of his head with the barrel of the SIG-Sauer. "Are you unable to comprehend that I will make you permanently inactive if you piss me off?"

Doug didn't even flinch, but he said sullenly, "I comprehend."

"What about sec men?"

"Sec what?"

"Security forces," Mildred said. "Sentries, guards."

"At one time we had a special division for that sole purpose, but all of us act in that capacity when necessary."

The wall curved lazily to the right and opened up in a low-ceilinged, colonnaded antechamber. They saw a metal pair of double doors topped by an arch bearing a long set of colored lights. Hovering before the doors, bobbing gently up and down on thin air, was a beetle.

Mildred and Ryan froze, both of them grabbing Doug and pressing their blasters into his back. They stared at the device. Its red photoreceptor eye stared back.

"What's it doing?" Mildred whispered into Doug's ear.

"Scanning us, or rather, the locator lozenges on the badges," the man replied in a normal conversational tone. "It transmits an invisible recognition beam. Your companion and myself are noted and logged as known installation personnel. However, since you are not wearing a badge—"

An unnerving *whoop-whoop* of a Klaxon caused Mildred and Ryan to jump and curse at the same time. The beetle drifted forward. "Make it back off," Ryan snarled, shoving the SIG-Sauer against Doug's neck.

Smiling, Doug said, "I can't. The automatic intruder-alert system has already been triggered." He crooked a finger over his lips and giggled. "She's been targeted for deactivation."

A needle-thin beam of white light shot out from a nozzle on the underside of the beetle, which touched the barrel of the gun in Mildred's hand. Sparks flashed and showered, and there was a loud electrical crackle. Crying out, she stumbled backward, dropping her ZKR. The mechanism swooped closer, needle beams stabbing with crackles of sound.

Mildred screamed and fell thrashing to the floor, covering her face with her arms. She tucked her legs up and shrieked, "Do something! It's electrocuting me!"

"Fireblast!" Ryan crashed the SIG-Sauer over Doug's skull, and even as he hurled the unconscious man away, he centered the blaster's sights on the beetle and fired five rounds in such rapid succession, the shots sounded like a single report.

The device fragmented under the 9 mm assault, metal and circuitry flying in shards. Its power pack flared in an orange halo of flame. Spinning crazily on an invisible axis, the beetle listed to the left, then clattered to the floor, the red light of its photoreceptor eye fading. The Klaxon still whooped.

Bending, Ryan pulled Mildred's arms away from her face. A red welt showed against the dusky complexion of her right cheek. She shook her right hand in irritation and pain.

"Are you all right?" he asked, helping her to her feet and handing her the ZKR. It was undamaged.

She took a long, shaky breath. "I think so. Electric shock, considerable voltage. Good thing I protected my eyes." She kicked the shattered, smoldering remains of the beetle. "Goddamn nasty little toy. Like a flying stun gun."

The lights over the lift door were blinking. "We're going to have company," Ryan said, tugging the badge from Doug's lapel.

They sprinted back toward the storage area, hearing the hydraulic hiss of door panels sliding open behind them. Ryan reflected that the prospects of their surviving inside the complex were moving from poor to zero. All the odds were stacked against them, but that was nothing new.

The explosive report of a gunshot sounded from the rear, and a bullet whipped between them, spinning end over end from the sound of it. The slug chewed off the corner of a varnished, ornately carved table on Ryan's right.

"You idiot!" bleated a male voice from somewhere behind them. "Don't shoot in here!"

Ryan and Mildred exchanged tight grins. The freezies wouldn't shoot out of fear of damaging the relics, but since they were under no such obligation, they unlimbered their autoblasters. Spinning, Mildred and Ryan triggered the Heckler & Koch MP-5 and the Walther MPL at the same time. The blasters roared into the trio of armed, business-suited men dogtrotting toward them in a flanking maneuver. A crate filled with light bulbs jumped and blew apart under the leaden hail. They didn't bother to gauge the accuracy of their shots. They fired, whirled and ran among a collection of life-size statues.

They changed direction twice, then sank down in the shadow of a giant television screen and electronics console. Male voices filtered to them, but they were too distant to be understood. The tones were undeniably petulant, like children ordered to perform an unpleasant task.

"There's got to be another way out of this rat's maze," Mildred panted.

"Speak for yourself, Mildred," Ryan replied.

"No, not us. Them. They're the rats. Hear them?"

"Yeah. They sound like bratty kids. And neither Doug or Bob were afraid of us, almost like they couldn't believe what was happening."

"Exactly," Mildred said. "John likes to say, 'crazy as a shithouse rat' to describe mental illness. I think we're dealing with the equivalent here. If you pack rats too closely together for too long, you get homicidal rats, suicidal rats, cannibalistic rats, insane rats. Not too different from the people in this place."

They stopped whispering when the sound of the voices grew louder.

"How's Doug?"

"How should I know? I'm not a medic. Where's Bob?"

"He was supposed to check out the merchandise. Somebody go look."

The voices drifted away, becoming distant and incomprehensible again. Ryan, suddenly realizing that he was very cold, repressed a shiver. It felt like he was squatting in the path of a frigid blast of wintry air. Wetting a forefinger, he held it up in several directions.

"Air movement that way," he whispered, nodding ahead of them. "Bastard *cold* air movement."

They crept in that direction and saw the shadowed, circular mouth of a hole in the floor about fifty yards away. Rising, they raced toward it, casting glances over their shoulders every few feet. It was more of a shaft than a tunnel. Icy wind blew up through a thickly meshed metal screen, stinging their faces, bringing water to their eyes and ruffling their hair. The frame of the hatch cover had a combination lock, but no handle or knob. Beneath it they saw ladder rungs affixed to one circular wall.

Ryan took aim with the SIG-Sauer and emptied the clip at the lock. He stood fast as ricochets whined and screamed around him. The 9 mm rounds smashed and shattered the combination lock, blasting the steel catch to scrap. He wrenched the hatch cover up and gestured to Mildred. "After you."

She didn't protest, but quickly climbed into the opening. Ryan followed her, not bothering to shut the cover after him. The men would have undoubtedly heard the shots, so as he scampered down the rungs, he swiftly ejected the spent clip of the pistol, took a spare from the harness and slid it into the SIG-Sauer's butt.

The ladder rungs descended about fifty feet. At their end, Mildred and Ryan dropped down and found themselves standing in the elbow of an L-shaped shaft. The shaft wasn't composed of rock, but of a lusterless, nonreflective metal, featureless except for ridges where sections of tubing joined. At intervals, wire-encased light bulbs glowed from the ceiling. It was narrow, not wide enough for them to walk side by side. The shaft stretched out almost as far as they could see, and the cold wind was stiff—to move forward, they were forced to lean into it. Far in the distance was a white circle, about the size of an old dime. A muffled, rhythmic throb set up steady vibrations in the floor of the tunnel.

"Air circulation shaft," Mildred gasped out, the wind nearly snatching her words away.

Ryan glanced upward and saw the head and shoulders of a man peering down into the mouth of the opening. He pushed Mildred forward, just in case someone topside started shooting.

They jogged along the narrow tube, Ryan in the lead, both of them maintaining a steady pace so their feet wouldn't slip on the smooth surface. He wasn't sure how long they navigated the passageway before a rattling roar came from behind them.

The din of bullets crashing into, ricocheting off and striking sparks from the metal was terrific, almost deafening. Mildred pointed the MP-5 behind her and fired a long burst, but the enemy fire didn't abate.

Fragments of slugs and chipped pipe shrieked through the shaft like angered hornets. Bullets buzzed all around them. Behind it all was the drumming hammer of a machine gun, a light caliber by the sound of it.

The two companions kept running forward, bent almost double so as to present smaller targets. Each time they passed beneath a light bulb, Mildred shot it out with her target revolver. It was a tiring effort, fighting their way through the frigid wind pressing against them broadside.

Ryan's free hand groped over the combat harness under his coat until it identified and closed around one of the V-40 grens. Detaching it from the harness, he hooked his thumb into the firing pin and tweaked it away.

He shouted, "Fire in the hole!" and tossed it behind him, over Mildred's head. Both of them increased their speed, running as fast as they could, not worrying about the bullets or losing their footing. Ryan counted to five under his breath. A score of yards later, they received violent blows in the backs that knocked them forward and off their feet.

The shock wave of the exploding grenade buffeted them to the shaft's floor, skidding them along for a few feet, bruising their knees and elbows. They lay where they had fallen for a moment, biting at the chilly air, listening to the fading, rolling echoes of the detonation and the feeble moans of the men who had been caught by it.

Rising a little unsteadily, Mildred and Ryan resumed their run, at a much slower pace. Their eardrums still vibrated, and their heads throbbed. Both of them had opened their mouths to equalize the pressure of the explosion, so neither one suffered hearing impairment. Ahead glimmered a circle of brilliant light, and the cold wind increased in intensity and strength. The throbbing noise grew in volume until they could feel it vibrating in their bones.

They emerged from the shaft, squinted their eyes against the brightness of artificial light and took two steps before stopping and staring.

Chapter Twenty-Two

All things considered, it wasn't the worst cell they had ever been imprisoned in, but it was a long way from being the best, too. It was more like a dungeon.

A single barred window, high in the adobe wall, was at ground level on the outside. Heavy flagstoned steps led upward to the single massive door through which the four of them had been shoved by the sec men. It bore a small observation slit in the center, covered on the outside by a metal grille and panel.

The cell was sparsely furnished with one bunk, made of crudely nailed-together two-by-fours and wooden slats. A thin mattress of sewn burlap bags lay upon it. A casual glance was enough to see that it was urine-stained and probably crawling with vermin.

Doc shouldered his swordstick and sighed. "Ah, to be in England now that durance vile is here."

Though the sec men had disarmed them, searching Jak and confiscating his knives, they hadn't bothered with Doc's swordstick. He had leaned on it, hobbling as he walked, complaining that he needed it for his lumbago. The only Helskel men who knew it concealed a sword blade were dead.

Fortunately the sec men hadn't mistreated them, though it was apparent they sorely wished to beat them. Hellstrom had evidently only given the order to incarcerate them, without adding a codicil concerning brutality to the command. No one seemed to be in charge, and since they were afraid of reinterpreting the patriarch's commands, Krysty, Jak, J.B. and Doc were merely herded into the cell.

Squeaking rats scurried about in the sour-smelling straw. A pair of ten-gallon galvanized metal buckets sat in a corner. One held brackish water, and a tin cup was attached to the wire handle by a small-linked chain. The other bucket was empty, intended to hold the prisoners' waste. Doc tapped it with his swordstick.

"In retrospect," he remarked, "I suppose our lack of breakfast is a blessing in disguise."

"Especially in your case," J.B. said. "Good thing you only had half a cup of coffee, or that bucket would be filled by now."

The Armorer was pacing off the dimensions of the cell. When he was done, he announced, "Twenty by eighteen. Downright spacious compared to some of the holes we've been thrown in."

Jak walked around the walls, his movements feline smooth and graceful. He pushed here and prodded there. He sprang up to the window, grasped the bars, hung from them a long moment, then dropped back down to the hard-packed earthen floor. He shook his head gloomily.

THE MORNING PASSED sluggishly. When no one else showed an interest in doing so, Doc stretched out on the bunk and napped, his swordstick held beneath his folded hands.

Krysty assumed a lotus position, sitting cross-legged, eyes closed, going through a relaxation exercise by balancing her breathing, her heart rate, and trying to reduce the flow of adrenaline through her body. It wasn't easy, though all of them had been prisoners before. Waiting to learn their fates wasn't a new experience, but repetition didn't make it any easier to endure.

She thought of Ryan and Mildred and repressed a groan of anxiety. She knew Hellstrom's threat to sacrifice all of them to the Anthill inhabitants was no idle boast. Human lives were, to the patriarch of Helskel, no more than a helpless insect in the wing-plucking hands of a sadistic child.

Outside the cell, the everyday business of Helskel went on. They heard merchants hawking their wares, raucous laughter, music and the roar of motorcycle engines.

Jak, noting the quality of light through the barred window, said, "Getting hungry. Hope give midday meal."

J.B., who sat on the flagstoned steps leading to the door, pointed to the rats cowering in a corner. "Mebbe them things are their idea of lunch."

Suddenly, unexpectedly, the small observation panel in the door opened. A sec man's face was framed behind the grillwork. "Everybody get away from the door."

Doc awoke with a snorting start, but he didn't rise. He lifted his head and blinked as J.B. and Jak moved to the wall beneath the window. The cell door opened just enough to admit a single figure. In the room outside, they glimpsed two sec men, blasters at the ready.

The door banged shut behind her, and Fleur regarded everyone with an emotionless stare. Her clothes were in disarray, her hair a wild, unbrushed tangle. A purpling bruise showed on her forehead, and her lower lip was puffy. Her right wrist was encased by a wooden splint, and her left hand was thickly bandaged.

Doc climbed to his feet and inclined his head in a courtly bow. "Welcome, my lady of war, to an exclusive club. The Honorable Order of Patsies."

Krysty stood and stared at Fleur. "I take it your beloved patriarch snapped his fingers, and you were magically transformed from warlord to scapegoat."

Fleur didn't reply. She simply stood motionless, like a mannequin, not even appearing to breathe.

"Or," J.B. offered grimly, "he transformed her into a plant."

"Plant?" Jak's face was puzzled. "What kind plant?"

"A spy," Krysty clarified, walking closer to her. "She was planted here to keep a watch on us, to report on any escape plans."

Fleur spoke, her voice hushed, like the rustle of coarse cloth. "I'm a prisoner, just like you. I was betrayed."

"Like you betrayed the Indians who rescued you from slavers?" Krysty snapped. "It's no sin to betray a betrayer."

"Or to kill a killer," J.B. said, a hint of menace entering his voice.

"Is that what you want to do?" Fleur asked calmly.

"Can you think of any reason why we shouldn't?" Krysty demanded. "You tried to kill Ryan. Twice, in fact."

Fleur didn't respond. She merely stood and stared. She was listless, as though her spirit had been more than broken. It had been stolen from her.

Shuddering, Jak turned away from the woman. "Dead already. Soul dead."

"Is that true, young lady?" Doc asked. He twisted the handle of his cane and unsheathed the blade.

Fleur's eye flicked toward him, but she didn't react.

"For if it is," Doc continued, "then you should have no objection to your material shell joining your astral self in the great ether. However, if a spark of vitality still resides within your soul, we may offer you a way to fan that spark into a full blaze."

Interest stirred faintly in her blue eye. "How?"

Plunging the sword into the earthen floor, Doc took note of how deeply it cut. "I have," he announced solemnly, "an idea."

J.B. cast his eyes ceilingward and groaned. "I was afraid you would."

Chapter Twenty-Three

The chamber was immense, nearly the size of the storage area above them, but built in an unusual cylindrical design. It was shaped like a hollow cone, with the apex funneling up overhead.

The chamber was trilevel, with two floors above their position. Banks of consoles ran the length of each. Brilliant overhead lights gleamed on the alloyed handrails, the glass-covered panels and meters. Chairs were attached to slideways so the console operators could be ferried from panel to panel. A quick count told Ryan that each level contained a dozen chairs. But none of the chairs was occupied.

Beetles flitted over the consoles, extensor cables manipulating dials, buttons and switches. Ryan quickly handed Mildred the ID badge he had taken from Doug, but none of the gadgets paid any notice to them.

Six chrome-capped glass tubes, each one ten feet long and three feet around, were positioned at equidistant points on the top level of the cone-shaped chamber. The tubes were filled with a churning, bubbling green liquid, flexible metal conduits extending from their tops and bottoms. The conduits extended from the bases of the tubes and disappeared into sleeve sockets on the deck.

It was very cold in the room, well below freezing. The frigid wind roared up from beneath, where the chamber's diameter was at its widest. Gingerly Mildred and Ryan peered over a handrail. Far below, perhaps a hundred feet, was a dark metal framework, surrounding six gargantuan fan units. Four of them were spinning, two were not, and Ryan estimated that the three fan blades of each unit were close to twenty feet long and ten wide.

Surveying the upper levels, they saw twelve open shaftways like the one they had used to reach the chamber.

Shivering and hugging himself, Ryan asked, "What the hell is this place?" The roar of the wind was so loud, he had to practically shout his question into Mildred's ear.

"I'm not sure," she shouted back. "An air circulation station, but it can't be the only one in an installation this size."

Eyeing the hovering beetles, Ryan said, "They haven't noticed us."

"They're probably not supposed to. More than likely their sole program is to maintain the operations."

"Why are those things doing it, since this place was designed for humans?"

"Lack of manpower to spare, easier to automate, I can't say."

Taking another look at the fan units below, Ryan said, "A couple of grens might knock those out, start warming this place up."

Mildred shook her head and gestured to the tubes of bubbling liquid. "That wind is almost gale force. Unless you find something to weigh down the grens, they'll probably be blown right back up here. Besides, those containers of coolant must be pumped into a conversion chamber below the fans. If we want to start a thaw, we need to prevent the flow of coolant."

Ryan lifted his blaster, but Mildred tugged at his arm. Her face was troubled. "This isn't right, Ryan. Our plan was to try and strike a deal with the Commander, remember?"

"Yeah, but his rats might gnaw us to death before we reach him. If this is only one of their stations, shooting out one or two of these coolant containers shouldn't putrefy the whole place, only show them what we can do if they screw around with us."

Mildred hesitated, biting her lower lip, then nodded. "Do it. We can't stay here much longer or we'll freeze."

Bringing the center of the nearest tube into target acquisition, Ryan squeezed the trigger of the SIG-Sauer. The report of the shot was completely swallowed up by the rush of the wintry wind, but the glass casing acquired a grayish smear. It didn't break or even crack. It was armaglass, or something very close to it. He cursed and fired again, aiming at the same spot. He expended three more rounds before he saw a small network of cracks appear, and he fired twice more before a trickle of green fluid began sliding down the tube's exterior and crawling down the conduit.

Immediately an overhead light went from white to red, and the beetles' smooth, hovering motions became hurried and frantic.

"Their instruments have registered a drop in the coolant level," Mildred shouted. "Time to go."

They chose a shaft at random and were grateful for the lessening of the cold and the thunder of the fans. Squeezing through the passage, the darkness grew almost absolute. The lateral shaft terminated in another elbow joint, and Mildred wasn't happy that it crooked downward rather than up.

"Makes sense, doesn't it?" Ryan asked, squatting at the lip of the upside down L and reloading the SIG-Sauer.

"Yeah, I guess so. The air has to be circulated to all levels of the Anthill. I'm just not crazy about climbing down into God knows what."

Putting his feet on the ladder rungs, Ryan replied, "Can't figure that it's much different than climbing up into God knows what."

After a few minutes of hand-over-hand descent, the shaft terminated in another elbow, joining with a passageway branching off to the left. They were able to walk side by side along this one. As they did they passed several smaller openings. Judging by the icy drafts that blew out from them, there were a number of other subsidiary shafts connected to more circulating stations.

Presently they detected a faint radiance ahead, and as they went farther down the shaft, the light grew brighter and they heard a series of noises. Ryan was able to distinguish the humming of generators and the murmur of voices. A metal-meshed grille stood in front of them. They approached it in a crouch and peered through the screen.

They looked down on a miniature city. They saw buildings with foundations of brick and concrete, narrow paths twisting and turning between the squat structures. None of the buildings looked like they could comfortably fit a child, much less a full-grown adult. It looked like a model of a predark city, shrunk in volume and reduced in scale. In the center was an obelisk tower made of white stone, stretching upward about twenty-five feet.

Mildred caught her breath in surprise, but she said nothing. The city, if it could be called that, was empty and devoid of life, despite evidence to the contrary. Both of them had heard voices. Ryan pressed his face closer to the grille, looking from the left to the right. Almost directly below them was a metal pole, and topping the pole was a rectangular green sign with white lettering. He read it aloud: "Pennsylvania Avenue."

Running a hand across her forehead, Mildred said, "Sweet Jesus. It's a scale model of Washington, D.C." She pointed to a white-domed building about thirty yards away. "That's supposed to be the Capitol Building, and that tower is the Washington Monument."

Ryan shook his head. "A bastard weird hobby. These freezies have way too much time on their hands."

"Crazy as shithouse rats," Mildred intoned.

After waiting a few minutes and hearing nothing, they decided to move. Feeling around on the inside of the hatch cover, Ryan found a slide lock and he pushed the bolt aside. The hinges were stiff, and he had to launch several kicks at the frame before it creaked open. They were about twenty feet above the floor, but only five from the arched roof of a strange building supported by Doric columns. There was the statue of a seated man inside it.

"A baby-sized Lincoln Memorial," Mildred said. "Appropriate in kind of a sick way."

Both of them jumped to the roof of the miniature memorial and clambered down to the floor. They walked carefully down Pennsylvania Avenue, looking for any movements or signs of life, straining their ears and eyes. The sound of their footsteps echoed unnaturally loud. Evidently the "city" wasn't equipped with the sound-absorbent shielding of the storage level.

"You know," Mildred whispered, "if I could have imagined a place that had become a refuge for survivors of the nukecaust, trying to evade death and retain some semblance of their former lives, this would be the place."

The ceiling was fairly high, perhaps fifty or more feet, tapering upward to armatures holding electric light fixtures. Very few of the buildings were more than six feet tall, and Ryan and Mildred felt uneasy striding among them like giants.

Ryan had only seen pictures of America's capital city, and walking through a toy version of it disturbed him for reasons he couldn't identify. Mildred, of course, had visited D.C. before skydark and remembered it well.

"'There were giants in the earth in those days,'" Mildred muttered, bending down to peer into the windows of a building.

"Don't you start. One of the reasons I accepted this job from Hellstrom was the prospect of getting away from Doc and his flashblasted quotes."

"Sorry," Mildred said. "It's only natural for the child of a preacher to quote scripture. Besides, if Doc was with us, he'd be talking some obscure shit about Gulliver and Lilliput."

The room containing the city was so long that its far end was indistinguishable in the shadows. There didn't seem to be any doors or any way out. Suddenly Ryan felt the fine hairs on his nape lift.

The cold, still air blazed with automatic gunfire. Bullets smacked into a building beside them, digging white pockmarks in the brickwork, shards scattering in every direction. Ryan and Mildred responded instantly, in lunging rushes for cover on opposite sides of the avenue.

Men in business suits, brandishing handblasters and autorifles, bounded toward them from all directions. Ducking behind a four-foot-high office building, Ryan fired the Walther MPL in a stuttering spray. He heard ricochets, screams and curses, and the snapping snarl of Mildred's MP-5.

A machine gun was unlimbered. The chatter of the weapon was amplified, and echoes of the rapid reports were sent booming back and forth. Out of the corner of his eye, Ryan glimpsed a shadowy shape and heard automatic fire. He flung his body to one side as a shower of rock chips swept against him.

He saw the man running toward him between two buildings, an autoblaster spitting flame, lead and noise, held at waist level. The Walther loosed three rounds and the man flipped backward, his chest blown out.

Another stream of autofire chewed the air over his head. Ryan tried to press his body into the building as the slugs stitched a red-hot path against the opposite wall of his refuge. Cordite smoke and pulverized stone filled the air.

Suddenly the autoblaster fire stopped. Ryan didn't wait and wonder why. He sprang away from the office building, holding down the Walther's trigger.

Only one man was out in the open, about thirty feet away. He was holding a small skeletal weapon Ryan recognized as a SIG-AMT autocarbine. He seemed to be having difficulty with its breech system, which Ryan, from prior unpleasant experience with the gun, could have guessed. The man saw him and swung the eighteen-inch barrel in a semicircle, trying to catch up with Ryan's sidewise lunge. Three rounds from the Walther broke his head apart before he managed to get his blaster operational again.

Ryan didn't see him drop. He was too occupied with angling his body toward a collection of several buildings and avoiding more slugs that burned the air all around him. Reaching the cover, he drew the SIG-Sauer and put it next to him while he popped a fresh clip into the MPL.

He didn't see Mildred, so he thumbed the transmit stud on the transceiver in his pocket. "Mildred, where are you?"

"About forty feet to your right," came the crisp response. "You made a head count yet?"

"Not yet. You?"

"Rough estimate. I think there's about fifteen of the opposition, not counting any you've put down."

"As far as I know," Ryan said into the mouthpiece, "I've accounted for two."

A man jumped from cover a dozen yards to his left, slapping the stock of a rifle to his shoulder. He was dead on his feet, with a skull smashed into three pieces, before he could squeeze the trigger. A single shot from the SIG-Sauer had drilled him through the forehead and blown out the back of his cranium in a welter of brain matter and bone chips. He went down without an outcry.

"Three," Ryan said. "What's your score?"

"Two definites, two maybes." There was a pause, and Ryan heard the crack of the ZKR. Her voice filtered into his ear again, tense and worried. "Make that three definites. Listen, we're already pinned down, and pretty soon we'll be outflanked and outgunned. I think we should split up."

Ryan didn't answer for a long moment. Mildred's expertise was crucial to the successful completion of their mission. It was a tough call to make, but each of them had to take fundamentally the same chances—both were important, and therefore both were almost equally unimportant, in terms of the risks to be faced by separating. It was the only way they really had a chance.

"Ryan?" Mildred's voice was urgent.

"Okay," he said. "We split up. We can stay in contact with the radios. I'll draw them away from you in a very flashy way."

"I'll give you covering fire if I can."

"No. Don't draw any more attention than necessary. Just wait for my next signal."

"Acknowledged," she replied tersely.

One thing Ryan knew better than anyone else was how to conduct a running gunfight. He leaped from cover, sparing one split second to survey his surroundings, then he raced through the miniature Washington, D.C., in a long-legged, yard-eating lope. He jumped over boulevards, pounded past the Capitol rotunda and sprang over the Potomac in a single bound. Voices yelled to his right. He spied four men, less than fifteen feet away, rising from cover, fumbling to bring their blasters to bear, faces registering astonishment.

Ryan swept them with a long burst from the Walther. One took several 9 mm hollowpoints in the face and throat, the others receiving theirs in the guts, their entrails shredding and splitting.

He didn't slow his pace, but he swerved back and forth, running in a broken-field fashion, trying to keep buildings at his back and sides at all times. Staccato pops filled the air, and bullets blasted chips of brick and masonry from the structures all around him. Flakes of stone and fragments of concrete stung the back of his neck and the left side of his face.

A dark-haired man ran to intercept him, a long-barreled revolver held in both hands. He assumed a two-handed combat stance, and with smooth, practiced motions drew a bead on Ryan.

The SIG-Sauer spit flame and noise, and three wads of lead centerpunched the man in the lower body. He staggered backward, dropping the blaster, arms windmilling as he tried to maintain his balance.

Another fusillade of shots chewed up the paint job of a building only a few feet in front of Ryan. Without aiming, he pointed the Walther MPL behind him and fired a strafing burst.

He felt a shock of impact in the muscle of his right shoulder, and he spun completely off his feet. His head reversed position with his boots and his back thudded heavily onto the floor with such force he couldn't see or breathe for agonizingly long seconds.

He choked back the burning bile sliding up his throat, and he bit his tongue against the pain. Rolling over onto his left side, gulping the cold air, he looked behind him, in the direction from which the shot had come.

The man who had shot him confidently exposed himself to check the quality of his marksmanship. The blaster looked like a Ruger rifle. Ryan planted two slugs from the SIG-Sauer in the man's dingy white shirtfront. He went down with a great yelp of pain and astonishment. Someone pulled him back behind the corner of a flat-roofed building.

Getting to his knees through sheer force of will, Ryan kept low and crawled behind the base of the Washington

Monument. The whole right side of his shirt was dark with blood. White-hot pain and nausea washed over him in a wave, but it passed. Gingerly he flexed his fingers, and though the movement tore a protest from his shoulder, the muscles, tendons and nerves still worked. He wasn't so much worried about the blood loss, but about crippling injury, temporary or not.

He seated the earpiece of the headset more securely and called Mildred. There was no reply, only the hiss of static. He repeated her name, and received the same response—static.

Refusing to speculate on the reasons why he couldn't contact her, Ryan opened his coat and checked the severity of the exit wound. The bullet had passed completely through his shoulder from the back. Under the circumstances, the raw, bleeding crater just beneath his collarbone was more unsightly than critical; the bullet hadn't taken much meat and muscle with it, and it had fortunately missed bone.

Still, the wound hurt like bottled hell, and it throbbed in cadence with his heartbeat. Sensations became rubbery, wavering. His eye remained open, but the miniature city blurred and receded in his vision. Footfalls and voices forced him to focus. He could hear men moving quickly toward his position.

"He's over there, behind the monument. Frank nailed him."

"And he nailed Frank. Let's be exceptionally careful, gentlemen."

The mechanical sound of firing bolts being pulled back was audible.

"Fuck this," Ryan mumbled beneath his breath.

He pulled one of the incendiary grens from his combat harness, jammed it firmly against the base of the obelisk and pinched away the pin. He got to his feet and trotted away in a fast backpedal, making sure to keep the replica of the monument between him and the freezies stalking him.

A quartet of blaster-wielding men crept around the monument, two to a side. One pair sighted Ryan and raised their weapons. The second pair sighted the metal egg at the base of the tower. They uttered cries of alarm and fear, and tried to scuttle away as fast as they could.

The base of the monument erupted in a blaze of flame, smoke and debris. Ryan felt the cold slap of the concussion. The obelisk shivered, swayed, and with a groan and grate of stone, the entire length toppled majestically down across metropolitan Washington, crashing into and crushing several buildings. Planes of smoke and dust rose in the air. Men screamed in pain and outrage, cursed in a homicidal fury.

Ryan turned and ran as fast as he could down another lane, sprinting low to keep his head down behind the buildings. Once, he was forced to squeeze into a very narrow alley and squat there as a column of dark-suited pursuers flashed past along the street. He didn't shoot at their retreating backs, reasoning that if he hadn't done enough to draw the heat from Mildred by now, there was no point in engaging in another blaster battle.

He noticed blood dripping from his left hand, slicking the butt of the SIG-Sauer and splattering on the artificial lawn. Fleur's knife cut on his shoulder blade had reopened, though Mildred's stitches and bandages seemed to be keeping the bleeding to a minimum.

He tried raising Mildred a third time on the comm unit, and when he couldn't, he removed the headset and stowed it in an inner coat pocket. Biting his lip to repress a grunt of pain, Ryan rose and moved through the drifting sheets of dust and smoke, wending his way between the buildings until he came to a barrier. Two very ornate, very tall double doors, bound with thick braces of brass, towered over him.

Emblazoned in the very center of the doors were two bordered disk-shaped symbols that depicted, in gold and black paint, an eagle with outstretched wings. One clawed talon gripped a sheaf of arrows, and the other held what looked like sharp pointed missiles. He recognized the images as altered versions of the great seal of the United States. There was an inscription printed inside the borders of the disks, and Ryan had trouble reading it, sounding out the words.

"Novus Ordo Secolorum," he muttered. "What the fireblasted hell is that supposed to mean?"

Chapter Twenty-Four

As far as Fleur knew, prisoners were fed only once a day, in the evening. She wasn't even sure of that, since most violators of Helskel's laws were either immediately chilled on the scene of the infraction or tortured to death. Actual jail terms were exceedingly rare, and based on little more than Hellstrom's whims.

But she was familiar with the two sec men acting as turnkeys, and she voiced a sneering opinion of their alertness and intelligence. Their names were T.J. and Tex, and she doubted either one would bother to check on them until mealtime.

Since she was the tallest of the inmates, Doc directed her to stand on the top step, blocking the observation slit with her back. If T.J. or Tex asked why she was there, Fleur was to tell them that her cellmates had threatened her life if she dared step farther into their dungeon.

J.B. and Jak moved the bunk a few feet down the wall and knelt on the floor, watching as Doc carefully slid his sword blade into the earth, slicing out squares. Meticulously J.B. lifted them out, keeping the hard topsoil intact and separated from the bottom layer of softer dirt. Jak and Krysty pawed through the heap of straw, examining and discarding individual stalks.

As the afternoon wore on, the process came faster and easier with repetition. They removed more and more squares of the hard-packed floor. The cell heated up, and all of them perspired freely.

By late afternoon they had dug a long square hole in the floor, a little more than a foot deep. It looked like a shallow grave, wide enough to accommodate three corpses.

Jak, using the sword, shaved off the excess loose dirt from the bottom of the squares until each one was perfectly flat and only three inches in thickness.

Noting the dimming quality of light through the barred window, Krysty whispered, "Better hurry. Be dark soon."

A bit reluctantly, but keeping their complaints to a minimum, J.B., Jak and Doc lay down on their backs in the hole. Jak, the sword beside his prone body, took the position nearest the door.

Krysty gingerly picked up the squares of earth and laid them over the men's bodies, fitting them together like the pieces of a puzzle. She rebuilt the floor from their feet up. When she reached their necks, she placed a hollow straw in each mouth. Before she laid the last chunks over their faces, she exchanged long looks with all three of them, smiling reassuringly. Jak gave her a wink, and J.B. mumbled around the straw in his mouth, "This had better work, old man."

"If it doesn't," Doc responded in a similar mumble, "then we'll be saving the gravediggers of Helskel time and effort."

Krysty fitted the squares over their heads, making sure the straws jutted between the edges. Rising, she fetched the water bucket and used the tin cup to dribble water over the cracks and uneven edges. With her hands she rubbed and smoothed the earth, mixing in the excess dirt and kneading out the cut marks. She very carefully broke the protruding straws almost even with the floor.

After washing the dirt from her hands, she moved the bucket back to its place and resumed her lotus position against the wall. Nodding toward Fleur, she mouthed a question. "Soon?"

Fleur responded with a short, terse nod, and Krysty closed her eyes to begin her preparations.

A rich warmth blanketed her as she followed the route of blood through her circulatory system, tracing the autonomic functions back to the controlling portion of her brain.

She slowed her respiration rate and concentrated on the mantra of power her mother had taught her.

"Earth Mother, help me. Aid me now, Gaia. Help me and give me the strength and the power."

Her heartbeat speeded up, then slowed, and at the same time she increased the amount of adrenaline into her bloodstream.

Krysty's mind went here and there through her body, adjusting it, manipulating it, honing and revitalizing her reflexes and responses. The warmth spread from the center of her belly, flowed through her arms and legs. Her fingertips and toes tingled with energy.

"Give me all the power. Let me strive for life."

She repeated the invocation, and in her mind's eye she saw a white blossom opening, the petals reaching out to engulf her. She felt as if she were floating, hovering between the solid material world and one made of warm, insubstantial light.

"Now, Mother of Earth, give me, I beg, the power to do that which is right. Let me render no evil. Give your daughter the power, the power, the power..."

There was a rattle from the heavy cell door. Fleur quickly moved away as it was flung open. The two sec men came down the stone steps. Tex was carrying a metal pail and a handful of wooden spoons. T.J. had his blaster in hand. They froze at the sight of Fleur sitting on the bunk and Krysty on the floor. Dumbly they looked around them, mouths dropping open.

"Where are the others?" Tex asked.

Krysty opened her eyes. She looked drowsy, and a dreamy smile played over her lips. "They had to leave. Had an appointment."

Tex dropped the pail, and what looked like a watery soup splashed up and out of it. He drew his Tec-10 and pointed it at Fleur. "How did they leave? Answer me!"

Fleur pointed to the window. "How else, you silly bastards? Through the bars."

T.J., face blank and stupid with shock, ran to the window, leaped up, tested the bars, then skipped around the cell, kicking at the pile of straw as if the three missing men might be hiding beneath it.

"This is ridiculous!" Tex snarled. "Just plain fuckin' crazy! They have to be here! You two bitches—on your feet!"

Fleur and Krysty stood and were herded out of the cell at gunpoint and into the adjoining room. It was small, barely more than a foyer, but a chained set of manacles dangled from a bracket bolted deep into the wall.

T.J. stood in the doorway of the cell, his back to it. Tex moved to the other side of the room. Both women were caught between gun barrels.

With a jerk of his head, Tex indicated the manacles. "Cuff yourselves," he commanded. "I want to hear them click tight."

Dark rust-colored streaks stained the floor beneath the manacles. People chained to the wall in the past had obviously left their blood as silent reminders of their suffering.

Still smiling a dreamy smile, Krysty put the iron cuff around her right wrist and snapped it shut. Fleur snugged the other manacle around her left wrist and sealed it with a loud click.

"Okay, you bitches," T.J. snarled, "where'd they go? Start talking, or we start shooting pieces off you!"

A motion behind T.J. caught Krysty's eye. Metal gleamed for a fraction of a second. T.J. made no sound, not even a startled gasp when the blade plunged through his back. His eyes blinked foolishly down at the inch of crimson-tinged steel sprouting from his chest.

Before those eyes went vacant, Krysty yanked her right arm forward in a short arc. The bracket holding the chain tore from the wall in a burst of powdered mortar and adobe. Her arm's arc ended when her fist connected with Tex's jaw.

The whole lower portion of his face skewed sidewise, the point of his chin skidding around and taking up position beneath his right ear lobe. His teeth spewed from his mouth like a handful of corn amid a torrent of blood, the crack of shattering bone sounding like a gunshot.

The force of the blow caused his torso to pivot violently at the waist with a loud grating of cartilage. Life went out of his eyes with the suddenness of a candle flame being extinguished.

As he fell, his face horribly out of shape, Krysty slid the thumb of her left hand into the space between the manacle and her wrist and exerted pressure. Muscles rippled up and down her bare arm. The cuff sprang open, twanging like the bass string of a guitar.

Jak, his white hair full of dirt kernels, withdrew the sword from T.J., who flopped face first at Fleur's feet.

Fleur was gaping at Krysty with mingled awe and terror. Her eye was wide, the azure iris completely surrounded by the white. The dreamy smile on Krysty's face had vanished. She advanced on Fleur, and the woman shrank in fear.

Grabbing her by the forearm and digging her fingers under the iron manacle encircling Fleur's wrist, Krysty wrenched it open. Fleur cried out in pain as Krysty flung the cuff aside. It clanged against the wall.

"That could just as easily have been your heart," she said softly, not releasing her.

Doc pushed his way forward, slapping dirt from his frock coat. He reached out to touch Krysty, thought better of it and said urgently, "My dear, she can help us reach Ryan and Mildred. She may prove useful to us."

Turning her head, eyes glowing with a jade flame, Krysty stared at Doc for a long moment. Then the blaze in her eyes faded a bit and she said quietly, "Let's get on with it. I haven't much time."

Doc took back his swordstick, and J.B. and Jak armed themselves with the sec men's blasters. The door of the building was barred on the inside, but rather than bother with the unlocking mechanism, Krysty kicked the door off its hinges. J.B. cursed at the loud splintering of wood and the screech of screws ripping from the wall.

Luckily the door faced away from the street and no one saw it sailing away or heard it hitting the ground. Though their chrons had been confiscated, J.B. estimated the time at around eight o' clock. It was early yet for the denizens of Helskel, too early for the riotous partying that seemed to go on every night.

As the five people made their way toward the armory, trying to keep to the darkness, the few people they encountered paid them no attention. Krysty led the way, with Jak bringing up the rear, checking their backtrack with quick, all-seeing glances.

Two men were guarding the armory. One was an X-scarred sec man and the other was a novitiate, obviously participating in an uneventful exercise. The sec man was trying to light a hand-rolled cigarette, his Tec-10 clutched under one elbow. The novitiate was standing at the corner of the flat-roofed, windowless building, urinating into the shadows.

Because of a steady breeze, the sec man was having trouble getting his lighter to stay aflame. He had his hands cupped around it. By the time his cigarette was afire, his eyes were swimming with multicolored spots from the dancing flame. He didn't see Krysty's bold approach, but he felt her hand fit itself around his throat and squeeze.

The sec man didn't gasp or cough or cry out. Fingers like bands of tempered, tooled steel closed around his neck, crushing his windpipe, his larynx, his esophagus and his top vertebrae all in a single clenching motion. The only sounds were a wet, mushy crunching of flesh and muscle mashing against bone and cartilage.

The novitiate heard the crunch, but he wasn't startled by it. He zipped up his fly and turned. When he saw the titian-haired beauty gripping his tongue-lolling mentor by the throat, his eyes bugged out and his mouth opened wide. For an instant he forgot all about the .38-caliber Colt M-1911 tucked in his belt slide rig.

By the time he remembered it, Doc had lunged around Krysty, sword blade extended. The razor point punctured the man's heart in a swift, darting thrust.

Jak and J.B. dragged the bodies to the side of the armory, hiding them behind a clump of sagebrush. The armory door was secured by a padlock, and neither of the guards had keys on them, so Krysty wrenched away the lock and a sizable portion of the doorframe.

Fleur knew the location of the light switch, so they shut the door behind them and turned on the overhead lights. The interior of the storehouse was stacked nearly to the ceiling with wooden crates and boxes. Most of the crates were stenciled with the legend, PROPERTY U.S. ARMY.

They moved down the main aisle, taking a check of the contents of open containers. M-16 A-1 assault rifles were neatly stacked in one, along with what had to be thousands of rounds of 5.56 mm ammunition. There were AR-18 rifles, 9 mm Heckler & Koch VP-70 semiautomatic pistols complete with holsters and belts, plus more than an ample supply of Tec-10s. Farther on they found bazookas, heavy tripod-mounted machine guns like the M-60 and the M-249, and several crates of grenades. Every piece of it, from the smallest caliber handblaster to the big M-79 grenade launcher, was in perfect condition.

J.B.'s eyes shone with unabashed longing. "Dark night," he said hoarsely. "I could stay here a year, just cataloging all this ordnance."

"You've got about five minutes," Krysty said in a quavering voice. She groped behind her and sat heavily on a box. A dew of perspiration had gathered at her temples, her eyes were glassy and her hands trembled.

"That's all, folks," she said weakly. "It's all I can do to stay conscious."

"When is the next guard changeover?" Doc asked Fleur.

"Not for a couple of hours. At ten. But we can't assume someone won't pass by and notice the guards are gone."

From behind them came Jak's triumphant announcement of "Found 'em."

While they had followed J.B. through the death-dealing wonderland, Jak had dropped back and fulfilled the original purpose of breaching the armory. He handed everyone their personal weapons and belongings. J.B. snatched a burlap bag from a wall hook and rushed deep into the storehouse, calling over his shoulder, "One minute. We can't pass up this chance to stock up on ammo and a few other odds and ends."

True to his word, J.B. emerged from the aisles a minute later, carrying a bulging sack. It clinked and jingled as he walked. "Everybody make sure they've got a full load before we move out."

"What about me?" Fleur wanted to know.

"What about you?" Krysty asked. "Can you handle a blaster with the shape your hands are in?"

Fleur lifted her shoulders in a shrug. "I'd like to help, as long as I'm sharing the risks."

Eyeing her a bit haughtily, Doc remarked, "You've certainly undergone an extreme change in attitude. Perhaps a bit too extreme."

J.B. rummaged around in his sack and came up with a paper wrapped cylinder about six inches long. He handed it to Fleur, saying, "Hold on to this. When I give the word, break it in half along the dotted line."

Examining it suspiciously, she demanded, "Why?"

"You'll see."

Opposite the armory was a tin-walled prefabricated building. According to Fleur, it was a billet, the quarters of the sec men. It appeared unoccupied, though the dim light of a kerosene lamp shone through the window. If they weren't home, then the sec men were patrolling the streets.

The five of them moved quickly through the streets, Krysty being helped along by Doc. She was nearly staggering from exhaustion.

They reached the shadowed rear of the saloon without being hailed by any passersby or seeing any sec men. Their Land Rover was still there, still sitting on flattened tires. The jukebox inside the saloon blared some discordant tune, full of wild guitars and heavy drums.

J.B. studied the wag compound across the dusty street. The chain-link gate was secured by a padlock, and beyond it two guards were loitering around the gasoline pumps. One carried a walkie-talkie slung over a shoulder by a strap.

"Now what?" Fleur whispered. "If we just stroll over, they'll recognize me, and the rest of you aren't exactly forgettable."

"Except for me," J.B. replied. "I'm what you call inoculated."

"Innocuous," Krysty corrected, a note of weary humor in her voice.

J.B. handed his sack and hat to Jak. He folded his spectacles into a coat pocket before taking it off and draping it over his right arm, the Uzi in his fist.

Mussing up his hair, he said, "Everybody get ready to move. You'll know when. Triple red."

He contorted his face into a vacant-eyed, imbecilic mask and started shuffling drunkenly across the street. He weaved, waved, stumbled, mumbled and cackled. When he reached the gate of the compound, he hung on to the interlocking wire links with his left hand and stared at the ground, muttering to himself and kicking at the loose dirt.

One of the sec men sauntered toward him, leaving his companion with the walkie-talkie. When the shaven-headed man was less than a foot away, he asked, "What are you doing there, joltbrain?"

Slurring his speech, J.B. said, "Lost my ma's locket."

"What?"

"Lost my ma's locket."

"Where?"

J.B. jerked his shoulder in the direction of the saloon. "Back there." He saw the sec man's partner respond to a call on the comm unit, unslinging it and holding it up to the side of his head.

The sec man scowled. "Then why the fuck are you looking for it over here?"

"Because—" The barrel of the Uzi poked through a link in the gate and pressed against the man's belly. In a quiet yet flint-hard voice, J.B. said, "The light is better over here. You got the key to the lock?"

Gulping, the sec man nodded.

"Very, very carefully, I want you to unlock the gate. Act like you're having a nice conversation with the jolt-brain."

The sec man fumbled inside his hair-covered vest, produced a small silver key, reached around the frame of the gate and inserted it into the base of the lock.

"Hey, Pooh Bear!" the sec man's partner bellowed from the compound. "Got an alert! Them outlanders escaped, chilled Tex and T.J.!"

The man opened his mouth to bellow a reply. J.B. saw the fear in his eyes change to panic, and the bellow became a grunt as a 9 mm burst squirted from the Uzi, catching him just above the groin. The impact slapped him away from the gate, and before his partner could do more than flail around to bring his Tec-10 to bear, J.B. shot him three times, just below the rib cage. Forty feet was long range for such a stunted blaster as the Uzi, but J.B. brought him down.

He unlocked the gate and pushed it open, hearing the running footfalls of his friends behind him. Krysty was reeling, her boots dragging in the dust, clinging to Doc, who had one arm around her waist.

J.B. ran a quick check on the nearest dune buggy, checking out its frame, the condition of the tires and the engine. The ten-gallon fuel tank was full. Jak pointed to the gasoline pumps. "Couple five-gallon cans there."

"Good. Go fill 'em."

The keys to the vehicle were hanging by a string from the rearview mirror. Relieved he didn't have to hot-wire it, J.B. nevertheless checked out the ignition, looking for an explosive charge. As he was doing so, Fleur said anxiously, "They'll just come after us, you know. Run us to ground like deer."

"Mebbe so," J.B. grunted. "Mebbe not-so. Electrical system is clean."

Everybody piled into the dune buggy, Fleur, Krysty and Doc squeezing into the back seat. Krysty sagged limply against Doc, her eyelids fluttering with the effort to keep conscious. J.B. started the wag, and it caught on the third try. The engine sound was steady, and though not loud, it carried a note of power. Putting it into gear, he steered around to the fuel pumps. Jak had just finished filling the two cans, and he heaved them onto the floorboards in front of the passenger seat.

He exchanged a quick nod with J.B., then produced one of his knives. He slashed through the pumping hose at a point just below the nozzle and gasoline sprayed in all directions. Jak leapt aboard, and the dune buggy rolled toward the open gate.

Down the street raced a group of sec men, about five of them. J.B. hit the brakes and half-turned toward Fleur. "You got that flare?"

"Yeah."

"Break it and throw it toward the fuel pumps."

She looked a little shocked, then a smile spread over her face. She snapped the cylinder between her hands, and a blinding reddish-white light splashed her with an eerie luminescence. The sec men were yelling at them, unslinging their blasters.

"Throw it!" J.B. shouted.

Turning in her seat, Fleur hurled the burning flare in an overhead half-loop, back into the compound. The spilled gasoline ignited immediately, and before J.B. floored the wag's accelerator, it was flashing in a foot-high flame trail toward the pump.

A mushrooming orange ball of fire roared angrily upward. The pumps were uprooted from the concrete apron and they rocketed into the night sky. The fuel storage tank beneath the compound exploded, ripping a ragged crater in the ground as if a giant fist had slammed up from beneath. It triggered a deadly chain reaction as the other vehicles in the compound were flung in all directions and overturned. The gasoline in their split tanks leaked out, then erupted in secondary explosions.

The shock waves thundered across Helskel, knocking people flat, pushing over merchants' stalls, shattering every window in the saloon.

A pillar of flame punched a hundred feet into the black sky over Helskel. The column of brilliant light spewed flying tongues of flame, and burning debris and wag parts rained onto the dusty streets and atop the nearest buildings. Hungry flames jumped from shack to hovel to geodesic dome to the rear wall of the saloon.

The sec men had been slammed to the ground by the concussion. They had their heads up and were staring at the conflagration like hypnotized moths. One tried to shoot at the dune buggy as it swung past, but Jak had his pistol out and working first. The .357 Magnum slug turned the sec man's face into a wet smear, and then J.B. floored the pedal, sending the vehicle roaring out of Helskel. Behind them, the lights of the ville were completely obscured by the inferno.

"How she handle?" Jak asked, speaking loudly to be heard over the roar of the engine.

"Great," J.B. said, smiling. The smile fled his lips. "I still miss the Hotspur, though."

Doc leaned forward, patting his shoulder. "Do not bother yourself over the loss, John Barrymore. If this were tit for tat, we have just paid Helskel back for its loss, and then some."

Chapter Twenty-Five

Out in the city, someone coughed and cursed. Ryan pushed against one of the tall doors with a shoulder, and it swung open silently on oiled hinges. Stepping over the dim threshold, he pulled the door back into place. He stood there, surveying the gloomy interior of the big, high-ceilinged room.

It was about sixty feet long, lined on three sides with bookshelves to the ceiling. There were comfortable armchairs, upholstered in red leather, scattered about, and a huge globe of the earth stood in one corner. At first glance the room appeared to be a combined library and office. The carpet was a medium blue, and a replica of the seals emblazoned on the doors was embroidered in thick gold thread. The lighting, from shaded lamps, was subdued. The only odd feature was a fireplace, logs glowing cheerily in the hearth.

An immense circular desk dominated the fourth wall. It was strewn with papers. Blinking in the semigloom, Ryan saw a man sitting at the desk. He was as motionless as a statue, not even reacting when the huge door had opened and closed.

He was dressed all in black, with a thatch of cropped white hair and a neatly trimmed gray mustache. His deep-set slitted eyes, in shadowed sockets, were without movement or the spark of life.

Ryan stared at him, not speaking, a little demoralized by the hush and vastness of the room. The man stared back. Finally Ryan raised both blasters and barked, "To your feet. Hands where I can see them. Quick!"

The man complied, silently and smoothly, without so much as a squeak of leather or wood. Ryan started to step toward him when the wall on his left seemed to explode like a grenade.

Splintery fragments flew in every direction, and something clipped him a stunning blow on the left temple. The whole side of his head went numb, and he reeled drunkenly, lurching to one knee. He stopped himself from falling, but he dropped the SIG-Sauer in the process.

His eyeball felt like it was spinning, and bits of dirt and pain-haze clouded his vision. He brought up the Walther MPL, lifting his head, searching for a target, tasting the coppery salt of blood at the corner of his mouth. He felt it crawling down the side of his face. Something heavy and metallic swung down from his right side, smashing across his wrist with nerve-numbing force. The blaster skidded quietly across the carpet.

Ryan sprang to his feet, reaching for his panga, and found himself face-to-face with Doug. Behind him he saw a man-sized recess between the bookcases. The man held a sawed-off Browning B-80 autoshotgun, and he snapped the bright brass out of the blaster's receiver. The shot had blasted a hole in the wall next to Ryan's head, and he had caught a spray of splinters.

The one-eyed man wiped his face on a coat sleeve and slowly dropped his hands to his sides. Doug stared at him impassively and said, "You asked about the Commander's location. You've found it."

The man behind the desk said, "Come here." His voice was very soft and completely flat. It was the voice of a man with few feelings and a lot of authority.

Ryan did as he was told, measuring each step. He didn't seem to have much choice, with Doug marching behind him. He noticed as he passed it that the fireplace was a fake, colored lights shining through molded plastic logs, strictly a decorative item. It cast no heat at all.

Facing the Commander across the desk, Ryan got a better look at him. He wasn't particularly tall, but his shoulders were very broad. His chin was squared, his jawline blocky. His eyes were a pale gray, like chunks of old ice. Thickish brows rose outward from twin creases above a hooked nose, and his short white hair grew down from high temples to a point on his forehead. He had unnaturally smooth white skin, with very few lines or wrinkles.

The shadowed depths of the Commander's eyes regarded him with an impersonal impassivity. "Who are you?"

"Ryan Cawdor."

"A citizen of Helskel?"

"No. I came from there, though. Against my will."

"Doug tells me you have a companion, a woman."

"Yes." Ryan didn't ask if Mildred had been captured or chilled. He kept his face and tone composed.

"How did you get in here?"

"The nose."

"Of course." The Commander's eyes opened a bit wider, then narrowed to slits again. "An unforgivable security oversight on the part of my aides. It has always been so." The words were delivered without heat, without change in timbre. "Why are you here?"

Ryan took a deep breath, wondering how much to tell him. "It's about your relics. Your artifacts."

"Indeed. What about them?"

"Lars Hellstrom wants them all to himself."

The Commander nodded, his expression vague and preoccupied. "I am aware of that."

He moved around the desk and extended his hands toward the fireplace, as if to warm them by the cold, colored light. "Why did he send emissaries such as you and your companion? Are you negotiators or are you assassins?"

Ryan sidestepped the question. "Hellstrom feels that you should share more of your bounty, and not hoard it all up here."

"No. Impossible."

"I'll convey that message to him, then."

"No, I'm afraid that's impossible, too. Your friends at Helskel will never receive word of the goings-on in this office. Not during *my* administration."

The Commander no longer looked vague or preoccupied. "You anarchist scum. You filth. You maggot. How dare you profane the sanctity of this high office with your person? I've dealt with prying busybodies like you before."

Ryan made a move to step backward, and the slide mechanism of the shotgun clanked loudly. He lifted conciliatory hands. "Look, I mean you no harm. I have nothing but admiration for you and your high office."

The Commander looked at him closely, with the detachment of a scientist examining an unfamiliar germ strain beneath a microscope. He gazed at Ryan steadily for what felt like a very long time.

Finally he smiled as if amused. "Perhaps I've been a trifle hasty. I am curious as to why Lars Hellstrom took such extreme measures to alter the terms of our trade agreement, and you may be able to advise me. After all, it's not as if you're a journalist."

He reached up and pressed his ice-cold fingers to the left side of Ryan's head. He brought the hand away and studied the blood. "You've sustained an injury. Several, in fact. You appear to be losing a considerable amount of blood."

"It's not as serious as it looks," Ryan replied.

"Losing any of the precious fluids of the body is serious, Mr. Cawdor. Go with Doug and he will see to your wounds. In the interim, we will try to locate your companion."

Ryan managed to keep the surge of relief from showing on his face. Mildred hadn't been apprehended or chilled and was still loose somewhere in the enclave.

With the hollow bore of the Browning staring him in the face, Ryan divested the combat harness of the remaining grens and ammo clips. Then Doug prodded him toward the door with the shotgun barrel. He marched Ryan out of the office and back into the miniature Washington, D.C. The smoke and dust had dissipated. A few armed men were in view, but when they approached, Doug waved them away.

"You fucked up this place and our personnel pretty good, Cawdor," Doug said petulantly. "You made a big mess that your elected officials will have to clean up. Same as it ever was."

"I liked it better when you spoke corporatese," Ryan replied. "As long as we're on the subject of gibberish, what does *Novus Ordo Secolorum* mean?"

Doug laughed derisively. "I can see that the educational level hasn't risen in America. It's Latin, meaning 'the beginning of a new order of the ages.'"

"Like this place?"

"Exactly like this place, Cawdor," Doug declared pridefully.

He directed Ryan away from the perimeter of the city, stepping over the Beltway. A beetle appeared, hovering silently behind and above Doug, following them like a guard dog. Ryan noticed that Doug was wearing another ID badge, identical to the one he had lifted.

When they reached a vanadium alloy wall, Doug aimed a small remote-control device at it. It was a simple sonic lock switch, of a type Ryan had seen before. There was a muffled, hissing sound. A large section of the wall moved forward, tilting back from its bottom edge. It slid out on pneumatic hinges, turning into an up-slanted ramp. Ryan was herded up the ramp and into a wide metal-walled tunnel. It was fairly long and obviously ran into the bowels of the mountain.

They walked for what seemed like a long time. Ryan saw that one section of wall to his left consisted of a glassy, smoke-tinted panel. He glanced into it, then halted. Doug didn't object; in fact, he snickered. Frightful life flapped behind the transparent panel. Within a darkened chamber recessed deep in the wall flitted a swarm of screamwings. The chamber was a specially designed habitat, with branches to roost upon and prey to pursue and kill.

However, these screamwings were larger than the creatures he had seen a few days earlier. Their scaled black bodies were nearly a foot long, and their wingspreads were more than three feet. They looked like depictions of demons he had seen in an old predark religious text. He couldn't understand why such dangerous animals were kept inside the facility—were they curios, conversation pieces, or something worse?

Turning to Doug, he asked, "What's up with the screamwings? The Commander's pets?"

"In a way. More like a project. We're working on a way to increase their size and reduce their birth mortality rate. The mothers tend to eat their young. That's one reason they're rare."

"Damn good thing. They're some of the most vicious predators in Deathlands."

Smiling a superior smile, Doug said, "We wouldn't be interested in them otherwise. Many of the mutations that veered toward polyploidism—"

"Polywhat?" Ryan asked.

A sneer lifted Doug's upper lip. "Polyploidism. Gigantism. Anyway, they were evolutionary dead ends, examples of a spontaneous doubling of the chromosomes. Most of the giant mutants aren't healthy, with extremely limited life spans. The screamwings, on the other hand, are perfectly adapted to their environment. They're a purer breed of killer."

"That's my point. Why make them larger and more numerous?"

"Microcircuitry, Cawdor, introduced into their brains, connected to the visual neural system. We'll be able to control specific behavior and they'll make an excellent offensive-defensive measure. They'll be completely expendable, too, since we'll always be able to breed more."

He gestured impatiently with the shotgun. "All of this is way beyond you. If the Commander wants to give you

a tour of our bioengineering facility, that's up to him.
Let's go."

They continued another hundred yards down the tunnel, then took a hard right turn and crossed a short catwalk that stretched over a cavernous workshop. Ryan saw
jigs, tooling machines, drill presses and equipment he
couldn't easily identify. Men handled pieces of metal of
all shapes that were spread out on tables. Many of the
metal pieces were frameworks that resembled the skele-
tons of human arms and legs. A number of others looked
like the molds and casings of the beetles.

Ryan stopped to survey them, but was pushed forward by Doug's shotgun. They reached the end of the
catwalk, walked into another stretch of tunnel and entered a room. The doorframe bore a square-armed red
cross.

The room was occupied by a white-coated man. He
had a kindly, smiling face, and he appeared to have been
expecting them. He looked to be about Doc's age, and he
asked Ryan to strip. He hesitated, and Doug pushed the
shotgun against his spine. The beetle hovered before the
open doorway.

Ryan took off his clothes, standing naked and shivering. His bones felt bruised, his flesh numb, his head light.
The man examined him closely, without voicing any curiosity about his wounds or his old scars. Removing
Ryan's eyepatch, he peered closely at the puckered
socket, but he didn't touch it. With remarkably gentle
fingers, he probed each injury carefully, tsk-tsking at the
stitches on his shoulder blade. With a tiny pair of scis-
sors he snipped them and removed them. While he en-
dured the pain and the cold, Ryan looked around the
room and saw very little except for an enclosed shower-

like stall that was shaped like a bullet. The top was a translucent semipointed dome.

The man said, "You are ready for the medisterile unit, Mr. Cawdor. Would you like me to investigate the availability of a new eye for you?"

Ryan couldn't disguise his surprise, or even his eager interest. "A new eye? You can give me a new eye?"

Frowning, the doctor said, "Why, of course. I'll have to see if there's one that we can match with the color of your left eye, but it shouldn't be too difficult."

"Never mind," Doug said sharply. "The Commander wants to see him PDQ. New eye, my ass."

The doctor sneered at Doug, curling his lip in disdain, and then directed Ryan to enter the bullet-shaped stall. The walls were tiled, and when the door was shut behind him, hissing sprays of warm disinfectant jetted from tiny nozzles on all sides. It was the first time in hours Ryan hadn't been cold, so he luxuriated in the welcomed heat. The fine streams of fluid scoured his body from the chin down, the churning spray of atomized liquid penetrating every pore, every cut, every wound.

Ryan felt his fatigue ebbing, as well as the pain. He assumed there was some sort of analgesic mixed in with the spray, and perhaps even a mood elevator, for his spirit lightened the longer he stayed under the streams. It was hard to believe he'd ever been hurt, considering the euphoric feeling rising within him.

The jets cut off and warm air whipped around him, all but making him break into a sweat. The heat dried him, and the doctor opened the door of the stall. Stepping out into the cold room was a distinct shock.

His teeth chattering, Ryan allowed the white-coated man to use an aerosol-can spray on his bullet and knife wounds. Wherever the spray touched, a film like a thin skin formed, adhering to his body.

"This liquid bandage contains nutrients and antibiotics and will nip any infection, Mr. Cawdor. It's composition is very similar to real flesh, and your body will absorb it as your injuries heal."

"Is that what you guys are made of?" Ryan asked. "Skin from a can?"

"Of course not! Our technique is far more sophisticated, far more—"

"That's enough," Doug interrupted coldly. "Get dressed, Cawdor."

Ryan did as he was told, noting that his knife and sheath had been removed from the belt. At least the transceiver was still tucked safely in his coat's inner pocket, and his weighted scarf hadn't been tampered with. As he replaced his eye patch, he asked, "Now what?"

Doug opened his mouth to reply, then cocked his head slightly, as though he were listening to whispered instructions. He pressed a spot at the base of his throat, just beneath his larynx, and said, "Acknowledged."

Ryan eyed him suspiciously, wondering if he was responding to ghostly voices only he could hear. "You didn't answer my question, Doug."

Doug grinned and squeezed the stock of the shotgun affectionately. "Now, despite your combat acumen, we'll find out if you can take it as well as you dish it up."

Chapter Twenty-Six

The city trembled with violence—gunfire, screams and shouted profanities. The hue and cry passed Mildred where she lay in the shadow of the National Gallery of Arts building.

She grinned wryly. Reliable old Ryan, who seemed to have a plan for every contingency, had drawn away the rat pack, his guns blazing like an action hero in some old movie.

She waited for a count of thirty, then began moving in a crouched duckwalk J.B. had taught her. The MP-5 kept banging her shins, and she realized why Ryan had passed on choosing it. It was bulky and a little unwieldy. She headed back toward the Lincoln Memorial, planning to return to the ventilation shaft and make her way to another level, hopefully to the primary circulation station.

The psychologist in Mildred despaired of ever reasoning with the Anthill inhabitants. The very existence of the cunningly crafted miniature model of Washington, D.C., indicated a severe disassociative disorder; it was obsessive-compulsive behavior taken to a frightening degree. The people inside Mount Rushmore had lived too long in isolation to feel emotions beyond contempt for the outside world or anger if their wants weren't immediately gratified. In that, they were very similar to the people of Helskel.

A shadow flitted over her, and Mildred froze in mid-scuttle, not daring to move or even breathe. A beetle skimmed slowly above the rooftops, not pausing or slowing as it floated past her position.

Doug's ID badge clipped to her coat had saved her from detection, but she realized it was a two-edged sword. The tracer lozenge on it could just as easily be used to pinpoint her location anywhere inside the complex.

After the beetle was out of sight, she began moving again. The heavy exchange of gunfire seemed to be tapering off to a sporadic crackle. Something rammed into her lower back. The air shot from her lungs, fierce agony filled her body and tears sprang to her eyes. She sprawled facedown across Constitution Avenue, crushing the six-inch-tall hedgeline around Stanton Park.

Mildred tried to push herself over, only to feel her upper arms vised by a pair of hands that felt like hydraulic-powered steel clamps. She allowed herself to be pulled to her feet, and she managed to keep her revolver in her hand. The force of the blow had knocked the headset loose, and it dangled between her legs.

Her assailant mashed her in a crushing embrace, fingers kneading her breasts. What little air remained in her lungs was squeezed out.

A hoarse, angry laugh sounded close to her left ear. "I found a black woman, didn't I? I heard they still existed, but I never thought I'd feel one."

Mildred sagged in the man's arms, shifting her weight into an unresisting, unstruggling mass. She went completely limp, and her attacker tried to reposition his grasp, hugging her close. His grip loosened for a split second, and she snapped her head back, butting the man's face with the top of her skull. She felt and heard the crushing of cartilage.

The man grunted, stumbled back a half pace, the tension in his arms lessening. Mildred wriggled free, dropping through his arms, landing on her knees and lunging forward. She lashed out behind her with her legs.

Her feet clipped the man's ankles, and he staggered backward. He kept himself from falling only by grabbing the cornice of the Supreme Court building.

Before he could regain his balance, Mildred flipped herself over and squeezed the trigger of the ZKR. The bullet caught the man in the neck just above the top button of his white collar. The slug traversed his throat, smashing vertebrae and exiting from the occipital area of his cranium. He backflipped over the building, propelled by the impact. Mildred saw his hands paw convulsively at empty air before he died.

The woman didn't rise for a long moment, striving to clear her body of its blurring pain. She breathed heavily, every inhalation hurting. Her heart pounded wildly. Finally, when the pain had faded to a tolerable level, she checked her headset. Her knees had cracked it, the earpiece breaking loose from its plastic casing, exposing the wires beneath. One of the wires had been snapped, and she didn't have the time to splice the ends back together. She and Ryan were incommunicado.

Using the pair of Senate office buildings as crutches, she slowly levered herself to her feet, biting her lip against the fierce pain lancing through her lower back. The man had to have kicked her there, probably with a bionic leg. She couldn't crouch, so she began a shambling walk.

She halted only because of an ear-knocking explosion behind her. The air shivered with the concussion. She heard screams and saw the Washington Monument swallowed by a cloud of smoke and flame. At least Ryan was still active, hell following in his wake.

After the echoes of the explosion and the crash faded, a mausoleum silence fell over the city. She found the quiet more disturbing than the noisy shouts and gunfire that had preceded it.

Gritting her teeth, clinging to buildings for support, Mildred changed direction. There was no way she could scale the Lincoln Memorial and climb back into the ventilator system. She could barely walk, and she couldn't help but fear a ruptured disk in her spine. There had to be another way out of the miniature city.

She staggered across Independence Avenue in the general direction from which her assailant had come. There had to be an entranceway somewhere.

Mildred paused to rest in Garfield Park. While she tried to distance her mind from the agony in her body, she gazed unfocusedly at the ground beneath her. She suddenly realized she was standing on real dirt—densely packed, but genuine soil just the same. An idea popped into her head.

Unsteadily she bent, dug up a handful of the dirt, rolled it and worked it between her fingers, crushing the larger clods to fine powder. She pitched it into the empty air, watching it whirl, the heavier granules separating from the dust. As the smaller particles settled, they drew into a neat vertical strip of light gray powder, about three feet wide. The band of dust slid across the ground, moving over and around obstacles, still keeping its vertical shape.

Rising painfully to her feet, Mildred followed the strip of powder through the city, losing it a time or two when it blended with other ground cover, but always managing to find it again. Inside of a minute she had reached the outskirts of the city. Where the Navy Yard and the Anacostia River should have been was vanadium alloy floorplates joining with a wall.

If she didn't fear injuring herself further, Mildred would have patted herself on her back for her ingenuity. She had guessed that an electrostatic field was a standard feature in every room and on each level of the installation. She had followed the invisible broom as it whisked the detritus toward a built-in dustpan.

The opening was about two and a half feet wide and two feet high, covered by a meshed screen. Kneeling before it, Mildred gripped the rim of the cover and tugged. It gave an inch or two, then popped out, connected by tiny hinges flush with the floor.

The duct was clean, made of a smooth metal sheeting that looked new. It stretched straight ahead, out of sight in the darkness. Taking a deep, nervous breath, Mildred removed a small pen-flash from a pocket, tested it, then holstered her revolver. Reluctantly she decided that the MP-5 would be an encumbrance in such a confined space. As it was, she feared the combat harness beneath her coat might slow her, but she didn't want to jettison the grenades or even the extra clips of ammunition. They could be crucial pieces of ordnance—if not to her, then to Ryan.

She took off Doug's ID badge, clipped it to the trigger guard of the autoblaster and flung it back toward the city, angling it away from the direction in which she had come. Distantly she heard it clatter against stone.

Lying flat, she elbow-crawled into the duct, holding the penlight between her front teeth. It was easier going than she imagined, due to the electrostatic field's reduction of friction, and it lessened the strain on her damaged back muscles. She could feel her flesh tingling and prickling from the field effect, as if a multitude of tiny ants crawled all over her.

It wasn't as cold in the duct as it had been in the ventilation shaft or even the city. There was no smell to speak of, beyond a faint whiff of ozone.

Half crawling, half sliding, Mildred moved forward, the light in her teeth dimly illuminating the darkness only a foot or so in front of her. There was a darker darkness ahead, and she approached it cautiously, every sense alert.

She reached the edge of the duct, where it slanted down at an angle, disappearing into yawning blackness. She groped around in the gloom before her and touched nothing but smooth metal. Mildred laid her head on the cold metal and groaned, then cursed her ingenuity.

It only stood to reason that dust, crud and other foreign particles would have to be swept somewhere, to a container very much like a high-tech Dumpster. Crawling back out the way she had come wasn't an option, but the concept of creeping headfirst into the chute frightened her more than the most monstrous mutie she had ever encountered.

Raising her head, she looked forward. The duct still slanted away into blackness. She placed both hands flat against the walls of the duct and pressed the sides of her feet against them. By pushing, it was possible to gain the leverage needed to keep from sliding uncontrollably down the chute, assuming, of course, the angle of the incline didn't become any steeper.

A few inches at a time, Mildred wormed herself into the downslanting duct, expanding her shoulders, using her hands and feet to grip the sides. She slipped a time or two due to the reduced friction on the metal surface. Once, she slid forward over a yard before she could brake herself.

Sweat collected on her face and beneath her clothes, and she was grunting with the exertion and pain in her lower back. Her teeth bit into the plastic casing of the pen-flash, nearly breaking it.

She kept at it, over and over with her hands and feet, losing all track of how far she had descended. Her feet and shoulder sockets began to ache, then screamed in silent protest at the strain placed upon them.

She experimented a few times, allowing herself to slide along under the momentum of her weight, sighing in relief at the ebbing of the pain in her back, shoulders and legs. When she began to pick up speed, she caught herself, came to a complete halt, then started the entire laborious process over again.

After the fourth moving rest stop, Mildred realized she was having difficulty slowing her descent. The incline of the chute had sharpened. She slapped at the sides of the duct, spreading her legs, pushing with her feet to stop herself, but the braking effect was marginal. She couldn't get a grip, and her body picked up speed. Then she was sliding out of control, diving headfirst down the black duct. She saw nothing below her but thick darkness.

She couldn't repress a cry of fright and the pen-flash fell from her mouth. It bounced from all four walls of the duct, the light jumping crazily, like a wild comet following a mad trajectory through the black gulfs of outer space.

The duct walls vanished beneath her gloved hands. Mildred clawed for a handhold, then she was diving headlong into a sepia sea. She didn't dive very long. A shattering crash numbed her body from the crown of her head to the tips of her toes. The darkness momentarily turned the color of blood. She was dimly aware that she was tumbling head over heels.

By the time her thrashing tumble ended, the world was spinning, tilting to and fro, and she wasn't sure if she was sitting up, lying down or standing on her head. She wasn't at all positive that she was alive.

When Mildred's senses finally regained control of themselves, she found she had landed against a soft heap of something and was in a half-prone, half-sitting position. Her head, her shoulders, her neck and especially her back, all ached abominably. She tasted blood sliding warmly from a laceration on her forehead, down her face and over her lips. Her hands smarted from the impact on whatever she had landed upon. The air was heavy and cloying, and she sneezed, sputtered and coughed.

Groaning, wanting to weep, she pushed herself away from the yielding heap and wobbled to her feet. Amazingly, despite the waves of pain washing over her, nothing seemed broken. As she stood, she felt a slight sinking sensation, as though her footing wasn't solid. She couldn't see what lay beneath her. The darkness was completely impenetratable. Patting herself down, she made sure all her personal equipment was where it was supposed to be.

She took a step forward, and something gritted beneath her boots with a crunch that sounded unnaturally loud. She sneezed, and that sounded frighteningly loud, too. Taking off a glove, Mildred reached down and felt

powdery granules, finer than sand, all around her. She
was in the central dustbin, the detritus dump of the Anthill. Though the motes irritated her nose and eyes, they
had cushioned her fall and probably saved her life.

Walking through the dust was difficult, like striding
through snow. She had to lift her feet clear of the layer of
grit and place them down carefully, or else a cloud of dust
would mushroom up and send her into a paroxysm of
coughing and sneezing.

Dabbing at the flow of blood from her forehead with
a sleeve, Mildred wetted a forefinger and tested the air
currents. She detected a faint movement from her left and
began a high-stepping shamble in that direction. She
groped through the blackness, both arms extended so she
could touch any hidden obstacles.

After a time she became aware of a peculiar click-clack
noise. It took her a moment to attribute it to the wooden
beads in the plaits of her hair. Normally a small, almost
unnoticed sound, the silence of her surroundings was so
complete that any noise seemed like a band striking up a
fanfare. She consciously tried to quiet her ragged
breathing.

Then, far away, Mildred saw a tiny white spark of
light. It was very distant, but she headed for it, the crunch
of her footfalls sending up ghostly, reverberating echoes.

Long before she thought she had come anywhere near
the source of light, she stumbled and saw the spark almost at her feet. It was the pen-flash, lying half-buried
in the acres of dust.

Gratefully Mildred picked it up and fanned the light
around. As she had expected, she saw nothing but gloom
and dust. She continued sifting her way through the
powder toward the air current. She walked only for a

short time before she felt the flow of air growing stronger. She stopped, right before she walked into a black metal wall. By shining the penlight around and groping with her free hand, she found a metal bracket in a flattened U shape, like a ladder rung. There were several more leading up the face of the wall, beyond the illumination range of her light.

Mildred swung onto the rungs and began to climb, ignoring the fires of pain the effort ignited all over her body. She estimated she had climbed less than twenty feet before the rungs ended at a narrow ledge, maybe two feet wide. She stepped out onto it, flattening her back against the wall, digging the fingers of her free hand into the uneven metal surface. She edged out in the direction of the air current. Affixed to the floor of the ledge, in regularly spaced intervals, were threaded strips of rubber. These helped her gain traction as the ledge angled upward.

The ledge made a sharp turn to the left after a few dozen steps, and its pitch descended steeply. Putting the pen-flash into her mouth, she crabwalked along it, hands gripping the wall tightly. Mildred wondered how deep beneath the mountain she was, and realized she couldn't hazard even an uneducated guess.

The ledge suddenly widened, opened and led out to a metal railed apron, and she realized with a leap of relief that she had been traversing some sort of maintenance walkway. There was still no sign of anything approximating a door. As she pushed against a wall, something brushed the top of her head.

Craning her neck to look up, she saw a length of heavy, rust-flaked chain, with a handle attached. She couldn't see what it was anchored to, but she grabbed the handle

and tugged gingerly. Nothing happened, so, using both
hands, she pulled harder, putting all her weight into it.

Mildred's effort was rewarded by a loud, shuddery
creaking, as of long-disused gears or pivots struggling to
turn. Feeble light suddenly appeared, a thread-thin out-
line tracing a tall rectangular shape in the wall before her.
Hand over hand, she hauled on the chain, and a wide,
flat slab broke away from the wall with a shower of grit
and rust. Grinding, screeching noises accompanied the
lowering of the slab as it slowly fell outward. Blinking
through the rust flakes swirling around her face, Mildred
saw the slab was like the drawbridge of a medieval cas-
tle, only this one was made of thick sheets of welded and
riveted iron.

With a shriek of metal clashing against metal, the slab
stopped moving, jamming at a forty-five-degree angle.
No amount of pulling, hauling or hanging on the chain
would budge it further.

The surface of the slab was by no means smooth or
featureless, so Mildred half crawled, half climbed up it.
Judging by the oxidized streaks, she was pretty sure it was
a very old accessway, a maintenance hatch to the detritus dump. It probably hadn't been opened in nigh on to
a century, perhaps considerably longer.

She struggled to the lip of the slab, grasping the edge
and carefully pulling herself to eye level to get a quick
recce of her surroundings. There was very little to see.
Mildred looked out into a small enclosed space, not much
more than a module with convex-curved walls. It was
bare, everything coated with a thin patina of dust that
had seeped out of the dump over the decades. So much
dust floated in the still air that the light from a ceiling
fixture was only a faint yellow blob. A spiral staircase

stretched up from the floor to a dark opening. The small room appeared to have been unoccupied for a long, long time.

Mildred pulled herself up, squirmed over, hung by her hands and dropped to the floor. She landed easily, dust puffing up from beneath her boots, but shivers of pain stabbed through her. But at least the room wasn't cold. In fact, it felt close to normal air temperature. That would explain why the module appeared to be in disuse. The cryonically altered people of the Anthill would find it very uncomfortable.

She considered staying where she was long enough to repair the transceiver, but the dust irritated her eyes and clogged her nostrils. She could even taste it. Without much surprise she saw that her clothing was completely filmed by gray powder, as though she had been dipped in ashes. She assumed her face was the same color.

At the foot of the staircase, Mildred peered upward. She saw nothing but a dim light, so she went up the steps, treading quietly and cautiously. The staircase curved up and around, like a corkscrew. There was a faint luminosity above, and it grew brighter the farther up the staircase she climbed.

She was pleasantly surprised when the last step brought her to a door with an ordinary, standard-issue, commonplace doorknob. Before turning it, she drew the ZKR, emptied it of spent cartridges and plugged fresh rounds into the cylinder. Thumbing back the hammer, she crooked her finger around the trigger, turned the knob and inched the door open. After peering and listening for several seconds, she opened the door wide enough to enter a corridor.

The walls were white and dingy and not composed of the vanadium alloy. The floor looked like dirty linoleum, with a black-and-white-checked pattern. This level was obviously part of the original floor plan, constructed well before skydark. Though the air was crisp, with a hint of a chill, it wasn't the Arctic atmosphere of the upper levels.

There was a sign on the wall, written in faded red letters, reading Know Your Emergency Exits! An arrow pointed to Mildred's right, so she followed it. The corridor curved toward a distant set of double doors that looked like an elevator stand, so she quickened her pace. As she passed a door, she heard a sharp, hissing sound, and she whirled.

A very tall naked figure stood framed in the door. She couldn't tell the sex of the figure, and her heart gave a great lurch. The body was gaunt and stripped of all fatty tissue. The texture of the pale skin suggested a pattern of scales, as if the figure had been spawned under conditions that were abnormal, even unhuman.

There was almost nothing human at all about the head above the tendon-wrapped neck. A coxcomb of thin blue-black hair twisted up from a low, sloping forehead. Eyes that were huge—red pupilless disks—blazed out of a narrow-chinned face. The nose barely qualified as a sharpened nare, and the lipless slit of the mouth gaped open, revealing spittle-wet, toothless gums.

Mildred immediately had the bore of her ZKR trained on the low forehead, when, in a high-pitched, squawky voice, the figure exclaimed, ''Took you long enough, didn't it! Where's my goddamn brains?''

Chapter Twenty-Seven

The inferno of Helskel smeared the dark sky with a glow that could be seen for miles. Even after the dune buggy had dipped down into a gulley, the orange stain could still be seen, like the aurora borealis.

Jak, standing and holding on to the roll bar, had been checking their backtrack. "Whole ville going up."

"What about pursuit?" asked J.B., crouched behind the wheel.

"No sign, yet. Too busy fighting fire."

J.B. switched on the headlights. The dune buggy had been running without headlights for the past hour, relying on the tracker instincts and night vision of Jak to find and follow the AMAC's trail.

Doc, Krysty and Fleur were still crammed shoulder to shoulder in the back seat. Krysty's head rested on Doc's shoulder in a sleep so deep it was almost a coma. The jarring and jouncing of the wag over the rutted, uneven ground had failed to stir her.

J.B. figured to follow the AMAC's tire tracks to a certain point, then cut over in the general direction of the cave. Trouble was, he wasn't sure how to find that certain point.

Worries swirled through his mind like a tornado. Though he hadn't seen one, the AMAC could be outfitted with a shortwave comm unit, and Hellstrom could have already been apprised of their escape. The closer they rolled to Mount Rushmore, the greater the odds of rolling into an ambush.

He wasn't sure if they could find the cave in the darkness, since he had only glimpsed its general location on Hellstrom's hand-drawn map. Fleur had never been allowed to visit the pickup point. According to her, it was a trip Hellstrom always reserved for himself and a couple of sec men. The closest she had been to the cave was the mouth of a canyon that led to it.

Consulting his chron, then the position of the stars and the moon overhead, he judged they had about seven hours of sheltering darkness left to them, seven hours to navigate ravines, hills and dry creek beds to locate a cave none of them had ever seen. Hell, they only had the word of a maniac the place even existed.

The dune buggy raced across the rugged terrain, and they made good time, much better time than the AMAC during their initial trip into the area.

Around midnight, J.B. stopped the vehicle briefly so everyone could stretch their legs and drink from the canteens they'd taken from a room off the armory. Krysty slept on in the back seat. Only Fleur thought her near-comatose state was unusual. The wag's fuel tank was half drained, so Jak refilled it from one of the gas cans. After half an hour they were underway again, Doc trading places with Jak in the shotgun seat.

They rode far into the night until they recognized the mouth of the valley that had been the site of their battle with the Lakota. It was about an eighth of a mile away. J.B. quickly switched off the headlights and silenced the engine. Half to himself, he said, "If Hellstrom's anywhere about, that's where he's laying."

Doc nodded. "I concur. He appears to be a creature of habit, and probably intends to camp in familiar surroundings, at least until morning. I suggest we reverse our course."

Jak leaned forward, his white hair shining like a tangle of silver threads in the moonlight. "Need recce, find out if there, if know we escaped."

J.B. agreed with the albino teenager. There was a chance Hellstrom and his party might be watching for them.

Getting out of the dune buggy, J.B. said softly, "We'll take a stroll in that direction. Doc, stay here with Krysty and Fleur. If you hear any shooting, and when you think you've waited long enough, haul ass out of here. Stay on triple red. Jak, since it was your idea, you can lead the way."

The two men walked toward the mouth of the valley but angled their path toward one sloping wall of the arroyo. The moon dropped a ghostly light on the rocky, brush-studded ground. Wind brought the faraway howl of a wolf, and the answering yelp of a coyote. At least, J.B. hoped it was a wolf and a coyote.

They clambered up the side of the valley wall and crept along its crest for a quarter of a mile. Then they lay forward beneath a small bush, propped on elbows, their blasters cocked and ready.

J.B. and Jak saw the AMAC, parked near the scene of the fight with the Sioux. There were no security lights blazing, and no sign of movement anywhere around the big armored wag. Straining their ears, they listened for any unusual sounds.

They heard a whispered conference somewhere below them, several men talking in hushed tones. Jak put his mouth close to J.B.'s ear and breathed, "Scouts. Spotted our headlights. Coming from a recce, reporting to sec boss. Don't know it's us."

J.B. had no reason to question what Jak had said. The youth's hearing was exceptionally, enviably sharp, and one question was answered, at least. Hellstrom wasn't aware of their escape from Helskel. The Armorer heard a number of feet scurrying alongside the bank of the arroyo. A patrol was moving out to investigate the mysterious lights.

A figure appeared on the crest of the slope, about twenty yards from their position. The shaven-headed sec man walked cautiously, and he was followed by another.

J.B. felt Jak tense beside him, but they remained motionless as the men approached. The first figure was no more than six feet away, boots crunching pebbles. J.B. saw him glance casually at their bush, glance away, then look back. As far as he could see, the man's expression didn't change.

The deep-throated boom of Jak's Colt Python came without warning, snatching a startled curse out of J.B. The bullet knocked the sec man backward. Before he hit the ground, the Colt hammer fell again and killed the second man. Yells and screaming curses sounded from the valley floor, and feet pounded on turf.

"Damn it all!" J.B. spit in disgust.

He got to his knees and fired the Uzi into the valley, not aiming, just hosing the shots. Bedlam broke loose. Autorifles and machine pistols cracked and stuttered, echoing in the valley, spitting slugs into the rim of the arroyo. The sec men below were shooting blind, but bullets tore into the ground near Jak and J.B.'s position all the same.

Pulling his companion's arm, J.B. urged him to his feet. The two men bent low and ran, sliding down the bank, trying to keep to the shadows.

"Think recognized us?" Jak panted.

"Who gives a shit?" J.B. retorted angrily. "They know somebody is around now. Why'd you blast the bastard?"

"Would have stepped on head, seen anyhow."

Not bothering to argue, J.B. tried to put more speed into his pumping legs. The shooting was dying down, and he heard shouted orders coming faintly on the wind. The voice was Hellstrom's. Then all was quiet.

They made it back to the dune buggy. Doc was at the wheel, the engine idling. When he spotted their figures rushing forward, he aimed the Le Mat over the windshield, then breathed an audible sigh of relief when he recognized them. Jak climbed in the back, squeezing next to the still-sleeping Krysty.

"Move over, Doc," J.B. said, elbowing the man into the passenger seat.

"Was it the patriarch you saw?" Fleur asked, a strange mixture of eagerness and anger in her voice.

"Does it matter?" J.B. replied, putting the buggy into gear and turning it northeast. He didn't switch on the lights.

Fleur sat back in the seat and stared at an invisible point beyond the windshield.

Steering the vehicle around a rock slide, J.B. said, "Got my bearings at least. The cave is in this direction."

For several miles the trail sloped gently upward into the Black Hills, and it became necessary to turn on the headlights. The dune buggy carried them swiftly up, then down into twisting ravines. It took more than an hour to navigate the wag through and around obstacles that would have given even the Land Rover a great deal of difficulty.

The sun slowly rose behind them, tinting the sagebrush and stands of gama grass a russet red. J.B. kept pushing on, even as they shivered in the predawn chill. As the sun inched higher, the heat rose in the rocky gorges and gullies around them.

According to the Armorer's chron, it was exactly six o'clock when the narrow ravine they traveled opened into a canyon. Sheer walls rose to nearly a hundred feet on either side, and they were grooved with deep horizontal lines, here and there forming ledges where the softer layers of strata had been eroded away.

The canyon floor was less than two hundred feet wide, and it wended off to the right, to a cave entrance. The opening was a lopsided triangle, twenty or so feet tall, fifty in width. Boulders were strewn all around, except for an unnaturally flat clearing immediately in front of the yawning black cleft carved into the canyon wall. It was about four hundred yards away.

Carefully J.B. steered the dune buggy close to the wall, beneath an overhanging ledge and behind an outcropping. It would be shielded from Hellstrom's sight if he came down the canyon, and from any eyes inside the cave. The stony floor was too hard to take their tire treads, so they couldn't be tracked that way.

After turning off the engine, J.B. turned to Fleur. "Is the front way the only way in?"

She shrugged. "As far as I know."

Krysty was awake now, dragging a hand over her eyes. "You sure this is the place, J.B.?"

"Hell, no, I'm not sure of anything," he replied gruffly. "But its location fits the general coordinates we saw, and unless somebody can prove otherwise, I'm going to assume this is the right place. Anybody got an objection?"

No one did. Disembarking, J.B. scanned their surroundings. Because Hellstrom had mentioned beetles guarding the place, a frontal penetration of the cave was out of the question. He saw a rough but scalable natural staircase curving up thirty or forty feet from the canyon floor and swerving over and down to a point directly beside the cave entrance. After a brief discussion, they decided to climb it.

As they headed up, J.B. was struck by the brooding majesty of the place; he could almost understand why the Indians believed a supernatural power guarded the Black Hills. The canyon was totally silent, the only sounds the grating of their feet on rock, their labored breathing and the occasional murmured word. The towering rampart walls seemed subtly charged with menace. Something eerie and uncanny existed here.

They had scaled perhaps half of the staircase's length, cautiously approaching a projecting granite slab they would have to squirm around, when Jak tapped J.B.'s shoulder.

The youth was peering intently at the canyon's opposite wall. "Hear something," he whispered.

"Like what?" J.B. whispered back.

A splitting crack shattered the silence, and a bullet sang past J.B.'s ear, bouncing off the cliff face behind him.

"Like that," Jak said calmly.

Chapter Twenty-Eight

Ryan could only judge the direction of the small elevator by the rising and falling sensation in the pit of his stomach.

First it descended, then smoothly switched to travel along a horizontal plane. Doug maintained a smug smile throughout, as if he expected Ryan to be impressed to the point of awe. The one-eyed man kept his face impassive, once sighing with impatience.

"Don't try anything, Cawdor," Doug warned. He touched his mastoid bone behind his right ear, then a spot on the base of his throat. "I'm wired for sound. Got a communic implanted in me. Mess with me and I'll have an armed squad waiting to blow your head off."

"Why did you let something like that be sewn up inside of you?"

Doug frowned, as if he had never contemplated the question before. "So I can be contacted when the Commander needs me. Why else?"

"Yeah, right," Ryan muttered. "Why else."

The doors slid open on yet another stretch of alloy-paneled corridor. The Commander was there to meet them. He greeted Ryan with a bleak smile that didn't indicate friendliness. He looked at the man's gray eyes and thought again of ice. There was no malice in them, but nothing else either. The Commander had gone beyond emotions; either they were frozen out of him, or he had never had them. There was no human warmth about him, probably not even in his blood.

In the brighter light of the corridor, Ryan saw faint pink lines on the smooth-skinned face that looked like old surgical scars.

"Continue the search for Mr. Cawdor's companion," the Commander ordered. "She somehow escaped the city. Your identification badge was found attached to a firearm. A check on the model, make and serial number showed it was one traded to Helskel over a year ago. So far, the woman has misled the search teams. They're very annoyed about it, so go and take charge of the operation."

Doug hesitated. "Sir, I shouldn't leave you alone with this renegade."

The Commander draped a paternal arm around Ryan's shoulders. The arm felt like a beam of steel. "Nonsense. We're going to have a talk, that's all, and your presence will inhibit our discussions. Be off with you now."

Doug scowled at Ryan, then turned toward the elevator. The Commander led Ryan down the corridor.

"Do you know who I am?" he asked in a conspiratorial whisper.

"The Commander."

"Short for commander in chief. A euphemism for President."

Ryan managed to keep his surprise from showing on his face. "President of what?"

Gesturing to the corridor, the man said, "This. The United States. You went through Washington and visited me in the Oval Office, didn't you?"

Ryan knew a bit about predark history, and this man didn't resemble pictures he had seen of the presidents whose terms preceded the nukecaust.

The arm tightened around Ryan's shoulders, and his shoulder wound screamed in pain. "Didn't you?"

"Yeah," Ryan said quickly. "When were you elected?"

The arm relaxed. "I wasn't elected. It was an office I assumed after the chain of command had been broken. This complex became the seat of government. It wasn't easy, making this place the nerve center of the country. But careful design, meticulous attention to detail and good, sound American craftsmanship paid off."

Nodding in agreement, Ryan asked, "How large is the complex?"

"The tunnels run all through the mountain, leading down beneath it. We have fifteen levels aboveground. I have lived here for—" the Commander frowned slightly, as though he were dredging his memory "—for many years. I still find it inspiring."

"An installation this size must require a lot of care, a lot of maintenance to keep it in operating condition."

"Oh, quite. The problems are many, and we devote a great deal of time to repair and improvement. But the topic is far too technical to go into now."

"Why did you retreat here in the first place?"

"I did not 'retreat,' young man. My reasons aren't open for discussion at present."

The Commander turned toward a doorway, still leading Ryan. The door slid aside at their approach. The room was very large, alloy-plated and was obviously a laboratory. It was staffed by men wearing white smocks, reading clipboards, checking gauges and thermometers.

Inside glass cases and fluid-filled jars were human internal organs: floating livers, pumping hearts, eyeballs, loops of intestines, and in one large cubicle was the naked body of a man. A metal framework extended from where the right arm should have been.

Ryan was both repulsed and fascinated. In glass-paneled cabinets were arms and legs, hands and feet and torsos, wires extending from the blood-rimmed stumps of necks, arms and thighs.

"Before your trade agreement with Helskel," Ryan ventured, "how did you acquire the organs and body parts you needed?"

"We managed to stockpile quite a number, primarily from personnel in nonessential positions. Spouses and children of staff members provided us with what we needed, at least for several decades. We began to deplete our supply over the last few years."

If Ryan's mouth hadn't been so dry, he would have spit. "Was it worth it, just so you could exist in this frozen prison?"

The Commander waved a hand around the room. "Hardly a prison, Mr. Cawdor. This installation is my gift to the country of my birth. It is devoted to bestowing order upon chaos. You have no idea how many years I have worked toward this. It's been a long life, a full life, a rewarding life."

Nauseated and angry, Ryan said, "You're a cyborg, a droid that never grows old."

"Not precisely," the Commander replied. "I have a new heart—my third—a few joints are prosthetic replacements, my face has undergone surgery to replace radiation-ravaged flesh, but I'm hardly a cyborg. Nor am I immortal."

"But if you can replace every body part that wears out—"

"We can't replace the brain, Mr. Cawdor, and liver transplants are sometimes successful and sometimes aren't. As you pointed out, the low temperature we must live in has definite drawbacks. We haven't conquered every vagary that preys on organic matter, though we've made a great leap in that direction."

As they progressed deeper into the laboratory, they passed more dismembered bodies in glass cabinets, then came to another door that opened onto a long, bare corridor. Their footsteps rang hollowly on the alloy-sheathed floor, and the lights were dim. They passed several doors.

"I don't come here often," the Commander said. "It tends to depress me."

They stepped through a tall, narrow doorway at the end of the corridor, and Ryan saw why the man didn't care to visit here. The cold was overwhelming, like a physical assault. It bit at his nostrils, his lips, his eyes, anywhere there was moisture. He raised the fur collar of his coat and lifted his scarf over his nose and mouth to protect them from the numbing cold. His eyeballs ached, and he was forced to take short, shallow breaths, worried the air would freeze his lungs.

The gloomy room was a crypt, where the living dead were entombed, frozen in time. There were over a hundred of them. They stood in orderly rows, each one upright inside a transparent armaglass canister, arms crossed sedately over their chests. With a twinge of surprise, Ryan noticed that not all of the encased people were men. There were a few women mixed in, mostly young. They wore only a simple drapery, and their bodies had the appearance of pale turquoise, not only in color but substance. The eyes were wide open and they seemed to stare, all one-hundred-plus pairs of them, straight into Ryan's mind.

"Who are they?" he asked. His teeth were chattering so violently, he was surprised his words were comprehensible.

Even the Commander seemed affected by the deep cold, tucking his hands into his pockets and slightly hunching his shoulders. "My people, the ones who contracted incurable diseases or went mad, or who refused to participate in the cybernetic implant program. They are scientists, engineers, military officers, doctors."

"This is a punishment, a prison?"

"No, only a rest stop. They are in cryogenic stasis and require no air, no food, no interaction with others. I doubt they even dream. But, as you can see, we take care of our own."

Ryan now understood what Doug had meant about over a hundred Anthill personnel being inactive. "Why not just shoot them and be done with it?"

"They have valuable skills, important information, abilities crucial to our survival. They held key supervisory and design positions during the construction of our complex and have much knowledge that we can draw upon."

"When you need to ask them something, you thaw them out long enough to ask a question, then refreeze them."

"Yes."

"I think they'd be better off dead."

The Commander nodded sadly. "Many of them think the same thing."

They went back along the corridor, and it took Ryan a long while to stop shivering. His teeth were still chattering intermittently when they stopped before a door. The Commander stepped aside, inclined his head in a short bow and waved one hand. Ryan walked across the threshold and was dazzled by bright light reflecting from plate glass and chromium fixtures.

They were in a long hexagonal room. The left wall was composed of sheets of frosty glass. Ryan glanced through one, down into a room below. It took his mind a moment to identify what his eye was seeing, and when it did, he instinctively recoiled. His hand grabbed at his empty holster. If he had been a wolf, he would have snarled and tucked his tail under his belly.

Ryan felt a great fear welling up within him, but not a natural, rational survival mechanism type of fear. It was a mindless, xenophobic cringing from a sight that was terrifyingly alien.

Below him, sloshing and floating in metal vats filled with a semiliquid gel were figures of horror. One resembled a young boy, about Dean's age. Judging by his lack of ears and the series of suction pads on the fingers, Ryan knew he was a stickie. However, he was malformed beyond the limits of a nightmare. He seemed to have neither joints nor muscles, and his flailing arms terminated in tentacles that suggested an octopus. The tentacles were disproportionate, far too short for his size, and the lower half of the stickie was a quaking, quivering mass of fatty tissue covered with undulating suction cups. The sight made him feel physically ill, bile working its way up his throat. He tried to back away, but the Commander put a hand against his back to keep him in place.

"Nothing to fear, Mr. Cawdor." The gray-eyed man's quiet voice purred with amusement. "They can't see you. They're kept in a constant state of sedation."

There were other figures in other vats, anthropomorphic, bloated bulks that bore no true resemblance to humanity. In one, a froglike head reared from the gelid contents. There were breathing slits at the sides of the head, and an inhumanly wide mouth was creased in a constant half-smile. Its round eyes were dull and fathomless.

Another gel-filled tank held a human figure, or the exact likeness of one. But the face was covered with coarsely matted hair, huge apish nostrils and snapping black eyes. It didn't move, but gazed up at the ceiling, as though lost in thought. There were many more, some so nauseating he couldn't bear to even glance at them.

"Genetic engineering is a program we began over a century ago," the Commander said quietly. "Have you ever heard of pantropic science?"

Ryan shook his head, too sickened to speak.

"Pantropy is a form of bioengineering, primarily theoretical, to reproduce a strain of humanity designed to live in different environments. After the bombs fell, the science took on a new meaning. It was no longer theoretical or impractical. The challenge was to adapt and modify humanity to survive in the new environment shaped by the holocaust. We experimented with human and animal subjects to create entities that could thrive in any physical condition, immune to radiation and other adverse environmental factors."

"You're making muties."

"Muties? You mean mutants, I take it. In a way you're correct. The subjects you see below were born with mutated characteristics. They were brought here and exposed to a mutagenic biochemical process in an effort to direct and control their altered DNA. You see, it makes little difference whether we get good raw material to start with. Let them be mutants or normals, we'll have our successes in the end.''

Not bothering to hide his disgust, Ryan turned to face the Commander. ''Why show me this?''

The Commander fixed his icy gaze on Ryan. ''To prove to you beyond a shadow of a doubt that your perverted, primitive kingdom of Helskel cannot hope to trick us, cannot hope to break our trade agreement and cannot hope to overcome us. We hold all of the power in this new world. Helskel exists only at our sufferance, at our whims. We can create new life. Helskel can only take lives.''

''Yet you rely on that perverted kingdom to supply you with human organs,'' Ryan snapped. ''Without Helskel, you probably would have died long ago, gone the way of all the other predark power-mad tyrants.''

Not responding to the comment, the Commander asked, ''What is the population of Helskel?''

''I don't know.''

''How high are you placed in its hierarchy?''

''I'm not placed at all. I'm here against my will. Hellstrom is holding friends of mine hostage. I don't want to be here any more than you want me to be here.''

''I don't mind your visit, Mr. Cawdor, despite the damage and disruption you have caused. A minor crisis, easily contained, can sometimes be stimulating. Did Lars Hellstrom send you to assassinate me?''

"Not exactly." Ryan sighed. "Though after meeting you and seeing this place, I don't find it such a bad idea. You've outlived your time."

The Commander regarded him blankly, then shook his head. "How can I possibly make you understand? You, a landless, lawless renegade."

Ryan looked at him keenly. "As far as I know, a renegade is someone who betrays a cause or a faith or a group of people who trusted him. From what I've been told, you held a high position of trust in the predark government. You and a few others—and not just your generation, either—are responsible for a war that destroyed most of the world and most of its population. You prey on your people in this installation, refusing to grant them a dignified death. I don't think I'm the renegade here."

The Commander didn't react, didn't reply, didn't respond. He pointed to a door at the end of the hexagonal room, and Ryan moved on. The door slid open on a gangway that bridged a twenty-foot gap of empty darkness. At the end of the gangway was a transverse corridor running to the left and right, as far as Ryan could see in both directions. Overhead lights shed a cold glare over the vanadium-sheathed flooring and walls.

The inward wall was pierced by an elevator stand, and the Commander directed him toward it. They got into the nearest lift and it propelled them smoothly upward, but only for a short distance. It stopped, and the door panel opened onto a vast dome-shaped chamber.

The Commander led him into it, past workers manning computer consoles, consulting printouts, all of them looking very industrious and intent. The room was crammed with the most advanced electronic instruments and equipment that Ryan had ever seen. Circuits hummed, and console and panel lights blinked. A bank of closed-circuit monitor screens ran the length of one wall. Most of them were dark, and as they drew closer to them, Ryan saw that each set bore a label that identified redoubts and their locations. With a start, he realized that though most of the screens were dark, the Anthill had at one time been plugged into all of the redoubts all over the continental United States. There were only a couple of screens that displayed images—dim, flickering black-and-white scenes of empty rooms and corridors.

"This complex was intended to be the nexus point of the Totality Concept," the Commander said, a faint hint of pride in his voice. "All the different spin-off projects like Whisper, Cerberus and even Chronos were to be centralized here. The departments were all to be controlled from here, from this colony."

His voice dropped to a whisper as he added, almost to himself, "Of course, the situation changed."

Turning to look at Ryan, he asked, "You have no idea what I'm talking about, do you, Mr. Cawdor?"

Ryan knew exactly what he was referring to, but he figured his best tactic was to play dumb. "Not a word."

"A pity. You would be exceptionally impressed by the elaborate technological marvels we managed to achieve during the last few decades of the twentieth century. But you don't have a frame of reference to understand even a fraction of what you're seeing."

As they walked farther into the room, Ryan saw a six-sided chamber, the armaglass walls tinted a greenish blue. The chamber was huge, the biggest mat-trans gateway he had ever seen. It looked large enough to accommodate a herd of mutie buffalo.

As they drew closer to it, Ryan saw a freestanding control console, facing the gateway's massive door. He managed to stroll near it, his eye flicking over the dials and buttons studding its surface. A small vid screen was placed directly in its center and it displayed the interior of a cave, looking out toward an irregularly shaped entrance. Beyond the opening was rock-littered ground. Because the image was in black-and-white, Ryan couldn't tell the time of day. However, since the illumination was so dim, he assumed it was moonlight, and probably sometime after midnight, maybe close to dawn.

A keyboard was attached to the edge of the console, and certain keys bore certain symbols. One key was inscribed with a triangle cut by three straight lines. It was the same symbol they had seen in the installation back in Dulce.

The Commander beckoned to him. "This way, Mr. Cawdor. The tour has come to an end."

Ryan was led across the room to a door. A red button was on the frame, and the Commander pushed it. The door hissed open, and the man waved Ryan in. They stood together in a very small elevator as the door closed behind them. The lift fell very quietly, and for only a short distance.

The door opened, and they stepped out between a pair of bookcases and into the "Oval office." The Commander didn't say a word. He went to his desk and sat down, staring at his prisoner with detachment. Ryan stood in front of the desk, staring back.

"Have you nothing to say, Mr. Cawdor?"

"What would you like me to say?"

"That you are impressed, intimidated even. That you have met your master."

"Is that what you are?"

"I am, but I'm interested in hearing you say it."

"Why? Will that save my life?"

The Commander shrugged. "I am afraid not. I toyed with the notion of simply releasing you, so you could carry the tale of your experiences back to Helskel, but I doubt Hellstrom would believe you. Once we locate your companion, she will fill that function adequately. No, I believe I will have you remain here with us."

"As a subject for your genetics experiments?"

"Perhaps."

"Or as an organ donor?"

"Again, perhaps."

"Or someone you can turn into a cyborg? Another one of your tools?"

"What else is man but a tool?" the Commander asked. "He has no other value. Humanity is self-destructive, suffering from an anarchy of mind and spirit. Free of the moral deterioration that paves the road to decadence, can you imagine the marvels humanity could accomplish?"

"I've seen some of your marvels," Ryan said grimly. "Shiny toys and freak shows."

The Commander affected not to have heard him. "In another century, maybe less, this world will cease to be a planet of strife and disorder, wallowing in bloodshed. It will be secure."

"The security of the grave," Ryan replied with bitterness. "A century ago you and your kind screwed humanity and left us to pick up the pieces." As he spoke, his right hand tugged at the hanging end of his scarf.

"The nuclear holocaust was actually a blessing," the Commander continued. "You have no idea of what it was like a century ago. The world before the holocaust was totally out of control, populations of useless people were expanding, chaos overwhelmed all the old political systems.''

Ryan slowly wound the slack of the scarf around his hand. "So you don't care about all the suffering, the horrors, the destruction. It was best for the world to be destroyed, especially since *you* survived it."

"Visionaries are needed. And there are things far beyond your understanding. The seeds planted a long time before are getting ready to take hold of the earth, getting ready for a new future."

"Hellstrom says that Charlie Manson's vision of the future was very much like this one. Like your own. How can you feel superior when you share your philosophy with a criminal maniac?"

The Commander's eyes were devoid of any emotional reaction to Ryan's question. He said, "The old world was ending anyway. It couldn't have continued."

Ryan slid the scarf across the back of his neck. The weighted end nestled just below his collarbone. He was ready, and he waited for his chance.

"Now, every action that affects the course of humanity will be dictated by us. Now, in a hundred years or less all the rules of the world will be *my* rules."

The Commander lifted his face and his eyes bored into Ryan's own. "A world," he continued smoothly, "you will never see. I am done being your host."

He reached across the desk toward a row of inset buttons. Ryan gave the scarf a jerk and whiplashed it across the intervening yards between him and the Commander. He had accurately gauged the length he would need. The weighted end of the scarf struck against the man's right temple with a loud cracking of bone, spinning him away from the buttons and hurling him heavily to the floor.

Ryan was around the desk before the body had settled, rewinding the scarf around his hand. The Commander lay on his left side on the carpet, one arm beneath him. An ugly, blood-oozing indentation interrupted the unlined smoothness of his forehead. He lay as Ryan had seen many corpses lie—boneless, mouth partly open, eyes wide and glazing over, an expression of shock frozen on his face.

Surveying the office in a sweeping, searching glance, Ryan saw his blasters, his grens and ammo clips stacked in a corner behind the desk. He snorted and muttered, "Stupes."

The arrogance of power never failed to astonish him. Those who wielded control always seemed to lose their objectivity, rigidly believing that their authority could never be challenged. They grew blind to other possibilities, to random factors, to wild cards. The Commander and Lars Hellstrom were so alike it was nearly comical. Or sickening.

Stepping over the body, he grabbed the Walther MPL, jammed a new clip into the SIG-Sauer and attached the grens to the combat harness he still wore beneath his coat. Jacking a round into the pistol, he decided to put a bullet into the Commander's ear just to make certain. Though the man had said they couldn't transplant the brain, it was remotely possible they could resuscitate him and repair a fractured skull.

He bent over, inserting the end of the baffle silencer into the man's ear. Over a century had passed since the crazy bastard should have been welcomed by Father

Death, but it was better late than never to force him to accept the invitation.

Just as Ryan's finger tightened on the trigger, the Commander moved. He convulsed beneath him, his hand streaking up, closing tightly around the barrel of the SIG-Sauer and yanking it to one side. Ryan tried to wrest it away, but it was like wrestling with an iron vise.

The Commander's expression was calm, almost serene, his icy eyes placid. "Killing me will serve little purpose. My death will not affect this place. The work will go on."

For an instant Ryan believed him, and he almost stopped trying to free the blaster from the man's grasp. Then a boiling anger came fountaining up out of him, and he erupted in a flaming, murderous fury.

His left fist smashed with all his weight behind it into the pale, unlined face below him. The head bounced against the floor, the nose flattening, blood splattering bright against the white skin. He kicked him in the groin, and as the Commander curled around his foot, he loosened his grip on the blaster.

Ryan snatched the pistol away, slashed sideways at the groping hand with the barrel, stooped over and shot the Commander through the forehead.

The man shivered, spasmed and went limp, hands dropping lifelessly to the carpet. The fingers scrabbled at the nap for a moment, then froze, curved like talons.

Breathing hard, Ryan stepped away from the corpse. His lips were dry and his face was damp. When he wiped away crimson droplets on the baffle silencer, he saw his hand was trembling.

He rubbed a drop of the Commander's blood between thumb and forefinger. It wasn't hot, warm or even tepid. Ryan grinned savagely and said, "Doesn't that just figure."

From the corner of his eye, he caught a shifting movement behind him. He whirled, the blaster leading the way. One of the tall double doors was opening, pushed from the outside.

Chapter Twenty-Nine

Mildred cocked her pistol and her head at the same time. "What?"

The lean, scaled figure before her capered impatiently, shifting from one foot to the other. "My brains, you were supposed to bring me my brains."

"I don't have your brains," Mildred said, not able to repress a smile despite the situation. "Don't you have any of your own?"

The figure blinked its huge eyes at her owlishly. "If I did, I wouldn't be waiting for you to bring them to me, now, would I?"

Nerves on edge, Mildred laughed shortly. "Logical answer. What kind of brains do you need?"

One of the bony shoulders heaved in a half shrug. "Yours will do. Yes, as a matter of fact, a woman's brain is preferable. It will balance out my own."

"What will you do with it if I give it to you?"

"Pop it out, of course, cook it over the fire in its own blood and juices. Then eat it."

Mildred, staring at the gaunt, scaled, sexless creature, felt clammy sweat bead her forehead. "Why?"

"Like I said," it replied, "to balance me out. I'm leaning too far in the direction of a single gender."

Mildred cast her eyes up and down its body. "Not as far as I can see."

It blinked at her again, and said, "Watch."

An awful groan came from its lipless mouth. Parts of the scaled body stirred and shifted, muscles crawling and sliding beneath the scaled flesh. The figure reeled backward, and Mildred, watching it, felt the marrow of her bones turn to water.

The muscles on the creature's arms and thighs thickened, and a fleshy pseudopod at the groin suddenly sprouted, like the bud of a flower. A testicle sac swelled beneath it. Mildred nearly cried out in horror, though the scientist in her was fascinated. She stared, spellbound.

The thing was a physiological gender bender, a hermaphrodite that could switch sexes at will. She knew that human hermaphrodites occurred naturally, if infrequently, though they were usually nonfunctional as both males and females. The genetic differences between men and women were very slight, only a matter of certain genes being switched on or off. In this creature's case, it could apparently switch them on and off, back and forth, at will. She had never heard of a mutie with this kind of ability, and she guessed that this thing was a product of genetic engineering. It wasn't clear in her mind why anyone would wish to deliberately produce hermaphrodites.

Clearing her throat, but not lowering her ZKR, she said, "Very impressive. Do you have a name?"

The creature's eyes narrowed a bit. When it spoke, its voice had dropped an octave. "Let me think. I was called Uni, since I was part of that program. That's not my real name, though. I can't remember what it was. Is."

"What program were you a part of, Uni?"

"The Unisex program, of course. You really aren't very bright, are you? Maybe I shouldn't eat your brain, after all."

Mildred smiled a slightly wan smile. "That's a start in the right direction. What was the purpose of the Unisex program?"

The reply was immediate, as if recited by rote. "To be fruitful and multiply."

"How many of you are there?"

"Just me now. Listen, I think I'll go back to my median nonstate. It takes a lot of effort to maintain one gender without the proper nutritional values."

"Please do," Mildred said, shuddering.

Tendons and muscles writhed, Uni's frame quivered, the shoulders narrowed and the primary male characteristics were absorbed back into its pale flesh. Mildred watched, no longer quite as fascinated, but no less sickened. Though genetic engineering wasn't her field, she possessed more than a layman's knowledge and could theorize about the process that had produced Uni. A developing embryo had been tampered with to artificially induce a bizarre form of consciously controlled hermaphroditism.

She could only guess at the purpose behind the experimentation. Since she had seen no females in the Anthill, it was probable that the Unisex program was designed to provide the complex with a stable population of organ donors. Uni and a few others like it could mate, give birth, switch genders, mate and give birth again. Only a few of the hermaphrodites would be needed to guarantee a controlled supply of offspring. However, she was pretty sure the program was a failure, that the Unis had been sterile in both genders. As it was, Uni's very existence was impressive. The Anthill geneticists had apparently invented a new biochemical coding system to substitute for DNA.

As interesting as Uni and its history was, Mildred couldn't afford to spend any more time with it. She had to find her way back to the upper levels and reestablish contact with Ryan. She needed to keep moving, not surrender to the desire for rest, or her injured muscles would lock.

Backing away down the corridor, Mildred said, "I have to be on my way, Uni. Nice meeting you."

"You have to go so soon?" Uni's eyes glimmered with disappointment. "I haven't talked to anyone in a long time. Feels like years. Maybe it has been years."

It shuffled toward her, and Mildred said pleasantly, "Stay back now."

Uni followed her as she walked backward. She didn't want to shoot the lonely monstrosity, but she couldn't devote her attention to what lay ahead of her if this thing dogged her heels. Though she pitied it, Uni was obviously—in its own words—unbalanced.

"You can't go that way," Uni piped. "Door is sealed. There's only one way topside."

Hesitating, Mildred scanned Uni's face, looking for indications of deceit. It was a futile exercise. "Can you lead me out of this damn place?"

Uni ducked its malformed head in assent. "You betcha. Follow me."

Mildred stepped forward, then paused and hefted her pistol. "Do you know what this is?"

"Sure."

"Tell me."

"A gun, right?" Uni sounded puzzled. "A revolver?"

"That's right, and I'm an expert with it. If you fuck with me, I'll blast your unbalanced metabolism into its component enzymes and amino acids."

Uni regarded her solemnly with huge eyes, then cackled gleefully. Opening the door, it beckoned with long fingers. "Come on, come on."

Grim-faced, Mildred followed Uni through the door into a room that was the exact opposite of the rooms she had seen above. It was filthy. Rusting pipes crisscrossed at all angles along the ceiling and walls. There was a cracked and dirt-filmed porcelain toilet affixed to a wall. The floor tiles were layered with ancient grease and layers of grime, in the shape of treaded boot soles. A long row of dilapidated metal lockers lined one wall. A few of the doors gaped open, revealing rotting military uniforms hanging from hooks. The place had been abandoned a long, long time ago.

A frayed copy of *Time* magazine lay open on the floor. She paused long enough to toe it closed. Before the coated stock cover broke into several pieces, she read a date of May 29, 1996. For some strange reason, the dirty and crumbling periodical seemed like a precious link to her past. Mildred stepped over it, fighting the impulse to burst into tears of grief.

Uni capered in front of her, its white body shining in the dim light. "This way, this way."

Mildred followed the creature through what had been a lounge or common room. There were couches, candy and soft-drink vending machines and a television set. The screen was perforated by what looked like bullet holes.

"Do you live here?" she asked.

"Sure," Uni replied. "For a long time."

"Alone?"

"Sure, all alone." Uni sounded troubled. "When the program was terminated, a man in a white coat showed me the way down here. He wanted the program to go on, said it had been stopped pre-prema—what's the word?"

"Prematurely?"

"Yes. He used to visit me here, examine me, bring me pills to eat. Then he went away one day and never came back."

"How long ago was that?"

Uni came to a stop, eyes half closing. It twirled a lock of blue-black hair around an index finger. A nervous habit, Mildred thought sadly. Like any other human.

"Don't know. Long time. He said I needed something for my brain. Said I needed a new one or something. Said he would get it. He left to get it and never came back. I waited a long time, and he never came back."

Mildred didn't reply, but she had a broad idea of what Uni was talking about and why the program was terminated. Because of Uni's inbred gender-bending metabolism, it probably had an exceptionally unstable mixture of hormones, not just testosterone and estrogen, but the ones affecting intelligence, as well, like vasopressin and acetylcholine. Uni's production of RNA and natural brain chemicals was inefficient, and the scientist had meant to rectify that. Uni had assumed it was to receive a new brain instead of a form of biochemical therapy.

"How do you live down here?" she asked. "Where do you get food and water?"

Tittering, Uni started walking again. "Plenty of food in little sealed packages. Lots of water in the drains."

They entered another room, this one very long and dimly lit, illuminated inadequately by overhead neon fixtures. It was a workshop, filled with heavy tables, tools, chain vices, band saws and cumbersome drill presses. Mildred's eyes roved over the objects on one of the tables, and she came to halt.

"Wait," she called. "I need a minute."

Uni stopped, staring at her from about ten feet away.

"Stay there," she instructed.

"Why?"

"Because I have something to take care of, and I don't need distractions."

Uni considered her words for a moment, then said reproachfully, "Won't hurt you."

"Is that a promise?"

Very seriously, very gravely, Uni made the sign of the cross over its bony chest, then kissed the little finger of its right hand. "Pinky swear."

Mildred was startled into laughing, but at the same time she wasn't about to place her trust in the creature, no matter how pathetic and harmless it seemed.

Removing the headset from her coat pocket, she took a pair of needle-nosed pliers from the table and set to splicing the broken wires together. It was an in-close job, with bad lighting, rust-stiff tools and a strained back to contend with.

It required several minutes, several experimental attempts and perseverance. Fortunately Uni kept its promise and didn't move, allowing her to concentrate.

Finally she heard the hiss of static in the earpiece. Though the circuit was engaged and open, Ryan didn't respond to her hails. She moistened dry, dust-coated lips and fought both the worry about him and the agony of her bruised back muscles. She turned to Uni. "Lead on."

They left the workroom and entered a similar, slightly smaller one. Uni led the way toward propped open ele-

vator doors. There was no car. The shaft rose above it.
Paralleling the cables and running up one wall into the
darkness was a metal ladder. Far above was a faint luminosity.

Uni stepped onto the ladder and began to climb.
Mildred snugged the ZKR into its holster and followed.
They went up in silence for more than a hundred feet
until they came to an opening, the elevator doors jammed
to one side by a length of pipe. The air was colder and
throbbed to the rhythm of engines and generators. The
walls and floors were sheathed with alloy. Beyond the
shaft were three entrances to corridors. One stretched
straight ahead, and the other two branched to the left and
right.

Uni moved down the central corridor. It was neon lit
and took several sharp turns and twists, like a maze. Even
though Uni claimed familiarity with the layout, it sometimes hesitated at the various forks and bends.

After several minutes the corridor terminated in a large
circular hatchway, rimmed by several concentric collars
of dark metal. Uni tittered and waved a hand in front of
it, and the hatchway irised open. The sound of mecha-
nisms grew louder, and the air was chillier. Beyond the
hatch was a short cylindrical tunnel that led them to an
identical hatchway. Uni opened this one in the same way,
by waving a hand over a concealed photoelectric eye lens.
The throb of generators deepened, until the air vibrated.
Feeling like she was breasting invisible waves, Mildred
stepped through the hatch and found herself perched like
a bird on a wire over what looked like a factory.

They stood on a narrow gallery. Above and below were
other galleries, and from them sprang a webwork of catwalks that spanned the vast area, all interconnected ver-

tically by a system of caged-in lifts. The lifts and walkways were constructed to give access to all levels of the enormous central circulating station and moisture condenser that filled the place.

Giant fan blades roared, and greenish liquid coolant bubbled and flowed through a confusing network of transparent tubes. Huge square conduits rose like sky-scrapers almost out of sight between a pattern of cool-ing coils. Water beaded and dripped incessantly from the metal surface of the condenser. It was very cold, very damp and dank.

Though the room was unoccupied, Mildred could see the subtle marks of use. Control consoles and banks of dials and switches surrounded the base of the gargan-tuan machine, and the chairs in front of them had deep hollows in the faded seat cushions.

Despite its size, Mildred could tell that the massive machine had been assembled in a rather piecemeal fash-ion. It wasn't symmetrical, and it was obvious that many of its working parts had been cannibalized from other machines. Evidently, when the decision to live in a near-freezing environment had been made, the original air-conditioning system was modified and reengineered. Though she couldn't see it from her vantage point, it was clear that the station was connected to a nuclear genera-tor. There was no other way such a massive machine could be powered.

Leaning over a guardrail, Mildred peered down at the floor. It was made of concrete and covered by several inches of standing, stagnant water. It drained sluggishly toward huge open grates scattered like giant poker chips over the floor. Resting on an elevated platform above the water was a row of six half-ovoid generators, filling the huge room with a penetrating subsonic song of pure power. Mildred could feel the sympathetic vibrations in the metal railing under her fingertips.

It could take hours to find a central switching console that controlled the generators. Besides, she was sure the station had back-up power sources and redundancies designed into it. To kill the Anthill, she would have to take out the generators. But what she wanted was to orchestrate a thaw, not deprive the entire complex of power. She checked over her complement of grenades and wondered if they were powerful enough to do the job.

Turning to Uni, she asked in a shout, "Is there another way out of here?"

Nodding, Uni pointed to one of the nearby lifts. "That one goes up."

"How far?" she yelled.

"I don't know," it yelled back. "Just up."

Studying the generators again, she eyed the thickness of their cast-iron casings and gauged that all four grenades might just knock out two of them. However, arranged in a semicircle around the last generator was a collection of clattering pumps, the armatures dipping up and down with a blurring speed. She recognized the rattling machines as air pumps, sucking oxygen from the outside and feeding it into the massive condenser. Her eyes followed the conduit and ductwork, and she recognized particulate filtration systems, coolant distribution and return networks built into them.

Before she took any action, she had to make one final attempt to contact Ryan. She pressed the transmit stud on the receiver and said, "Ryan, come in. Ryan, respond. Goddammit, why won't you respond?"

This time she received an answer.

Chapter Thirty

J.B. rolled behind the outcropping and came up with his Uzi in firing position just as two more steel-jacketed wasps stung the canyon wall overhead. The outcropping was over seven feet wide at its base and provided enough cover for everyone, as long they sat scrunched up, knees folded against their chests. Unfortunately it wasn't very high, barely four feet tall.

Jak cautiously peered at the opposite wall of the canyon, the only place for the shots to have originated. The sniper was well hidden. If it hadn't been for the teenager's keen sense of hearing, J.B. might have been chilled.

Jak ducked aside as another bullet ricocheted off the granite shield, but he had seen a glint of sunlight on a gun barrel. "Spotted him."

"An Indian?" J.B. demanded.

Jak shrugged. "Only saw gun."

Krysty passed the Steyr SSG-70 to Doc, who passed it to Jak, who passed it along to J.B. Pushing his spectacles onto his forehead, J.B. brought the rifle to chin level, settling the rubber-cushioned stock into his shoulder. He peered through the image-enhancing scope and followed Jak's direction to the reflected light.

He spotted it and took slow aim, centering the cross hairs, waiting for the sniper to show more of himself than just his gun barrel. Jak said, "I'll speed along."

He lifted his head until the top of his white mane rose above the edge of the outcropping. J.B. glimpsed a dark arm and head through the scope and squeezed the trigger of the rifle. The report sounded like a giant twig snapping in two.

"Think got him," Jak whispered.

Almost at the same second, a dark shape slithered over the lip of the canyon wall and fell with a clatter to the stones below. J.B. saw it through the scope and identified it as an SA-80 automatic rifle.

"It's Hellstrom's people," he said grimly. "They must have figured out who we were and came after us."

"He'll send men up on both sides to block us off in two directions," Fleur said fearfully.

Peering over the outcropping, Jak said, two across from us, hear at least two more above us."

Doc craned his neck, looking up the canyon wall. "We have been cast in the roles of the proverbial fish in a barrel. They will not have to expose themselves to point their weapons down and shoot."

"Mebbe so," J.B. said, pulling his sack to him. "Mebbe not so."

He pawed around in the bag and pulled out an oval gren, the thin metal walls encircled by rubber rings. He tossed it experimentally in his hand.

"What are you planning to do with that?" Krysty asked.

"Take care of the coldhearts above us."

"You'll have to arm it and throw the damn thing straight up, J.B. There's no guarantee it won't just drop back down and blow up in our laps!"

J.B. smiled. "This is a DM-19 incendiary gren with a phosphorus filler. It has a pull-cord arming device, but detonation occurs when the casing breaks."

"So?"

J.B. tossed the grenade to Jak, who caught it gingerly. He turned his back to the outcropping and leaned as far back as it would allow. He looked straight up, holding the Steyr to his shoulder.

"Jak, when I say 'now,' I want you to throw the gren straight up, over our heads. Try to put a little effort into it so it'll land on the top of the wall, but it doesn't matter if you do. Just make sure you throw high and straight."

J.B. flattened himself against the rock and fitted his eye over the scope. He waited, watching and listening. There was a faint clink of metal against rock and he said softly, "Now."

Jak lobbed the bomb up in a straight line. J.B. followed the gren's vertical flight through the scope, and when it lost its momentum and began to drop, he waited until the small object was level with the edge of the canyon wall before squeezing the trigger. He was right on target.

The blast of the detonating gren echoed across the canyon and back like a thunderclap. A fireball bloomed, and tongues of flame curled in all directions. Everyone below felt the slamming concussion. As the echoes of the explosion still reverberated, clattering rock fragments and screams of agony added to the noise.

Shielding his eyes from the falling rock chips, Jak looked up and said with a grin, "Flash-fried 'em."

A pair of automatic rifles began chattering from the opposite wall, striking and ricocheting from the outcropping. J.B. hitched over, saw the men on the facing edge of the canyon and fired the Steyr at them. After one man fell, arms windmilling, and the other dived for cover, J.B. said, "Time to move. I'll lay down a covering fire."

As the friends broke from their granite hiding place, J.B. propped his Uzi atop the boulder and depressed its trigger, sending a steady stream of bullets to chew up the topmost edge of the opposite wall. He kept the sec man up there pinned down, afraid to raise his head, until the five people had reached the bottom few feet of the stone staircase.

J.B. grabbed his sack and scrabbled out on the ledge, climbing, crawling and sliding. He heard voices shouting from the mouth of the canyon, and he recognized one of them as Hellstrom's. Evidently he had sent a scout force ahead, holding back the remainder of the sec squad.

Fleur, Krysty, Doc and Jak had taken cover behind rock tumbles beside the cave entrance the moment they'd jumped from the stone staircase. J.B. slid down to join them, hopping from ledge to ledge. Although the exchange of gunfire and the gren explosion had happened in a very short span of time, he feared that whoever or whatever lurked inside the cave had been alerted. He expected a swarm of beetles to swoop from it immediately. At the very least, he expected Hellstrom and his sec men to charge down the canyon, weapons blazing.

J.B. managed to join his friends behind the rocks on the right side of the cave opening before either one happened. He didn't have to wait long before six shaven-headed, X-scarred men raced down the canyon, blasters flaming, heading straight for them. They fanned out and took cover without hesitation. The sec men kept up a cone-shaped firing pattern. Bullets whined from their stone shelter and exploded against the rocky wall over their heads, sprinkling them with dust and gravel.

"As long we stay down, we're safe," Krysty said. "But if we try to make a run for the cave, we'll make excellent targets."

A bullet dug a gouge in a rock very close to Doc's head. The shot had come from above, and Jak returned the fire with a double blast from his Colt Python.

Krysty and J.B. exchanged hard-eyed, knowing looks. It was only a matter of time before the sec men got in position to lob grens at them, or the sniper above would pick them off.

Doc chuckled mirthlessly, peering out between the open spaces in the rocks at the men shooting at them. "This reminds of the time I took my daughters to see Buffalo Bill's Wild West Show."

Fleur stared at him as if the white-haired man had suddenly decided to turn senile, but Doc continued. "The climax of the performance was a stirring scene of settlers beset by bloodthirsty Indians. When events looked their darkest, the gallant Colonel Cody led the U.S. Cavalry in a charge to rout the savages and set things aright."

No one responded to Doc's story. J.B. had only the vaguest idea of who Buffalo Bill Cody had been, and at the moment he wasn't inclined to solicit Doc for further information about him.

A movement on the canyon rim caught his eye. The head of the Helskel sniper was silhouetted against the blue of the sky, and sunlight gleamed dully off the gun barrel as he brought it into firing position.

As J.B. raised his Uzi, the sec man's head suddenly acquired a new and different shape, and the automatic rifle in his hands tumbled down the face of the cliff. The crack of the rifle shot was lost in the echoes of the gunfire from the men on the canyon floor, but the Armorer definitely heard the volley of shots that followed it.

Bullets punched gouts of dirt from around the sec men's cover, and they shouted in surprise and fear. J.B. scanned the towering walls and saw at least half a dozen copper-skinned men on horseback, men with feathers in their long black hair, paint on their faces and blasters in their hands. He recognized Touch-the-Sky among them.

J.B. stared at the band of Sioux as they poured a withering hail of autofire down on the sec men from above. He turned to Doc and said, "That ain't your Colonel Cody *or* the U.S. Cavalry."

"I'm not going to complain," Krysty said, smiling with relief. "Are you?"

J.B. wasn't going to complain, but he did wonder whether the Lakota, after chilling the sec men, might end up blasting them down. He doubted that Touch-the-Sky's arrival was to pull their fat out of the fire. More than likely he was taking advantage of the opportunity to rid the Black Hills of white intruders once and for all.

Jak and Krysty opened fire on the sec men while they were occupied by the Sioux. They were spread out all over the canyon floor, and half of them shot back at the Indians while the other half blasted away at them. But most of their shots went wild, since they were trying to dodge and duck the death belching from the rifles above.

Seeing that the sec men were thoroughly occupied with the Lakota, J.B. said, "Let's hit the cave."

"No time like the present," Doc said, rising stiffly to his feet.

The five people climbed quickly over the rocks and sprinted for the cave opening. The few hasty shots directed their way kicked up dirt and rock, but none came uncomfortably close. As far as J.B. could tell, the bullets didn't come from above.

As they darted inside, J.B. risked a backward glance and saw the Lakota astride their ponies, swerving away from the edge of the canyon and galloping toward its mouth. If Hellstrom lurked anywhere back there, the Indians' pounding arrival would flush him out.

The cavern had a huge, irregular dome shape. The sunlight slanting into the canyon reached only a few yards past the opening. Beyond that, darkness was a congealed mass, and none of them moved toward it.

"Remember what Hellstrom said about the beetles," he warned.

They remained at the mouth of the cave, hunkering down on either side of it, not shooting, just watching, waiting and listening. The sec men didn't fire at them. They had to be aware of their situation, being trapped in the middle between the guns in the cave and the guns of the Sioux, but they stayed where they were, behind cover.

"J.B.," Krysty called, "shouldn't we look for that mat-trans gateway?"

"I don't want to bump into those flying mechanical bugs in the dark. Besides, we should stay and finish it with Hellstrom."

Jak grinned ruefully. "Nervous too about going back there blind."

Fleur snorted. "We may not have a choice, if our men make a charge."

"'Our' men?" Doc echoed, angling an eyebrow at her. "I was under the impression you felt thoroughly disaffected from your former fraternity."

"You're welcome to go out there and join them," Krysty said in a tight, cold tone. "If you think they'll let you. Of course, if they do, I'll chill you personally."

The roar of an engine floated up from around a bend in the canyon wall, and mingled with it was the crackle of gunfire and yipping war cries. A few seconds later the AMAC jounced into view, with hard-riding Lakota flanking it, shooting at its armored hide and uttering fierce screams. A warrior was crouched on the roof, clinging to the periscope. As the wag drew closer, J.B. recognized the Indian as Touch-the-Sky. Though the windshield was tinted, he assumed Lars Hellstrom himself was behind the wheel.

The sec men were rising to their knees, believing the AMAC was making a rescue run and would brake, allowing them to board it. The vehicle didn't stop, didn't even slow. It sped past the sec men, and they howled in anger and terror. The Lakota had used the big armored wag as mobile cover, and when their ponies paralleled the sec men's position, they directed their fire into them. The return fire was sporadic.

Though a couple of the Sioux pitched from their saddle blankets with bullet wounds, the remainder leaped from horseback and grappled hand-to-hand.

The AMAC kept coming on a straight course for the cave entrance, bouncing over loose stones. J.B., Krysty and Jak triggered their blasters, and ricochets sparked from the front bumper guard. The windshield acquired a few stars, but it didn't break. Nothing less than armor-piercing rounds could wound the vehicle, and though there were some in the sack, there was no time to load them into their blasters.

Snatching a gren from his sack, J.B. armed it and flung it in the AMAC's path, trying to place it beneath a tire. A red-yellow bouquet of flame bloomed beneath the wag, and the dulled thunder of the detonation rumbled loudly. Still, the exploding gren did little to impede the vehicle's progress.

Whirling, J.B. shouted, "Move, goddammit!"

He began to run into the blackness, hearing his friends sprinting beside and behind him. The engine roar seemed to fill the cavern. He heard a woman shriek, very briefly, and he cast a glance over his shoulder.

The AMAC rocketed through the cave opening, and the driver cut the wheels sharply to the right, stomping the brakes at the same time. The resulting skid wasn't controlled, and the rear end floated around in a 180-degree turn. A wave of sandy soil crested from beneath it, the vehicle thrown off balance in the loose dirt when the brakes were applied.

The swinging rear end slapped against Fleur, swatting her off her feet and flinging her to the right. The rear of the AMAC hit the rock wall hard, with a shrill squeal of metal grinding into stone. It lurched violently to a halt.

The woman was pinned between the armored wag and the stone wall of the cavern. There was no need to dwell on the sight; the life had been crushed out of her body in a microsecond.

J.B. and his friends kept running through the dark throat of the cave, and within a few dozen yards they couldn't see their hands in front of their faces.

"Everybody link hands," Krysty said.

The Armorer had a small pen-flash in his pocket, and after the human chain was hastily assembled, he took the point. The light was hardly more than a needle of white incandescence, piercing only a few feet of the cloying blackness. The cavern widened, and the ceiling grew in height. Irregularly formed stalactites hung from above. The light glinted off mineral deposits embedded in the fissured walls. The walls were also decorated with faded, crude paintings and carvings, representations of bizarre figures and shapes. They were obviously very old.

"Petroglyphs," Doc whispered. "Now I see why Touch-the-Sky didn't care to enter this place. It's a holy spot."

The *clink-crunch* of stones came faintly from behind.

"Hellstrom isn't worried about holy spots," J.B. said softly. "If he gets a bead on us with one of those SA-80s, he can cut us to pieces without getting close."

"Turn out light," Jak urged, staring behind them. "Wait until gets into range. Chill him big time."

J.B. complied and they were plunged into absolute blackness, which lasted only for a moment. In the gloom before them shone a fiery red orb, casting a blood-colored luminescence over their faces.

"Dark night," J.B. managed to husk out.

Chapter Thirty-One

Before the door had opened more than a few inches, Ryan was bounding across the office toward the recess between the bookcases. Putting his back to the elevator doors, he held his breath and waited, the SIG-Sauer held in a two-handed grip.

Doug strolled past him, the Browning autoshotgun angled jauntily over a shoulder. His pace slowed when he saw no one at the desk, then it quickened. Peering around the edge of the bookshelves, Ryan watched the man reach the front of the desk, look around, then do a violent double-take. A gasp of horror escaped his lips and he rushed clumsily around the desk, bending over to check the Commander's bullet-blasted corpse.

Ryan crossed the carpeted floor on the balls of his feet, sacrificing a certain amount of stealth for speed. He didn't use his guns. He got behind Doug, gripped the man's neck in both hands and twisted sharply. He didn't hear the snap of breaking vertebrae, merely a faint metallic creak. Doug choked out a half-gagged curse and his hands came up, locking around Ryan's wrists. The one-eyed man could feel his flesh and tendons being ground against bone, and it was all he could do to bite back a cry of pain.

Levering himself to his feet, still gripping Ryan's wrists, Doug turned, facing the double doors and suddenly bending forward at the waist, flipped Ryan over his back. Rather than resist the maneuver and risk having his arms dislocated or torn from their sockets, Ryan kicked off from the floor, landing on his back but cushioning the fall with the soles of his feet.

Doug staggered forward, off balance from the lack of resistance. He had no choice but to release Ryan's wrists or fall face forward.

In the instant his upper body was still bent forward, almost parallel with the floor, Ryan performed a backward half-somersault, kicking up with both legs, the soles of his combat boots slamming into Doug's face. The man straightened, half-blinded from the blood springing from his flattened nose and split lips. He staggered back and fetched up hard against the desk.

Ryan continued rolling, ignoring the pain in his shoulders, and came to his feet with his left fist driving into Doug's belly with all his strength behind it.

The man bent forward, clutching at his stomach, and Ryan slammed his right fist behind his adversary's left ear. He sagged, and the one-eyed warrior chopped the back of his neck with the edge of his palm.

If he had been a normal man, Doug would have died. But he was only half-stunned and struggled to pull himself erect. Ryan jacked his right knee into his opponent's forehead, and pain exploded up and down his leg, from ankle to thigh.

But Doug fell facedown, and while Ryan bit his lip to keep from groaning, the man forced himself over, fighting to get into a sitting position. His face was a mask of dark pink blood, and his expression was one of dazed, confused hurt. Drawing his blaster, Ryan moved behind him and put the bore against the back of his head.

"The woman," he said, voice quavering with the effort to control the agony in his knee and wrists. "Did you find her?"

Doug buried his face in his hands. He began to sob—dry, shuddering heaves that racked his body.

"Answer me!" Ryan pressed the pistol harder into his skull. "The woman!"

Voice muffled by his hands, choked with grief, Doug stammered, "Couldn't. Didn't. Don't know where. The Commander is dead."

"And so are you."

Ryan squeezed the trigger of the SIG-Sauer. The 9 mm round broke open the back of Doug's head, but it didn't exit from the front. The blaster bucked, the unexpected blowback nearly snatching it from his fingers. The force of the shot slammed the man's upper body forward, face hitting the floor between his knees. Metal gleamed in the mixture of clotted brain matter, synthetic flesh and blood.

Letting out his breath, Ryan knelt with difficulty, quickly examining the body. Though partially deflected by the metal plate in his skull, the bullet had still done enough damage to chill him. As it was, he doubted that anything less than a point-blank shot would have accomplished the job. He found his sheathed panga on Doug's belt, and after pulling it free, he took the man's ID badge from his lapel and unsteadily climbed to his feet.

After attaching the badge to his coat, Ryan drew the headset from his inner pocket and put it on. When he seated the earpiece Mildred's voice said "—won't you respond?"

"That's what I'm doing, Mildred."

"Ryan?" Her voice was filled with elation, but there was a throbbing roar in the background, and it sounded as if she were shouting.

"Yeah, it's me. Are you all right?"

"You have to speak up."

Raising his voice, Ryan asked again, "Are you all right?"

"More or less. You?"

"The same."

"What?"

Impatiently Ryan asked loudly, "Where the hell are you?"

"I don't know exactly, but I've found the primary cooling and circulation nexus. Where are you?"

"On the level where we split up. I've got Doug's ID badge and you can find me by the locator lozenge."

Voice troubled, Mildred replied, "I don't think there's a computer tie-in down here. I'll have to go up, get my hands on a badge so I can access it. Listen, I can take out a generator down here, probably start a thaw. At the very least it'll be a diversion."

"Do it," Ryan said. "On the level directly above me is some sort of a control room, with a mat-trans gateway. That'll be our escape route. I'll wait for you up there."

"What about J.B. and the others?"

"I don't know. There's a vid circuit upstairs connected to the cave, but when I checked it out a little while ago, there was no sign of them."

Mildred's response was so long in coming that Ryan almost called her name. Then her voice filtered over the earpiece. It was unsteady.

"If they're not there, what are we going to do?"

"We'll think about that later. First we have to get out of here. Blow the generators."

"When?"

"As soon as you can. I won't make my move until you've made yours. I'm sure all sorts of alarms, bells and whistles will go off, and that'll be my signal. Acknowledged?"

"Acknowledged. You know something?"

"What?"

"We need to put more thought into planning our field trips."

"Understood. Standby."

He waited until he was sure she'd signed off before allowing himself the luxury of a groan. Ryan sat back to wait, trying to massage the soreness from his wrists and knee.

Chapter Thirty-Two

Turning toward Uni, Mildred shouted, "You have to go back. It's not safe in here."

Uni narrowed its big eyes. "Why not? I've been here plenty of times."

Waving toward the row of generators below, she answered, "I'm going to blow those up. There's no telling what will happen."

Staring first at the generators and then at Mildred, Uni asked, "I don't understand."

"You don't have to. Just get back below. I think you'll be okay. I'll give you a minute to get started."

The red disk shaped eyes moved from her face to the generators, then back to her face. "What about my new brain?"

Mildred swallowed hard, feeling pity well up like a lump in her throat. "You don't need one, honey. The one you have is just fine. Now go!"

Uni moved a few faltering steps toward the round hatchway, then turned, beaming broadly. "Come back when you're finished, okay?"

Mildred nodded. "I'll do my best. Be on your way now."

Uni flipped her a quick salute and scuttled through the hatch opening, swinging the heavy cover closed. Mildred counted to sixty under her breath, trying to give Uni as much time as possible to get away from the area. As far as she or Ryan knew, destroying one generator might trigger an atomic chain reaction that would result in a do-it-yourself Hiroshima.

Mildred moved around the catwalks, heading for the optimum position from which to throw the grenades. Though her hand-eye coordination was excellent, she didn't possess the muscle strength or the experience to throw one of the deadly explosives very far. Her best bet was to get right over the generators and drop them straight down.

She was able to reach a point on one of the walkways that was almost directly above the generator connected to the pump array. Best of all, it was only a couple of long steps to a lift cage. She examined the control box inside of the cage and saw that it was a simple lever: to go down, you pushed the lever down, to go up, you pulled it up.

Mildred unclipped two grenades from the combat harness, an incendiary and a fragmentation. She hoped the combination of shock, heat and about three thousand ball bearings spraying out at six thousand meters per second would accomplish her task.

Leaning as far out over the vibrating railing as she dared, Mildred held both grenades in her right hand. She armed them by pulling away the pin levers. She opened her fingers, letting both of the devices fall away toward the rows of generators fifty feet below. Then she bounded for the elevator, slamming the gate shut and grabbing the lever. Before she could jerk it up, the brutal sound of detonating high explosives and ripping, rending metal filled the vast room.

The lift cage shook violently, rattling and clattering. Water, chunks of concrete and metal flew upward in a fiery column, battering the underside of the catwalks. Mildred got a blurred image of a layer of fire clinging to the handrails and grillwork. The double concussion slapped against her eardrums.

The angry, deafening shrieking of ruptured metal replaced the thunder of the explosion, and blinding clouds of white vapor spewed up from below, billowing and rolling like heavy fog. It doused the flames and coated all of the walkways with a patina of frost. Mildred inhaled just a bit of the supercooled air, and for a moment she gagged herself blind, the soft, wet tissues of her throat afire with agony. She slammed the cage lever as far as it would go in the up position, and with an electrical whine the elevator shot upward. It rose, rattling and shaking, past level after level.

Once, she hazarded a look over the gate and saw nothing but an expanse of white clouds, as though she were rocketing high in the air, far above the earth. Then, over the hum and the rattle, she heard the warbling and wailing of alarm Klaxons. Quickly she drew her revolver. She had no idea where she was going to end up, but she was at least on her way.

The lift clanked to a jolting halt. Pushing aside the gate, Mildred stepped into a small alcove fronting a tunnel from which a group of men emerged. They wore white coveralls and were frantically donning breathing masks. They stumbled to unsteady, fearful stops when they saw Mildred and her blaster. She almost shouted "Freeze!" but thought better of it and commanded, "Don't move!"

The man in the lead wore a badge identifying him as MIKE. He sputtered and stammered behind the mask. "Pl-please, we've got to get down to the station!"

Snatching the badge from his coverall pocket, Mildred said, "First things first, Mike. Show me the nearest computer tie-in."

Mike pushed his way through his companions, moving toward the rear of the tunnel. Mildred said, "The rest of you can go about your business."

They made a concerted rush for the lift cage, and Mike stopped in front of a wall panel. "Here."

"Complex display," Mildred announced.

The wall panel flashed with light, and a diagram of the complex appeared. "Where are we?" Mildred asked.

Mike pointed to a throbbing green dot.

"Locate Doug."

Another dot began to throb. Counting the levels, Mildred saw she was far below Ryan's location. "Where's the nearest lift, Mike?"

"Out the doors, a hundred feet to your right. To get to Doug's level, all you have to do is say into the tie-in, 'Doug.'"

"Handy. You may go now."

Mike bustled away, and Mildred went through the doors at the end of the tunnel. She called Ryan on the transceiver and told him, "On my way."

"Good," he responded. "J.B. and the rest should be here soon."

"Are you sure?"

"No. Watch your back."

"Watch yours."

Chapter Thirty-Three

When Ryan heard the first alarms, he picked up the Walther MPL and the SIG-Sauer P-226 and walked painfully toward the private lift between the bookcases. Pushing the red button with the barrel of the Walther, the door panels rolled open and he stepped inside. A push of the button on the inside wall closed the doors and started the elevator moving smoothly upward.

When it sighed to a gentle stop, he poked the button, the door panels opened and he stepped out into a scene of utter, screaming panic and pandemonium. He stood for a moment, grinning, relishing the energy of dazed, almost stupefied terror crackling throughout the control room.

He did a quick scan of the huge, dome-roofed room, his senses on full alert, his warrior instincts tingling from the waves of tension coursing and cresting through the place.

Men ran to and fro, back and forth, going from computer terminal to readout station to dial-and-button-studded consoles. All of them were screaming and shrieking to be heard over the rising and falling banshee notes of the Klaxon. Ryan picked up snatches of shouts and yells.

"Coolant core breach! We've lost two generators—"

"Why aren't the backups on line—"

"Goddammit, my board shows a total circulation system failure!"

"Main pumps and conduits are gone! Reserve processors and the temperature and humidity controls are locked—"

"Where's the Commander? The temperature will rise to critical levels in five hours—"

Ryan stepped into the control room, walking around the running, panic-stricken men, heading toward the gateway chamber. He almost reached it with no one noticing him. A man bending over a flickering monitor screen glanced up and snarled. He shouted something, but no one heard him. One of his hands fumbled at his waist and came up gripping a long-nosed automatic made of blued steel.

Simultaneously Ryan brought up his SIG-Sauer and dispatched a 9 mm round into the man's stomach. That drew attention to him, and a group of men spun in his direction. Already on the verge of mindless flight, it took them an instant to identify him as an intruder, as a danger.

Ryan kept walking, swinging the Walther toward them, holding down the trigger. He sprayed bullets into the middle of the group and could hear their screams above the warbling of the alarm.

The burst of autofire was the signal for the men in the control room to go berserk. They milled around mindlessly, ducking beneath consoles and panels, some stampeding madly for an exit. The few who were armed were bowled over by their terrified comrades.

A short, stumpy-legged man bolted around a corner, trying to run past Ryan, who reached out and grabbed the man's necktie, swinging him around in a wide arc. The man clawed desperately at Ryan's hand, his face ashen with terror.

Ryan released the tie and the man floundered backward, toward the gateway, and fell up against the freestanding console pedestal. The one-eyed man stepped in close, ramming the muzzle of the SIG-Sauer under his fleshy chin, forcing his head back at a painful angle. His ID badge proclaimed him to be HOWARD.

"Are there beetles in the cave, Howard?" he snapped.

"Only one," the man gasped. "Programmed for surveillance and defense."

"Can you override the program from this console?"

Howard stared at him as though he were insane. "Why?"

"Answer me!"

"Yes, there are manual overrides here."

Hauling the man away from the console, he turned him around to face it. "Show me."

J.B.'s face stared at him from the small screen in the center of the panel. Behind him, Ryan could make out Krysty, and his head went light with relief.

Howard fiddled with a button or two and announced, "The beetle is controlled from here now."

"Can you speak through it from here?" Ryan demanded.

Howard's trembling finger touched a square grid. "Talk into that. The communication channel is open."

"J.B., Krysty," Ryan said loudly, "can you hear me?"

On the screen, J.B., and Krysty's expressions went blank, then lit up with relief. Both of them started talking at once, so Ryan had to say, "Is everyone with you? Jak and Doc?"

"Yes, lover," Krysty replied. "Where are you?"

"In the Anthill. Have you found the gateway in the cave?"

"No," J.B. answered. "The place is as black as a swampie's hind end."

Turning to the terrified Howard, Ryan said, "Where's the gateway in there?"

"Only a few hundred yards ahead. You can guide them to it with the beetle."

"Do it."

"We copy that, Ryan," J.B. said. He glanced behind him. "I think Hellstrom's on our heels, though."

"Forget him."

"Where is Mildred? Is she with you?" Doc asked.

"Not yet," Ryan replied.

J.B.'s lips compressed. "What do you mean?"

"We'll talk about it when you get here. Follow the beetle to the gateway chamber, get inside and I'll transport you all here."

"Then what?"

Ryan grinned mirthlessly. "Then we'll plan our next field trip."

He watched both the screen and Howard's hands, as under his ministrations on the controls, J.B., Krysty, Doc and Jak followed the beetle to the mat-trans unit. It was an exact double of the huge one in the control room.

"No controls here!" Jak exclaimed as they reached it.

"They're up here," Ryan responded.

He glared at Howard. "Aren't they?"

Howard nodded several times and flipped up a cover on the console. Beneath it, inset into the surface, was a set of buttons and tabs.

When his friends were inside, with the armaglass portal secured, Howard keyed in the transport sequence. Ryan watched the screen, through the beetle's electronic eye, as tendrils of white mist crept up around the figures inside the chamber. The tendrils were shot through with crackling fingers of static electricity. A very bright light began to glow behind the glass.

From the chamber in the control room a sound like a fierce rushing wind grew, rising louder and louder. Light flashed on the other side of armaglass walls. The light swelled, growing in intensity in tandem with the hurricane noises. Both the light and sound faded at the same time.

Howard fidgeted with his tie. "Are you done with me?"

Ryan ignored him, running around the console and grabbing the handle of the gateway chamber. Mat-trans jumps usually had a debilitating effect, making the jumpers weak and often sick for a while. Ryan hoped that this short jump wouldn't incapacitate his friends. He might need their firepower.

When he popped open the door, he saw Jak, Krysty, Doc and J.B. struggling to rise. They looked a bit dizzy, a little disoriented, but not faint or sluggish. Ryan helped Krysty to her feet, and she held him in a crushing embrace.

J.B. struggled to his feet, helping Doc up. He grinned, but there was worry in his eyes. As was his habit, he had taken off his spectacles before the jump. "Good to see you. Where the hell's Millie?"

"Right here, John." Mildred pushed her way into the chamber and grabbed J.B.'s face with both hands, kissing him passionately. Ryan noted that it was probably a good thing J.B. wasn't wearing his glasses. Mildred's face was caked with dried blood, and she was covered by what looked like a gray dust. The plaits of her hair were snarled in a wild, Medusa-like tangle.

She met Ryan's glance, looked him up and down and said, "You look like shit."

Jak and Doc, feeling a little left out of the reunion, moved to the chamber door, peering around it at the control room beyond. The alarm Klaxons had fallen silent, and the abrupt quiet was almost as nerve-scratching as the warbling tones.

"What's plan?" Jak demanded. "Take over place, give up or what?"

"I hope it's a 'what,'" Doc muttered, blowing on his hands. "I do not find the climate congenial."

"I want to get the fuck out of this frozen nightmare," Ryan declared. "We can make a direct jump back to that installation in New Mexico from here. Just have to punch a key with that strange triangle symbol."

"What'll keep the freezies here from following us?" Krysty asked.

Ryan shook his head. "Luck mebbe."

Jak, in an urgent whisper, said, "Men with blasters, creepy-crawling here."

Ryan cursed, peering over Jak's head. A few of the Anthill's staff had recovered from their shock, armed themselves and were moving toward the gateway.

J.B. dug around in his sack and with a triumphant snort produced a small plastic-shelled sphere. "Here's a piece of luck, Ryan."

Looking at it, Ryan said, "A gren. We'll need more than that."

"This *is* more than that. It's a Misar MU 5-G fragger, with a kill radius of about thirty feet. We're talking about a handful of hell here. More than that, it has a time pencil fuse."

That captured Ryan's attention. It was an old device, developed over a hundred years before. A thin-walled metal tube, similar in shape to a pencil, was inserted into the gren, and a turn of a small screw atop the MU 5-G crushed the tube, releasing a corrosive liquid, which then ate through a wire restraining a sprung firing pin. It was the next best thing to a clockwork time bomb.

"Great," Ryan said, taking it from J.B.'s hands. "I'll ask you later where you picked it up. The rest of you cover me and get ready to jump."

Ryan shouldered the door of the chamber open and made a run for the console. In a far corner, a trio of men had barricaded themselves behind an overturned table. One of them saw him and shouted. Gun barrels shifted his way.

Emptying the Walther's clip in their direction, Ryan saw wood shredding and bodies twitching. A few bursts of gunfire came from across the control room, and he triggered the SIG-Sauer as he ran. He heard J.B.'s Uzi and Krysty's Smith & Wesson blasting from behind him. The big room trembled with shattering glass and the sound of metal being punctured. Bullets punched through the air around him, ricocheting away from the armaglass of the gateway chamber.

Skidding to a stop at the console, Ryan ducked low as he worked with the gren, turning the knurled timing screw until he heard a crunch. He placed the sphere on the floor next to the hard plastic support pedestal, then raised his head up to punch in the destination. As he did, movement flickered across the monitor.

It was Lars Hellstrom, standing before the mat-trans unit, holding an automatic rifle in one hand and a revolver in the other. The right sleeve of his white coat was black with blood.

Ryan spoke into the speaker grid. "Lars. Wondering when you'd show up."

Hellstrom's reaction was almost comical. He skipped around, glaring wildly up at the beetle, face contorting. His mouth worked for a long second, with no sounds coming from it. Finally he bellowed, "Cawdor? *Cawdor!* You deceived me! You betrayed me!"

"Sorry, Lars, but after thinking it over, I'm afraid I must refuse your job offer. The hours stink, and the pay is lousy."

Hellstrom began to tremble, eyelids flickering, spittle collecting at the corners of his mouth. In a voice that shivered with the intensity of the emotions he was struggling to control, he said, "You stupe bastard. You stupe, suicidal bastard. You don't know what you've done."

Ryan snarled out a laugh. "I know exactly what I've done. I've cut off this sick trade between you and this monument of predark insanity. You're cast back out onto Deathlands, to survive or to die on your own. I hope you die, and if we ever meet face-to-face again, I'll make sure of it. That's not a threat, Lars. It's a fucking prophecy."

Hellstrom stood frozen, his body quaking violently, a thousand changing sparks of light dancing in his dark eyes. Then he threw back his head and screamed, a howl of agony, terror and rage torn from the roots of his soul. Saliva sprayed from his mouth, one hand clawed at the side of his face, the long nails tearing gouges from his hairline to his chin.

"I'll track you down, Cawdor!" he shrieked. "I'll find you and I'll keep you alive for years, in constant, unending pain! You'll promise me anything, give me anything, do anything, just so I'll chill you! And if you die before I find you again, I'll dig up your stinking corpse and spend my days pissing in its mouth! Your punishment begins now, Cawdor! It will never end!"

The tone, the crash of his strident voice, the unregenerate, unforgiving madness in his eyes almost caused Ryan to drop his blaster in surprise. To witness Hellstrom losing his iron control and flaming up in a torch of insane fury was a more fearful picture than he had imagined. For a moment he contemplated making a mat-trans jump to the cave and finishing his business with the patriarch of Helskel.

"Ryan!" J.B. shouted. "Come on, dammit!"

Peering over the console, he saw J.B. and Jak standing in the open door of the mat-trans unit chamber. They were staring past him, and Ryan heard the slap of running feet on the smooth alloy flooring, rushing up from behind.

He half turned, sweeping the ranks of the business-suited men with a prolonged burst from the SIG-Sauer. They screamed as the hail of full-metal-jacket rounds ripped through them. The few who weren't drilled scrambled for cover, flinging ineffectual pistol fire in his general direction.

"Ryan!" Krysty's voice was high and tight with tension.

But Ryan wasn't satisfied with the carnage. The Anthill still stood, a symbol of everything vile, depraved and self-serving that had survived the nukecaust. He wanted to claw the mountain stronghold down, stone by stone, crush it into rubble and stomp it flat.

He fired another four rounds at the stumbling, mewling straw men and roared, at the top of his voice, "I'll be back, you ice-blooded bastards!"

Ryan slapped the destination key, the one bearing the triangle symbol, and raced across the room to the gateway chamber. Jak slammed the door behind him, and the jump mechanism was triggered.

Everyone but Mildred eyed him strangely. Threats and vows of vengeance were uncharacteristic of Ryan Cawdor. Turning to J.B., he asked, "What was the setting on that time pencil fuse?"

J.B. shook his head. "About two minutes."

"Then we've got about thirty seconds left," Ryan said grimly.

"Let's pray to Gaia that's enough time," Krysty murmured fervently.

The metal disks in the floor and ceiling of the mattrans chamber shimmered, the glow slowly intensifying, like a condensed fire. A fine mist gathered and wafted down from the overhead convertor assembly. A vibrating hum arose, climbing quickly to a high-pitched whine.

Men began to shout out in the control room, their blasters cutting loose with slugs that splattered against the armaglass walls of the chamber. J.B. squeezed Mildred's hand reassuringly. The mist sparked and thickened, curling down to engulf them.

Ryan pulled Krysty close to him, pressing his cheek against the soft caress of her hair. They had conquered many hellpits in Deathlands, and they would conquer this one.

He hoped.

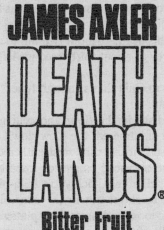

**A downed American superplane throws
Stony Man into a new war against an old enemy.**

STONY MAN™ 25
SKYLANCE

When the Air Force's pride and joy, America's advanced
top-secret reconnaissance plane, is shot down in western
New Guinea, Stony Man is dispatched to do the impossible:
recover the plane or destroy it. Caught in the cross fire of a
raging civil war, Bolan's army goes up against the shock
troops of a first-world industrialist fighting his private war
against America....

Available in November at your favorite retail outlet.